K,

It's a pleasure working with you. I hope you enjoy my first stab at writing.

The Floating Man

by William Crawford

Copyright © 2013 by William Crawford

This is a work of fiction. Names, characters, businesses, places, events and incidents are either the products of the author's imagination or used in a fictitious manner. With the exception of historical figures and events used in a fictitious manner, any resemblance to actual persons, living or dead, or actual events is purely coincidental.

All rights reserved. This book contains material protected under International and Federal Copyright Laws and Treaties. No part of this publication may be reproduced, distributed, or transmitted in any form or by any means, including photocopying, recording, or other electronic or mechanical methods, without the prior written permission of the author, except in the case of brief quotations embodied in critical reviews and certain other noncommercial uses permitted by copyright law. For more information visit: http://the-floating-man.com

CHAPTER 1

John Hill was coming home.

Turning off Interstate 95 South, he guided his Mercury Grand Marquis onto US 17 North. Up ahead, a familiar signpost loomed. Only twenty-five more miles to Beaufort, South Carolina.

Home.

He smiled at the thought.

A beautiful, sunny June afternoon. A new beginning.

Home.

Max Baker—his editor at the *Washington Post*, a big bear of a man sporting a bushy walrus-style mustache—had tried his best to persuade John to stay on, noting that he was well on his way to becoming a Washington institution. At thirty-two, John already had several major investigative pieces under his belt. In a few years he could be another Bob Woodward. But John would not be persuaded. The previous fall he had suffered a grievous loss: both his parents were killed in a car crash. Suddenly, all his career success, his achievements—none of that seemed to matter. It all seemed shallow and inconsequential.

John Hill was coming home.

His thoughts went to the Pulitzer Prize he shared with Sheila Jefferson, his investigative partner. Working together, they had uncovered a scheme in the defense department to rig contracts during the rebuilding of Iraq. In the aftermath, several high-ranking military officials were forced to resign.

Thinking of Sheila brought some sadness—another blow to his psyche. When Sheila quit the *Post* to join the staff of the National Security Council, it ended any chance for a romance, compounding the emptiness he felt in his life.

Sheila was an intimidating woman: a tall, statuesque brunette with a figure that was almost like the cartoon caricatures found in superhero comic books. Almost.

Those looks, coupled with a no-nonsense, standoffish exterior, did not make her many friends those first few months at the *Post*. The general opinion in the office was that Max had hired her for her looks. Men, with the exception of jerks like Ted Dody, now the *Post's* Paris bureau correspondent, were too intimidated to approach her. Women universally shunned her, perceiving her looks to be both a career and marital threat.

John was the first to see through her facade. Paired together for an investigative piece on waste and abuse in farm subsidy programs, he saw what Max had seen: a first rate investigative reporter with the instincts of a veteran. Behind that facade, John found a lonely woman trapped by her beauty, as if it were a disfiguring liability. Sheila, longing to fit in, to be one of the guys, became close to John, professionally; over the next two years the two of them worked as a team on several stories.

The hurt look on Sheila's face when he broke the news of his move back to South Carolina would forever be seared in his mind. John knew there was a mutual attraction between them, but Sheila was intent on climbing the rungs of the Washington power structure. He was not.

Sheila's job involved compiling intelligence reports into briefing papers for the head of the NSC, Henry Smith. As national security advisor to the president, he was one of the wise old men of Washington, having served in both Republican and Democratic administrations. John could not see a future for the two of them. An investigative reporter whose job was to ferret out government secrets, romantically involved with a staffer for the NSC, whose job was to protect those secrets—not going to happen.

And the simple truth of the matter? He was tired of the rat race. Tired of chasing down one big story after another.

Looking in the rear-view mirror at the crow's feet forming around his eyes, he realized the physical and psychic toll stress was taking on his body. The excessive drinking of late didn't help matters much either.

John's solution was to move back to his old hometown, reconnect with the people he grew up with and lead a slower-paced life. His first job had been interning for James Campbell, editor of the Beaufort Sentinel. During high school and summer breaks from college, James showed John the ins and outs of small-town reporting. The great-great-grandson of the founder, and last surviving male heir of the Campbell name, James was a portly Southern gentleman of seventy with a head of wispy white hair that seemed to have just weathered a windstorm. John had always kept up with his mentor, who was like a father figure, calling him frequently. During one of those calls he learned that James had developed heart problems and was considering selling the Beaufort Sentinel. He saw a chance to break away from the rat race, and took it.

Taking a leave of absence from the *Post*, John made several trips to Beaufort to discuss the matter before he and James agreed on terms. James stipulated that he wanted a continuing role, something akin to Editor Emeritus, when physically able. John added a further proviso: James must stop in from time to time to provide insights into Beaufort society. This had delighted James. They sealed the deal with a drink on the front porch swing of James' home as the sun slowly set over Beaufort.

John smiled at the memory as he turned onto US 21, minutes away from the Sentinel.

John Hill was coming home.

CHAPTER 2

James Campbell took a look around the office. He wanted to soak in his last few moments as Editor of the Sentinel before John arrived.

He went slowly down the stairs into the basement where old newspapers were archived in wooden camphorwood storage chests along the side and back walls. Sweating profusely, he chuckled to himself at the mess John had made. A week earlier, John had removed the papers from the chests for 1830 and 1831 to look up articles about President Jackson and the Indian Removal Act—one of John's pet projects.

James bent down to pick up the papers strewn across the floor and stopped dead in his tracks. He felt his heart flip into what his doctor would later call a supraventricular tachycardia heart rhythm. Collapsing to the floor, James clutched his chest as his heart pounded furiously. He waited for the dangerous rhythm to stop, but instead, it speeded up. As it reached two hundred beats per minute he felt a fear he had never felt before—the fear of dying. Panic, mixed with copious amounts of sweat, broke out all over James Campbell's body.

Got to get up the stairs, reach the phone . . . don't want to die in the basement.

Clutching his chest, afraid his heart was going to explode,

James turned onto his side. Slowly, in snakelike fashion, he slithered towards the stairs, not moving at anything faster than a snail's pace for fear of causing his heart to jump into an even more dangerous and faster rhythm. He reached the stairs. It seemed like an eternity. In reality, only a couple minutes had passed.

James raised his right arm and reached for the banister that seemed to float in front of him like a lifeline tossed from the deck of a ship. He grabbed hold. Slowly, he raised himself up. His heart raced faster. He stood for a minute . . . not moving . . . expecting the worst . . . but nothing happened. He lifted his right leg onto the bottom step. When he lifted his left leg, it happened—his heart stopped with a huge thump. It felt as if someone had punched him in the chest, right over his heart muscle. The dangerous racing tachycardia was suddenly broken; his heart snapped back into a normal rhythm. But the suddenness startled James. As he lowered his left leg it landed on the edge of the step and slipped off.

All James' weight shifted to his left side. In his panicked condition he lost grasp of the banister and fell backwards, spinning counterclockwise. His head struck a large filing cabinet, creating a shallow inch-long gash just above and behind his left temple, knocking him unconscious. He fell onto a three-foot stack of newspapers that cushioned his fall and created a makeshift compress for his wound.

* * *

John pulled up in front of the Sentinel and looked up at the two-hundred-year-old red brick building he was now the proud owner of. He went inside to look for James before unloading his worldly possessions from the small U-Haul. Calling out, he received no response.

That's strange.

James knew he would be arriving this afternoon. He looked around the office and noticed a cup of coffee on the editor's desk. He went over and felt it.

Still warm.

Beginning to get a little worried, John shouted out James' name, over and over. He searched the front and back living quarters.

No James.

He searched the upstairs. Still no James.

John went downstairs to the basement. And there, lying on newspapers scattered across the floor, he found him. Rushing to his side, John noticed blood seeping from a gash in James' head. He leaned over and called to him but got no response. He pressed a hand to James' chest, feeling for a heartbeat, but could feel none. He ran back upstairs and dialed 911. After his frantic explanation, the operator dispatched paramedics and instructed John in the application of CPR. He ran back down the stairs and immediately started chest compressions. After thirty compressions he checked for breathing: finding none, he bent down to give James mouth-to-mouth breaths.

As John began mouth-to-mouth breathing, James' eyes opened up.

"I never expected you to take advantage of an old man this way."

"I thought you were dead," John said, jumping up in shock.

"That kind of makes it even sicker, don't you think?"

James put his hand to his head. John helped him to a sitting position against the filing cabinet.

"Stay right there, James. Don't try to get up, I called the paramedics. They should be here any second."

"I didn't have a heart attack. I had a heart arrhythmia and fell, hitting my head."

"James, you didn't have a heartbeat."

"That's because you couldn't feel it through my Rubenesque figure."

Attempting to get up, James fell back to a sitting position as paramedics arrived. Within minutes he was placed on a stretcher and loaded into the ambulance for the short ride to Beaufort Memorial.

CHAPTER 3

It was nearly seven in the evening before the doctor would let John in to see James. He was sitting up in bed watching an old movie starring Humphrey Bogart.

"How many times have you watched that movie?"

"At least two hundred. I know all the lines by heart. If they ever film a remake, I've got the Casper Gutman character sewed up."

"I'm sure you do," John said, pulling up a chair to James' bedside. "So tell me, what did the doctors say?"

"Mild heart attack. Probably from the shock of seeing you on top of me," James said with a pretend scowl. "My doctor says I was lucky I didn't have a stroke, my blood was frothing around like a washing machine. They want to do something called an RF ablation. Zap some cells on my heart that cause the arrhythmias." James hit the mute button on the remote. "Going to snake some thin wires through my groin and neck arteries first thing in the morning. A minor procedure. The doctor says he's also going to clear a small blockage, maybe put in a stent while they're at it. Said I'll be back home in a couple days. Sooner, if I wasn't so fat and old."

"You need anything? Maybe something to read? Newspaper, magazine, book?"

"Get me the latest issue of Cosmo, if you would."

"Really? Cosmo?" John looked a bit amused.

"Positively," James said, beaming. "I like to keep up with what the women of today are thinking."

"I'll get you a health and fitness magazine."

James looked at John sourly.

They talked for a while about the Beaufort Sentinel and plans for smuggling James his beloved scotch and water. After a half hour, John could see that the day's events had taken a lot out of his friend. Rising out of his chair he told James to get some rest, and squeezed his shoulder before turning to leave.

"One more thing, John . . . uh . . . if you would. I know it's not my paper anymore."

"What?" John interrupted gently.

"Could you *please* clean up that mess in the basement? You know how anal I am."

"Bye," John said with a laugh and shake of his head.

As John reached the door, James, in a surprisingly strong voice said, "*Wait.*"

He turned and looked back at his mentor.

"Thanks for today," James said.

John blew him a kiss and slowly closed the door behind him.

"By gad, sir, you never cease to amaze me with your antics." In perfect mimicry of Sydney Greenstreet's fictional Casper Gutman, James' words followed John through the closing door.

CHAPTER 4

Thirty-two-year-old John Hill sat on a stack of old newspapers, breathing in the smell of crumbling bricks in the musty basement of the Sentinel. The moldering decay made him think of James' physical decay. Sitting amidst the scattered remains of history from so long ago reminded John of how transient life was.

Once we're gone, we're all just history. That's if we've done something with our lives that history will take note of.

This last thought made John realize that maybe coming home was an admission of defeat rather than reconnecting with the people he loved. He thought of James, lying there in a pool of blood. Turning his attention to cleaning up the mess and cleansing his mind of negative thoughts, he picked up the bloodstained newspaper which had so recently served as a pillow for James' head. The date was Friday, June 4, 1830.

Indian Removal Act - Savages offered new territories west of Mississippi!

Federal Government to negotiate with Indians to voluntarily move to lands west of the Mississippi river. President Jackson says the Act will "separate the Indians from immediate contact with settlements of whites and enable them to pursue happiness in their own way and under their own crude institutions."

William Crawford

The Act

Be it enacted by the Senate and House of Representatives of the United States of America, in Congress assembled, that it shall and may be lawful for the President of the United States to cause so much of any territory belonging to the United States, west of the river Mississippi, not included in any state or organized territory, and to which the Indian title has been extinguished, as he may judge necessary, to be divided into a suitable number of districts, for the reception of such tribes or nations of Indians as may choose to exchange the lands where they now reside, and remove there; and to cause each of said districts to be so described by natural or artificial marks, as to be easily distinguished from every other.

Our beloved President went on to address those presently assembled at the signing:

"And is it supposed that the wandering savage has a stronger attachment to his home than the settled, civilized Christian? Is it more afflicting to him to leave the graves of his fathers than it is to our brothers and children? Rightly considered, the policy of the General Government toward the red man is not only liberal, but generous. He is unwilling to submit to the laws of the States and mingle with their population. To save him from this alternative, or perhaps utter annihilation, the General Government kindly offers him a new home, and proposes to pay the whole expense of his removal and settlement."

Turning the pages of the bloodstained newspaper, John came across an article about a Mr. Owens: stabbed in a fight over the honor of his wife by one Mr. Andrews. It seems that an attending doctor proclaimed for all to hear that Mr. Owens wounds were not life threatening, whereupon Mr. Owens promptly expired. Mr. Andrews was later found not guilty of murder, based upon the testimony of all present that the good doctor had proclaimed Mr. Owens wounds to be of the non-lethal variety.

Delving further into the old newspaper, John found a curious article with the following headline:

Floating Man from France to perform aerial stunts this Saturday

The Floating Man

Henri Richaud, the amazing Floating Man, will be demonstrating his antigravity device in Union Square this Saturday, June 5, at 1:00 p.m. Mr. Richaud amazed the crowd in Savannah last week by floating above their heads and performing several passes over the assembled throngs, who gazed in awe and some terror. The device that Mr. Richaud has invented appears to work by some sort of electrical means, utilizing the repellant force of gravity. In an interview with the Southern Times, Mr. Richaud, who has been performing along the Eastern Seaboard of our great country, said he hopes to cap off his summer tour by performing for President Andrew Jackson on the lawn of the White House. Mr. Richaud, who served in the armies of Napoleon, and was a colleague of the late great French scientist, Pierre-Simon Laplace, hopes one day to make a conveyance capable of transporting several passengers. The Honorable Pastor Leonard Pearson fears that this machine, which in his words, "defies the laws of nature and man," is perhaps the result of a collaboration between Mr. Richaud and evil forces. Pastor Pearson does not discount the possibility of witchcraft being involved, though his is a minority opinion in the community.

John reread the article several times. It had to be some kind of joke. Did James' ancestor, Robert Campbell, enjoy playing practical jokes on his readers? The notion seemed absurd. John began looking through the newspapers scattered around him for the Friday, June 11, 1830 edition of the weekly Beaufort Sentinel. That edition would undoubtedly have a lengthy article on Henri Richaud's performance in Beaufort.

After nearly an hour of looking through several stacks of newspapers, John gave up and went upstairs—showered, and brewed a pot of coffee.

Sitting at the kitchen table in the back of the Sentinel—which doubled as his home—doubts again seeped back into John's mind about his decision to return.

Home. Am I home? Or am I just running away?

John had always believed that a person's life had meaning. Now he was not so sure. Was he a man without purpose, without love? At the exact instant he thought those negative thoughts, a sunbeam streamed in through the kitchen window and splayed across the table.

Looking at the sunbeam, John was suddenly transfixed by one lonely speck of dust, dancing as if in a spotlight. As he stared, this one solitary mote of dust, became, for a moment, suspended in the sunbeam. A crazy irrational thought, one that would shake John to his core and bring him back to some sort of grounded reality entered his brain. This speck of dust was the soul of Henri Richaud trying to communicate with him. As if on cue, the speck of dust moved horizontally across the sunbeam. Reaching the edge, it reversed direction, directly back in front of John's eyes. At that moment, the speck of dust became Henri Richaud, the Floating Man, racing high across a sun-drenched field over the throngs assembled below. As if by magic, John looked down and noticed a mass of dust motes nearer the surface of the table. In his mind the assembled masses watched in awe.

Looking back at the dust mote soul of Henri Richaud floating before him, he watched in amazement as it floated towards his face. When it was mere inches in front of his eyes it ascended upward, disappearing above the sunbeam.

An instant later a cloud moved across the sun, extinguishing the sunbeam and completing the transformation of John Hill. If one speck of dust out of the trillions and trillions of specks of dust could hold such purpose and meaning, surely he could find some meaning in his life.

At that moment John Hill silently made a vow.

Henri Richaud, whoever you are, I will find you. I will dedicate my life to finding your story and bringing it to the world. I make this promise to you and to myself.

CHAPTER 5

Ecole Militaire School, Paris, France, 1785

Professor Pierre-Simon Laplace leaned back in his chair. The thirty-six-year-old mathematician and astronomer, world renowned for his mathematical formulas explaining the stability of the solar system, relaxes after a full day of classes.

Elected to the French Academy of Sciences at the age of twenty-four after being rejected the previous two years, may explain why Laplace is imperious with his colleagues—for whom with but a few exceptions, he has nothing but disdain. Professor Laplace is generous however, with students under his tutelage: frequently engaging them, socially and intellectually.

Sitting comfortably across from him today are two of his most prized pupils: Napoleone (as he was known before he dropped the 'e' at the end) and Henri Richaud, son of a wealthy vineyard owner from the port city of Bordeaux, in the southwest of France.

In his own mind (and perhaps correctly) Pierre-Simon Laplace is the most brilliant scientist of his time, and never ceases to remind others of this fact.

"Did you know I am referred to as the Newton of France?"

"I was not aware of that, Professor. Were you, Napoleone?" Henri looked over to his friend, the future Emperor of France with a smirk.

"I cannot say with certainty that I have heard the phrase either."

"Oh, come come boys, I tell you every day. In fact, it is more than a little demeaning to be known as the Sir Isaac Newton of France, when I have more knowledge of the universe than he ever had. He should be known as the Laplace of England, no?"

"That may be true, sir. But then again, Newton does have the misfortune of being dead now for almost sixty years. And I *believe* he remains dead to this day." Fifteen-year-old Henri Richaud leaned back to his left, stretched out his legs and languorously threw his right arm over the back of his chair. He looked over at Napoleone, anticipating an amusing retort, and was not disappointed.

"Professor, if it assuages your hurt feelings a little, I believe I can safely say that one day Henri will be known as the Alessandro Volta of France."

"It would assuage my feelings more, my dear Napoleone, if he were known as the Luigi Galvani of France," Laplace said in a mocking Italian accent while looking intensely into Henri's eyes.

Henri, a bit unnerved by the Professor's intense stare, looked down.

"You do not think highly of Galvani's theory of electrical fluid in animal tissue, Professor?"

"Henri, I do not think that making dead frog's legs jump by connecting them to metal strips a profound discovery. That is equivalent to the first woman who chopped off the head of a chicken and watched it run around the barnyard. You two are my brightest pupils. But Henri, I believe your work on bioelectrical energy will eventually lead you to a dead end." Professor Laplace nodded at Napoleone and continued: "Napoleone is right. Better to be known as the Volta of France. Right now he is working on electrical current, and batteries which will one day power marvelous new devices."

"But Professor, why not study both in parallel? Animate and human electrical energy fields along with inanimate electrical energy fields. Surely all living things are subject to the same forces of gravitational attraction and magnetism as are the planets of the solar system. We all exert a physical effect, no matter how minutely, with everything around us."

"Henri, your point is well taken. But I am afraid I am busy at the present time, fixing the orbits of Jupiter and Saturn, along with proving the stability of the Solar System to my esteemed members of the academy. Who, I might add, are too insufficient to understand my explanations without having it spelled out to them mathematically, like some dumb child. And Henri . . . once I have done that, and as soon as I am done fixing the speed and motion of the moon, I will work with you on your unified theory of the effect of animate and inanimate objects on the magnetic field. Should take me no more than a week. In the meantime, why don't you two work on proving mathematically why animate objects such as yourselves tend to wobble and tilt on their axis, instead of orbiting smoothly through their course of studies here at Ecole."

* * *

Back in their living quarters the setting sun sent shards of light through the window. Napoleone sat on a chair, looking over at Henri, who lay on his bed trying to catch the last glimmers of sunlight on the book he was reading. The book, *Dangerous Liaisons*, published less than three years earlier, had caused quite a stir in France. Through a series of fictional letters, it told the tale of two ex-lovers and rivals: the Marquise de Merteuil and the Vicomte de Valmon; following them as they used sex to manipulate and exact revenge on those around them. Written by Choderlos de Laclos, a captain in the engineering section of the French army, it was an immediate sensation, selling over a thousand copies in the first month of publication. It was said to be a favorite of Queen Marie Antoinette.

"Henri, what are you reading?"

"*Dangerous Liaisons*, by Laclos."

"Ah, Laclos, he is a good military man. An artillery expert, graduated from the Ecole Royale D'artillerie de La Fere. I will probably study under him one day. A bit of a decadent pervert, if his writing is any indication."

Henri, still reading, casually said to his friend, "Why my dear Napoleone, you do not believe all is fair game when it comes to love and war?"

For some reason this remark seemed to strike a nerve in Napoleone. His voice rose in pitch. "Where is the honor in everyone deceiving and provoking jealousy in each other? Using sex as revenge instead of remaining virtuous is not my idea of the way human society should behave. It is why our aristocracy is so despised. There is no honor. Our whole society is rotting from within, and everyone seems to be content on drinking, partying, and dancing their lives away."

Putting his book down, Henri turned onto his side and propped his head up with his hand. "I could not agree with you more. And our beloved king better be careful. If he raises taxes on the poor any higher, there will be nothing left for them to do, but to die or revolt. And if you are going to starve to death, you might as well go out with a bang. An admittedly different type of bang than our aristocratic friends are going out with. And of course, using sex as a weapon will not work if the masses revolt. But then again, I suppose you have to work with what you have. And Laclos does make for some very enjoyable reading."

Napoleone shook his head and grinned.

"I can see that it does, my dear friend. Go play with your pistol and I will stick with my artillery."

Henri smiled back mischievously.

"Napoleone, must you always have to have the bigger explosions?"

"It makes up for my lack of aim."

A cloud suddenly crossed Napoleone's face. He turned serious and changed the subject.

"Tell me something, Henri. Why is it that when I came to Ecole, you were the only one that did not make fun of my Corsican accent? Everyone picked on me but you. And you certainly did not have to make my fight yours. Why?"

Henri raised himself to a sitting position and faced his good friend. He looked down for a few moments to gather his thoughts before looking back up.

"I guess it must have seemed strange to you. It certainly seemed strange to me. I had never seen you before in my life, but there you were, in the courtyard of Ecole with your bags at your feet, surrounded by jeering students. I heard the commotion, so being a curious fellow, I walked over to see what all the fuss was about."

"I was about to get my ass kicked, that was what all the fuss was about! And then you came and did a most remarkable thing."

"A brilliant thing," Henri added.

"In hindsight, I suppose you are right. But at the time, it did not seem to me to be so brilliant."

"You did not think it brilliant the way I walked right up to you, telling those other boys to get out of my way?"

"Admittedly, it was brilliant the way you took charge and said, 'Out of my way. Leave this one to me. I know how to handle this one.' The way you took command of the situation. That part I have no problem with. Nor the part where you winked at me, letting me in on whatever you were planning, and then grabbing me by the collar. Up to that point, Henri, your plan was brilliant."

"And whispering into your ear? Was that not also brilliant?"

"That was brilliant too. Even what you whispered into my ear, while I would not characterize it as brilliant, was at least satisfactory to me."

"So we are quibbling then with the execution of the plan?"

"Yes! Yes, exactly. Your strategy was perfect. The execution? Not so much."

"Well it was the first time I had ever punched anyone in the face."

Both boys looked at each other and broke out laughing.

Henri continued: "You know, if I had met you earlier we might have had time to practice. But Napoleone, you played your part most convincingly. I loved the way you rolled your eyes back into your head, pretending to be knocked out."

Napoleone, still laughing, managed to say, "I *was* knocked out, dammit!"

At that moment, Henri looked stone-faced at Napoleone. Softly, with some regret, and in a most sincere tone of voice, he said, "Napoleone, I am so sorry. I always thought you were acting. It pains me to realize that you missed out on the most brilliant aspect of my plan."

"I will, of course, accept your apology for knocking me out, although I have the strange suspicion that you are sorrier for my not watching the finale of your performance, of which, I am sure, you will presently fill me in on."

Napoleone made a grand sweeping gesture with his hand.

"Please, if you will, Henri, on with the finale of your most brilliant plan."

"Seems like a letdown in retrospect, knowing that you were not witness to it. I merely told your tormentors that if anyone had a problem with this Corsican, they were to see me. I alone would deal with you. And if they did not, they would get what I gave to you. Then I told them all to get out of my sight because my thirst for blood was not yet assuaged."

"You *actually* said your thirst for blood was not yet assuaged?"

"Probably not. But something to that effect."

"So Henri, you still have not told me why you would involve yourself in my difficulties. Why?"

"This is going to sound strange to you, and I hesitate to tell you, for fear that you might misinterpret what I am about to say. Then again, I do not know if I have an interpretation to explain it either, but here goes. When I saw you standing there with your bags at your feet, surrounded by that callous uncaring mob, I saw my mother standing there."

"I am so sorry for your mother, Henri."

"Thank you, Napoleone, for your little joke, but no, mother did not look like you. It's just that the first memory I have of my mother is her carrying a sack of groceries at the market. My mother has a palsied leg which makes walking very difficult. Each step for her was and is very painful to watch. After taking a step, she would set down her sack of groceries. All the villagers were milling around, much like the boys circling you on your first day. I watched my mother move, step by step, struggling to stay upright and carry that heavily laden sack. Nobody would help her, but everyone stared as she slowly made her way down the market street. Then out of nowhere, I saw my dad running up to her. When he got to her side he stopped and hugged her for a very long time. He leaned into her, kissed her gently, and relieved her of her sack. She laid her head on his shoulder and he wrapped his arm around her, helping her down the street. With my dad by her side she appeared to walk normally, as if her palsied leg had magically healed. That's it. I guess that is why I helped you. I love you like my dad loves my mother."

"More like a brother, perhaps?" Napoleone looked at Henri; he averted his eyes and looked down at his feet.

"Yes, I suppose, more like a brother. Of course."

"And that is why you helped to rid me of my Corsican accent?"

"I suppose so. Tried to anyway. I could not help my mother. As a small child I prayed every day for God to heal her. But apparently he has more important things to do, and leaves us to fend for ourselves."

"Henri? Maybe God brought us together. Maybe God has a plan for the both of us. We just cannot see it at the moment."

"Perhaps." Looking up with a slight smile, Henri continued; "But Professor Laplace does not believe in God."

"No, Henri, he believes in God. He believes he is God."

CHAPTER 6

In the basement of the old eighteenth-century building, home to the weekly Beaufort Sentinel since its inception in 1828, John continued his search for the elusive Friday, June 11, 1830 edition. He was puzzled. Robert Campbell, the original editor of the Sentinel until his death in 1886 at the age of eighty, was meticulous in archiving his old editions—a tradition that his son, Robert Jr. did not carry on.

Each year's editions were stored in virtually identical, golden-brown camphorwood chests, adorned with brass corners and locking hasps, the year stamped on each brass faceplate. Native to China, Indochina, Japan, and Australia; camphorwood chests were widely used by seamen of the nineteenth century. The wood gave off a pleasing scent which repelled insects and moths, making them excellent for storage. The chests were chronologically stacked on shelves that lined the side and back walls of the Sentinel.

James, especially proud of his great-great-grandfather's attention to preservation, renewed the tradition of archiving each year's editions in camphorwood storage chests when he took over the helm in 1970.

When he first showed John the newspapers from his forbear's 1828 storage chest, John had been amazed at their remarkable condition. This was due to the type of paper the early newspapers were printed on. Up until the late 1870s, the Beaufort Sentinel was printed using rag linen, as were most newspapers of the era. James explained that rag-linen paper was actually made from a mash of boiled down clothing. The paper contained no acid or wood pulp, making it much more stable than later editions from the 1870s. That, along with storage in the camphorwood chests, explained their remarkable condition.

Given the elaborate storage and archiving system, John was mystified as to why he could not find the next few editions of the Sentinel following the one on Henri Richaud's flight—the one that James' head had so fortunately landed on.

A week prior to James' accident, John had removed the papers from the 1830 camphorwood chest. He had been doing research for a historical piece on the forced removal of Indian tribes from the early colonial states, culminating in the long march of the Cherokee nation from their homes in the southeastern United States to Oklahoma. The forced march of the Indian peoples to Oklahoma, known as the Trail of Tears, resulted in the death of anywhere from eighteen hundred to four thousand Cherokee out of a total population of approximately seventeen thousand.

As John restarted the search for the missing edition, the initial euphoria he felt upon discovering the news of a man floating above throngs of people, dissipated. Doubts about the significance of the event crept into his mind. Unable to find any additional information in the archives, John began to feel that maybe Henri Richaud was just one of a handful of early hot air balloonists.

A quick Google of hot air ballooning revealed that many of the first balloonists were indeed French. Perhaps it was not just coincidence that Henri Richaud was also French. The first recorded flight of a hot air balloon occurred over Paris on November 21, 1783. On that date, the Montgolfier brothers built and flew a balloon that reached a height of several hundred feet. Only a few days later on December 1, 1783 a hydrogen filled balloon piloted by Professor Jacques Charles and Nicholas Louis Robert flew almost two thousand feet over Paris: staying aloft for over two hours before landing in a small town twenty-five miles away. A French balloonist floating over Union Square in Beaufort, South Carolina, certainly would have been an amazing sight. And one not likely seen before by the residents.

But there were still those missing editions of the Sentinel.
John's mind raced.

Wouldn't an editor of a paper know about hot air or gas balloons even if he had never seen one? Surely, someone who would write a lead article on the Indian Removal Act as Robert Campbell had done would also keep up with the latest scientific developments. And balloons had been invented almost fifty years earlier.

John momentarily vanquished his self-doubts. In earnest, he began a systematic search through several years of the Sentinel.

The preceding two years of the Sentinel were complete, but the 1830 editions beginning with June 11 were incomplete. There was a missing gap for the period of June 11 through September 17. The one other missing paper was the Friday, New Years Eve edition.

John decided to go through the 1831 and 1832 storage chests. In the 1831 chest he found two installments missing, and one in the 1832 chest. Curiously, in both years there was a missing edition in June, approximating the June 5, 1830 anniversary of the Floating Man's appearance in Beaufort. The June 3, 1831 and June 8, 1832 editions, along with the December 30, 1831 edition were missing.

John put all the facts together. First, there were the missing editions in 1830 corresponding with the summer tour of Henri Richaud, aka the Floating Man. Second, the editions that would have celebrated the anniversary of the events of June 5, 1830 were missing in the 1831 and 1832 editions. And third, the end of the year edition of the paper was missing in both the 1830 and 1831 editions. Putting it all together, John came to the conclusion that something indeed remarkable had happened in the summer of 1830.

John played devil's advocate one more time as doubts again crept back into his mind. Perhaps Robert Campbell had removed editions of the Sentinel that referred to the event in order to write a book of his memoirs. Hot air and gas balloons were still in their infancy and this would have certainly been a significant event in his life. But something in John's gut told him that there was more to the story than a simple hot air balloon over the square. John reread the original story from the June 4, 1830 edition.

After going over the article line by line, John became convinced that by 1830 a hot air balloon could not be mistaken for a device that in the words of the editor, "appears to work by some sort of electrical means, utilizing the repellant force of gravity." This was a once in a century story of great historical significance—of this he was positive. One that would require all his investigative talents. From his years at the *Washington Post*, John was used to tracking down witnesses on big stories; but in this case, all his witnesses were dead.

CHAPTER 7

It was late in the day when John finished working up a plan of action for investigating what he labeled, "The Case of the Mysterious Henri Richaud aka The Floating Man." After listing what he knew, what leads to follow, etc., he relaxed for the first time that day, settling into his vintage, leather club chair with a whiskey on the rocks. Both whiskey and chair were nicely aged. John took a sip and gazed out the large picture window of his office, watching the sun slowly lower its gaze on the residents of Beaufort. He was alone with his thoughts for several minutes when the back door opened and closed. He heard a tinkling of ice cubes in a glass, water running for a few seconds, and then the creaking of old oak floorboards as footsteps came towards him from behind.

"You're late tonight." John did not turn as James settled into the matching leather chair next to him, plunking down his usual scotch and water on the cocktail table between them.

"You know, Thelma used to love sitting on the porch, watching the sunset." James, a widower, had lost his beloved wife a year earlier to lung cancer. "I would of course join her on the swing chair. Did that every day in the summer, rain or shine, for almost thirty years."

"Sounds beautiful. Like a Norman Rockwell painting." John raised his glass, clinked James' glass and made a toast: "Here is to

Thelma, God rest her soul."

"God rest her soul," James said, almost in unison.

"I'm sorry, my friend. Our little Saturday evenings must pale in comparison."

"Are you *kidding* me? I hated it. Every day getting attacked by bugs. Never seemed to bother Thelma, but they were all over me. Something in my sweat glands. I looked it up once. Something called carbolic or carboxylic acids. Can't remember exactly, but I have it in prodigious quantities. I think that's why Thelma always had me join her on the porch."

"To keep the skeeters away from her."

"Exactly." James pulled out a bag of broken-up pieces of dark chocolate. "Want some?"

"No thanks, I'm good," John said, raising his glass to take another sip.

"You know, it's lucky for you I didn't find out about the beneficial effects of dark chocolate on the arteries and heart before I sold you the paper."

"Does the doctor know you're eating that stuff?"

"They don't know everything. I've been out less than a week and already I feel twenty years younger." He took another sip of scotch and water. "Besides, I'm following doctor's orders as we speak. A drink or two helps protect the heart."

"Eating chocolate and drinking scotch sounds like a pretty brutal health regimen to follow."

"I'll survive. We all have to make some sacrifices," James said, turning to face John. "And speaking of sacrifices, thanks for cleaning up that bloody mess in the basement."

"Funny thing about that bloody mess," John said, turning serious. "You literally landed on the story of a lifetime."

"How so?" James said, looking a bit confused.

John related the discovery of the Floating Man article and the missing editions of the Beaufort Sentinel. When he finished, he got up and brought his friend the June 4, 1830 edition of the Sentinel.

James read the article. He put the paper down and looked quizzically at his friend.

"So what do you plan on doing next?"

"First, I plan on refilling our drinks." John got up and grabbed James' raised glass.

"Easy on the Scotch. Doctor's orders."

Returning with drinks in hand, John settled back down and gazed out at the last few rays of sunlight.

"Second, I'll see if I can track down the interview the *Southern Times* did with Henri Richaud. Savannah was mentioned in the article as a place where Richaud performed the week previous to coming to Beaufort. And since he was traveling up the Eastern Seaboard he would have undoubtedly stopped in Charleston. So it makes sense to research some old archived papers from around that time. I guess I should also do some research on this French scientist, Laplace, who apparently was a colleague of Henri Richaud's. Hopefully there will be some record of his meeting Andrew Jackson . . . if his tour made it to Washington. I'm still close with Max Baker, the editor of the Washington Post. And an investigative reporter I did some articles with, Sheila Jefferson, now works for the NSC. I know she's busy, being on the staff of the National Security Council, but I'm sure she could pull a few strings and get someone at the National Archives to help me with some research."

"You won a Pulitzer Prize with her, didn't you?"

"Yep, sure did."

"And if I remember correctly, she's very hot as your generation puts it so crassly?"

"Correct on both counts. Beauty and generational colloquialisms. So tell me, James, is there anything I've missed as far as my investigative plans are concerned?"

"Seems from your perspective you have everything covered. But if it was me doing the research, I would first look at the missing editions that are probably stored in my basement along with the other editions my great-great-grandfather archived in the house."

"Excuse me?" John looked like he had just been hit in the head with a brick.

"My forebear was very anal, but also quite advanced for his time. Of course he would have a backup copy, just like we have today. His version of a flash drive was identical camphorwood storage chests."

* * *

"Well that's the strangest thing. This certainly is turning out to be quite a mystery, John."

They had gone through the 1830–1832 camphorwood chests stored in the basement of the ancestral Campbell family home and came up empty. Every edition missing in the archives back at the Sentinel was also missing from the chests stored in James Campbell's home. John was too stunned to say anything.

"There's a reason for this," James said. "An explanation. We just have to find out what it is. It's just part of the puzzle. My grandfather was too meticulous. In fact, I guarantee you that if we go through every other chest we will not find any other missing editions of the paper. And if there is one here or there, it's probably related to this Henri Richaud. But why? John, this is such fun. You must let me join you in this quest."

James put an arm around his crestfallen friend, continuing to babble as they walked back upstairs. "You wouldn't want such a mystery to be solved immediately, would you? What satisfaction would there be in that? C'mon, John. It's like the search for the Maltese Falcon. I'm Casper Gutman, the Sydney Greenstreet character to your Sam Spade. Does it matter if we have to spend more time searching for our little bird? It's only an expense of time and money." Chuckling, James added, "Your money, to be precise."

James opened the door for John to leave.

"I don't mind a reasonable amount of trouble, but didn't your Gutman character spend seventeen years looking for the Falcon, with no result?" John said, standing on the porch.

"Well, well now, what's this?" James replied in his Casper Gutman voice.

"Did you memorize *every* line from the movie?"

"Positively! Oh, and John, happy anniversary."

Looking confused, John asked, "What are you talking about?"

"Today is the fifth of June. The anniversary of Henri Richaud floating over Beaufort."

John stared for a few moments at the closing door before turning to leave. His thoughts on a man and events nearly two centuries old.

CHAPTER 8

Midnight, Paris, France, June 19, 1792

    Paris on the eve of the third anniversary of the Oath of the Tennis Court was on fire with rumors of a march to Tuileries Palace and a possible assassination of King Louis XVI. It had been almost three years to the day since deputies of the Third Estate, representing commoners, declared themselves the National Assembly of France in defiance of King Louis XVI. In the following days, a majority of the clerics of the First Estate along with a handful of nobles of the Second Estate joined the commoners.
    On June 20, 1789, after being refused admittance to their assigned assembly hall, the deputies of the Third Estate moved to a nearby tennis court and unanimously adopted an oath that asserted sovereignty resided in the people themselves, not with the king. The 577 members agreed to stay assembled until a constitution was written and adopted. One week later, King Louis XVI capitulated and summoned representatives of all the Estates for the purpose of writing a constitution. In the following weeks, as he saw his support crumble, King Louis XVI ordered the remaining Clergy and Nobility to join the Third Estate.
    But if the king thought these actions would quell the

revolutionary ardor rampant across France, he was rudely reminded otherwise less than a month later. On July 14, one thousand Parisians stormed the royal fortress prison known as the Bastille, looking to free those imprisoned by King Louis XVI. Bernard-Rene De Launay, Governor of the Bastille, hoping to avoid a bloodbath, surrendered to the assembled mob on the condition that he and his men would be spared harm. De Launay was escorted under protection of the leader of the insurrection to the Hotel de Ville. Unfortunately for de Launay, the crowd had other ideas. A heated argument over his fate ensued at the steps of the Hotel de Ville. Governor De Launay soon sealed it.

After being insulted by a man called Desnot, he shouted, "Enough! Let me die!" De Launay then kicked the man in the groin and was repeatedly stabbed and shot. He suffered his final ignominy at the hands of a Parisian butcher, who cut off his head and placed it on a wooden pike to be carried aloft through the streets of Paris.

Now, three years later, in the fateful summer of 1792, Napoleone and his friend, Henri Richaud, had a ringside seat on events that would ultimately lead to the overthrow of the monarchy and the execution of King Louis XVI. In a small second floor Paris apartment overlooking the public square of the king's Tuileries Palace they reminisced about old times and the amazing events that had rocked France the past few years.

Napoleone regaled Henri with his exploits on the island of Corsica. After failing in an attempt to seize the Citadel of Ajaccio (his hometown) from the French garrison stationed there, he narrowly escaped back to France where he found he was listed as absent without leave. He then spent the next few weeks politicking legislators to get reinstated as an officer in the French army.

"So let me see if I understand you," Henri said, leaning forward in his chair. "You become lieutenant colonel in a battalion of the Corsican Volunteers and try to seize the French citadel at Ajaccio. You stir up the whole island against you and flee back to Paris where you are absent without leave from the army, and get reinstated. After attacking French troops."

"And I got promoted to captain," Napoleone grinned.

"I don't understand how that happens," Henri said, shaking his head.

"It's all a game of politics. Everything has been screwed up here the last few years; you just have to know who is calling the shots, day-by-day. I spent more time at the Legislative Assembly then I did at the officers' quarters."

"And more time on leave than on duty," Henri replied.

"They value my expertise as an artillery theoretician." Napoleone smiled and leaned back in his chair. "And what about you, Henri? What have you and Professor Laplace been up to?"

"I've been helping him with the mathematical approach to his laws of universal gravitation. Setting up equations to explain the motions of the centers of gravity of the various bodies in the solar system. But I am more excited about electromagnetic force. I believe that it is possible to use the attractive and repellant force of electromagnetic fields along with centrifugal force to levitate an object. After all, aren't the planets, in reality, levitating?"

"So no more jumping frog's legs?" Napoleone said in a jab at his old classmate.

"No, Professor Laplace was right about Galvani. Volta's line of research on electrical batteries is much more promising in the field of electromagnetic levitation."

"Why not work on refining hot air balloons? Monsieur Montgolfier flew over Paris almost ten years ago. And others since have done the same," Napoleone replied.

"Yes, yes, I was there! I saw the Montgolfier brothers' balloon take off. But when it landed over five miles away the pilots had to walk back. I want to be able to control where I am going."

"But can you control gravity?" Napoleone asked earnestly.

"I believe you can, by reducing and increasing magnetic fields through centrifugal force."

"And what if you cannot?"

"Well . . . then I guess I will just have to put a horse aboard my balloon so I won't have to walk back," Henri said, laughing at his own joke.

Napoleone shook his head. "Still the same old Henri. You will never change."

"And you, my friend, are still the same old Napoleone. Always out looking for a fight, regardless of the side. You hate us French, but yet you fight for us . . . sometimes."

"Speaking of fights, have you heard what is going to happen tomorrow?"

"I have heard rumors."

"They are more than rumors, Henri. According to my contacts, the Girondists are going to stage a demonstration at the Assembly. Afterwards, they plan to march on the palace to protest the removal of their cabinet ministers and overturn the king's veto of their decrees. And Santerre has been plotting for the past few weeks and plans to lead his people in a big demonstration."

"If I were the king, I would abdicate and leave Paris."

"He can't, Henri. He tried leaving France a year ago to the day and was dragged back to Paris. He is for all intents and purposes under house arrest. I fear that tomorrow may see the end of the monarchy."

"Is it that serious?"

"Henri, this has been building for weeks. Every section of Paris has been planning armed demonstrations for the anniversary of the Oath of the Tennis Court. I don't see how the municipal authorities or the National Guard can stop them. You see how they've ignored the law against armed demonstrations. My sources in the Royal Court tell me that the king took confession and prepared his will. He even gave last souvenirs to his closest friends to remember him by."

"And which side will you be on, Napoleone?"

"I support the Republic but hate mobs. The king should be subject to the rule of law, not to Santerre's mobs."

Napoleone became lost in thought, remembering the mobs that had chased him from his home in Corsica.

CHAPTER 9

Paris, France, June 20, 1792

On the morning of June 20, festive crowds gathered outside the National Assembly building and the Tuileries Palace. After the storming of the Bastille in 1789, King Louis XVI moved the seat of power from his palace at Versailles to Tuileries in Paris. The Estates General, now the National Assembly, followed suit and moved into the Salle du Manege (formerly Louis the XV's indoor riding arena, situated next to the palace).

Antoine Joseph Santerre, known as the King of the *Faubourgs* (suburbs) was leading a group of demonstrators—the largest of many assembled that day to petition the assembly. Santerre, a wealthy brewer from the *faubourg* Saint Antoine, and hugely popular, was a man of paradoxes. Rough in manner, he could be at turns brutal and cruel, or kindly and generous. Like a chameleon, he would blend into the background of any situation and take advantage of the moment at hand. Three years earlier he had led the battalion that stormed the Bastille. When insulted by the Governor of the Bastille, Santerre ordered his lieutenant, Mathieu Jouve Jourdan to saw off the Governor's head. Now, along with Jourdan and eight thousand of his followers, Antoine Joseph Santerre pressed to gain admittance to the Assembly. His plan was to present a petition protesting the recent removal of several members of the king's cabinet, and after gaining their blessing, march on to the palace where he planned to assassinate King Louis XVI.

Inside the Assembly building, legislators debated letting the crowds in. One of the legislators noted that armed petitioners had been let in on previous occasions. This prompted another legislator to cry out: "For God's sake, there are eight thousand of them and only seven hundred forty-five of us!" The matter was quickly settled when a legislator allied with Santerre replied, "If eight thousand citizens are waiting, twenty-four million French men and women are waiting for me too!"

With that, the crowds were let into the Assembly building.

Napoleone and Henri, let into the gallery of the Assembly building earlier—thanks to Napoleone's political contacts with the legislators—watched from above in amazement as thousands of Parisians marched through the main hall. At the head of the parade, women and children danced and sang, holding wooden spears called pikes in one hand and olive branches in the other—signifying war or peace. Intermingled among grenadiers and armed National Guardsmen were men and women brandishing all varieties of weaponry: long wooden pikes, forks, axes, scythes, clubs, swords, large daggers, etc. A huge banner that read, "Liberty! Tyrants tremble; the French are armed" was held up high by several women. Another banner held aloft read, "Tremble tyrants, your reign approaches its end."

The celebration in the hall went on for nearly thirty minutes until a loud roll of drumbeats silenced the masses. All eyes were drawn to the assembly hall entrance. Under a phalanx of upraised swords walked Santerre, followed by his bodyguards.

Napoleone and Henri watched intently as Santerre walked up to the bar of the Assembly and addressed the legislators.

"Today will decide whether we live as free French men and women under a constitution or as slaves under a monarch. Dear legislators, you are the protectors of our freedoms and I humbly thank you for allowing us to present our petitions of grievances. I also present to you on behalf of the citizens of France, this flag, the symbol of the republic which we cherish and love so much. For which we will lay down our lives to preserve and protect."

The crowd broke into thunderous applause. Singing and

dancing ensued as Santerre moved to consult with his trusted lieutenant, Jourdan.

Napoleone turned and whispered into Henri's ear: "The man next to Santerre, Mathieu Jouve Jourdan, has been with him for years. He is very good with a knife. A butcher by trade and reputation. At Bastille, he cut off the head of Governor De Launay for insulting Santerre. He bears watching, Henri." Henri silently nodded as they both continued to watch Santerre and Jourdan.

After the demonstration and speech by Santerre, the President of the assembly, Francaise de Nantes, rose and donned his hat in a gesture of respect. This was followed by a nod of assent from Santerre, at which time the crowd began to withdraw from the Assembly.

* * *

Tuileries Gardens, 3:15 p.m.

Santerre and Jourdan, followed closely by Henri and Napoleone, walked among the crowd down the narrow courtyard off the Rue Saint-Honoré that separated the Assembly from the gate leading to the gardens of Tuileries Palace. Henri looked around and noticed people of all ages and description: old crippled war veterans, market porters dressed in their finest clothes, women bearing bouquets of flowers, children running and playing. All seemed to have great joy etched on their faces, marching with their signs and banners aloft, extolling the virtues of freedom, liberty, and the constitution.

Henri turned to Napoleone. In a loud voice so he could be heard above the mass of people, he said, "This looks more like a festive occasion rather than a dangerous demonstration. I do not think we have to worry about the king's safety."

"Henri, look behind you about fifty yards." Napoleone pointed to the left, down the courtyard. "Over there, Henri, through the crowd. Look closely. See the cannon?"

Henri squinted and then nodded as the cannon turned onto the narrow courtyard off the Rue Saint-Honoré.

Napoleone put his hand on Henri's shoulder and spread his other hand across the crowd. "Now, block out the old men, women, and children," Napoleone instructed Henri. "Tell me, what do you see? Look at the men carrying pikes. Look at their faces."

"Yes, I see it now," Henri replied, looking at the men carrying weapons sprinkled among the festive crowd: their faces hardened, jaws set, eyes fixed with a determined look.

A man dressed like a market porter, carrying a saber and wearing a conical red liberty cap, ran up to Santerre and Jourdan. The three huddled for a few minutes before the man with the saber ran off towards the gate leading to the gardens of Tuileries Palace.

More and more people funneled into the narrow passageway separating the Assembly building and walls of the palace grounds, pressing up against the gate. They found the usually opened gate closed; a single cannon pointed out at the crowd from behind it. People continued to stream down the passageway. The suffocating crowd became increasingly agitated and began to pound on the gate. In an effort to calm the crowd, municipal officers ordered the removal of the cannon—to no avail. The pressure of the crowd broke down the gate; they jubilantly streamed into the gardens of the palace grounds.

Upon learning of the gathering of a large number of demonstrators at the gate to the palace gardens, measures were taken to increase the number of battalions protecting the king. Ten battalions were placed on the terrace of the palace overlooking the gardens. Several more were stationed around the palace at various points and one was stationed inside, along with over a hundred gendarmes of the Paris police.

The crowd marched by the palace facade. The terrace above was lined shoulder-to-shoulder with National Guardsmen.

The Royal Gate, a large double gate secured with a heavy iron bar, was now the only barrier to entry into the palace. Directed by Santerre, several men went to the Royal Gate to argue for an audience with the king. As heated discussions ensued, more demonstrators showed up. Just as it appeared that the guardsmen inside the courtyard had gained the upper hand, Henri looked over at Santerre, standing some twenty paces behind the Royal Gate, and saw him nod to one of his lieutenants. Immediately, an extremely long pike with a tri-color ribbon attached was raised high into the air. It stayed aloft for thirty seconds and then was lowered. The cannon that Napoleone had earlier pointed out to Henri was brought up and aimed at the gate. Suddenly, a booming voice from inside the courtyard rang out.

"Do not fire! We will open!"

The iron bar holding the double gate was raised by several guardsmen and the gate swung open. Instantly, the crowd poured onto the courtyard leading to the grand staircase: several were trampled to death, having fallen in the onrush.

At the foot of the grand staircase Santerre and Jourdan paused, whereupon two men confronted him loudly.

"Monsieur Santerre, are you going to break the law and enter the king's residence?"

Santerre replied in an equally loud voice for the crowd to hear: "Bear witness that I refuse to go into the kings' apartments."

Napoleone, after observing this, said to Henri, "That was a setup if I ever saw one."

"No doubt. It looks like he has an alibi for the assassination of the king," Henri replied.

"So who will be the assassin? Jourdan? He is still by Santerre's side. Or maybe that market porter with the saber and red liberty cap?"

"Napoleone, look!" Henri pointed to a man running up the palace steps. "Jourdan is moving away from Santerre and entering the palace. I will follow him. You stay with Santerre."

"Alright, stay close to him Henri. And be on the lookout for the porter with the saber. If you lose sight of Jourdan, go to the king's apartment."

After giving Henri directions to the king's apartment, Napoleone left to follow Santerre, who was huddled with some of his men at the base of the grand staircase.

Everywhere, inside and out, chaos ensued. People were turning over furniture, breaking vases, ripping paintings from the walls. More ominously, several men dragged a cannon up a flight of stairs and were only stopped when it got caught in a doorway, preventing further passage of the crowd. The cannon was dragged back down the stairs to let the impatient crowd continue their rampage through the corridors and rooms of the palace. Overwhelmed by the sheer size and fury of the crowd, National Guardsmen and gendarmes alike stood by helplessly as they watched the spectacle unfold before their eyes.

Meanwhile, Henri followed Jourdan up the stairs to the royal apartments. Several in the crowd had already beaten down the doors leading to the first two apartments and were at the door to the third—behind which, King Louis XVI waited with several of his ministers and guards. Henri watched transfixed as several men began pounding on the heavy door with axes. Soon, one of the panels began to give way. Seeing the futility of the situation, the door was ordered open by the king. In a mad rush, protesters streamed in, filling the room to capacity.

One of the ministers to the king addressed the crowd in a loud voice: "Citizens, recognize your king, respect him. The law commands you do it. I will perish; we will all perish rather than allow the least harm to be done to him."

A few moments of confusion followed. This allowed one of the guards to move the king to a window recess, where he could be better seen by the crowd outside the palace and better protected within.

The next several minutes were a blur. Henri searched the crowd for the market porter in the red cap. Amidst shouts from the crowd directed at the king to overturn his recent decisions, followed by the king's response to respect the constitution, Henri struggled to move about the royal apartment. He finally located the man in the red cap, brandishing his saber, constantly moving in what appeared to be an attempt to better position himself for an assassination attempt. Also particularly aware of the man's movements were the National Guardsmen and gendarmes of the Paris police. Transfixed by the efforts of the porter to get in position for a saber thrust, Henri completely lost track of Jourdan. He finally realized to his horror that the movements of the porter were a diversion.

Henri furiously looked for Jourdan, finally spotting him on the other side of the apartment. Smiling, with one arm around a small girl in a soft red cap (the French symbol of liberty) was Jourdan: holding an exceptionally long wooden pike with a sharp metal spear attached to its end. Henri was perplexed for a moment as he slowly moved through the crowd from one end of the apartment to the other, towards Jourdan.

Meanwhile, the king remained surprisingly calm amidst all the threats being hurled at him, answering each in a calm deliberate voice. This was the only thing keeping the king alive, Henri thought.

Now, about twenty feet from Jourdan, he watched nervously as Jourdan removed the red liberty cap from the little girl's head and placed it over the head of the spear. Continuing to fight through the crowd, Henri struggled to get closer. As he closed to within fifteen feet, Jourdan placed the long pike, its sharpened end hidden by the red cap, into the hands of the little girl. Next, Jourdan moved an old army veteran behind the girl.

Still about ten feet away, Henri watched as Jourdan whispered into the girl's ear. As Jourdan got behind the old veteran and grabbed the end of the pole, Henri realized what was about to happen. With an exceptionally loud voice the girl sang out; "Long live the nation and long live our king."

The trio, holding the pole with the red liberty cap at the end, moved forward diagonally from the corner of the room towards the king. Henri now found himself directly behind Jourdan but still too far away to stop the outcome. As the crowd cheered for the king to take the red liberty cap, Henri began roughly moving people out of his way. He managed to get within five feet of Jourdan.

It was too late!

The pole was lowered to within a foot of the king's chest. The king grabbed the hat and placed it on his head to the cheers of the crowd. Jourdan pulled back on the pike to make the fatal thrust into the king's heart. While making this backward movement to get more leverage into his thrust, several people behind Jourdan moved to the side.

Henri saw his last, only hope.

Amidst deafening cheers of *Long live the nation! Long live liberty!* and *Bravo!* Henri dove forward, his fists striking directly behind Jourdan's knees. This, along with the momentum of Jourdan pulling back on the wooden pike caused him to tumble backwards over Henri. The deadly pike rose harmlessly skyward towards the ceiling. With all the attention focused on the king, nobody in the crowd realized what had just occurred.

Jourdan hit the back of his head on the marble tile floor. He looked at Henri lying beside him; in a daze he asked, "What just happened?"

Henri looked into Jourdan's glassy eyes. Thinking fast, he said, "You just killed King Louis XVI. You must leave, now! Quickly! Make your escape!"

Henri, smiling to himself, helped the befuddled Jourdan to the door of the king's apartment and watched as he stumbled down the hall towards the stairs.

Outside the king's window, Napoleone could hear the abusive threats being hurled, as could Santerre who watched and waited nearby. Suddenly, the threats turned to cheers of *Bravo! Long live the nation! Long live liberty!*

Santerre smiled. He thought to himself that Jourdan must have completed the job. Lost in a reverie, he was snapped out of it when Napoleone walked up to him.

"That is disgusting!" Napoleon said.

"What are you referring too?" Santerre tentatively asked.

"That!" Napoleone pointed up to the king's window where Louis XVI appeared with the red symbol of the French revolution perched atop his head. "How could the king tolerate those buffoons?"

Santerre looked up in horror, his mouth agape. "I don't believe it." He turned and entered the palace; Napoleone followed on his heels. Going up the stairs leading to the corridors of the Kings' apartments they met a still befuddled Jourdan, going down.

"Jourdan, what happened up there?" Santerre shook Jourdan by the shoulders.

Looking like a confused wild man, Jourdan replied, "The king was assassinated! I need to find Santerre."

"Jourdan, I am Santerre," he replied, looking directly into Jourdan's eyes and gripping him by the shoulders.

Jourdan broke away and stumbled down the stairs, continuing to mumble, "I need to find Santerre."

Santerre, with Napoleone behind him, reached the king's apartment and entered. Inside, they found the king by the window, sitting on a raised chair, taking a drink from a bottle that was offered by one of the mob filling the room. Through an equal mixture of cheers and jeers, people still pressed the king to reinstate the decrees of the National Assembly. The king tried several times to speak above the noise. His guards were having a hard time holding back the crowd. Santerre realized the crowd was turning to his advantage. The right words would tip them over the edge and ensure the king's demise.

Before Santerre could speak, Napoleone, his hand on a knife

hidden in his waistcoat pocket, gave a sharp jab into Santerre's back. He whispered into his ear: "You may have the king killed my friend, but you will not live to see him hit the floor. The republic is in your hands. If you are willing to die for your cause, now is your moment in history."

Santerre, with a determined look on his face, shouted to the crowd; all eyes instantly turned towards him. "What the devil are you all talking at once for? That is not the way to be heard. We are not going to leave here."

As Santerre spoke these words, Napoleone dug the blade a little deeper into his back.

Santerre continued; "Don't you hear that the king wishes to speak? Let us show him some respect. Your majesty, I apologize for the discomfort we may have caused you, but your people wish their petitions to be heard in the heartfelt manner in which they were presented. You need have no fear from your people. I will be responsible for your safety."

After Santerre spoke, the fervor of the crowd dissipated. The municipal officers (including the mayor) seized the moment: persuading the crowds to disperse and leave the palace.

Outside, on the garden grounds of the palace, Napoleone found Henri.

"What happened in there to Jourdan? We saw him stumbling down the stairs saying the king had been assassinated. He had a wild-eyed look and didn't even recognize Santerre."

Henri smiled and put his arm around Napoleone. They walked to their favorite café off the Rue Saint-Honoré. Two friends; arm in arm, sharing their exploits of the day.

* * *

Two months later, on August 10, 1792, the Tuileries was stormed again. King Louis XVI escaped by secret passageway to the Assembly building where he remained a prisoner until his trial and execution the following year.

* * *

January 21, 1793, Revolution Square, 10:00 a.m.

It was a cold, wet, dreary day when the royal carriage arrived at Revolution Square (formerly called Louis XV Square). After a two-hour procession through the streets of Paris, lined shoulder-to-shoulder with citizens, King Louis XVI calmly stepped out and gazed up at the scaffolding and guillotine that awaited him. Twenty drummers, lined in front of the scaffolding, did a soft roll of the drums. Santerre, now the chief commander of the National Guard of Paris, escorted King Louis XVI up the steps of the scaffold.

In the crowd, watching events unfold, stood Henri Richaud with his mentor, Professor Pierre-Simon Laplace.

"Well Henri, there is no saving the king this day," Laplace said, placing a comforting hand on Henri's shoulder.

"What bothers me more than anything is that Santerre is the one leading him to the guillotine. I wish Napoleone had run him through with his knife."

"Would it have mattered, Henri?" Professor Laplace said as King Louis XVI walked resolutely up the steps to the platform that held the guillotine and his executioners.

"No, I suppose not."

"Just like the planets in their orbits. We all have our predestined fates, Henri."

Henri and Professor Laplace watched as their king reached the platform and turned to address the crowd.

"I die innocent of all the crimes laid to my charge; I pardon those who have occasioned my death; and I pray to God that the blood you are going to shed may never be visited on France."

The king continued to speak, but a National Guardsman on horseback loudly exhorted the drummers to beat their drums and drown out the king. At the same time, the crowd urged the four executioners to get on with their business.

The king was dragged onto the bed of the guillotine; almost immediately, the blade came down, severing his head. The youngest of the executioners, a lad of eighteen, seized King Louis XVI's head by the hair and walked around the scaffolding. Holding the severed head up high, the crowd roared back their approval.

Both Henri and Professor Laplace looked on in disgust.

"If this is what a revolution for freedom looks like, I think I would rather be a slave," Professor Laplace said to Henri.

"I think it would have been better if the king had died at the hands of the mob back at the palace. Was it preordained that I save the king from a murderous mob in June, only to have him murdered by the state?"

"Perhaps you are right after all, Henri. Unlike the planets, we decide our own fate."

"And the fate of France?" Henri said sadly. "I fear that the king's last words—like his life—will not be honored. 'I pray to God that the blood you are going to shed may never be visited on France.'"

* * *

And so began a reign of terror that would see France drenched in blood: swallowing up, one after the other, the leaders of the revolution. Meanwhile, Henri and Professor Laplace retreated to the professor's estate in the countryside where they continued their research, avoiding the political upheavals of Paris.

Henri never again saw Napoleone, the close friend of his youth.

And Napoleone?

He navigated the turbulent currents of French politics, dropped the 'e' off the end of his name and became an Emperor.

CHAPTER 10

Beaufort, South Carolina; Present Day

John got up the next morning at five and made himself a pot of coffee. He poured a good strong cup with a splash of Baileys, went over to the kitchen table, sat down and looked out the window, waiting for sunrise. He liked rising early: watching the sun slowly come up, bringing life and light into his small rustic kitchen. Thinking about the revelatory sunbeam and dust mote of the other day, John smiled and shook his head—then quickly cringed as his thoughts turned to James' accident.

Scary, how quickly one's life could change.

Just a few days earlier he had been thinking of doing a book on the life of Chief John Ross: the one-eighth Cherokee who in 1828 became the first (and only) elected chief of the Cherokee Nation. When President Andrew Jackson forcibly removed the Cherokee from their lands, Chief John Ross was the one who led them on the thousand-mile march to Oklahoma.

It was a propitious coincidence. The newspaper containing the article on the Indian Removal Act of 1830 (part of John's research) also contained the article on the Floating Man. If not for James' fall off the basement steps and that particular newspaper serving as the resting place for his head, John most likely would not have read all the pages.

Funny how a chain of events could lead your life into a totally new direction.

After pouring another cup of coffee, John brought his laptop to the table and began his investigative research. He looked up and printed nineteenth-century maps of the Eastern Seaboard from Florida up through Georgia, the Carolinas, and Virginia, including Washington D.C. He was researching the availability of newspapers from 1830 when the back door off the kitchen opened with a squeak.

"Help yourself to some coffee," John said without turning to see James enter.

James made himself a cup and sat down, placing a battered leather briefcase on the table. Without looking at John he said, "Turn your laptop off."

"Why? Did you *find* something after I left last night?"

"No. But I couldn't sleep. That was quite a story you laid on me last night. I kept thinking about that Floating Man, Henri Richaud, and the missing newspapers. It spans the whole summer of 1830. I have a theory about that."

"Which is?" John closed his laptop, moved it to the side and propped his elbows on the table in front of him.

"I don't think there are any missing editions." James paused for a moment before continuing: "At least not for the summer of 1830. There's only one explanation for the months of June through September being missing in both the office and the house. . . . They didn't exist."

"You're saying the paper was suddenly shut down for those months?"

"I believe so. My great-great-grandfather was quite an adventurer later in life. He traveled all over the world. The first trip he took was to France in 1833, which is quite a coincidence under the circumstances."

"I was thinking about coincidences before you came in this morning. What are the odds that the same edition I was looking for, containing the Indian Removal Act, would also contain the story about Henri Richaud? But anyway, please, go on."

"When my ancestor was away on his travels, his son, Robert Jr., would take over the paper. You could always tell by the style of writing. But Robert Junior was only around seventeen or eighteen years old in 1830. So my guess is that after seeing Henri Richaud perform on that Saturday in June, Robert must have accompanied him on the rest of his summer tour."

"That seems logical. But wouldn't he have written about it? Something like that is a journalist's dream."

"*Exactly*. Old Robert wrote about all his travels. Kept them stored in a separate chest. I checked that chest this morning. Nothing on Henri Richaud. And something further puzzles me."

"What's that?"

"The journals of his trips are very detailed and read like a novella, except for Robert's trip to France in the summer of 1833. Now, I realize that this was his first adventure, but the journal is very antiseptic. There's no life to it. Let's pretend that my wildest speculation is true: that Henri Richaud accompanied my dear old ancestor to France. That would have been one hell of a journal. If Robert went alone to France, it still should have been one hell of a journal. A young man, first time abroad in one of the most enlightened countries in the entire world . . . it doesn't make any sense. I made you a copy. You'll see what I mean. Dead. No life in the writing whatsoever."

"Quite a mystery we have. Guess I better fire up my laptop and see if I can find some small-town newspapers from 1830 where our Frenchman might have visited."

"Actually, that's why I'm here. I told you I couldn't sleep last night, so I did a computer search of newspapers along the Eastern Seaboard. Here, let me show you." James opened his briefcase and took out a few papers. "Very few editions from 1830 exist along the route that our Henri Richaud would have taken. No papers from Savannah exist. The Southern Times . . . well, we're in luck. The State University at Albany has a few from 1830, as does the Library of Congress. The Southern Patriot, which was published in Charleston from 1825 to 1848, is in the Library of Congress; January through July of 1830 is on microfilm. The Charleston Courier and two other Charleston papers from that time are on microfilm at the University of South Carolina. If you don't mind, I'll take the liberty of checking those out. Your best bet is the Library of Congress. I found several papers from Jacksonville Florida all the way to Virginia that are archived there." James handed John the printouts. "You can look up Max and Sheila while you're at it."

"I don't know what to say."

"Say thank you."

"Thank you. But there's just one small problem."

John thought about the problem of running a newspaper while doing an investigation and realized instantly that he was staring the solution right in the face. To a beaming James Campbell, former editor of the Beaufort Sentinel, he said evenly, "I hope you're ready to take on the rigors of publishing again. I would feel a little guilty if you were to suddenly drop dead."

"Come, come now, John, admit it... you're just a selfish bastard who would miss our evening cocktails together."

"True. Very true. But seriously, are you physically up to it? I don't want to put your health at risk. We can always shut the paper down for a month or two. We do have a precedent in that regard."

"Nonsense. The doctor says it's okay to add a little more activity. Besides, I have these." James pulled a handful of cocoa beans out of his pocket and popped one in his mouth.

"Ah, yes. I forgot. The magic beans. Dark chocolate wasn't good enough."

"Not magic, my dear boy. Purely scientific. These beans come from the Kuna Indians who live on the San Blas Islands off the coast of Panama. For centuries they were isolated from the mainland; these beans form a large part of their diet. They lay the beans on the ground and let the sun roast them naturally. Scientists studying this tribe found they have no incidence of heart disease and cancer. And guess what? When they move to the mainland, they get heart disease. Why?"

"Let me guess.... Beans."

"Exactly! Or more precisely, no beans. In fact, a long term study of old men like myself found that there was a fifty percent reduction in mortality for those men who regularly consumed cocoa. And these beans are shipped directly from the San Blas Islands. So no need to worry about me."

"And what does your doctor say?"

"Oh, *him*? ... He thinks I'm nuts."

CHAPTER 11

Washington D.C.

Despite his protestations and magic cocoa beans, it was over a month before John felt James was up to running the paper alone. The story of a lifetime could wait. Besides, after almost two hundred years, it was not going anywhere. And John had already lost his parents. Losing his mentor and surrogate father figure would be too devastating a blow for him to bear.

On a mid-July morning, John finally felt safe enough to board the seven forty-five flight out of Charleston. After landing at Reagan National, he took the Metro Blue Line to the Capitol South Station and walked the remaining block to the Capitol Hill Suites. It was close to eleven by the time he had checked into his room overlooking Saint Peters Church. Around the block on Independence Avenue was the Library of Congress and the United States Capitol. Further down Independence, less than a mile from the Suites, stood the National Museum of the American Indian.

Before the discovery of the Floating Man, John had planned on visiting the museum to do research on Chief John Ross and the forced removal of the Cherokee. He thought of John Marshall, the famous Chief Justice of the Supreme Court, who issued a ruling against the removal, and Andrew Jackson, who infamously said in response: "John Marshall has made his decision; now let him enforce it! . . . Build a fire under them. When it gets hot enough, they'll go." After finishing up at the Library of Congress, perhaps he would stop at the museum and do some research on the Cherokees and John Ross, their legendary Chief.

John was scheduled to meet Rachel Leeds, a research assistant with the Library of Congress at one in the afternoon. Max, his old friend and boss at the *Washington Post*, had given him Rachel's number during a phone conversation a couple days earlier. John had called Rachel the next day and told her what newspapers and issues he was looking for. He said he was doing a historical piece on colonial Indians and wanted a perspective about events along the East Coast in the summer of 1830, coinciding with the passage of the Indian Removal Act. He felt a little silly using a cover story, but old habits die hard.

Standing on Independence Avenue, John paused to check his watch. He prided himself on being punctual. He was several minutes early, and felt uncharacteristically nervous. Was it the anticipation of discovering something more on Henri Richaud? Or the ambivalence he felt about being back in Washington? Perhaps both. He looked up at the Thomas Jefferson building, named for our third president who donated his extensive book collection to the Library of Congress after the British burned the original library in 1814. Built in the style of the Italian Renaissance during the late 1880s, the three-level edifice was finally finished and opened to the public in 1897. A renovation one hundred years later restored it to its original splendor.

He arrived at the researcher entrance, located one floor beneath the microfilm collections reading room, ten minutes early. Exactly at one, a tall young lady dressed in business attire opened the door.

"Hi, I'm Rachel," she said, extending a hand to John. "Hope you weren't waiting long."

"No, not at all," John lied, adding, "It's a pleasure to meet you." Which wasn't a lie. Taking her hand, he was instantly captivated: intelligence radiated from behind her large, luminous blue eyes; her smile was warm and welcoming. She appeared to be fresh out of college.

How did Max come to know Rachel? He wondered to himself.

"Max told me to give you my undivided attention," she said, leading John by the hand, up the stairs to the reading room. "Any friend of Max's is a friend of mine."

"Same goes for me." John couldn't help himself: As they reached the top of the stairs he asked, "How do you *know* Max?"

"In the biblical sense." Rachel turned around and stifled a laugh at the embarrassed look on John's face. "We have been living together for the past month."

"Sorry, I didn't realize. You know, I've known Max for years, but I always thought he was married to his job. I don't think I've ever asked him about his love life. Strange, isn't it?"

"That's what Max likes about you. You don't pry into friend's lives. Only people you are doing a story on. And I hope you never do a story on me."

"Now that sounds very intriguing. You have secrets worth investigating?"

"Doesn't everyone?"

"Not me. I'm sure Max told you how I burned out and threw away a promising career."

"He told me you had a midlife crisis. A few decades early, I would say." Rachel paused a beat before continuing; "But Max is a big believer in second acts. He thinks you'll be back better than ever once you sort your life out."

"I'm afraid I pushed his belief in my salvation to the max, bailing on him like I did. Sorry, that was an awkward pun."

"John," Rachel said, giving him a hard stare. "If you were a woman I would say you were a bit of a drama queen. Anyway, that's all in the past. We're looking forward to having you over for dinner tonight. Max took the liberty of inviting Sheila, he knew you wouldn't mind."

"No, not at all."

Rachel opened the door of the machine-readable collections room. John noticed a reserved sign on the door. Organized on a large table were a dozen or so rolls of microfilm and several reading machines. Rachel sat down and motioned for John to sit next to her.

"I loaded the microfilm for the Southern Patriot on the machine in front of you. The machines we use now are probably different than the ones you may be familiar with. You can watch me load the Charleston Courier roll on this machine, and I'll give you a quick refresher on how to use it." Rachel demonstrated how to load the roll and use the microfilm reader. "The rolls are set out alphabetically, and I took the liberty of including other papers published along the Eastern Seaboard during the months of June through September of 1830 that I thought might interest you. You're probably anxious to get to work, so if there are no questions, I'll check back with you in about an hour. If you need me for anything, just hit extension 4874 on the phone. Any questions before I leave?"

"Just one. How did you and Max meet?"

"He picked me up on a playground by offering me a bag of candy."

"*What?*"

"John, I'm a woman. I saw the way you looked at me. You were thinking I was a little young for Max."

"No, no, I never . . . well yes, I did kind of wonder how old you were. I pegged you as just graduating college."

"Well, that's true, sort of. I did just graduate with my doctorate in library sciences. But I'm not as young as I look. Rather than play that embarrassing game of having you guess my age, I'll just come out and tell you. I'm thirty-nine."

"Amazing what exercise and a good diet can do these days."

"And it helps to get eight hours of sleep each night."

"I wouldn't know about that," John said, as Rachel rose from her chair. "I guess I better get started here and get as much accomplished as I can."

Rachel squeezed John's shoulder. Before she turned to leave the reading room, she said, "I'm really looking forward to dinner tonight. We're starting out with an arugula salad followed by baked salmon with tomato concasse. And then a midnight run along the Reflecting Pool to burn off some calories. On second thought, maybe we'll skip the run and settle for after-dinner drinks."

John wistfully watched a receding Rachel exit the room: happy for his friend and former boss who finally had some balance in his life, sad for the lack of balance in his own life. He stared at the empty doorway for several moments before snapping to and getting to work.

On the first microfilm reader, John looked at the May editions of The *Southern Patriot*. Published from 1825–1848, the *Patriot* was a daily newspaper out of Charleston. John had a hunch that the interview mentioned in the Beaufort Sentinel June 4 article would have probably occurred towards the latter half of May.

He flew through the first three weeks of the paper, focusing on the front page. Things got weird when he reached the Friday, May 28 edition of the *Patriot*. There, on the lower half of the front page, was a big blank block that took up almost a quarter of the page. After looking at the rest of the May 28 edition, John looked page by page through the May 29 and May 31 editions. There was no Sunday, May 30 edition. The *Southern Patriot*, like many papers of the era, did not publish on Sundays. John noticed that on the second page of the Monday, May 31 edition, there was a small section in the upper right portion of the newspaper that also contained a blank block, as if it had been cut out.

For the next half hour, John went through each edition of the *Patriot* starting with May 1. When he finished, he had documented three other small sections that were apparently cut out or blanked out. He printed out the pages with missing sections, hopped over to the next machine and began going through the *Charleston Courier*, a tri-weekly newspaper. Charleston, just up the coast from Beaufort, would have undoubtedly been the Floating Man's next stop on his tour up the Eastern Seaboard. Once again, John found several small sections of the newspaper that appeared to have been cut out. The front page of the June 18 edition of the *Courier* had a large quarter section of the paper cut out, leaving another blank section on the microfilm. John printed each of these pages and was loading up the *Charleston Mercury* for June of 1830 when Rachel walked in.

"Find anything interesting?" Rachel asked.

"*Very*. Maybe you can help me find an explanation for this." John slid the printouts to the corner of the table and Rachel leaned over to take a look.

She turned and looked quizzically at John. "What am I looking for?"

"Nothing." John smiled. "Maybe you can explain why there are all these blank sections, as if someone had cut them out."

"That's weird. On rare occasions when we have the only copy of a newspaper, and no other copies exist, there might be an article that someone cut out back when it was printed. But these newspapers aren't rare. Several other institutions have copies of the Charleston papers."

"So what is your best guess?" John asked.

"I haven't a clue. Why don't we load a couple more newspapers and see what else we find?"

"Good idea. I just loaded the Charleston Mercury."

"Let me load up these other readers while you flip through yours."

Rachel loaded three more readers while John looked through the *Charleston Mercury*. After she had finished loading the rolls, Rachel hopped on one of the readers. Thirty minutes and four rolls later, they had discovered several more pages with blank sections. Moving quickly now, searching only for blank sections, they finished every roll of each newspaper originally requested by John, along with a few more that Rachel had pulled. In total, they printed up sixty pages with blank sections. John had the idea of seeing if there were blank sections in the same newspapers earlier in the year of 1830. Rachel left, returning a few minutes later with several rolls of microfilm for February and March. After another thirty minutes of scrolling, they were both stunned to find no other instances of missing sections.

John thanked Rachel for her help and returned to his room at the Capitol Hill Suites. It was five in the afternoon. Tired and disappointed, John decided to take a nap before leaving for dinner with Max, Rachel, and Sheila.

CHAPTER 12

At six fifteen, John's cell phone awakened him from a light sleep. He looked at the display and saw James name.

"James, what's up?"

"What the *devil* have we gotten into?"

"What do you mean?"

"I looked all day at microfilm and some original newspapers at the university and only got one small item out of the Charleston Observer from June 26." James paused for a beat. "And the rest were all blank sections. As I got to the latter part of 1830, the blank sections became fewer and smaller. Damn strange thing. I looked at previous years and no blank sections. What about you? Any luck?"

"Nada, zilch. All blank sections here too. You said you *found* an item?"

"Two letters to the editor concerning the performance of Henri Richaud in Charleston. One by a reader named Daniel Rutledge and the other by Harriott Pinckney Horry, a lady with quite an illustrious lineage. When you get back, I'll tell you the history of the Horry family and Hampton Plantation. But let me read you the letters. First is Mr. Rutledge's letter: 'I attended the performance last week of the illustrious Henri Richaud and his Floating Machine. He seems like a most genial fellow, but his machine was most terrifying. With the sound of a hundred thousand hummingbirds, I watched awestruck as his floating machine hovered over our heads and then would dart from one end of the field to the other. All the while that humming noise seemed to penetrate every part of my body and left me with a tingling sensation. Most terrifying, for myself and those gathered, was when the Frenchman rose to a height of what appeared to be several hundred feet. He remained there, suspended; then, to our horror, he came hurtling straight down towards us and the earth: stopping mere inches from the ground. Daniel Rutledge.'

"The next letter is from Harriott Horry: 'I would like to say how delighted we are at Horry House to have here residing, our most esteemed guests: Henri Richaud and his chronicler and companion, Robert Campbell, Editor of the Beaufort Sentinel. Mr. Richaud is a French intellectual of the highest merit. His magnificent conveyance is a wonder, based on the sound scientific principles of the late scientist Pierre-Simon Laplace of France and the gravitational laws of Sir Isaac Newton. We have been delighted to share our home with Mr. Richaud and have very much enjoyed his witty conversations of his youthful years with the late Emperor of France, Napoleon Bonaparte. It is to my most solid satisfaction that I am to accompany Mr. Richaud and Mr. Campbell on their journey to Georgetown next week. Harriott Pinckney Horry.' "

James paused briefly. "That's it. Confirms my theory about the missing editions of the Sentinel though."

John was wide awake now and sitting on the edge of the bed.

"If your grandfather was chronicling the journey of Henri Richaud, there has to be some memoirs. Yet you didn't find anything."

"I have all his travel memoirs laid out chronologically in a separate storage chest. Maybe since this predates the rest of his travels, he stored it somewhere else. But John, I've run out of places to look."

"Well, we still have other private libraries and universities that have copies of the same papers. And we now know which editions to look for."

"The ones with blanks."

"Yep."

"John, who would ever imagine... a cover-up from the 1830s?"

"I've been trying not to think of that, but I guess there is no other explanation. Listen, I have to get ready for dinner. Look forward to hearing the story of this—what's her name?"

"Harriott Horry. See you when you get back."

John hit end and got ready for dinner. He thought about where this story might lead but realized he really didn't have a clue, other than to find newspapers, somewhere, without the missing sections. At least the Library of Congress had a complete list of institutions (universities, private libraries, historical societies, etc.) with holdings for these newspapers, down to the year and edition available. Several editions with missing sections were available from multiple sources. It gave John a headache: the thought of running all over the country searching for a few missing articles. Maybe at dinner his friends would give him a different perspective or line of attack on this investigation.

CHAPTER 13

At seven in the evening, John was dropped off by taxi at Max's colonial style home in a fashionable section of Bethesda. Waiting to greet him at the door was his old friend. Noticing that the rotund Max had not only shed his mustache but also quite a few pounds, John couldn't resist taking a light jab at his former editor.

"Max! Good to see you. Or what is left of you."

"Atkins diet." They shook hands and Max ushered John inside. After a minute of requisite small talk, Max said, "Why don't you go into the kitchen and say hello to Sheila and Rachel while I make you a drink. Is it still whiskey?"

"You've got it. And a couple rocks."

John went into the kitchen and exchanged hellos with Rachel and Sheila. He asked Sheila how her job with the staff of the NSC was going. Okay, she said. He asked how she liked working for Henry Smith. Rarely saw him was her reply. Sheila congratulated John on his new job as editor of the Sentinel . . . sort of.

And then Rachel turned to Sheila and said, "I was helping John at the library today while he browsed through some old southern newspapers from 1830. He uncovered a most curious thing. Do you want to tell Sheila the story, John?"

"No, you go right ahead. There's a lot more to the story; I'll save it for after dinner. But go ahead and whet Sheila's appetite while I keep your boyfriend and my whiskey company."

John and Sheila shared slightly bemused smiles before he turned and went back into the study. He sat down on an old leather chair and picked up the drink that Max had placed for him on the cocktail table.

"Max, it's really good to see you. You don't know how much I've missed you."

"Is that why you didn't call until two days ago?"

"I was just too embarrassed to call. There were several times I picked up the phone, but I just couldn't bring myself to call."

"Yeah, you were a mess. I figured getting away from the rat race of Washington for a little while would be the best thing for you to do. That's why I didn't call either. Didn't want to stir up old ghosts. Speaking of old, how's your friend doing?"

John told Max about discovering James unconscious and bleeding in the basement. He laughed when John told him of James' sudden revival and response to his CPR efforts.

"I have to meet this guy, sounds like a real character."

"Actually, he thinks he *is* a character," John said with a straight face. "Casper Gutman from the Maltese Falcon."

"Oh, hell John, now I definitely have to meet him."

"Positively, James would say. A line from the movie." John leaned in a little closer, as if speaking conspiratorially. "But the most amazing thing, Max, is that James *literally* stumbled onto the story of a lifetime when he fell down the base—."

"Some historical piece on the removal of the Indians during colonial times," Max interrupted. "Rachel told me. She also told me about some missing sections in newspapers. That's rather odd, don't you think?"

"Yes, it is. But that's not the real story. Wait until after dinner Max, it gets weirder, a whole lot weirder."

* * *

Over dinner of baked salmon with tomato concasse the old friends relived their glory days at the *Washington Post*. Max told a story for Rachel's benefit of the time he was seated on the campaign bus of then candidate George W. Bush and had accidentally spilled his whiskey flask on W's shirt. The future president's aides were in a frenzy. Rumors had just been spread, presumably by someone on Al Gore's staff, that W was hitting the bottle again due to the pressures of the campaign. It seems George was just minutes away from a meeting with some leading southern evangelical ministers, and reeking of whiskey was not on the candidate's agenda. Max had admired how good-naturedly the then candidate took it all, as his staff whirled around him, frantically trying to find someone with the same size shirt.

Sheila told Rachel about John and their initial frosty relationship at the *Post*. John admitted being a bit of an ass in prejudging Sheila based on her looks, but he tried to blame it on her provocative attire and the power of her feminine ways, eliciting chuckles from Rachel and Sheila. After much deliberation, all agreed that John had in fact been an ass, and that Sheila would look provocative even if she wore an oversized, dirty grey sweatshirt and pants. The subject ended abruptly when Rachel gave Max a stare after he added that Sheila would even look provocative in a pair of mom jeans. With that, dinner was adjourned. Max was put in charge of mixing drinks while everyone moved to the sitting room.

* * *

John told them the story from the beginning. How he had found James lying in the basement after he had fallen and struck his head, landing on the June 4, 1830 edition of the Beaufort Sentinel. How he had read the bloodstained paper and stumbled upon the story of Henri Richaud, and how he stared at a sunbeam and made this story his life's mission. The latter revelation drew raised eyebrows. John recounted the search for the missing newspapers at the office and at James' home. The missing sections on microfilm at the library, and the call earlier in the evening on the additional piece found by James.

Max was the first to comment. "It's almost *too* unbelievable. If it wasn't for that last piece and those missing sections of microfilm, I would think that this editor of the Sentinel was having some fun with his readers. Creating some sort of hoax to entertain the locals on a slow news week."

Sheila added, "The part that gives me goose bumps is the description of the sound of this floating machine as the humming of a hundred thousand hummingbirds."

"That would freak me out today," Rachel said, looking over at

Sheila. "Imagine what those people back in 1830 felt like when they saw and heard that thing."

Sheila turned to John. "Is there any description of this floating machine?"

"None from the two small articles we have so far."

Max asked Sheila, "Is there any way you can find out if there are any files on this Richaud fellow in one of the intelligence archives?

"Beats me, Max. I can give it a try. I'll do a search through some of our databases. It wasn't until the FDR administration that the government centralized records. Before then, each branch and agency of the government was responsible for maintaining their own records, and unfortunately, a lot of them were lost or destroyed as a result."

Interested in this line of inquiry, John interjected, "If the government way back in the 1830s was trying to cover-up what hap—"

"That's too fantastical to imagine," Max interrupted. "The Jackson administration rounding up all these newspapers and censoring them? Kind of hard to believe."

Rachel leaned toward Max and said, "They rounded up all the Indians and got rid of them."

"And let's not forget the Dreyfus affair in the 1890s. The French government forged documents, threatened witnesses and faked depositions, all to keep an innocent man imprisoned on Devil's Island," Sheila added.

John asked everyone to play along with him for a second.

"What if, putting everything else aside for a moment, the government did have an interest in covering this up? After all, this is a foreigner that seemingly possessed a technology, far in advance of anything previously known to science. They would have collected as much information as they possibly could about this fellow and his antigravity device. There would have been files stored somewhere, and possibly even the machine itself."

"The most logical place would have been the White House, or maybe the War Department," Sheila said.

"That's where you should start then," Max said, turning to Sheila.

Sheila reminded Max: "You forget that all records were

consolidated during the FDR administration. It would be harder than finding a needle in a haystack."

"But something that secret and sensitive would have been kept separate, don't you think?" John asked.

Rachel, eager to add to the discussion said, "That's assuming the records were not already missing or destroyed, and long forgotten."

After a lot more back and forth and what ifs, Max asked John, "So where do you proceed from here? What are your next steps?"

"I have a list of institutions that have copies of these missing editions. If there was a cover-up or government program to censor these records, I doubt they were as efficient back then as we are today. But then again, there were not as many records to destroy. So, first I search those records and see if anything further pops up and see where that leads me. Also, maybe Sheila can find out if there are still any government records, located somewhere, on Henri Richaud."

"And I can continue to look through the records at the Library of Congress," Rachel said, quickly adding, "If you don't mind?"

"Not at all. I could use all the help I can get."

Sheila, acting like the investigative reporter she once was, said, "John, why don't you make copies of everything you have and we can all do a little. I'm sure Rachel has contacts at other libraries and universities so you don't have to run around the country. I can use my contacts in government, and Max has his, which shall go nameless so that I don't have to have them arrested for leaking government secrets."

Max smiled at Sheila. "So you don't have to arrest *yourself*."

"That too." Sheila smiled back.

"Sounds like a plan," John said, rising from his chair. "It's getting late. I'd like to get an early start tomorrow at the library."

"It's getting a little late for me too," Sheila said. She got up and turned to John. "I'll give you a ride back to your hotel."

"Isn't that a little out of your way?"

"I don't mind if you don't."

"Not at all," John said, taking hold of Sheila's hand.

After the requisite goodbyes, John and Sheila got into her car and drove off. During the short drive they asked each other subtly about their personal lives. Both were quietly pleased to discover that neither was seeing anyone romantically.

Sheila was first to dive into the pool of romance.

"You know, John, before you left so suddenly from the Post, I thought that we were on our way to developing a closer relationship."

"I know," John responded. "I just felt like it wouldn't have been fair to you, considering how messed up I was. And then you joined the NSC. That kind of ended any chance of a love affair."

"Don't you think you kind of overstate how messed up you were. *Christ*, half the reporters on staff drink too much, and you wouldn't believe who is sleeping with who in Washington."

"I don't know. I thought it was a big enough problem, and I didn't want to jeopardize your career."

"John." Sheila turned and gave him a withering look. "I'm a big girl. Rachel told me earlier that she called you a drama queen. But I think you're more like one of those throwback men of an earlier age that thinks women need to be sheltered from life's unseemly side."

"Gee, thanks, Sheila. So basically, I screwed up our love life before it ever began is what you're telling me. I feel so much better. I think I'll get drunk and celebrate."

"There's always second acts in the theatre of love. Even for drama queens," Sheila said as she put her hand on John's leg and squeezed gently.

"Sheila, you missed the turn for the Capitol Hill Suites."

"I know."

Sheila smiled and looked straight ahead as she turned into the underground parking garage of her apartment building.

* * *

John had the best night of his life. Sheila had no complaints either. And the next morning—

John awoke to the sound of the shower turning on. He got out of bed, walked into the bathroom and asked Sheila, "Would you like a little help with the soap?"

"Come on in."

Sheila turned around and handed him the bar of soap. "You can suds up my back, and if you're good, I'll let you do these babies." She grabbed her perfectly shaped breasts, gave John a quick peck on the lips and turned back around.

John washed Sheila's back and then moved his hands around and massaged her large firm breasts, letting the soap fall to the floor.

Sheila moaned softly. She pushed back into John's hard erection as he continued to gently massage her breasts; her nipples swelling and stiffening under his touch. "Hmm harder, squeeze harder."

John entered her from behind, thrusting and squeezing harder as the tempo of their lovemaking increased exponentially.

In between hurried breaths and moans she urged him on. "Harder, harder."

John, lost in the moment, letting go of all the pent-up frustrations and disappointments of his life, thrust harder and faster. Sheila, muscles taut, hands braced against the shower wall, pushed back in rhythm to meet his thrusts until they finally came together in an explosion.

They slowly slid to the floor of the tub; Sheila lay back on John, his hands still tight around her breasts. They lay there for a short while, letting the warm water of the shower rain over them, lost in the moment, until Sheila said, "John, excuse me dear, but do you mind—my tits, please?"

John quickly let go as he realized he was still holding on tightly to her breasts. Looking at the deep red marks from where his fingers had dug in, he said apologetically, "God Sheila, I'm sorry. I must have gotten carried away. Does it hurt?"

"Hell yeah it hurts!" Sheila said as she lifted herself up. Standing over John, still lying in the tub she continued, "Let me dig my fingers into your balls and tell me how it feels."

"I'm sorry. I don't know how I got so carried away."

"You don't know *how* you got so carried away?" Sheila said incredulously as she put her hands on her hips. "Seriously? Look at me." She tucked her stomach in and thrust out her chest, a panic-stricken John looked up helplessly.

Sheila couldn't help but break out laughing.

"My God, Rachel is right. You are a drama queen."

John, smiling a little too shyly for a thirtysomething year old man, got to his feet. They stepped out of the tub and dried each other off.

Sheila examined herself in the mirror.

John watched, commenting, "That's gotta hurt."

"I think it looks sexy," Sheila said, examining the red marks. "It's something to remember you by when you're back in South Carolina." Sheila turned and faced John, caressed his head with her hands. As John placed his hands on her hips she continued: "Every time I see these marks or jiggle a little and feel the pain, I'll think of you." Sheila paused for a moment and then added with a lascivious sneer, "It'll make me hot."

"And what happens when the marks disappear and the pain goes away?"

"It'll be time for round two. After a few more rounds with me, you'll be crying uncle and begging for your old job back so you can spend the rest of your life with me."

CHAPTER 14

John spent each day at the Library of Congress, and each evening in sexual congress with Sheila. And after a week, all John had for his troubles were more blank sections and a sore dick. But John was ecstatic. He was in love and on a quest. Every little bit of missing newspaper was a clue to him. Max's girlfriend Rachel had been a godsend. Even working after hours at the library.

From the missing sections of various newspapers they were able to establish that the story of the Floating Man had spread as far south as St Augustine, north as far as Richmond, and west to Atlanta. James continued his research at the University of South Carolina and a few historical societies. Rachel called other libraries and universities and had researchers looking through their copies. So far, none had reported anything other than the same ubiquitous missing sections.

Sheila did a search through several government databases as far as her security clearance would allow. Using key words: Henri Richaud, the Floating Man, Simon Pierre La Place and antigravity, she had come up empty-handed. She asked colleagues with connections at the CIA to see if there was a file anywhere in Langley on the subject, but again came up empty-handed. Max, likewise, through his contacts came up empty.

* * *

Friday at half past noon, John, Sheila, Max, and Rachel met for lunch at Le Bon Café, just around the corner from the Library of Congress on 2nd Street SE. With its signature blue and white striped awning, Le Bon, a Parisian-style sidewalk café, seemed the perfect place to meet on John's last day in Washington. Sheila, arriving first along with John, chose a table on the sidewalk to enjoy the summer weather. Max was only a minute behind. Last to arrive was Rachel, who worked the closest to Le Bon. John pointed out that she was just conforming to the laws of physics.

"Very funny, John. Maybe I'll just make you wait before telling you what I found," Rachel said, sitting down in a chair next to Max, who handed her a menu.

"Rachel, you *found* something? What did you find?" John leaned over and looked anxiously at Rachel.

"I'll tell you what I found. . . . NOTHING!"

Rachel leaned back, smug, enjoying John's tortured look.

Max turned to Rachel. "Ouch, that was cruel."

"Well," Sheila said, "it seems we've all been striking out."

Max asked John if James had found anything further.

"Nothing. In addition to the universities in North and South Carolina, he's looked at several private collections. Nothing but those blank sections everywhere we search."

Sheila put her hand tenderly on John's thigh and asked, "I thought James had a bad heart. Is all that running around good for him?"

John shrugged. "I told him to take it easy, but he says that this has been the best thing for his heart. He really seems to enjoy the search. He tells me in every conversation that it's like the search for the Maltese Falcon."

"That's kinda weird," Sheila said.

"Not really," John replied. "He's a dead ringer for Casper Gutman, just minus a few pounds."

"*Who?*" Rachel asked.

"Sydney Greenstreet," Max replied.

"I thought you said he looked like some guy named Casper?" Rachel now looked totally confused.

"Sydney Greenstreet and Casper Gutman are one and the same person, dear," Max said helpfully. "Sydney Greenstreet played the character of Casper Gutman in a famous black and white movie starring Humphrey Bogart. It involved the search for a jewel encrusted statue of a falcon."

"And how did it turn out?"

"Don't ask," Max replied, feigning irritation.

* * *

Halfway through lunch, Rachel was taking a bite out of her Tuna Provencal when her smartphone rang. She put her sandwich down and answered. She didn't recognize the caller at first, then said, "Oh yes, Frank from Florida U." Rachel listened intently. "That's great. I'll check it out as soon as I get off the phone." A long pause, followed by a few uh-huhs and then Rachel ended the call by saying, "Yes, absolutely, please do, and thanks so much, Frank." A shorter pause, another uh-huh, and then, "Okay, bye now."

Everyone waited expectantly for Rachel to tell them about the call as she bent down to grab her iPad out of her handbag. Rachel turned on the iPad and began talking while pulling up her email. "That was Frank Schwartz from the University of Florida at Gainesville. He found a small article on Henri Richaud from a copy of the Winyaw Intelligencer out of Georgetown, South Carolina."

Everyone huddled around Rachel; all eyes glued to the iPad as she opened the attachment. The article in the *Winyaw Intelligencer* was from July 5, 1830. They all followed along as Rachel read the headline: "Floating Man shot at over Waterfront!" She paused for a moment before plunging ahead with the article.

"Henri Richaud, known as the Floating Man from France was performing his aerial maneuvers along and over the waterfront in downtown Georgetown when musket fire rang out. It was not known if he was struck by any of the musket balls, but several eyewitnesses said that immediately afterwards, the Floating Man, with a companion on board, was observed flying in an erratic manner over Winyaw Bay. It appeared that he was having trouble controlling his device, and this led to speculation that perhaps one of the shots had struck either the machine or Mr. Richaud. Spectators said that the shots appeared to come from behind the crowd, perhaps from the roof of one of the buildings located along the waterfront. Several federal soldiers who had accompanied John Eaton, President Jackson's secretary of war, fanned out in the direction of the shots, several more raced out on horseback in pursuit of the Floating Man's machine.

"Secretary Eaton, in attendance for the demonstration of the antigravity device at the request of President Jackson, would not comment, other than to say he was here only to observe and officially welcome Mr. Richaud on behalf of the president.

"Later in the day, witnesses reportedly saw smoke rising from a forested area southwest of town in the direction of Mr. Richaud's line of travel. Of peculiar note was the observation of Mrs. Lillian Pembroke, wife of Reverend Pembroke, who insisted she saw Mr. Richaud's companions (including a woman and Negress on horseback) ride off to the south, down Island Road, accompanied by several Cherokee Indians, before the shots were fired. As of the date of this publication, no further details on the fate and whereabouts of Henri Richaud and his amazing antigravity device are known."

As John and his lunch companions excitedly talked over these new developments, no one noticed the well-dressed couple at the next table, quietly sipping espressos. The couple listened intently through earpieces built into their eyeglasses, connected wirelessly to a directional microphone and recorder—both concealed in the woman's stylish purse that sat next to her on the table.

"The mystery deepens," Max said as they finished lunch and prepared to leave. "Is our man Henri dead or alive? And who is this other companion of his?"

"And now we have a secretary of war involved—another lead to follow," Rachel added.

"And what mystery would be complete without a few Indians thrown in. Right, John?" Sheila got up and gave John a kiss on the cheek. "See you at dinner."

Everyone went back to work, except John. Alone at the table, he pulled up the email that Rachel had forwarded and began to read the article . . . over and over again.

CHAPTER 15

John arrived back in Beaufort shortly after noon on Saturday, met at the Charleston airport by James. It was a hot, July day, with angry clouds overhead that threatened to burst at any moment. James dropped off John with an invitation to join him for lunch after he settled in. John accepted. Two hours later, after a light lunch, both men adjourned with drinks in hand to James' front porch swing just as the sky opened up. Amid thunder and pouring rain, the two sat and talked about the events of the past few weeks. James seemed a bit drawn in the face. John was worried that the excitement may have been a little too much for him. He urged his friend to take it easy now that he was back, but James waved that suggestion away, saying he would like to continue on at the paper while John concentrated on "the investigation" as they both referred to it.

As what appeared to be an all-day rain continued, along with occasional lightning and thunder, John asked James about the "Hairy woman."

"It's Horry. Harriott Pinckney Horry," James said. He paused to take a sip of his scotch and water. Sheets of rain came down, casting a grey sheen over the landscape. "Kind of looks like a scene from an old black and white movie, doesn't it?"

"The rain does seem to lend a film noir cast to everything,"

John said. Leaning over to joke, he added, "You aren't going to go into your Sydney Greenstreet character, are you?"

"Maybe," James replied. Changing the subject he added, "So, did you call Sheila to let her know you arrived home safely?"

"Am I supposed to?"

"You're a couple now, aren't you?"

"I didn't think of it that way, but you're right," John said, continuing to sit dumbly with drink in hand.

James laughed, shook his head and looked down. "I don't know how you ever became an investigative reporter, as clueless as you are."

"*What?*" John looked at James with a baffled look on his face.

"Go! Go inside and call her. . . . Jeez."

"Right, sorry. It's just that I was . . . never mind," John stammered as he got up and went inside to give Sheila a call.

He returned a few minutes later, plopped back down on the swing, and turned to James. "Now for the Hairy woman."

"Horry. But first." James raised his empty glass.

John dutifully got back up and went inside with it.

Returning with refilled glasses he sat back down.

"Now, can we talk about Harriott . . . Pinckney . . . Horry?"

"Very well. Let's talk. I'll tell you straight out, sir, that I like talking to a man who is judicious in his speech and gets right to the heart of the matter," James said in perfect Casper Gutman voice.

"Now that was good. I have to hand it to you. Even Mr. Greenstreet himself would have been impressed."

"Thank you," James said, glowing like a little kid.

"You know, James, considering the atmosphere and the old black-and-white quality the rain is lending to this scene, I think it would be appropriate to tell the story of this lady in character."

"Seriously?"

"Positively." John smiled and raised his glass.

Raising his glass in a return salute, James said, "A toast to plain speaking and clear understanding."

Both men took a sip. James put his glass down and began the story of Harriott Pinckney Horry in the voice of Casper Gutman from the *Maltese Falcon*.

"Harriott Pinckney Horry comes from one of South Carolina's most illustrious families. Born into high society, there are actually two Harriott Pinckney Horrys: mother and daughter. The mother, coincidentally, died in the same year as Henri's visit to Horry house, better known as Hampton Plantation. But, my dear boy, I'm getting ahead of myself." James patted John's knee and stared at him with the same bulging eyes that were so characteristic of Sydney Greenstreet's characters. John looked on, spellbound by the metamorphosis of his friend.

"The story begins in 1744 when Daniel Horry purchased six hundred acres in the Saint James Santee Parish district of Charleston, near what is now present-day McClellanville. The Low Country, as it is still called today, was the home of great wealth and power for the aristocratic elite of South Carolina. A rich loamy soil created by clearing the cypress swamps allowed the native indigo plants, which grew wild up and down the coastal plains, to be cultivated. Fortunes were made off the dye it produced, and hundreds of miles of canals were dug, crisscrossing the great cypress swamps. Daniel Horry's wealth began to grow. Toward the latter part of the 1740s, Daniel built a beautiful Georgian-style mansion along the banks of Wambaw Creek. The envy of all the other planters.

"In 1763 old man Horry died and left the plantation to his son, Daniel Huger Horry. The young son was just as industrious and shrewd as the old man. By the mid-eighteenth century, worldwide production of indigo began to increase dramatically. Daniel, the young newcomer, was shrewd enough to foresee that prices would soon fall precipitously. The young man replaced his father's indigo and began cultivating rice: ideally suited for swampy lands. Daniel was fortunate that among the slaves his dad had acquired were several from Senegal's rice growing region of West Africa. One slave, Eboe John, was particularly adept at planting and harvesting rice. Together, they grew a long golden grain that was known throughout the world as Waccamaw Gold.

"Soon the coastal areas of South Carolina became the largest rice culture in the world. Rice replaced indigo as King of the Low Country, and Daniel's profits increased exponentially. Of course, alongside this enormous wealth came the great evil of our time.... Slavery. But even in this evil enterprise, Daniel excelled. He had an uncanny ability to take other planter's castaway slaves and make them profitable by treating them a bit better, and working alongside them. By the eve of the Revolutionary War, his hard work and the soaring price of rice had helped increase the family holdings to several thousand acres and several hundred slaves."

James paused to savor a sip of scotch. He looked out at the sheets of rain hammering the landscape. His thoughts became lost in the grey misty veil that enveloped them.

John waited a few moments before softly interrupting the silence. "Where do the Horry women come into the story?"

James snapped out of his reverie.

"The younger Daniel married his second wife, Harriott Pinckney, in 1768. Her father, Charles Pinckney—who died a decade before the marriage—had risen through the political ranks to become Chief Justice of the then Province of South Carolina. During the Revolutionary War, the planters, including Daniel, went off to fight the British, leaving Harriott in charge to run Hampton plantation. Hampton became a refuge for friends and relatives, including Daniel's mother, the widow Eliza.

"In 1780 the British captured Charleston and searched the nearby plantations for a local planter named Francis Marion, who had been a large thorn in their side for two years. Marion, a neighbor of the Horry's, led a band of local men in resistance to the British. Having learned guerrilla tactics from the Indians, he and his men set up ambushes and then retreated back into the cypress swamps, which they knew like the back of their hand."

As James paused to finish his scotch and water, John blurted; "The Swamp Fox!"

"*Precisely*. The name was given to him by the British commander, a man named Colonel Banastre Tarleton, who had the unfortunate duty to try and capture him."

"Right! The Leslie Nielsen character from the old Disney series. I remember the theme song: Swamp Fox! Swamp Fox! Tail on his—"

"You know my good man," James interrupted. "If you wish for me to keep speaking in character, you must quit with your inane banalities."

"Sorry. Please continue, Mr. Gutman."

"Well then, as I was saying before you so rudely interrupted me with your unfortunate remark about some obscure character actor, this neighbor of the Horry's was being hunted by the British and took refuge in the main house on Hampton Plantation. It was the young daughter and namesake of Harriott Pinckney Horry who woke a sleeping Francis Marion and led him out the back door, while her mother—then twenty-one years old—flirted with Colonel Tarleton in a most provocative way, buying the Swamp Fox just enough time to swim across Wambaw Creek and hightail it through the rice fields."

"Close call, huh?"

"Close call *indeed*. And the kicker is that Harriott's mother proved to be so charming and provocative, dare I say, indiscreet, that the completely smitten colonel ordered his men to take nothing from the house during their search for Francis Marion. Quite unusual for the British. But then again, so were the Horry's, mother and daughter."

"Quite a story," John said. "I thought you were going to throw George Washington in there somewhere."

"Actually, he came a little later, in 1791 during his southern tour. And in 1793 when Eliza, the matriarch of the family, died, he offered to be a pallbearer at her funeral."

"Seriously?" John asked incredulously.

"Positively," James said, taking a folded sheet of paper out of his shirt pocket. "Let's reread the article I found last week, shall we?"

James unfolded the paper and placed it on his lap. John leaned to the side and stared down at one of the only known articles on Henri Richaud, and the only one connected to Harriott Pinckney Horry. Both silently read the short article from the June 26, *Charleston Observer.*

I attended the performance last week of the illustrious Henri Richaud and his Floating Machine. He seems like a most genial fellow, but his machine was most terrifying. With the sound of a hundred thousand hummingbirds, I watched awestruck as his floating machine hovered over our heads and then would dart from one end of the field to the other. All the while that humming noise seemed to penetrate every part of my body and left me with a tingling sensation. Most terrifying, for myself and those gathered, was when the Frenchman rose to a height of what appeared to be several hundred feet. He remained there, suspended; then, to our horror, he came hurtling straight down towards us and the earth: stopping mere inches from the ground. Daniel

The Floating Man

Rutledge.

I would like to say how delighted we are at Horry House to have here residing, our most esteemed guests: Henri Richaud and his chronicler and companion, Robert Campbell, Editor of the Beaufort Sentinel. Mr. Richaud is a French intellectual of the highest merit. His magnificent conveyance is a wonder, based on the sound scientific principles of the late scientist Pierre-Simon Laplace of France and the gravitational laws of Sir Isaac Newton. We have been delighted to share our home with Mr. Richaud and have very much enjoyed his witty conversations of his youthful years with the late Emperor of France, Napoleon Bonaparte. It is to my most solid satisfaction that I am to accompany Mr. Richaud and Mr. Campbell on their journey to Georgetown next week. Harriott Pinckney Horry.

John turned to James after he read the article.

"Did you print out a copy of that attachment Rachel sent you?"

"Of course."

"Get it . . . *please.*"

"Be right back." James rose and went inside. He returned a few minutes later with two copies of the attachment from Rachel's email, and a refreshed scotch and water. They reread the article from the Georgetown *Winyaw Intelligencer* that had caused so much excitement before John had left Washington.

After he finished the article, James turned to John: "I don't know why I didn't think of it the other day. The other companion must be Harriott Pinckney Horry."

"And the Negress? Perhaps one of Harriott's slaves. But what about the Indians?"

"No clue," James replied.

They fell silent, watching the rain, thunder, and lightning. Their thoughts lost in a mystery, so close geographically, so distant in time.

CHAPTER 16

The next two weeks passed without any new articles appearing. Rachel, continuing to plug away at the Library of Congress, was coming up empty—so were her contacts across the country. Nothing was reported other than the ubiquitous missing sections.

Initially buoyed by the discoveries in Washington, John started to get discouraged. After only two weeks back in Beaufort, James' concern for his friend was so great that he surreptitiously got Sheila's phone number from John's cell phone. Sheila was surprised when she got the call from James, but appreciated his concern. She had planned to visit in a couple weeks. After getting off the phone with James she decided to move her plans up.

Sheila gave John a call. He didn't protest when she said she had vacation time coming and wanted to spend it with him. She didn't mention the call from James—it would be their little secret, as she had put it.

John met Sheila at the airport in Charleston on Saturday morning. After a warm embrace, he struggled with her luggage, remarking that it seemed she was planning on more than a two-week visit.

"Don't get your hopes up, buddy," she replied as John loaded her luggage into the trunk of his Grand Marquis.

Sheila stepped into the passenger side and buckled herself in, commenting on John's choice of ride: "I see you drive an old man car," she snickered.

"What? Who? What's an omackar?" John said in a mock old man's voice.

"Well at least you can see above the steering wheel."

Sheila smiled and relaxed as John turned off I-526 and headed south, down Savannah Highway, towards Beaufort. In less than an hour and a half they were crossing over Huspa Creek on US Route 21 into Beaufort; minutes later they pulled up to the Sentinel on Boundary Street.

Waiting at the front door to greet them was James. He winked at Sheila and took her by the hand, leading her across the threshold.

"So good to see you, my dear. You're even more beautiful than John described. Something I thought would be quite impossible."

"Why thank you, James," Sheila replied in a Southern belle voice—having been briefed by John on James' love of hamming it up.

"You know, if you were a little younger, I might kick John to the curb. I always wanted a Southern gentleman," she whispered.

James continued to lead her by the hand.

"Well . . . then I will just have to lay the charm on a bit thicker to compensate for my advancing age."

"Thanks for the help, James," John called out as he struggled with Sheila's two suitcases and bag.

"Sorry John, you'll just have to manage without me." Turning to Sheila, he said loud enough for John to hear: "It's my heart dear, too much stress will kill me. And right now you have my heart pumping at about its limit."

Shaking his head, struggling to get the luggage up the stairs to the bedroom, John yelled back; "Laying it on a bit *thick* don't you think?"

"Positively not. Age does have its advantages in the laying on thick department," James said loudly, and then whispered conspiratorially to Sheila: "Come my dear, let me show you around. You didn't tell John about our little secret did you?"

"Of course not. You know I'm in the secrets business, don't you?" Sheila whispered back.

James rubbed his hands together like a little kid.

"We're going to have so much fun, even with John here."

"I know. Wish we could get rid of him for a little while. He's such a bump on the log. Do you say that expression down here?"

"We do now."

John came back down the stairs and interrupted their conspiratorial whisperings.

"What are you two cooking up down here?"

"Nothing, dear. Just talking about how much fun we're all going to have."

"Just watch out for James. He looks harmless, but in reality he's a wolf in sheep's clothing. He plays that heart angle like a Stradivarius."

"I was just about to show Sheila the Beaufort Sentinel archives in—"

"I would love to see your grandfather's newspapers," Sheila interrupted.

"Great-great-grandfather," he said, taking Sheila's right hand in his left and leading her down the stairs, leaving John in his wake.

James went over the archiving system of Robert Campbell, his twice removed grandfather and founder of the Beaufort Sentinel. He and Sheila examined the very first storage box made of Camphorwood with the year 1828 stamped on its brass plate. He proceeded to show how his forebear devised an intricate shelving system and hoist, allowing for each storage box to be slid easily out of its rack and onto a wooden platform assembly that slid in parallel tracks on the floor, alongside the shelving unit. The top of the assembly had a long wire rope threaded over a pulley, extending down and coiled several turns around a large wooden drum with a handle. James explained to Sheila that by using the drum hoist—as he referred to it—one man could easily take down any of the storage chests.

Sheila took hold of the wooden assembly and moved it along the track toward the end of the row of shelves at the northeast corner of the basement. When she got to the corner she found intersecting parallel tracks along the adjoining wall. She moved the assembly along the east wall of the basement a couple more feet before coming to a stop.

James proudly interjected; "I built those tracks along the east wall when I took over the paper in 1970."

"I can tell," Sheila said, stopping to wipe her forehead. "It's much harder to push along the newer tracks."

Feeling a bit chastened, James said in a soft almost inaudible voice, "Well I suppose after the new tracks are broken in for another hundred-fifty years, it will slide just as easily as it does along the old tracks."

"I suppose." Sheila's gaze went from the tracks in the floor to the top of the racks in the northeast corner of the basement. She looked to the left, at the storage boxes along the north wall and then at the boxes along the east wall. She pointed to the boxes along the east wall and turned to James. "These are the storage boxes you started in 1970, right?"

"Right. The ones along the north wall go in order from 1828 to the year of my great-great-grandfather's death in 1886. I started the ones along the east wall in 1970, when I took over."

"And the ones from the 1970s are a bit lighter in color. *Correct?*"

"They'll darken over time. I'll be long gone by the time that happens, but John here—" James turned and looked at John. "If he continues on long enough, he may notice a change."

"And you and your double g are and were very anal in your meticulousness, right?"

"Double g." James smiled at Sheila. "I like that. From now on, old Robert is double g."

John looked at the shelves of storage boxes along both walls, furrowed his brow and fixed his gaze on Sheila.

"You're getting at something. What is it, She?"

Sheila walked up to the racks at the northeast corner and pointed up.

"There on the third row. See it? On double g's rack is a newer storage box." Moving her arm to the right, Sheila continued, "And adjacent to it, on James' rack, is an older storage box."

With a disappointed look on his face, James said, "John? How could you be so careless?"

John, in mock protest replied, "Don't look at me. My research on the removal of the Cherokees only took me up to 1835."

In a hurried penguin-like fashion James waddled over to the beginning of the archives, his face a mask of concern, growing redder with each step. James scanned each row and moved down the line, as Sheila and John looked on amused.

A little more than three-quarters of the way down, James suddenly stopped and turned to John and Sheila. "Over here . . . 1865 and 1866 are in reverse order."

John and Sheila walked over to James. John put his hand on James' shoulder.

"There's an innocent enough explanation for that. 1865 was the end of the Civil War and the year of Lincoln's assassination. Probably years ago you looked at that period and simply reversed the two."

"Not very likely," James replied, giving him a hard stare.

"I would be inclined to agree with John, if we didn't have the new and old box mixed up at the corner," Sheila said. Turning abruptly, she walked up the stairs. "C'mon fellas, we need a drink."

James looked at John and shrugged. "Never argue with a lady."

CHAPTER 17

The editor's office of the Sentinel was small but cozy, with wide, well-scarred oak plank flooring. Opposite the door, in front of the window, was a large old, oak desk—in use since the 1920s. A stuffed eagle stood perched at one corner, standing watch. James comfortably settled himself into the high-back leather desk chair, arguing once again that age did have its benefits, few though they might be. John and Sheila sat opposite James, in mission style oak armchairs. Wooden slats ran down the backs and under the wide flat armrests. Fitted on the bottom of each chair was a well-worn, black leather cushion. Between the chairs sat a small table, large and high enough for John and Sheila to place their drinks on without having to contort themselves. Along the wall to John's left were two mission-style mahogany bookcases built by the Globe-Wernicke company circa the 1890s. Cheap in its day, these stackable cases featured beveled glass fronts that swung up and under the top of each case, and were now quite expensive. On a table along the other wall sat a bronze replica of Remington's bronco buster. Above Remington's idealized version of a cowboy astride a rearing horse hung an oil painting of a cypress swamp; a lone man in the foreground paddled a canoe down a winding narrow canal. In the background, on a small sliver of land, the figure of a black woman stood in front of a cabin; smoke curled skyward from its chimney.

Sheila looked around the office, absentmindedly twirling her right index finger in a rock glass loaded with whiskey and ice. After a few seconds, she took her whiskey-soaked finger and stuck it in her mouth, and then slowly pulled it out, making a soft popping sound at the end.

Noticing both men staring intently at her with not-so-subtle leers, Sheila said, "Enjoyed that, huh?"

She tilted her head back and poured the drink into her mouth, gargled loudly for several seconds, and then swallowed. Lowering her head, she gazed around the room a second time.

"Nice décor you boys have here. Early Norman Bates period would be my guess." She looked at James and then John before adding, "You guys done with your little reverie? I think it's time to get back to reality."

"Reality is starting to scare me a little," James said. "I think I much prefer watching a beautiful young woman drink. Don't you, John?"

"You're right on both counts as usual, James. But . . . ." turning to Sheila, John continued; "we do need to focus on what might be going on here."

James spoke in a whisper, as if someone might be standing just outside the office door: "I don't even know if it's safe to talk about this here. The government was obviously censoring newspapers all across the country."

"James, that was almost two hundred years ago," Sheila said.

"The government didn't move those storage chests two hundred years ago," he replied, still whispering.

"You've got a point there. So what do you suggest we do?" John asked James.

"I don't know. I just feel confused . . . violated. Someone going through those storage chests has suddenly made me very nervous."

Sheila decided to try and lighten the mood a little.

"I've got it! We'll speak in code. Ifthey Hethey overnmentgay isay isteninglay, histhey illway riveday hemthey utsnay."

James looked at John, totally perplexed.

"I have no idea what she just said, do you?"

"Not a clue. Must be something they taught her at the NSC."

Sheila smiled. "It's Pig Latin. I said, if the government is listening, this will drive them nuts."

John rolled his eyes. "Okay, let's get serious now. I don't think we're in any danger looking into a man who has been dead for at least a hundred years. Whatever secrets the government is trying to protect, I don't think it holds any physical danger for us," John said, trying to reassure James, who seemed to be in need of some bracing.

John stood up and went behind Sheila's chair, kissed the top of her head and put his hands gently on her shoulders.

"She, honey, is there any possibility that your inquiries may have tripped an alarm bell somewhere, and activated . . . I don't know, seems silly, but some group within the CIA or the National Security Agency that has an interest in this?"

Sheila looked thoughtfully out the window that stood behind James.

"I've been running through my mind everyone I talked to about this. I figured if there was anything to this story, and if I talked to enough people, it might shake something loose. But I think the bigger possibility involves all the searches I've conducted on the computer. The NSA is basically just one giant eavesdropping organization. If there were any secrets to be protected, an alarm would be triggered by a keyword, like, Floating Man, Henri Richaud, et cetera."

James now seemed a little more relaxed; following Sheila's train of thought, he chimed in: "So what you're saying is that by searching government databases using keywords, you may have triggered an alarm somewhere in the nooks and crannies of the intelligence bureaucracy and activated some part of that bureaucracy into action."

"Possibly. But it doesn't have to be a computer search. The NSA monitors every call, every cell phone, every email. They even listen in at thousands of public places. Assuming these keywords trigger an alarm, it could have been triggered when Rachel called us on her cell phone, or when John talked to Max, or when you called John at the hotel to tell him about Harriot Horry. In fact, that could be another one of the keywords programmed into the NSA network."

"Who would be in charge of programming that into the network or database?" John asked. "Wouldn't there be a department responsible for that?"

"That's the problem. There is no *one* department. There are literally hundreds of intelligence cells. Anyone of them has the power to hack into the system and program what they want for their own needs... totally unknown to the rest of the bureaucracy."

"So what happens when one or more of these keywords triggers an alarm?" James asked.

"The conversation gets analyzed to see if it's relevant. The owner of the cell phone or computer is identified and tracked."

"*Tracked?*" James said.

"Yes, of course."

Sheila removed John's hands from her shoulders, got up and turned to face him, looking pale and worried.

"Once a caller or device is identified as being relevant, every call he or she makes is monitored. Every movement is traced via GPS chips that are in our smartphones."

"Now I'm back to being scared," James said glumly, slumping back in his chair. "In your learned opinion, Sheila, who is monitoring us?"

"James, I haven't the faintest idea. That's the beauty of intelligence agencies. Nobody knows what is going on. There are off-budget super-secret intelligence groups that hire other off-budget cells, all compartmentalized from each other. Some of these cells have no idea who they are working for or what their purpose is. They just get assignments, and money. The president, directors of national intelligence and the CIA all have plausible deniability if anything goes wrong, because they literally do not know what is going on. It's like a self-perpetuating beast with tentacles that keeps growing and sprouting new tentacles, with no central direction or authority."

With the revelation that an unknown, unseen hunter was possibly tracking them like game, the Floating Man and his amazing machine receded from their thoughts. As the midmorning sun crept into afternoon, the three of them sat mute, alone with their thoughts and libations.

CHAPTER 18

The silence among the three was abruptly broken by Frank Sinatra's rendition of "Fly Me to the Moon."

John stared at his cell phone that sat on the table as Frank continued to croon . . . *on Jupiter and Mars*. Slowly, as if waking from a deep sleep, John reached for the phone. . . . *hold my hand*. He picked it up, saw Rachel's name on the screen . . . *baby, kiss me* . . . and answered.

"Hi Rachel, what's up?"

John put the phone on speaker and placed it on the desk. Sheila scooted her chair close, while John sat on the desk, and James leaned back with his eyes closed.

"A lot more of nothing that means something."

"How so? By the way, I have you on speaker so Sheila and James can hear."

"Well you guys are going to love this. It seems we have several institutions that have missing inventory when it comes to the dates we're looking for. This wasn't all done in the distant past—at least not at these libraries."

Rachel paused to let the news sink in.

John took the moment to add, "We also have some news on our end, but go ahead."

"Alright . . . I got a call from Vincent Silver. He's the curator of newspapers and periodicals at the American Antiquarian Society in Worcester, Massachusetts. I sent an email request asking that he look at several South Carolinian newspapers with dates corresponding to the missing sections. Anyway, Vincent called, a bit perturbed. Said that the papers we requested were missing, along with several micro cards that they use instead of microfilm. He was *really* upset that several original newspapers were gone."

"Is he sure? Maybe they just got misplaced over the years."

"Nope, he's very anal, just like your friend, James. Sorry James."

"That's alright," James said, "anal doesn't bother me."

"Me neither, James." Sheila leaned over and patted James hand.

After the laughter died down and the color in James face returned to its normal pink complexion from the reddish purple hue it had taken on, Rachel continued: "Vincent said he completed an inventory of all nineteenth-century newspapers and periodicals a month earlier. There's no way he could have misplaced them. He seems to think that maybe we had something to do with it."

"I guess in a way we have," John said.

Sheila quickly leaned over the phone to speak, putting her hand out in front of John as a stop signal.

"It seems we have very little to show for all our research and running around. Just a lot of missing articles and newspapers. I don't see much point in continuing."

"Well can't you dig a little deeper using *your* sources?" Rachel asked, unable to hide her annoyance.

"The short answer is no."

Sheila could imagine the surprised look on Rachel's face at this turn in the conversation. "Anyway, I don't feel comfortable talking about all this right now. Why don't we meet back in Washington next week and discuss it."

Sheila nervously looked at James, then John, and made a zip-it motion across her lips.

"Alright . . . we can meet next week." On a more hopeful note, Rachel asked, "What was the news you had, John?"

"Nothing really, pretty trivial . . . uh, we'll talk next week. Bye Rachel, say hello to Max for us."

Sounding puzzled, Rachel said, "Okay, sure. I'll see you all . . . next week then. Bye."

After Rachel disconnected, James got up and said, "I need another drink. In fact, I think we all need another drink. We're not very good at this spy business. We almost spilled the beans over Rachel's phone, which is probably tapped . . . or whatever you call it in the spy game."

"I bet all our phones are tapped, or whatever you call it in the spy game," John said.

He and James looked over at Sheila.

"Why are you two looking at me? I'm just a staffer, for Christ's sake." Sheila got up from her chair. "We don't need another drink . . . we need to get drunk."

* * *

They went over to James' house, adjourned to the front porch swing and started in on a very expensive, twenty-three-year-old, single-barrel Kentucky bourbon that James had been saving for a special occasion. The skies turned a hue of silver and black. As they dulled their senses, a summer shower pounded all around— obscuring them from prying eyes.

CHAPTER 19

Lying on his back, John awoke fully clothed late Sunday morning, amazed that he had only a slight headache. Lifting himself up part way on his elbows, he looked over at Sheila, lying on her side in bra and panties—snoring loudly. A bit of drool hung from the lower edge of her mouth, a tangle of brown hair covered her eyes. John gently brushed her hair back and watched her sleep. He thought of an old saying: If you think she is still beautiful in the morning when you wake up, then you're definitely in love ... or something to that effect. Maybe it wasn't an old saying, but he was *definitely* in love, and he'd realized it from the moment he first saw her striding into the newsroom of the *Washington Post*.

While Sheila continued to snore away, John got up, showered, dressed, and fixed breakfast. He brought in a tray of scrambled eggs mixed with mushroom and onion, along with an English muffin and a glass of orange juice to his snoring beauty.

Snoring beauty awoke, rubbed the sleep out of her eyes and raised her head. She looked up at John through unfocused eyes. Seeing double, she closed one eye.

"Jesus, the room is spinning. I haven't tied one on like that since ... ever." And she promptly let her head fall back to the pillow.

Within seconds she was snoring again.

John smiled, grabbed half the English muffin and left the tray on her nightstand. It would give him time to do some grocery shopping, take care of some errands around town, and most importantly, think.

* * *

John drove by James' house on his way back to the Sentinel. He pulled into the long circular drive. James gave him a slow wave from his front porch swing. John waved back, got out of the car and walked up the front steps.

"Still some coffee in the pot," James said as John sat down.

"No thanks."

John began gently rocking the swing. They sat quietly for a few moments. Breaking the silence, John said, "I think maybe we ought to back off of this investigation for a little while until we know what we're up against."

"It just seems so absurd. Why would somebody care if we found a few newspaper articles about a man who has been dead for over a hundred years . . . even if that man did discover a technology that would be advanced by today's standards?"

"I don't know. And whatever it is that we don't know, maybe they don't know either. Or maybe they don't want us to discover what they do know."

John rocked the swing a little harder.

"And who are they? Another mystery."

"Well James, I think it's safe to say that whoever they are, they're listening in on our phones and monitoring our computer."

"If this is some sort of secret cell of an intelligence agency wouldn't our homes be wired with listening devices and wouldn't they have one of those GPS tracking devices on our cars? How far does it extend? Or am I just being a bit too paranoid?"

"Maybe we're collectively spooking each other. I suppose there could be an innocent explanation for the misfiled storage chests and the missing inventory. But then again, given everything we know, the best explanation is that we're being eavesdropped on because we stumbled onto something we shouldn't have," John mused, failing to convince himself he was overreacting.

"Maybe someone is hoping we discover something, lead them to something," James said. Slapping his hand on John's knee, he added, "Give it a rest on the rocking."

"Sorry. I guess at this point we just have to assume that our every move is being followed. I don't think it's being paranoid to assume for safety's sake that everything we say on our phones or even inside our homes is being recorded and analyzed. I think it's prudent not to talk about this inside your house, the office, or on the phone, until we find out."

"How would we find out, without they, whoever *they* are, finding out also?"

"I've been thinking about that problem and have an idea that might work. But I need to talk to Max face-to-face... in Washington. Find a safe place. Until then, we should be completely paranoid and avoid talking about this anywhere."

"What about here on the front porch swing?"

Both men laughed, but the conversation from that point on avoided any mention of missing newspapers, Henri Richaud, or government conspiracies.

CHAPTER 20

Late in the afternoon, Sheila finally got up. She ate cold scrambled eggs and took a bite out of the soggy piece of English muffin from the tray John had left. She took a long languorous shower with the water as hot as she could stand, and then right before getting out, cranked the water all the way to cold.

Goosebumps broke out over her body. She toweled off and slipped into one of John's bathrobes hanging on the back of the bathroom door. The robe fit her five-foot-eleven frame perfectly. She tied it loosely so that the front was not completely closed, showing off the plunging cleavage of her large shapely breasts—a touch of areola peeked out on the left.

She admired herself in the mirror while combing back her long brunette hair and tying it into a ponytail. She smiled, remembering how people at the *Post* thought she was such a snob, so aloof from everybody else.

Most men were afraid to approach her, to treat her like a normal person—so intimidated by her looks. The ones that did were usually just jerks hoping to score.

Women, on the other hand, shunned her and saw her as a threat. Even hated her in some instances. They were always cordial in a stiff, formal kind of way, but they never included her in any activities where the girls might get together and talk about their husbands or boyfriends. She always heard about parties after the fact. Never invited; she thought women took a perverse pleasure in telling her how much fun they had had at these get-togethers. As a result, her life before John had been very lonely and sex starved.

She thought about the first time she met John. She immediately sensed he was different. Stiff at first, and a bit standoffish like most of the men she encountered, John loosened up once they began to work together. In fact, he even apologized, confiding that he initially didn't like her and thought she had obtained her position through her looks. In return, she confided in John what a detriment her looks and figure could be.

At first he didn't believe it, until she did an experiment and proved it to him. She told John to watch their coworkers' reactions as she loaded the copier and pretended to fix a jam. One by one each of their male coworkers stopped and watched, as if under a spell, as Sheila bent over to pull the tray out and load a couple reams of paper into the copier. Her simple movements had the opposite effect on female coworkers, who looked on in disgust.

She pretended to hit the copy button and acted perturbed when nothing happened. She stood up straight, placed her hands on her hips and took a deep breath, accentuating her large breasts and flat stomach. Then she scratched her head and looked puzzled. Right on cue, two of the biggest a-holes in the department made a beeline over to help her. As they arrived she pressed the copy button, turned around and said, *"All fixed,"* before striding back over to John.

She remembered how John had struggled to find a diplomatic response.

"That was quite a demonstration of the . . . power of a large . . . of the feminine figure."

She had immediately put him at ease with her quick response.

"You mean I have big tits."

John finally loosened up and replied, *"Magic tits. They attract and repel at the same time. Defying the laws of gravity."*

From that point on they were totally comfortable with each other and could share anything without being embarrassed.

* * *

By the time John finally walked through the door, Sheila was charged up, ready to unleash the passion that had been building up in her over the past two weeks and a day. Hearing John pull up she stood waiting inside the doorway for him, loosening the robe to allow a glimpse of her half-exposed breasts and well-manicured pubic area.

John immediately smiled and remarked on the heat in the office. He went to turn on the air conditioner but was blocked by Sheila. Quickly grabbing his hand, she half-led, half-pulled him upstairs to the bedroom. The cinch of her robe became untied as John trailed behind, his hand firmly in hers.

They entered the bedroom.

Sheila swung John around violently.

With his back to the base of the bed, she immediately grabbed him by the lapels of his shirt and ripped the top three buttons off, remarking tartly that he could finish the rest. She bent over, undid his belt and unzipped his pants, pulling them down sharply to the floor along with his boxers. Squatting down and grabbing the base of his fully erect penis, she bit down lightly on the head; her tongue, cushioning the bottom row of teeth moved back and forth on the underside of his shaft. She quickly withdrew, stood, and faced him—a wild look in her eyes. She put her hands on his chest and pushed him hard onto the bed, laughing at the shocked look in John's eyes as he scooted himself further back so his legs didn't hang over the edge.

"I've been waiting two weeks and a day for this."

With feline grace she hopped up onto the bed, kneeling astride and over the supine John. She let the robe fall from her shoulders, revealing her swollen breasts with their hard pink nipples.

"Are you ready for these?" she said, glancing down at her outthrust breasts.

"Are those fully recovered from our last encounter?"

"You tell me," Sheila said, bending over John. Her hands grasped the brass bar of the headboard; she swung her breasts side to side, slapping them across John's face, mashing them right and left, straight down, smothering him. She rose up a little, and John took the opportunity to grab both breasts. After much resistance from Sheila, he succeeded in pushing her back onto her haunches.

Sheila put her hands over John's, still cupped around her breasts, peeled them off and said, "Are my magic tits strong enough for you?"

"Too strong, I surrender. I'm your slave oh mighty warrior queen. What is your command?"

"Shut up and fuck me hard."

* * *

In a small windowless room in an old government building in Washington, the well-dressed man and woman from the Le Bon Café sat listening and watching as John flipped Sheila over and turned her onto her front, pulling her into him as she raised to meet him, propped on her knees and elbows.

The thin young woman with delicate features and short blonde hair looked on in disgust and fascination at the scene unfolding before her.

"Warrior queen? Magic tits? Who the fuck talks like that?"

"People say silly stuff when they're in love, so what," her partner replied.

The man with the crew cut leaned over one of the monitors as the woman used a toggle switch to zoom in on the genital area of John and Sheila. He looked away and addressed his partner, scorn showed on his face.

"Did you have to use up *all* the cameras in the bedroom?"

"I saved a couple for the rest of the house and office. It's not like these bozos have a clue as to what they're doing."

"They look to me like they know what they're doing," the man said as Sheila changed position onto her side, lifting a long lean leg in the air so John could enter. John placed his right leg on the floor, allowing more leverage for thrusting. "What a body on that girl. She must have been a gymnast until her boobs got too big, don't you think?"

"I think you're disgusting, and so is she," the woman said as they listened to Sheila moaning in the background, and watched as she grabbed John's right hand and placed it on her left breast.

"Squeeze that big titty. Push harder . . . that's it, that's it."

The woman zoomed in on Sheila's reddening breast.

"Those magic tits won't be so tough when I get through with them."

"Yeah?" The man said, watching the action and getting aroused. "What will you do to her?"

"I'll scratch the shit out of her with my razor sharp nails, and punch holes in those big balloons and let some air out. Then when she's holding those bleeding fun bags I'll kick her in her fucking cunt."

The man turned to his partner with a look of both puzzlement and fear.

"What's with all the hatred? I know we sometimes have to kill people, but with you it's genuine hate: men or women, especially women. Where does that come from?"

"You really want to know?" The woman continued to stare in rage at the lovemaking on the screen in front of her.

"Yes . . . I do."

In a flat emotionless voice, with the sounds of passionate lovemaking as backdrop, she told the story of how she was raped by her dad from the age of nine until she was seventeen.

Then, the incident happened.

"My mother, who was beautiful like this fucking cunt on the screen, with the same perfect body, was the life of every party. Every man wanted her. I looked up to her as some sort of feminine ideal. Every night I would go to bed, rubbing my chest, praying for the tit fairy that never came. One night, when I was seventeen, my dad was raping me for the umpteenth time. I opened up my eyes—literally. I had always kept them tightly closed so I wouldn't have to see the bastard's leering face. But that night for some reason, I opened them and found myself looking past him, at the light coming from my bedroom door that was open a few inches. There behind the door, looking in with a gleam in her eyes was my mom. My mom! She had been watching all those years and did nothing! Nothing! I had been too ashamed to tell my mom what was happening, but she knew all the time. All those years . . . nothing."

"And that is when the incident—"

"I killed them. When they were asleep I crept into their bedroom. I stabbed my dad first. It only took a few stabs, but the noise he made woke up my mom. She jumped on my back, screaming like a banshee. As my dad lay choking, gurgling on his own blood, my mother threw me off him. She stood there in front of me, naked, screaming; she started raining blows down on me. I stabbed her repeatedly but it seemed to have no effect. She kept screaming, *'you fucking little cunt'* over and over again, hitting me in the head with her fists, and I kept stabbing her, but I guess the knife was just penetrating those big tits of hers and not hitting any organs. Finally, when I was about to pass out from all the blows, I managed to thrust the knife under her left breast and penetrate her heart. It got very quiet. She looked at me with a strange look, blood covering her body, running down that perfect body, dripping from her breasts, dripping down her ribcage, down her legs, and she just stood there for what seemed like . . . forever . . . and then a look of pure hatred crossed her face. I snapped out of whatever state I was in, and . . . I kicked her as hard as I could between the legs. And she fell over on her back . . . dead."

CHAPTER 21

On Monday morning, James escorted Sheila and John around town, pointing out historical buildings and adding little tidbits of local gossip. So much gossip, in fact, that it caused Sheila at one point to remark in her Southern belle accent, *"Why James, you're just like an old woman."* To which James had smiled and retorted, *"No, but I was married to one for thirty years."*

Their little tour took them to the Campbell Museum on West Street. Remembering Sheila's term for his very late descendent, James remarked, "The museum was founded by my late double g. It's not the original building though. That was gone by the forties." He led them across the sidewalk and was about to walk up the steps of the museum when he saw Elmer Gaskins out of the corner of his eye, standing to the side.

"Why Elmer, good morning to you." Both men looked genuinely pleased to see each other.

"It is a good morning, isn't it?" Elmer walked over to the trio and turned first to John. "Hello John, you're up and about kind of early." John had a slightly chagrined look on his face. Elmer turned his attention to Sheila. "And you must be, Sheila. James has told me all about your attributes . . . journalistic wise."

Elmer, only forty, but looking sixty due to a perpetual two-day facial growth and oddly fitting blonde toupee, ran his eyes up and down Sheila before continuing. "I heard all about how you met John at the Post, and if you don't mind me saying so, I think you could have done better. No offense, John."

"None taken, Elmer," John replied.

Elmer's eyes stayed riveted on Sheila.

"Well, it was awfully nice to meet you, Miss Sheila."

"Yes Elmer, awfully nice." Sheila shook Elmer's extended hand, trying unsuccessfully to hold back a grimace.

"Well I better be getting back to those gutters. Better to be painting one than in one, right, John?"

Elmer gave him a wide grin, revealing yellow teeth that included a gap for a missing bottom premolar, next to the canine on the right side.

As Elmer shuffled off, John remarked sarcastically, "A delightful fellow."

"He used to be our version of Otis, the town drunk from the Andy Griffith show," James explained to Sheila. "I got him a job at the museum doing minor repairs: yard work and other odd jobs. He's pretty much cleaned up his act. From time to time he falls off the wagon and I find him passed out in some nook or cranny of the museum. But other than an acerbic tongue, he's pretty harmless."

Sheila's brow furrowed, remembering something. "Otis's last name was Campbell."

James paused at the top of the steps. "What?" he replied, with a look of mild surprise.

"Otis, the town drunk from Mayberry, his last name was Campbell."

"No relation," James replied. And ever the Southern gentleman, opened the door for Sheila.

Once inside, he introduced them to Maggie Jones, busily cleaning the front of a large glass case. Behind the glass, hung a beautiful bejeweled antebellum dress and a striking green morning suit with red velvet trim worn by the Southern aristocracy.

"I don't know what I would do without you," James said to Maggie, who glowed proudly in return.

Sheila thought she detected some chemistry between the two, and wouldn't have been surprised if there was something going on between them. After a few minutes of small talk, James tenderly put his hand on Maggie's shoulder and whispered something too low for Sheila to hear. Maggie's luminescent smile increased in wattage.

Definitely an item, Sheila thought.

For the next half hour, James shepherded them around the museum and its eclectic collection. He paused at a collection of Indian weaponry displayed along the back wall, near the far corner of the museum. Next to the display was a locked door that James pointed at.

"This is one of Elmer's favorite hiding places. A small storage room that he can lock from the inside." He turned to John. "You might find this interesting." James grabbed a spear off the wall and handed it to John. "That was used mostly for spear fishing," he continued while John handled the spear and examined the tip.

Sheila pointed to a long slender wooden pipe. "What's this?"

James took it down and handed it to Sheila. "It's a Cherokee blowgun made of river cane."

"Did they hunt people with it?"

"No, they only used it for small game."

James took down a small, elaborately woven quiver and pulled out a wooden dart. Showing it to Sheila he explained, "When the Cherokee wanted to hunt a squirrel or raccoon, whatever, they would place this dart in the pipe. This fluffy white fringe at the end is made of bull thistle down. It's soft enough to glide through the pipe but dense enough to block air from passing through. Powered only by lung capacity."

John hung the spear back on the wall and examined the blowgun.

Sheila looked up at James and asked, "Why so many artifacts from the Cherokee? They were primarily in the northwestern part of the state."

John answered for James.

"I started doing research on the Indian removal when I discovered that James' illustrious predecessor wrote quite a good deal on the plight of the Indians. As a matter-of-fact, he was a good friend of the Chief of the Cherokee tribe, John Ross."

"Follow me," James said. He walked along the side wall about a quarter of its length, stopping at a large portrait. "Here's Chief John Ross."

"He looks like a white man," Sheila observed.

"One-eighth Cherokee, elected by the tribe. The man saved a

lot of lives when Andrew Jackson had his army march them over a thousand miles. You may have heard of the Trail of Tears. Once we solve this floating man riddle, John is going to go back to his research on the treatment of the Indians. Chief John Ross presented this portrait to Robert, sometime in the 1850s. He died in 1866. Framed next to it is an edition of the Cherokee Nation's newspaper, the Phoenix, from the first year of publication in 1828. The Cherokee didn't have a written language until 1821. A Cherokee scholar named Sequoyah developed an alphabet with eighty-six characters. Virtually the entire Cherokee nation became literate within the space of a few years. They had their own written constitution, courts, schools, paved roads, and modern houses. They did everything they could to fit in, including fighting on the side of the government, and this is what they got for all their efforts."

James moved a few feet down and pointed to a document behind glass in a large ornate frame.

"The Indian Removal Act of 1830: President Andrew Jackson's gift to the Indians. This is one of the original copies signed by Jackson himself."

"What a bastard."

"You're absolutely right, Sheila, what a bastard," James said, walking off.

* * *

On Monday morning, John and Sheila found themselves on Fripp Island, pulling off Tarpon Blvd at the southeast end of U.S. Highway 21. Just a thirty minute drive from Beaufort, James had offered them his beachfront rental home, insisting the two of them needed to make up for lost time. With barely enough time to pack they were literally pushed out the door by James: John, in shorts and tee shirt; Sheila, stuffed snugly into a pink tube top and matching shorts.

John pulled the Marquis onto a long drive. They soon found themselves in front of a massive two-story, cream-colored stucco with green slate roof. A large deck wrapped around the oceanfront and sides of the home. Jutting out from the southeast corner of the deck was a gazebo that had a Sand Live oak at the center.

Stepping onto the deck, looking out at the ocean and secluded beach, Sheila remarked to John that this could not possibly be the right address.

"Only one way to find out," John said as he slipped the key into the lock of a double sliding door that led to the large living area of the house. Pretending to have difficulty with the lock, John turned to Sheila with a disappointed look on his face.

"I guess you're right, She. The key doesn't fit." And then, with a sudden startled look on his face John shouted, "Oh my God! Where did that pit bull come from?"

"Where!" Sheila screamed and jumped into his waiting embrace.

"Just kidding." The key turned and the door opened.

"You didn't fool me for a second. I just wanted a hug."

Sheila gently bit the bottom of John's earlobe, then blew sensuously into his ear and pulled back, looked longingly into John's eyes.

"Right," John said, and began to slide the pink tube top up over her breasts.

"Don't you think we should go inside?" Sheila said breathlessly, not offering resistance as the tube top slid over her upraised arms.

"Why? We have our own private beach," John said, bending over to pull down Sheila's shorts, while she, now topless, worked on John's tee shirt. Soon they were writhing around on the deck in passionate embrace, both silently thanking James as they made up for lost time.

* * *

After their primal needs had been satiated and following a quick dip in the ocean, John and Sheila lay naked on separate chaise lounges, looking out at the gently undulating surf.

Holding John's hand, Sheila turned her head and said in a soft tender voice, "Honey, why did it take you so long to come to me? You must have known I wanted you."

John kept staring straight out to sea as he pensively answered. "I don't really know. I've thought about it a lot, and the only thing that I can come up with is that I'm afraid of success, or happiness . . . or both. For some reason, that seems to make sense to me, but then again it doesn't."

"Why would you be afraid of happiness? Of this? What we have right now?"

"Maybe I'm more afraid of losing it. It's like back at the Post... after each big story, all the accolades, I would go into despair and drink myself senseless. I couldn't face the fact that I would have to climb back up the same hill. What if the next story didn't pan out? What if the praise stopped coming? Same thing with you. Sure, I wanted you the instant I saw you. Every man does. After we started working together I fell in love with the person behind the facade. But it's better to be unhappy than miserable. If we had fallen in love back then and it didn't work out... I don't think I could've survived the pain."

"We're in love now, John," Sheila said, gently fingering the palm of his hand.

"I know. And sometimes, in the quiet, it scares me to death."

Sheila got up from her chaise lounge and moved over to John's, swung one leg over and sat astride John. She bent over and kissed John gently on the forehead and held his head in her hands. "Look at me," she said, staring with a determined look in her eyes. "I'm not going anywhere. So unless you have some weird sick perverted side that I'm not aware of, I'm yours for the rest of your natural life. So do you?"

"Do I what?"

"Do you have a sick perverted side that I'm not aware of other than being a little rough in bed, which quite frankly, I enjoy. So that's it, that's my perverted side. What's yours?"

"Well, I do occasionally toss off to Victoria's Secret catalogs."

"Really?"

"Occasionally."

"Anything else?"

"Field and Stream."

Sheila doubled over in laughter and fell on top of John.

"Oh my God. You're into sheep!"

"Elk, actually. Sometimes an antelope will strike an enticing pose and send me over the edge."

After their laughter subsided and the midday sun began its rise, the two fell asleep on the chaise lounge: Sheila enveloped by John's embrace—only to be awakened by a curious older couple who happened to be strolling along the beach, thought they might be

dead and walked onto the deck to investigate. Or so they said.
That was their story and they were sticking to it.
As they left, Sheila turned to John.
"Guess we're not the only perverts on the island."

CHAPTER 22

The rest of the week was spent taking long walks on the beach, snoozing on the chaise lounge and making up for lost time. On one midnight walk, Sheila found a couple of loggerhead turtles laying their eggs. Unlike the older couple encountered earlier, she gave them a wide berth to ensure their privacy. On Wednesday they managed to get in a round of golf. John was initially impressed by Sheila's swing. Less so by the end of the round when he found himself losing by three strokes. It was little comfort to John that she had been on the women's team at UCLA. But aside from golf and dinner at the Beach Club, most of the week was just spent in and around the house, lying on their chaise lounges, reading. At the small general store a short walking distance away, Sheila picked up Patricia Cornwall's latest *Scarpetta* novel. John, under the guise of doing research for his soon to be, maybe someday book on the removal of Native Americans from their homeland, purchased *American Lion*, a biography of Andrew Jackson by Jon Meacham.

Thursday, after a light dinner, they repaired to their usual spots on the deck overlooking the ocean. With the sound of the rolling surf it was not surprising that they didn't hear John's cell, ringing on the coffee table inside. As darkness descended, they went for a swim and made love in the rolling surf. When John's cell rang a second time, the two lovers were caught in the silvery shards of moonlight that danced on the surf and cascaded over them, advancing and retreating to the rhythms of their love.

Back inside, they showered off the salt film and John became aroused again. In answer to Sheila's look of surprise, John confessed to popping a Viagra earlier in the evening. Thankfully, John climaxed just as both the hot water and Sheila were about out. It was almost midnight when they emerged from the bathroom, with matching ivory-colored Egyptian cotton towels wrapped around their waists. John headed for his cell phone—ringing for a third time. He reached it just as it went to voicemail.

John saw that Rachel called, Max also, twice after Rachel. He went to the front living room, sat on the sofa facing the ocean and checked his voicemail. Sheila joined him, stretching her feet across his lap. John had such an excited look on his face that it caused Sheila to rise up on her elbows.

"Honey, what is—"

John put his hand up to silence her.

Sheila studied John's face as he continued to listen to his voicemail.

He turned to her and put the phone down.

"It's Rachel, she found something big."

"Aaand?" Sheila dragged out the word and rolled her hand for him to continue.

"She said she was researching Jackson's secretary of war, John Eaton, in the rare document section, and came across a document on the capture of Henri Richaud and his removal to Washington. She said it would blow our minds. She's leaving the library with a copy and will scan and send it as soon as she gets to Max's. That's probably what the next message from Max is about."

"I thought we were at a dead end. This is so cool," Sheila said, rising up to a sitting position, leaning over John and the phone. "Guess Rachel didn't listen when you told her to lay off the investigation."

"You know Rachel. There's no stopping her once she gets ahold of something."

John put his hand back up. The second message played.

A shadow seemed to fall across his face. He turned pale and put the phone down.

"It's Max. Something happened to Rachel. She's at George

Washington Hospital. He said he's on his way there now."

"Oh my God!"

Sheila put her hand over her mouth. Tears began to pool in her eyes. She searched John's face for clues as he listened to the last message from Max. She didn't have to wait long to confirm her worst fears.

John hit end, tossed the cell on the floor, his head fell to his chest trying to hold back tears.

He exhaled.

"Rachel's dead."

CHAPTER 23

John and Sheila sat in the back of Saint Peters church, a block down from the Library of Congress on C Street. When they had talked the previous night, Max told John that Rachel would often come to Saint Peters on her lunch hour and say her rosary. Now they were listening to a priest praying over Rachel as she lay closed up in her white casket.

John couldn't get something Max said the night before out of his head. At the wake, John and Sheila offered their condolences to Max as they stood by Rachel's open casket. Obviously racked with grief, Max commented that Rachel's favorite color was white, and even though the design was spare, her casket had an adjustable bed to raise or lower the body. It was an odd thing to say, John thought. But people at such moments were often at a loss for words.

John remembered commenting on how beautiful she looked in the violet floral dress she was laid out in. Laid out in. Another awkward phrase used when one was dead. As these and other inane thoughts flickered across his cerebral cortex, the image of Rachel adjusting the floor of her casket played in his mind. The priest sprinkled holy water on the casket; John imagined Rachel raising herself up so she could hear better. Rachel, with her critical mind wanting to correct the priest on a subtle point of liturgy, suddenly opened the top of the casket.

John was snapped out of his strange reverie and into the present by Sheila's elbow.

The casket wheeled past, down the aisle and out the church as the choir sang "In Paradisum."

"May angels lead you into paradise; upon your arrival, may the martyrs receive you and lead you to the holy city of Jerusalem. May the ranks of angels receive you, and with Lazarus, the poor man, may you have eternal rest."

John thought how much more dignified it sounded when sung in Latin. In English, the words lacked a certain solemnity, seemed beneath the occasion.

* * *

John drove in the procession to Mount Olivet Cemetery. Sheila broke the silence that had shrouded them since the beginning of the funeral mass.

"Do you buy the story that this was a simple mugging gone wrong?"

"Of course not," John replied.

"Max seems to think so."

"I don't think Max knows about Rachel's call, or the discovery she made."

The funeral procession turned into Mount Olivet and arrived at the gravesite. John pulled over to the shoulder of the narrow cemetery road and put the car in park. He turned to Sheila. "How do we tell Max that we may have inadvertently caused Rachel's death?"

"In private," Sheila said, opening the passenger door and getting out.

They walked over to the large gathering of people at the gravesite. Close to a hundred, Sheila thought. John thought it closer to fifty. Throughout the short ceremony, Max kept his head down, not acknowledging the presence of anyone, as if he wanted to be alone in his sorrow.

At the end of the ceremony several people tossed roses on the casket as it was lowered into the ground.

Max inexplicably turned and left.

He walked towards two cemetery workers dressed in grey coveralls, standing near a large old oak tree some thirty yards distant. All eyes were riveted on Max as he talked, out of earshot, to the cemetery workers. One of the men walked over and grabbed a shovel that was leaning against the oak tree and handed it to Max. Returning to the gravesite he plunged it into a pile of dirt near the grave and threw a shovelful on top of Rachel's casket. He then turned and handed the shovel to the person closest to him.

Max walked slowly to his car.

One by one, the mourners—including John and Sheila—took a shovelful of dirt and placed it on top of Rachel's casket.

Returning to the car, John was about to drive off when he noticed Max running over. He rolled his window down.

Max put his hand on the car roof and leaned his head down, pausing for a few moments before speaking.

"John, Sheila, I want to thank you both. I know this whole funeral has been kind of rushed. Normally there'd be a repast for everyone to gather, but I just can't face all these people right now."

"We understand," Sheila said.

John nodded in agreement.

"Rachel's parents, two sisters, and a few of my relatives are coming over to the house. . . . Not looking forward to that."

Max looked away before continuing. "Hopefully, they won't linger too long." Clearing his throat, he looked in at John and Sheila. "I would like you two to come over later, say around nine o'clock tonight. And bring your bags. I don't want you staying in a hotel, when I have a guest bedroom."

"Are you sure, Max? You might want your privacy at a time like this," John said.

"No . . . no, I don't want a lot of people, but I don't want to be alone either. Besides, I need to talk. I don't think what happened to Rachel was a random act of violence. Do you?"

"No, we don't think so either," John said.

As they drove off, neither John nor Sheila were aware of the slender young woman dressed in black, standing by the side of the cemetery lane, staring intensely as their car passed by.

CHAPTER 24

Framed by bookcases, Max sat in a wingback chair by the window of his study, filling in details of Rachel's murder for John and Sheila. From library records and surveillance video, the police established that Rachel had worked late, leaving the Library of Congress a little before eight. She left the southeast entrance, walked south to the corner, and turned east onto Independence Avenue. She reached 2nd Street Southeast and was attacked crossing to the east side of the street.

The attacker, described as between five foot eight and five foot ten, slender to medium in build, wearing a blue Chicago Cubs baseball cap and windbreaker, crossed 2nd Street in the opposite direction. As Rachel and her attacker met in the middle of the intersection, Rachel was stabbed once in the chest.

The surveillance camera showed the attacker taking the briefcase from Rachel's hand and continuing across to the west side of 2nd Street. Rachel is seen hurrying across to the east side. Once across the intersection, Rachel ran south several feet before collapsing.

While she lay bleeding to death on the sidewalk, her attacker, on the opposite side of 2nd Street, calmly walked south towards C Street before going kitty corner across C Street. There was a rental car parked a quarter block down; the attacker got in on the passenger side and it sped off east down C Street.

The car was later found dumped at the end of E street, with no further sighting of the attacker and his or her accomplice. The police checked rental records and dusted for fingerprints, but Max felt certain they were not going to find anything.

By the time paramedics got to Rachel, she was in shock from blood loss. The knife had pierced her heart. She bled to death before reaching George Washington Hospital.

Max slowly got out of his chair, went over to the window at his left and looked out at the night sky.

"By the time someone at George Washington called, she was already dead. . . . They didn't tell me that."

Max turned around. The light from a torch lamp near the window cast a shadow across his face, highlighting the sallow quality of his cheeks. Grief seemed to have aged him overnight. John noticed Max's drawn face, with new wrinkle lines etched at the corners of his dark-rimmed, sunken eyes. He was at a loss for words. Head held low, he could only listen.

"I raced through red lights to get to her and she'd already died." Collapsing back into his chair, Max added, "I never had a chance . . ."

His voice trailed off. His head slumped to his chest.

Sheila—lost in her own train of thought—didn't hear a word of Max's dash to the hospital. Her mind was stuck on the spot where Rachel had collapsed.

"There's a Kinko's right around there . . . on 2nd Street," she blurted out, more to herself, but loud enough for John and Max to hear.

Max's countenance turned from sad to surprise. His head popped up with a jolt.

"That's where she collapsed: in front of the FedEx Kinko's store next to Le Bon Café where we had lunch a few weeks ago. Maybe she was going to Le Bon to pick up some sandwiches before she drove home. I wondered why she was going in the opposite direction of her car."

"I think she was going to the Kinko's," Sheila said.

Max looked at them with a baffled look.

"She called right before she left the library," John explained. "She found something she thought was important."

"Rachel was going to scan and send it to us as soon as she got to your place," Sheila added.

"Why didn't she just do that at the library?"

"I don't know, Max, maybe she got spooked," Sheila said. "Did she seem nervous, or act different the past couple of weeks?"

"Well, your last conversation weirded her out. She thought you were all a little paranoid, but that didn't stop her from digging. In fact, it kind of spurred her on. That's why she stayed late every day: so she could do her own research. The library had been giving her a bigger and bigger workload the past few weeks. Budget cuts they said. Rachel was getting a little pissed off, thought she was shouldering the brunt of it while other staffers seemed to be skating as usual."

"Maybe it was intentional," John said. "To keep her from snooping."

"Well if it was intentional, it had the opposite effect," Max replied.

Sheila walked over to John, whispered in his ear. She walked over to Max and did the same before speaking aloud.

"I'm sorry we brought this up."

John added as if scripted, "We didn't mean to get you worked up about this."

"No, no . . . that's alright. I just need some time to grieve. Let it all sink in. Think I'll turn in. It's been quite a shock. You two don't have to follow suit. I left fresh towels in the guest bathroom, and you know where everything is in the kitchen. Thanks again for keeping me company."

Max got up and gave Sheila's shoulder a tender squeeze as he walked past. Sheila looked up and gave him a sad smile; her eyes following him all the way to the bedroom.

John and Sheila shared a quiet nightcap and then turned in for the night.

CHAPTER 25

The next morning, the three of them met in a private conference room at the *Washington Post*. A windowless room with no phones and no pictures—just four white walls, a white ceiling, a white door, and an empty white table. The only real color added to the room was Sheila's sleeveless, yellow sundress with crossover straps that tastefully revealed a hint of cleavage.

"Christ!" Sheila said as she looked around. "I feel like I'm in a waiting room in heaven."

"More like a room in a psych ward," John added.

"We've become increasingly more paranoid," Max said. "We added this room shortly after you two left. It's regularly swept for bugs. And no one is allowed to bring any electronic devices in here, just a notepad and pencil. Can't be too careful, especially with Rupert's outfit trying to run this town."

John and Sheila brought Max up to speed on the events of the past couple weeks. He already knew about the missing inventory from Rachel. Sheila told him about the discovery of the storage chests in the basement of the Sentinel being switched.

"So—" John let out a deep breath and lightly slapped his hands on the table, fingers spread far apart. "Let's assume the worst. That everything we have been doing has been tracked. Let's assume our phones are tapped. Our homes are bugged . . . everything. All our conversations have been recorded. What do we do?"

"First off," Max said, "we get some prepaid disposable cell phones that can't be traced. That's easy enough. I'll take care of it."

"Somebody, somewhere, will still pick up our conversations if we mention keywords like the Floating Man or Henri Richaud," Sheila replied.

"Let's compile a list of words that might trigger a search and use code words for them, like Charles de Gaulle for Henri," John suggested.

"Perfect," Max replied.

After a few minutes, they had compiled a list of code words and turned their attention to other topics.

"What do we do about being bugged?" Sheila asked. "If we check for bugs, we'll let whoever is bugging us know that we're on to their game."

John said they probably already knew. To what extent they couldn't be sure.

Max faced John and asked, "What about your friend, James? Do you think his place is bugged too?"

"I don't know. We've kept him out of it, except for his running around to a few libraries in North and South Carolina. He found that article connecting Henri Richaud, excuse me, Charles De Gaulle with that Harriott Horry, I mean Horrible Hairy woman. Better get used to this code stuff."

"Sheila," Max said, pointing a finger at her as if he were still her boss. "Why don't you ask your boss to make some—"

Sheila interrupted. "I don't think that's such a good idea. I feel a lot of guilt about asking around in the first place and setting this whole thing off. I should've kept my mouth shut."

"I've been giving this a lot of thought," John said. "Let's proceed on a few assumptions. First; whoever is spying on us knows we suspect something. Again, to what extent, we can't be sure. Second; let's assume that the Beaufort Sentinel is bugged, along with Sheila's apartment and your townhouse. On one hand, we can't check for bugs without tipping our hand; on the other, we need some safe places to talk without running all around to different meeting places. So, here's where it gets a little dicey with the assumptions." John swiveled nervously in his chair, paused—a bit uncertain of himself. "Let's assume that James' home, along with the rental on Fripp Island are both bug free."

Sheila looked up with a pained expression. "You can't assume that!"

"Hear me out. We assume it so we can take a calculated risk and have them checked out for bugs. We leave your apartment, the Sentinel, and Max's townhouse alone."

"Don't have to worry about my townhouse. I'm moving into another one very soon. Blame it on grief caused by too many memories, which would also be the truth."

"Even better," John said to Max. "When Sheila and I are home at the Sentinel, or any of us talk on our regular phones, only mention the case in general terms. Pretend we're not making any progress."

"We're *not* making any progress," Sheila interjected.

"Yes we are, I think. Something you told Max earlier about the storage cases made me think we may have missed something. I'll explain later."

"Go on, John." Max was eager to hear where all this was leading.

"Max, you obviously have a team, or connections to do a sweep. Have your guys sweep James' home and beach house for bugs. If they're clean, then we can proceed with our plan."

"Our plan? I didn't know we had a plan." Sheila said.

"If we're being hunted we need to find out who's doing the hunting, draw them out into the open."

"And we do that, *how?*" Sheila asked.

"First, if we don't find anything further on Mr. de Gaulle, we make something up. I'm getting pretty good at this code stuff."

"Okay, I think I'm following you," Max said. "Go on, but let's skip the code stuff."

"I agree," Sheila said. "If anything would tip someone off that we were on to them, it would be talking about Charles de Gaulle staying with that Horrible Hairy Woman searching for the broomstick."

"Broomstick is the floating machine, right?" John asked.

"Forget it, honey."

"Yes, forget it, honey." Max turned to Sheila. "Sorry dear, but I have known John longer than you, so you will just have to find another term of endearment. Go ahead, honey." A big grin spread across his face as Max shook off his grief, if only momentarily.

"Thank you love, and thank you dear." John nodded to Sheila and then Max before continuing: "We set up surveillance around James' home and the beach house. Also, we should set up surveillance at a safe distance to cover the Sentinel, front and back. Then we have Sheila go to her boss and tell him about our suspicions concerning Rachel's death, and its relationship to our research on de Gaulle—excuse me, Richaud. Sheila tells him about her fear that the Sentinel is being bugged and asks if he can arrange a team to debug it."

"Sheila's boss, Henry Smith, wouldn't be involved in this," Max said dismissively. "He's one of the old wise men of Washington. Henry goes all the way back to LBJ, serving both Democratic and Republican administrations."

"Henry wouldn't be involved, but he might set the ball in motion when he goes down the chain of command and orders an investigation. Maybe the same team that bugged the Sentinel— assuming that it's bugged—will be sent down. Or a team not involved in any way is dispatched to sweep the Sentinel of bugs; it doesn't matter. We get them on tape from our own surveillance. Later, we let slip that we discovered something, and ... I don't know, tell them it's at the beach house. Then we wait and see who shows up. The same team from the earlier sweep or a different one."

"Sounds a little risky, but it might work," Max said.

"I like it. Let's do it," Sheila replied.

Before leaving the conference room they agreed to continue their cross-country hunt in libraries and private collections for articles on Henri Richaud. But with Rachel's discovery of the missing inventories, they now knew they were not hunting alone. Plus, the loss of Rachel meant the loss of her contacts as well. Max said he would mount a search using *Post* resources at various bureaus. Max was particularly interested in having Ted Dody, his Paris bureau correspondent, investigate Henri Richaud and his mentor, Pierre-Simon Laplace, the Newton of France.

And finally, John told Sheila and Max his suspicions concerning the storage chests that were out of order. John couldn't remember exactly which two years were switched, but Sheila was certain of their position on the storage rack. In any event, John's hunch—more a hope than a hunch—was that whoever had been snooping around was looking for a specific issue or date in the Sentinel archives. If that was the case, there would be a missing issue. All they needed to do would be to check the storage chests of James' forebear that served as his backup collection. It was all predicated on the very big assumption that James' house had not been bugged or under surveillance. They all agreed that it was the only promising lead they had.

CHAPTER 26

Three days later.

Sheila was making a pot of coffee in the kitchen of the Sentinel building. Although it was almost seven in the morning, John was still asleep. Sheila looked out the kitchen window. As she rinsed out a coffee mug she noticed a hand bobbing up and down. Leaning over to look out the window, she saw James jumping up and down, flailing his hands. Dressed only in her bathrobe, she went to the back door and stepped outside. James immediately grabbed her hand and pulled her several feet towards the side of the building before Sheila pulled back and stopped his progress.

"Come! Come quick!" James leaned into Sheila and whispered in her ear. "They're here."

"Who's here?"

"The team." As he continued to whisper, James took Sheila's hand and tried to pull her along without success.

"Some kind of spy you are, James," Sheila said whispering back.

"Sorry." A pinkish hue spread across James' face as he continued in a low hushed tone; "What should I do?"

"Kiss me," Sheila said, giving James her best wanton look.

Aghast, James face continued to redden, jowls quivering. "What? Why?"

Sheila whispered, "Because we're having an affair."

James stood dumbfounded as Sheila threw her arms around him and began kissing him on his now crimson cheek and neck.

"Oh, darling, darling, I need you so. John will be asleep for at least another hour."

"Of course my little sparrow," James said, finally catching onto the game. He again took Sheila's hand. "Let's retreat to our little love nest, where we can—"

"Not so fast Casanova, I'm naked under this robe." Sheila reared back, laughed and turned to go inside, but James held tightly to her hand.

"Shouldn't you stay in character?" he said with the most sincere, innocent look he could muster.

One withering look and he knew the jig was up. He let go of her hand, smiling sheepishly. Sheila went inside. She quickly threw on a tee shirt, shorts, and sandals, and returned—steaming coffee mug in hand.

They covered the five blocks to James' house in a hurry. Sheila was surprised that James had no trouble keeping up with her long strides. She was less surprised when she caught him glancing sideways at the rhythmic bouncing of her breasts. Men were all alike no matter what their age; she wished she had put on a bra instead of rushing to get out the door.

Once they got to James' house she understood his anxiety. Several men were roaming about, and equipment was lying everywhere.

"See what I mean? It's like an invasion."

"Wow! I thought it would only take a couple guys holding a scanner to sweep a house." Sheila put her hands on her hips and looked on incredulously. "Well, get a load of this—*Damn!*" She turned to one of the men carrying what looked like a large black suitcase. "Excuse me; is all of this really necessary?"

The man put the suitcase down and said, "It's not like in the movies."

"I guess not. I thought you just swept a room to find a listening device hidden in a phone, lamp, hole in the wall, whatever."

"Kinda sorta, but it's a little more complicated than that. There are several types of bugging devices. You've got your primitive acoustic devices, starting with the neighbor listening with a glass against the wall—I think we can rule that one out—on up to more sophisticated devices that are usually located around windows, air ducts and outlets. Then you have your VLF or ultrasonic bug that converts sound waves into ultrasonic signals transmitted to a receiver and converts them back into audio."

At this point, Sheila was sorry she had asked; the man continued to drone on.

"You also have your RF. That's your radio frequency bugs. Those are easy to find, but hard to trace back to whoever planted it. Then you have your optical and hybrid bugs, but I won't bore you with that."

Thank God! Sheila thought. Impressed though she was with the man's ability to ignore her curves, she was less impressed with his one-sided conversational skills. *Maybe he's a good dancer,* she inanely thought as he relentlessly continued on—anything to block out the droning noise.

"Now, wiretapping is the way to go. You've got your hardwired tap, but that's pretty easy to trace back to a listening post. I would put my money . . . well, actually it's your money, more specifically the Post's money, whoever's money it is, I would put it on a soft tap. That's really the only way to go, if you have the resources that is. And from what Max has told me, resources are no problem."

Jesus Christ, shoot me now dear God, put me out of my misery. I've got to put an end to this.

"That's what your enforcement and intelligence agencies mostly use. They're the ones that have access to the phone company's servers. If that's the case, I sure wouldn't want to be you. Although, on the other hand, your soft tap is easy enough to . . ."

I can't believe I'm doing this, Sheila thought as she scratched her left breast at a phantom itch. But once her nipple hardened and protruded through her tee shirt, it had the desired effect she'd prayed for.

"Anyway," the man continued, losing his train of thought, "we need all this equipment to detect the various frequencies that the uh . . . well, I better get back to work. This could take more than a day. It depends of course on the number of—"

"Well, I better let you get back to work then. Thank you so much. That was fascinating," Sheila lied, holding her hand out to the man.

With a look of newfound respect and confidence in his bearing, the man took hold of Sheila's hand and was not at a loss for words as he bid her adieu.

"Any time Miss, it's a fascinating subject. Now there was one time, must have been about three, no, maybe five years ago . . . no, I take that back, it was three years ago. I remember, because my son Jimmy had just entered kindergarten. Or was it first grade? That would have made it two years ago. Anyway, we had this warehouse, fifty thousand square feet, honeycombed with offices at the north end of the structure. Well, I looked at that and said . . . ."

Sheila picked up a gun, put it in her mouth and pulled the trigger. It still did not stop. She took a knife and committed Hara-Kiri. Still it droned on. She was not about to do the itch thing again.

CHAPTER 27

No bugs were found at James' home or at the beach house on Fripp Island. Using their prepaid cell phones, Max told John that along with the surveillance equipment in place inside and out of both homes, a team was working on setting up surveillance equipment at a safe distance from the Sentinel building. As they were talking, an idea occurred to John. He had been thinking of how to check the misarranged storage chests in the basement of the Sentinel without tipping off whoever was spying on them. When Max reminded him that there was no solid evidence that the Sentinel was bugged, John got a little testy.

"You know our lives may be at stake here, Max. Don't tell me that just because there were no bugs at James' homes that there are no bugs at the Sentinel. Already you want to ditch the plan and change our assumptions?" John's voice became shriller, "That's easy for you to say, sitting safe and sound in your little cocoon back in Washington."

"John, I'm not trying to change our plans. And I'm not in a little cocoon as you put it. I'm staying in a rental. My home of nearly ten years, which may also be bugged, is on the market. And as for lives being at stake . . ." Max paused and slowly enunciated each word to make a point that was not needed. "I don't think you have to remind me of that."

"I'm sorry, Max. I think we're all a little stressed out."

"Apology accepted," Max said brusquely. "What is this idea you have?"

With calmness returning to his voice, John said, "I need your team to set up surveillance inside and out of a building that James owns. A week ago he was showing Sheila the historical museum he runs, established back in the late 1800's by Robert Campbell. It has a varied assortment of historical pieces of that era: Indian artifacts, historical documents, period clothes, tools used on the plantations—basically a little bit of everything. Well, I've been struggling to find a way to look at the misarranged storage chests without arousing the suspicions of whoever may or may not be watching. An idea came to me—assuming the Sentinel is wired from top to bottom."

"Let me guess," Max interjected. "You want to donate or lend the storage chests to the museum."

"You've got it. It would actually make quite a good exhibit. Display a newspaper from each decade showing how writing style and journalism changes over time. The museum already has the original printing press that was used at the Sentinel, and Maggie, the lady who runs the museum for James, is bored out of her mind. I'm sure she would love the challenge of designing a new display."

"Okay. So now you can get into the chests without anybody watching, then what?"

"First, before we move them we have Sheila raise a stink with her boss about being bugged and her suspicions concerning Rachel's death."

"Our suspicions," Max quickly added.

"Right. Our suspicions. Anyway, Sheila's boss will hopefully order a sweep of the Sentinel. With the surveillance you've set up, we'll get video of the team that is sent. Once that is done, we'll wait awhile. And then, using our regular phones we'll talk about a discovery we've made in the archived papers. Papers which will be residing in the museum."

"So anyone listening in will undoubtedly send a team to investigate—"

"And we'll capture them on video."

"What if they're the same team?"

"Then we know who we're dealing with," John said matter-of-factly.

"No, then we're *fucked*," Max replied.

"That, too."

CHAPTER 28

Sheila stopped by the museum to see if Maggie needed any help on the exhibit—soon to include the storage chests from the Sentinel. Walking towards the office she saw the incredibly boring bug man.

Trapped!

The loquacious member of the sweep team at James' home was trotting down the stairs that ended just outside the entrance to Maggie's office. With images of their last encounter racing through her head, and too late to take evasive action, Sheila decided to confront her nemesis head on.

Giving him the brightest smile in her repertoire, she strode over to him as he reached the bottom step and got uncomfortably close; their chests nearly bumped as she took his hand. "Well *hello* again! It's so good to see you."

Taken aback by her forwardness, the boring bug expert responded weakly.

"Ah . . . yes, it's good to see . . . me . . . you. I was . . . just . . . finishing up my work here."

The bug man began to recover and hit his tedious stride.

"You *know*, installing bugs is almost an art form, not as diffi—"

Sheila broke in and nipped his soliloquy in the bud. "I found our conversation last week fascinating. I was telling my boyfriend all about VLF and RF bugs, soft taps versus hard taps. My boyfriend used to be a journalist. Still thinks he is one. John, that's his name, my boyfriend, graduated from Northwestern University where he majored in journalism at the Medill school of Journalism. He started working for the Washington Post in January of 2002. I *think* it was 2002. I remember it was after 9/11 happened. Or was it right before? No, it couldn't have been before, could it . . ."

Sheila looked into his eyes; the bug man was beginning to wilt. With the battle won, she continued the relentless assault on her tormenter.

" . . . you know, it must have been after, because I started there in 2006. John, my boyfriend, told me he had just celebrated his fifth year anniversary at the Post. Oh my God!"

Sheila gaped as if shocked by a meaningless revelation.

"It *was* before 9/11! So, where was I? Oh . . . so I started at the Post in 2006, I went from . . . . . ."

Sheila droned on for another five minutes before mercifully putting the bug man out of his misery. She entered Maggie's office and closed the door behind her.

Looking up from her desk, Maggie noticed the smug look on Sheila's face.

"Well, whose goose did you cook today?"

"That obvious, huh?"

Maggie motioned for Sheila to sit down.

Sheila scooted a chair close to the desk and reenacted her encounter with, and narrow escape from the bug man.

"Oh my god," Maggie said as she hunched forward and leaned towards Sheila. "That man is the most *boring* man in the world. That's why I'm holed up in here. And that didn't work. Now I'm trapped, cornered."

Maggie held up her hand with her fingers fanned out.

"Five times he's come in here. The last two times I was quick enough to pick up the phone and pretend I was having an important conversation."

Maggie shook her head. Both women leaned back and laughed.

The ladies basked contentedly in a few moments of silence, suddenly punctuated by the door opening—whereupon both sprang.

Elmer found the two of them draped over the desk sideways, a look of panic on their faces as they fought over the phone.

"I'm sorry if I interrupted something," he said uncomfortably.

Relieved, both ladies sat back down laughing.

"I won't even ask," Elmer said, shaking his head. "What you ladies do behind closed doors is none of my business"

"We were having phone sex and got a little carried away," Maggie said for Sheila's benefit. Both ladies continued to laugh as Elmer shook his head, looking on as if both had lost their minds.

"I just wanted to tell you that I finished moving the buffalo. So now you have plenty of space for the newspaper chests when they arrive. If you don't mind, I think I'll call it a day, unless you have something else for me to do."

"No, that's fine, Elmer. See you tomorrow."

As Elmer began to leave, Sheila jumped up.

"Elmer, wait a second. I was just going to talk to Maggie about something, and I think you should hear it too."

Elmer sat on the edge of the desk and looked at Sheila.

"This new exhibit comes with a bit of danger." Sheila talked slowly and chose her words carefully. "I don't want you two to work late or to come in too early. And if you notice anything out of place, let me or John know immediately."

"Talking about that spy shit," Elmer said evenly.

"How did you know?"

Maggie replied for him. "I told him."

"And how did *you* find out?" Sheila looked incredulously at both of them.

"James told me."

Maggie's head raised a little. Her face took on an air of importance not previously there.

"They're sleeping together," Elmer added.

"Elmer!" Maggie shouted.

CHAPTER 29

With everything in place, John and Sheila flew back to Washington and met with Max at his new apartment. Sitting around the kitchen table, each with coffee mug in hand, Max brought them up to speed on the investigation of Rachel's murder—no speed.

Nothing but dead ends.

Max had asked John to bring a recording of Rachel's last message. John took it out of his pocket, placed it on the table, and slid it over to Max. Max raised his index finger, got up and walked out of the kitchen, returning less than a minute later with an iPad. He scrolled through a few files, moving his fingers across the screen until he found what he wanted. Not a word was said as Max placed the recorder next to the iPad and played Rachel's last message. After the message reached the end, Max continued to make adjustments on the screen. John and Sheila silently looked on.

Max finally looked up from the screen and broke the silence.

"Just had to make a few adjustments, syncing the audio in the right places. iMovie—great app."

Max pushed the pad across the table.

"Just hit play."

Sitting back, lost in thought, Max closed his eyes. His former employees watched and listened to Rachel's last moments. The audio and video ended: frozen on a close-up of Rachel lying outside the entrance of the FedEx Kinko store.

Both John and Sheila had watery eyes. One lone tear broke loose and trailed down the side of Sheila's cheek.

Max sat stonily, staring at her. He spoke in a slow resolute voice.

"Take that. Play it for Henry Smith."

CHAPTER 30

Sheila sat in the waiting area just off the north lobby entrance to the west wing of the White House. Her meeting with Henry Smith was scheduled for ten o'clock. Although the national security advisor was technically her boss, she had only met Henry Smith a handful of times. Normally, she submitted her reports to Ed Maxwell, the deputy national security advisor whose small office was adjacent to Henry's corner office.

Sheila looked nervously at her watch. Fifteen minutes early. She hated waiting. Ticked off, she began to fidget, wishing she had brought something to read. As fate would have it, Ed Maxwell stepped out of his office to get a cup of coffee and noticed Sheila waiting. He knew she had an appointment that morning, so maybe fate wasn't involved. Ed offered her a cup of coffee which she gratefully accepted. After asking how she took it, he added cream and sweetener.

"I've never seen you so jumpy. What's up?" he asked as he handed Sheila her coffee.

Looking distraught, Sheila said, "I've got five minutes with Henry and a story that takes at least ten."

"So? You used to be a reporter, lead with the headline. Short punchy statements. From the little you've told me, it shouldn't be a problem."

Sheila smiled nervously, saying everything with her eyes. Eyes that held fear and hope at the same time.

"In fact," Ed said, "I just got off the phone with Henry; he doesn't have anything scheduled until ten fifteen, so—" Ed walked over to Henry's office door. "Let me peek in." He opened the door and poked his head in, saying something that Sheila could not hear. Ed turned around and motioned for her to get up. As Sheila entered, the national security advisor to the president got up from behind his desk and motioned her to a high-back chair in the sitting area where a sofa and two more high-back chairs were arranged.

Ed and the national security advisor remained standing until she sat down. The gesture made her more, rather than less nervous.

"Thank you for seeing me, sir," she said, setting down the coffee cup on the small table next to her chair.

"You can call me Henry, Miss Jefferson."

"Thank you. And you can call me Sheila."

"Well then, that's settled. Now, what did you want to see me about that's so urgent."

Praying that she didn't sound like a lunatic, Sheila took a deep breath. Exhaled. In an even voice, overly fast in cadence due to her nervousness, she said, "I'm being followed. My friends are being followed. One of them has been murdered. We uncovered a government cover-up that happened a long, long time ago, and I'm afraid it's still going on. I fear my apartment is bugged, along with the home and office of my boyfriend and the home of the editor of the Washington Post."

Unable to read the national security advisor's stone face, and fearing that she did indeed sound like a lunatic, Sheila stood and took Max's iPad out of her handbag. She pressed play and handed it over to Henry Smith. Ed Maxwell got out of his chair and stood beside Henry's chair. Sheila searched both men's eyes, darting back and forth between them, trying to read their expressions.

A minute later the video ended. Henry passed the iPad nonchalantly to Ed, who handed it back to Sheila. Ed sat back down and Henry pressed his hands together in a steepled shape; his fingertips pressed against chin and mouth.

After a few moments he spoke.

"Write me up a report of what this is all about." He turned his head. In a very loud voice he shouted at the door: "Stella, come in here for a moment!" Henry turned back around; in a smiling aside to Sheila, he said, "She just hates when I do that."

For the first time since she'd arrived, Sheila relaxed a little.

The door to Henry's office opened. A heavyset woman of about forty appeared, looking unperturbed.

"Stella, be a dear and see if I have any openings later this week."

"Four o'clock Wednesday is open," Stella immediately said, as if she had to suffer fools gladly all her life.

"Pencil Sheila in, will you?"

"I will. Just make sure your meeting with Senator Fischer doesn't run long. You know how he can ramble."

"Damn. Thanks for reminding me. Make sure you break in around three fifteen and say the president needs to see me."

"Right." Turning to leave, she paused for a moment before turning back and asking, "Anything else?"

The national security advisor made a hand gesture for Sheila to stand. "Sheila needs a workstation." He put his head down, picked up some papers and said to Sheila's exiting figure, "See you Wednesday at four."

* * *

Henry Smith read Sheila's report over lunch. She had stumbled upon a deeply embedded cell of the intelligence apparatus involved in ancient history. After lunch, in between appointments, he made a few phone calls to the Directors of the CIA, NSA, and DIA. He assigned his deputy, Ed Maxwell, to shuttle between agencies and dig up whatever he could. A day later a report from the Defense Intelligence Archives was lying on his desk. Henry read the report in amazement. The head of the Defense Intelligence Agency, General Eric Stebbins was called into Henry's office.

"How is this possible?" Henry said, holding the report up in the air.

General Stebbins, sitting in the same chair that Sheila had sat in a day earlier, replied evenly, "It's possible."

"How come I've never heard of it?" Henry asked, looking troubled.

The general shrugged. "I never heard of it either, until today."

"And the president?"

"Nope. As far as I know he doesn't know."

"How is this possible?" Henry said again, skeptically.

"It's possible."

"We're repeating ourselves."

"It's your meeting, Henry."

"Okay, just give me your analysis of what's going on."

"In a nutshell it's quite simple. For over fifty years we have been trying to reverse engineer alien technology from the Roswell crash of '47. There's a super-secret section of Area 51 designated by President Truman dedicated to that purpose."

Henry interrupted; "I know there's a secret section of Area 51 that we don't have clearance for. The rest is all conjecture. The Roswell crash is just a nice mythology that boosts the local economy."

"You don't have clearance." Eric smiled smugly.

"And you do?" Henry said suspiciously.

"Henry, I'm the Director of the DIA. If I didn't have clearance . . . who would?"

"How about the president," Henry said with indignation.

"When and if he ever needs to know, he'll know," the general said calmly. "Shall I continue?"

"Please," Henry said entreatingly.

"So," the general continued, "we have this technology that has flummoxed us for over fifty years, and we have this Frenchman, Henri Richaud, who apparently built a crude device, based, perhaps, on the same principles as alien spacecraft. If we could recover his plans or his device, we could use it as a bridge to help us understand the more advanced device, alien spacecraft, UFO, whatever you want to call it."

"And we've been searching for these plans and device for almost two hundred years?"

"From what I've been able to determine, a search was started by the Jackson administration and continued off and on until the outbreak of the Civil War, when it was abandoned for more immediate concerns. After World War I, someone at the Department of War found the file, and the search was renewed. We came close to unlocking the secret in 1925, but a fire at a chateau in France destroyed some records that may have contained the plans for Henri Richaud's device."

"So you're telling me that the story of the Roswell crash and alien technology is *real*? And that there's a DIA cell searching for this device that may work on the same principle?"

"No I'm not," General Stebbins said firmly.

"General, what did you just tell me?"

Henry was not used to being trumped by anyone but the president, and the look on his face showed it.

"Not a thing." The general smiled unsympathetically, and then added, "You don't have clearance."

CHAPTER 31

At approximately the same time Henry Smith and General Stebbins were meeting, a small piece of the puzzle arrived via email into Max's inbox at the *Post*. Ted Dody, Max's Paris correspondent had been searching for information about Henri Richaud by researching his mentor, Pierre-Simon Laplace. It turned out that there were suspicious circumstances occurring in France that mirrored those in America.

Dody began his search in the village of Arcueil—located five miles from Paris—where in 1806, Laplace purchased a home. Adjacent to Laplace's home was that of another famous scientist, the great chemist, Claude Louis Berthollet. Together, they formed a scholarly society known as the Societe d' Arcueil. The country homes of Laplace and Berthollet were, in reality, the first serious research labs set up anywhere in the world. Scientists from the French, Austrian and London academies of science frequently visited and contributed to the research being conducted there. From documents that Dody had uncovered, the research was funded by the French government on direct orders from Napoleon.

Dody enlisted the help of the London bureau chief. He uncovered documents revealing that both the British and Austrian governments were concerned about the possible military applications of research being done at Arcueil. Reports from

London noted that there were several French battalions stationed around the village as well.

Dody found two other notes of interest concerning the research at Arcueil: the home remained in the Laplace family after the famed scientist died in 1827, and many of the original research documents were lost in 1871 when the house was looted.

After the break-in, the Laplace family moved the remaining documents from Arcueil to the family chateau of Saint-Julien de Mailloc, where the main repository of Laplace's research papers already resided. Unfortunately, all of these, along with the remaining documents from Arcueil, were lost in a fire that destroyed the chateau in 1925.

Dody found a living connection to the chateau when he located the son of the last caretaker, living in the nearby village of Lisieux. Jacques Allegre, a surprisingly fit ninety-five-year-old, was the only son of Philippe, who from 1900 until 1925 was superintendant in charge of the research papers stored there. Dody was able to talk with him briefly by phone before his granddaughter ended the call. Jacques revealed a bit of the history of the chateau, and also agreed to meet Dody the next afternoon in Lisieux. He told Dody that when his father Philippe arrived at the turn of the century, all was peaceful at the chateau. Scholars would infrequently visit and go through the vast archives of the Societe d' Arcueil stored there, but things started to change after the Great War. Jacques' father revealed to him that there was an increased interest by scholars after the war, coinciding with several attempted break-ins at the chateau. On one occasion, Philippe noticed that boxes were misplaced, and the lock to the door of the great library appeared to have been tampered with. It was at this point that Jacques' granddaughter interrupted the call, apologizing that it was time for her grandfather to take a nap.

CHAPTER 32

Lisieux, France

The next afternoon, Ted Dody arrived at the country cottage of Jacques Allegre, located just outside Lisieux. There to greet him not so warmly at the door was Jacques' granddaughter, Adrienne. She introduced herself and reluctantly led Ted to the sitting room. There, on a small sofa surrounded by beige plaster walls framed in rich cedar beams, sat Jacques, hunched in front of a small stone fireplace, a shawl wrapped around his shoulders. Adrienne led Ted to a small rocking chair to the right of Jacques, who in contrast to his granddaughter, smiled warmly when Ted greeted him in perfect French.

"I like staring at the fire," the old man said as Ted sat down. "It stirs up memories. Memories that flicker and fade. The flames help me to remember. I want to remember. At my age, memories are all I have to hold on to."

He turned his head, looking up and down at his visitor, sizing him up.

"Tell me monsieur Dody. What memories can I conjure up for you?"

Ted decided to come right to the point.

"I'm interested in the research that was done at Arcueil."

"Are you familiar with the Societe d' Arcueil, monsieur Dody?"

"I know it was formed by Pierre Laplace and Claude Berthollet, along with Alexander von Humboldt, Jean Biot, Louis Thenard, and Joseph-Louis Gay-Lussac. The laboratories were quite sophisticated for their time. Most of the leading scientists of Europe dropped in on occasion to share research and ideas."

"Dropped in on occasion," Jacques said to himself. "I like that. Yes, monsieur Dody, it was all that and much more. In the beginning, Laplace and Berthollet had lofty goals. France was the center of the universe in those days for the arts and sciences. Laplace felt that if there was a central focal point where scientists could gather and bounce ideas off each other, the advances then occurring across Europe could be greatly accelerated. Promising students from all across the continent were recruited to conduct experiments under the guidance of the great scientists of the day: Count Volta, Lagrange, Sir Humphry, along with many, many others."

Jacques stared into the fire and coughed a weak laugh.

"Yes, scientists dropped in on occasion as you put it."

"What about Henri Richaud?" Ted asked the old man.

"You know of Henri Richaud?" Jacques turned and stared into Ted's eyes, trying to divine his motives.

"A little," Ted stared back.

Jacques broke off the stare and returned to the fire.

"Then you undoubtedly know enough to leave the poor man alone."

"I know that his secrets contributed to the death of a friend of mine."

"How so?"

Ted told the old man the story from beginning to end: how the article on Henri Richaud aka the Floating Man was discovered, the missing newspapers, the further articles that surfaced, on up to the murder of Max's girlfriend, Rachel.

Throughout the telling, the old man remained riveted by the fire. When the story was finished, Jacques turned back towards Ted; his old eyes seemed to come alive after having consumed some of the flickering flames.

"So Henri made it to America after all." Jacques' smile and flickering eyes retreated as fast as they had appeared. "Only to again be taken prisoner by the state."

Adrienne came over to her grandfather from the kitchen. Jacques slowly got up from his chair and walked with his granddaughter from the sitting room to the kitchen.

At the precipice to the kitchen the old man turned and faced Ted: "Come monsieur Dody, time for lunch. And then I must nap. A good story needs anticipation, no?"

From the crestfallen look on Ted's face, Jacques felt he had to say something more. "Don't worry, monsieur Dody. You will have your story. I may be an old man, but I am not going to die on you."

* * *

After lunch and a one-hour nap, the old man returned to the living room. Dody had spent the intervening time reading the latest edition of Le Monde. As Jacques entered, Ted began to rise but was quickly lowered back into his rocker at the wave of the old man's hand. Before sitting down, the old man went to the fireplace and placed a well barked log on the burning pile. He picked up a short black stoker and poked at the logs. Soon the flames were dancing.

After melting back into the sofa, Jacques reminded Ted: "Remember, monsieur Dody, the flames help me to remember."

"Do you remember the flames from the chateau in 1925?"

The old man turned his attention away from the fire and looked coldly at Ted.

"I was just a boy, but yes, I remember. I see it every time I look at the flames. Instead of providing warmth, it gives me the chills. Maybe that is why I need this shawl. So much history and knowledge lost. My father thought it for the best, but apparently he was wrong. The killing continues."

"Your father burned down the chateau? *Why?*"

Ted leaned up in the rocker and pivoted so he could face Jacques.

"He knew the history. And he knew the nature of man, monsieur Dody. After the Great War, it began again . . . with you Americans. Especially with you Americans. The first wave descended after your civil war, but it was nothing like after the Great War. So many visiting scholars with bad hips and knees, all with beautiful silver and brass handled canes. At the forward, flat end of the handle was a small circle with elaborate etchings around it. On the side was an ornate round knob. Aim the circle at a document, press the knob, and then turn it to forward the film hidden inside. My dad confiscated quite a few of these spy canes, once he caught on. I still have one. I'll show it to you later, if you like."

Jacques paused for a moment before getting up again, unnecessarily stoking the fire a bit more before returning to his perch.

"But I get ahead of myself. No? Back to the beginning: the Societe d' Arcueil." The old man fixed Ted with that stare again. "But first, monsieur Dody—"

"Please, call me Ted."

"I will, if you accept my ground rules. I am to understand that you are a journalist for the Washington Post, yes?"

"Yes. I'm the correspondent for the Paris bureau of the Post."

"That is a big paper. This is a big story. It will be a big story here, and in America."

Ted for the first time addressed Jacques with his family name.

"Yes, monsieur Allegre, it would be a big story. But I'm just helping with an investigation that—"

The old man interrupted before Ted could finish. "It's an investigation *now*, monsieur Dody, but later?"

"I'll concede your point, monsieur."

Ted saw his chance at hearing the story begin to fade.

The old man turned back to the fire.

"I am not comfortable with this." He slumped down, crossing his arms over his chest.

"Your story could save lives, Jacques," Ted said softly, deliberately using the old man's first name in an attempt to separate the emotional distance between them. "Rachel's murder has set in motion certain activities which we hope will expose this conspiracy, once and for all. We have people in high positions discreetly helping us. We are not naked here, Jacques. We won't leave you or your granddaughter exposed."

"As a journalist you are required to protect your sources, are you not?"

The first crack in the old man's armor was showing, but he still sat with crossed arms, staring at the fire.

"Absolutely," Ted replied.

"And how will you do this, monsieur?"

Ted now saw light at the end of the tunnel. He explained how he had gathered his information to date and would use that as source material, excluding Jacques and his granddaughter as sources. For the information that could have only come from Philippe, he asked Jacques if his dad had left him any correspondence.

Jacques called Adrienne. After a private discussion between the two, she left, returning shortly with both handwritten and typed letters from Jacques' father, Philippe. Ted asked if he could make copies of these to use for stylistic purposes. He then told Jacques his plan to type up a letter in the style of Philippe on the same make and model typewriter that Philippe had used.

Ted would say he made the copy from the original, disclosing that he had uncovered it in the private collection of a London historian who wished to remain anonymous. To make the copy harder to prove a forgery—since every typewriter, even of the same make would leave its own fingerprint key—he would make successive scans to reduce the quality of the copy.

At that point, Jacques interrupted to say that he still had in his possession the typewriter his father used. Ted said that would pretty much seal the deal as to authenticity, adding that it might be wise to ditch the typewriter afterwards.

Jacques had no objections, saying the sentimental value would be lost on the younger generation once he was gone. He turned to monsieur Dody, and for the first time, called him by his first name.

"Ted, please help an old man. Go tell Adrienne to bring her laptop in here, and also that old typewriter. I don't know how you are going to find a new ribbon for that old thing, but then you are the journalist, which is almost the same as being a spy, no?"

Ted smiled and left to find Adrienne.

CHAPTER 33

The Secrets of Chateau Saint-Julien de Mailloc

Staring into the flames, Jacques summoned up memories from his distant youth. Adrienne sat nearby in the kitchen, ready to transcribe her grandfather's words into type.

"The village of Arcueil was home to the great chemist, Claude-Louis Berthollet. During the early years of the revolution—long before the formation of the Societe d' Arcueil—the army ran into a shortage of gunpowder. The Directory, then running France, called upon Berthollet to head a commission entrusted with finding a substitute for potassium nitrate, more commonly known as saltpeter. Berthollet's solution for the dwindling supply of saltpeter was to use potassium chlorate. The Directory funded a laboratory in Arcueil for Berthollet's use. He was very much in favor; and then came the coup of Eighteen Brumaire."

Jacques paused for a moment, turned to Ted and raised his right index finger.

"Question! What is Eighteen Brumaire?"

Ted thought of Max's retelling of Sheila's boring bug man and silently prayed that this was not going down the same road. Debating whether to show boredom or feign interest, he chose the latter.

"I have no idea, Jacques. What is Eighteen Brumaire?"

The old man's face glowed. His voice became stronger.

"It is the ninth of November, 1799. Year eight under the French Republican Calendar."

His watery eyes glistened. He paused a few seconds. Then he smacked the palms of both hands on the cushion of the sofa.

"So!" he grunted. "Simply put, the coup of Eighteen Brumaire is the coup that brought Napoleon to power."

"And what happened to Berthollet when Napoleon came to power?" Ted asked, trying to move the story along.

"His funding increased. Napoleon was a much better politician than general. Always on every side and against every side at the same time, he knew intimately of Berthollet's research."

"So!" Jacques grunted again.

An affectation that Ted found a bit unsettling.

"Berthollet, utilizing the reactive property of various chemicals in all sorts of combinations and quantities kept making bigger and bigger bombs, no? Some of his bombs were so big, Napoleon worried Berthollet would blow himself up along with the village of Arcueil and all its inhabitants. Question!"

Fuck me! Ted thought, as Jacques held up that finger again. Ted felt an itch in his most sensitive area. An inadvertent smile crossed his face as he remembered Max's story of Sheila's bug man.

"When was the War of the Third Coalition?" Jacques with those gleaming watery eyes again taunted Ted.

"Jacques, forgive me, I don't even know what the War of the Third Coalition is."

"1805," Jacques said triumphantly. "The British were assembling another coalition of countries to fight the French. These European wars were off and on for decades. So! Napoleon decided to invade Great Britain. He assembled an invasion force of almost two hundred thousand men on the coast of Boulogne. In order for the plan to work he needed to achieve naval superiority. The only way to do that against the British with the mightiest navy in the world was to have cannon that fired a greater distance, with more accuracy and explosive power than the British. So! Before the invasion, Napoleon went to Arcueil to see Berthollet's work. He was impressed by the explosive power of the bombs developed by Berthollet but disappointed in the size, which rendered them useless as cannon projectiles aboard ships. In short, Napoleon lacked a delivery system. Instead of being able to confront the British navy head-on, Napoleon was forced into a complex ruse to distract them, which ultimately failed. Leading to, as every French and British schoolboy and girl learns, Lord Nelson's defeat of the French naval forces at the Battle of Trafalgar."

"Lord Nelson was killed," Ted added cheerfully.

"Small comfort," Jacques replied glumly.

"Where do Pierre Laplace and Henri Richaud enter the story?"

"Very prescient, Ted," the old man said, his watery eyes gleaming. "During the early years of the revolution, Henri Richaud, along with his mentor Pierre Laplace—the greatest scientist of his day—retreated to Laplace's home, fifty kilometers southeast of Paris. From there they conducted research, away from the buffeting winds of revolution. Many discoveries were made. But most remained secret. For some reason unknown to my father, Henri feared retribution from the Directory and was adamant about not sharing any of his research."

Jacques got up from the sofa. He added another log to the fire, waving away his granddaughter Adrienne, who attempted to get up and assist. After stoking awhile, Jacques, finally satisfied, sat back down.

"So! At the end of 1805, with his plans thwarted, and Berthollet going a little off kilter with his fascination for bigger more explosive bombs of little value, Napoleon remembered his old teacher and roommate back at Ecole Military School. He devised a plan whereby Berthollet would go to Laplace and convince him and Henri to join him at Arcueil. There they would form a society where scientists could conduct research in relative harmony, unencumbered by the politics of Paris. And most importantly for Henri, in anonymity.

"The whole enterprise was funded by Napoleon's government. From 1806 to 1808 it was just as Berthollet had promised. Scientists from all over Europe would come and conduct research, and in the evenings relax and commiserate. The Societe d' Arcueil became like one of your country clubs in America, no? Instead of golf during the day, it was research. At night, fine dining. And afterwards, the great men of science retreated to a great study at the center of the village. Cigars, the newest fad among the intellectual elite, were smoked. And wine was consumed in moderately large amounts. Along with the cigars, wine, and fine cuisine, came beautiful women. Berthollet could explain the funding for the laboratories, along with the food, wine, and cigars, but he could not explain the women. Only Henri, with his inquisitive mind, wondered about the high ratio of young beautiful women in the village of Arcueil compared to that of the general population. The other scientists, so astute in breaking down molecules and explaining the orbits of planets, were totally oblivious to the matter behind the charms these young ladies proffered."

"How do you *know* all this? Is this all from memory?" Ted looked a bit dubiously at Jacques.

"You worry about my memory?" The old man pointed to his head. "It is all up here. I remember because I heard all these stories from my father. Every night at bedtime, he would sit up with me and tell me a story about the secrets of the Chateau Saint-Julien de Mailloc. Each story was told to me many, many times over the years. That is how I remember. Do you remember Goldilocks and the Three Bears? Little Red Riding Hood? Why? Because these were your favorite bedtime stories. Am I right?"

"I never thought of it like that, but that would be a perfect way to get a small child to remember something important."

"Very good, Ted. Now you see. Let's get back to the story."

Jacques paused, staring at Ted before continuing.

"So! All was peaceful in the village of Arcueil those early years. The scientists were safe in their cocoon, isolated from the political and military machinations of Napoleon. By 1808, France held sway on the continent. Austria, Prussia, and Russia—the great European powers had all been eliminated as military threats. Only Britain remained.

"Then in 1808, Napoleon, under the guise of invading Portugal, moved his armies through Spain, which was then an ally. He placed his brother Joseph on the throne. Deposing the Spanish monarch caused an uprising by the Spaniards—more than Napoleon had anticipated. This allowed Britain to land an expeditionary force in Portugal. Napoleon's forces suffered their first loss in years at the hands of the future Duke of Wellington."

Adrienne entered the room with a tray of tea, interrupting the old man's story. After Adrienne set down a cup for both of them,

Ted took the moment to steer the story back to Henri.

"Jacques, during those years at Arcueil, what was Henri Richaud up to? Was he merely an assistant to Laplace?"

Smiling with those gleaming watery eyes, Jacques veered away from the military troubles of France, back to Arcueil.

"Henri was the greatest of them all! Even Laplace, with his tremendous ego, was deferential to him. The pupil had supplanted his master. But Henri was very secretive about his work, and leery of trusting others. He and Laplace had witnessed the execution of King Louis XVI. Henri had taken it especially hard. His work at Arcueil was compartmentalized among each of the scientists. Only Henri knew the sum of the parts."

"What was Henri's line of research? His specialty?" Ted asked.

"He had none!" The old man leaned over to Ted and pointed his finger. In staccato emphasis he jabbed each word; "And-he-had-everything!"

"How so?"

"Henri was interested in everything. His intellect knew no bounds. At Arcueil he was the conductor of a great orchestra. And all the great scientists of the day were merely his musicians: each playing a part to make up a whole. Henri would go around to each of them, refining their theories, correcting their formulas, suggesting new lines of research. Giving them all the credit. Berthollet on his chemical reactions. Volta on his electric batteries. Refining Laplace's masterwork, Mécanique Céleste. On and on, with each great scientist Henri flitted about, steering them to help create his great symphony."

"Antigravity," Ted said evenly.

"Yes . . . but even more. A unified field theory, one hundred years before Einstein."

"That's not possible," Ted said with certainty. He leaned away from Jacques.

Jacques leaned closer to Ted as if talking in conspiratorial tones.

"He developed the idea of black holes. Look it up! It is in every biography of Laplace!"

"Even if that is so, where is the proof? Where are his papers?"

"My father burned them along with the Chateau. But the proof is in the work done at the Societe d' Arcueil, supervised by Henri but published and credited to the great scientists that gathered there."

"But Jacques, even Laplace's great formulas have flaws."

"Henri purposely left mistakes in each of their works. In all their great formulations, an error here and there. He loved riddles and constantly invented mathematical puzzles for the others to solve. Testing them. In each of their works is a puzzle."

"But Jacques, why would he do that?"

"Because he feared that someday, someone as smart as him would come along and figure it all out. His only hope was that man would evolve and shed his more primitive instincts."

CHAPTER 34

Sitting beside the desk of the national security advisor to the president, Sheila went over the story from the beginning. Henry Smith studied her face intently as he listened. When she had finished, he swiveled in his chair, both hands grasping the armrests, legs crossed. Never breaking his gaze, he spoke in a quiet, calm tone.

"I don't want you or your friends involved in this any longer."

Matching his gaze and tone, Sheila spoke one word: "Why?"

"Sheila, this is way past your pay grade. I'm afraid it's past mine also."

"How is that possible, sir?"

Henry Smith, advisor to the president, shifted uncomfortably in his chair, re-crossed his legs and shifted his gaze momentarily.

"I'm not exactly sure." He paused. "And I don't know who is pulling the strings."

"Wouldn't you want to find out?"

Henry, again fixing his gaze on Sheila, said firmly, "Oh, I'll find out."

"We can help you." Sheila searched his eyes for any sign of deception. Finding none, she repeated, "We can help."

"There are too many people at risk already. And now we have this Dody fellow, and the old man and his granddaughter. Now they're also at risk."

"And what about my apartment? Max's home? John's? Do we live in fear of having everything we do and say being recorded?"

"If someone is bugging you, they will eventually lose interest if you drop it."

"Sir," she said, locked in like a laser on Henry, "can we ever be sure?"

Unable to maintain eye contact, Henry Smith looked away.

"No, I suppose not."

Sheila decided to take the gamble that she, Max, and John had discussed over lunch prior to her meeting with Henry Smith. They had left it up to her whether to trust her boss. She took a deep breath.

"We have a plan."

Sheila laid out their plans for getting whoever might be spying on them on tape. She told the national security advisor about the surveillance that was already in place, and their idea for planting something to act as bait for their pursuers. After finishing, she sat back in her chair and crossed her arms and legs in what looked like a defensive posture, but was in reality, one of relief, of unburdening herself.

Henry stared evenly at her. "You took quite a gamble telling me this. I hope I can live up to that trust."

"That's not very reassuring, sir," Sheila replied.

"It wasn't meant to be. And please; from now on call me Henry, unless we are with the president. Hopefully that will not occur." He drummed the desk with the fingers of his right hand. "I'll give you a phone and secure line. Only call me if absolutely necessary. Just so you know up front, it has a GPS chip. If for some reason you don't want to be tracked, leave it at home. Naturally, you will remain on leave for an undetermined amount of time."

He paused for a moment, then opened his desk drawer and got out a pad of paper. He wrote a few names down and slid it over to Sheila.

"These are the names of a few FBI agents I would trust with my life; but you shouldn't take that to mean you can trust them with yours. I know Max, and I know he has his own contacts in the FBI that he trusts. Give this to him. At his discretion he can choose to avoid any that are on the same list as his, or if it makes him more reassured, use them. In any event, I'll be fine with whatever he decides."

"Thank you." Sheila put the paper in her purse. "And the sweep of our homes?"

"Right. I think I'll give that to another agency head. I don't think he's involved, but someone in his agency is. If someone is bugging you, that might flush them out into the open."

Sheila subconsciously tilted her head and arched one eyebrow.

"And *what* agency would that be, Henry?"

"I'm sorry. You'll just have to trust me. If not . . . well, so be it."

On that note the meeting was adjourned. Sheila left as uncertainly as she had arrived. Henry picked up the phone and made a call to the Defense Intelligence Agency. Colonel Stan Weatherly, aide to General Eric Stebbins answered.

CHAPTER 35

Lying in bed, staring at the ceiling, Ted thought about Jacques' incredible story. Along with Adrienne's printed copy, he had discreetly recorded the story on tape. It was close to ten when the old man had finished.

Ted looked at the clock on his nightstand: three in the morning. He had read Adrienne's transcribed copy while listening to the recording, thinking without result that it might make him sleepy.

But Ted wasn't tired.

His thoughts raced back two hundred years. Ted imagined Henri stroking those great scientists' egos: steering them, using them, for his own end. And these great men of science, not even aware that they were being used like marionettes, with Henri as their puppeteer. Ted closed his eyes. He could see Henri feverishly working as Napoleon's armies roamed across Europe. And then, just as the Emperor was at the height of his glory, Henri had made his breakthrough, unveiling his amazing machine. He could imagine the awe and pride that shone in the eyes of those great men of science as Henri told them how their research had been responsible for this amazing discovery. Of course, Napoleon had his spies, and rushed to Arcueil when he heard of Henri's invention.

And there the old man abruptly stopped the story. If Jacques were a young woman, he would be a great prick tease, Ted thought. His only worry was that the old man would die in his sleep. He wished he could just interview him and skip all the descriptions of the laboratories, and the great study, and the beautiful women . . . well maybe the beautiful women could stay. Ted smiled as that thought crossed his mind.

And then he thought of Adrienne, who was not so bad herself: thin, with large black luminous eyes set in an angular high cheekbone face, surrounded by a luxuriant tousled head of jet black hair that cascaded over her shoulders. Maybe it would be okay if this storytelling of Jacques' dragged on for a few weeks. The old man seemed to relish the company, and even though he had some annoying habits like grunting, *So!* and shouting *Question!* he could put up with that as long as he made progress with Adrienne. Yes, this could get *very* interesting, Ted thought as he drifted off to sleep.

CHAPTER 36

Sheila spent a restless night back in Beaufort, tossing and turning in bed. John snored peacefully next to her. It wasn't the July heat and humidity that was bothering her as she lay naked under a thin sheet, but rather the unshakeable feeling that they were being watched. Well, soon they would know. As Sheila turned from her left side, onto her back, the sheet dipped down, exposing her left breast. Very self-consciously, Sheila pulled the sheet back up to her neck, thinking to herself that at this rate, she would never get any sleep. They should have taken James' advice and stayed at Fripp Island, which was free of bugs.

She stared at the ceiling.

She felt as if someone was staring back.

Someone was.

* * *

The well-dressed woman from Le Bon, clad only in an overly long tee shirt, sat hunched over a desk, working toggles that manipulated the pinhead sized cameras placed in various spots of the bedroom. She grew increasingly frustrated as she got fewer and fewer glimpses of the naked body that lay beneath the sheet. A misplaced rage continued to build inside her. She zoomed in for a close-up of Sheila's face, lying in bed with open eyes that stared back at her from the screen. Mixed in with that rage was an outsized, twisted, sexual desire.

What had that psychiatrist called it?

She thought for a moment, trying to remember. Sexual rage disorder was part of it, along with a bunch of other gobbledygook. Fixated, zooming in even closer—Sheila's eyes completely filling her screen—the words of her long dead psychiatrist came back to her.

Because of the abuse you suffered, you have a severe psychosexual disorder. The components of which include an extreme rage, while at the same time a love for your mom that borders on a sexual addiction. Along with these raged-tinged sexual urges, are feelings of guilt and shame.

The memory of killing her mom and dad flashed across her mind. She was quickly rewarded with a glimpse of the long lines of Sheila's exposed left side as John turned away from her, tugging at the sheet. The camera slowly panned up the length of her long leg, zoomed in, lingering awhile at the arch of the pelvic bone leading to Sheila's flattened stomach and pubic mound before pulling away to reveal a gracefully sculptured thigh, ending at a muscled but well rounded bottom. The camera panned slowly up again, slightly revealing the outline of her ribcage, ending on the curve of her breast that lay piled high without spilling over.

She watched Sheila's chest slowly rise and fall with each breath. The woman became increasingly aroused, moving the camera to Sheila's well-toned arm, the end of which lay underneath the sleeping Sheila's head. The woman focused on the armpit, deeply indented, with her breast resting above, as if providing shade. The camera pulled back. The image on the large, flat-screen monitor revealed her full length.

The well-dressed woman in the long tee shirt slipped her hand below, and leaned back in her chair. A twisted smile was etched on her face, mixed with equal amounts of ecstasy and hate.

CHAPTER 37

The next morning, on the way over to James' for breakfast, John and Sheila had their first fight. Sheila couldn't shake the uneasy feeling she had of being spied on, and insisted that they spend the next week on Fripp Island—at least until the sweep team had arrived. John was equally insistent on keeping up the appearance of a normal routine. Sheila thought this absurd; they had already tipped their hand.

Arriving at James' house, barely speaking, the atmosphere remained tense, despite James' best efforts to lighten the mood. Sheila barely touched the omelet that James prepared, while John chomped furiously, as if the soft concoction was a tough piece of steak. James did his best to play mediator, but it quickly became apparent that even Henry Kissinger with his shuttle diplomacy would be no match for these two.

Midway through breakfast, Sheila abruptly got up and asked James if she could stay at his place on Fripp. James quickly assented and Sheila was out the door. James watched her leave. John remained immobile, except for the chomping of his food.

* * *

On the drive down US Highway 21, Sheila was already feeling a little guilty about the argument, but she would be damned if she was going to give John the satisfaction of an apology. And besides, it was not easy living in a fishbowl, knowing that somebody might or might not be spying on you. The not knowing part was the worst, Sheila thought as she pulled into the drive leading to the beach house.

* * *

John was still over at James' house when Max called and brought him up to speed on Ted Dody's visit with Jacques Allegre. Ted was trying to get closer to Jacques' granddaughter and felt that this would lead to more revelations from Jacques, who he believed was holding some things back. Maybe as he and Adrienne grew closer, Jacques would let his guard down a little more. Ted also described the old man's habit of jumping from story to story, and worried that Jacques was perhaps a little senile.

James listened intently to John's side of the conversation, which consisted mostly of *No kidding? That's amazing*, and *Unbelievable*. By the time the conversation ended, James was on the edge of his seat.

"Well? What did he say?"

"He said that our man Henri was part of a society of scholars: a genius who developed a unified field theory before Einstein, leading to the discovery of antigravity. He also said that he loved riddles and purposely left mistakes in all his scientific formulations. Other than that, not too much. He also said Ted plans to meet with the old man again. Perhaps as early as tomorrow."

"How disappointing. He only developed a unified field theory and antigravity. I would've thought he would've at least discovered the secret to time travel."

"Yeah, our Henri was a real slacker. At least now we know the magnitude of his discoveries."

"It was the real deal then. Not just a balloon with a propeller, which is more along the lines of what you originally envisioned," James said.

"And one more thing," John said sadly. "The place where all his scientific documents were stored was burned down in 1925 by Jacques' father."

CHAPTER 38

Ted spent the morning at an open-air market with Adrienne. The two kept up a constant chatter as they moved from stall to stall, picking a red pepper here and a green pepper there. Adrienne apologized for her initial coldness and confided in Ted that her grandfather was rather fond of him. In between a cucumber and a bunch of grapes, Adrienne revealed that Jacques had talked about giving Ted a great gift. Ted thought to himself that this could be the Holy Grail. After nearly two hundred years, he, and he alone, would be in possession of Henri's secrets.

Ted turned to Adrienne.

"The gift that I'll treasure most is our friendship."

He did not see the slight wince that passed across Adrienne's face. She recovered in an instant and smiled warmly. The two stopped at an outdoor café and shared a couple espressos. Adrienne pretended to listen while Ted talked about his career at the *Washington Post*. The only part of Ted's biography that piqued her interest was when Ted spoke of being approached by a high-ranking official in the Defense department with an offer to become his official spokesman. She probed Ted for the name and position of the official, but he fended her off. It was an offer he never seriously considered, he explained. Besides, working for the government would be antithetical to his role as a journalist.

"So you consider yourself a defender of the truth?" Adrienne asked.

"More like a searcher for the truth," Ted replied.

"And what if the truth hurts? Or if the truth has the power to kill?" Adrienne picked up her cup and held it just below her mouth, blowing softly on the hot espresso.

"The truth should never be suppressed. What we do with the truth is always another matter. Sometimes we have to trust the innate ability of man and time to move towards the arc of justice." Ted thought his use or misuse of the Martin Luther King quote was close enough. He moved his hand across the table, placed it over Adrienne's.

"Perhaps you are right, Ted, but for you Americans, history is very short." Adrienne picked up Ted's hand, rubbed her finger over the back of it and brought it to her lips. She gave it a quick kiss and put it back down, smiling slyly. "Such a beautiful day. We don't get many days like this. Blue sky, warm sunshine."

Ted wasn't ready to take the bait. "It's a shame we have to let it go to waste. But Jacques will probably be waiting to tell me the further adventures of Henri. Your grandfather is quite the storyteller. He makes me feel like I'm an eyewitness to the events."

"Isn't that the point of a good story?" Adrienne sipped her espresso and bored her dark soulful eyes into Ted's. "And what makes a good story a great one?"

"I don't know. How about a love interest?" he said, his resolve beginning to weaken.

Adrienne met his gaze. Neither one blinked. "Suspense. Anticipation," she said softly. "And while your anticipation simmers, why don't we play the love interest part of the story. Let's not waste such a beautiful day. I know a secluded spot under a shade tree where we can lay out a blanket and add a little spice to a loveless story."

"And Jacques?" Ted asked.

"Jacques is a big boy. When we're not back for lunch, he will just smile to himself and make his own lunch."

Adrienne took Ted's hand and the two set off down the small village lane.

CHAPTER 39

Sheila made the short drive from Fripp Island and turned onto Bay Street. She had spent a sleepless night, her first one alone since coming to Beaufort. She was almost ready to throw in the towel and rejoin John back at the Sentinel. Almost.

One more night alone and he will come to his senses, she thought. If not, then she would have to be the one to cave. *Electronic bugs be damned. Whoever is watching better not be prudes, because they will definitely be getting an eyeful.*

But she was getting ahead of herself. She parked the car and walked towards the Campbell museum to meet Maggie for lunch.

She walked up the steps of the museum and thought of Henry Smith's parting admonition not to involve anyone else. He had put his hands on his head and visibly groaned when she had mentioned Maggie and Elmer. Then it was *bye* with a backward wave of his hand.

Sheila noticed Elmer sitting off to the side of the entrance, his back to the wall, a paper bag in his hand.

"Smells good, Elmer."

Elmer scratched the bridge of his nose with an extended middle finger.

"Cute," Sheila replied, and stepped inside. Maggie was waiting for her in the office.

Everything was set for acceptance of the camphorwood storage chests and the opening of the new exhibit. They were just waiting on a sweep team to check for bugs at the Sentinel. Surveillance cameras were in place in and around the museum, and thanks to James' loose tongue there was no longer any pretense that they were for the protection of the many artifacts residing there.

Maggie went to the small fridge and got out two cans of sweet tea. Sheila reached into her handbag, removed two chicken salad sandwiches purchased from Alvin Ord's and slid one across the desk to Maggie.

"I see Elmer is in fine form today. He gave me a one fingered salute," Sheila said matter-of-factly as both women unwrapped their sandwiches.

"For Elmer, that's a term of endearment. Consider yourself blessed," Maggie said. "You don't want to see his bad side. He can be a *mean* drunk."

Sheila began to respond, but was interrupted by the ringing of her cell phone. She picked it up and answered. It was John. She listened for a moment. "I'll be right there." She whispered to Maggie; "They're here."

Leaving her sandwich behind, she rushed out the door and bounded down the steps.

CHAPTER 40

Sheila ran as fast as she could to the Sentinel, five blocks away. She needed to burn up a little of the pent-up energy inside her, but didn't factor in the stifling heat and humidity. She arrived at the steps to the Sentinel, sweating and out of breath, regretting her decision not to drive the short distance. Bursting through the door, she ran into a slender young woman with short blonde hair, standing just inside, holding a small scanner device.

"Sorry, excuse me," Sheila said breathlessly.

"That's okay," the young woman said, fascinated by a sweat bead rolling down Sheila's neck, continuing down the right side of her chest, then veering off to find the centerline of her cleavage before disappearing beneath the lines of her V-neck tee. She fixated on the rapid rising and falling of Sheila's chest for an uncomfortable length of time before finally looking up and smiling into Sheila's eyes.

"Are you okay? Looks like you have asthma or something."

A bit taken aback, Sheila stammered, "No . . . I was . . . just doing a little jogging and didn't realize how hot and humid it was . . . is."

Sheila felt unnerved by this woman with the short-cropped hair, grey eyes, and small rodent-like teeth, who seemed to be probing her with her eyes.

"Well, I better get to work," the young woman said, turning to walk away.

Sheila stopped her. "Where is all your equipment?"

Holding up her small scanner device, she grinned: "This is all I need." And then she turned and walked towards the center of the room, holding it like a divining rod.

John came into the office area from the back living quarters and saw Sheila looking perplexed.

"Hey She, what's up? You know I couldn't sleep last night. Why don't you spend tonight here?"

"I don't know . . . maybe. Maybe you can join me at the beach house," Sheila said distractedly, looking at the woman walking slowly around the office area of the Sentinel.

"What's bothering you, Hon," John asked.

"Our team at James' house had a roomful of equipment. This young lady has a little scanner device. Does that make sense?"

"It does if they are the ones spying on us. Or maybe the government has far more sophisticated equipment." John brushed aside a lock of Sheila's dark brunette hair that was sweat-matted against her cheek.

"They?"

"A guy is in the other room. He has the same scanner device."

"Maybe you should watch him, while I watch her."

Sheila gave John a quick peck on the cheek before softly saying *go* and nodding towards the door to the living area.

* * *

After a few minutes, Sheila decided to pepper the young woman with questions on electronic surveillance devices to test her knowledge. She remembered some of what the boring bug man had told her about radio frequency bugs versus ultrasonic ones. She was sure the woman was a phony, but walked away disappointed when the young woman knew exactly what she was talking about. She left the woman alone for awhile to do her work—or pretend to.

A few minutes later, the woman appeared to pay particularly close attention to one of the phone jacks at the corner of the office. Sheila quietly crept up on the young woman as she squatted in the corner, and hovered over her.

The young woman working on the phone jack noticed Sheila

out of the corner of her eye. She smiled to herself, pretending not to notice Sheila bending over her as she removed a telephone transmitter from her pocket.

The young woman shouted, "Found one!" to her partner in the other room. At the same instant, she jumped up and turned, her elbow landing squarely on the right side of Sheila's breast.

"Fuck!" Sheila grimaced, grabbing her breast.

"Oh my! I didn't know you were there. I'm so sorry," the young woman said, smiling to herself.

"My fault. I shouldn't have crept up on you. What did you find?" Sheila asked, still clutching her breast.

"It's a modular telephone transmitter. Looks like an ordinary double jack, but this one has a splitter on it. This baby can transmit up to a thousand feet or more. The third telephone wire acts as an antenna."

John and the other man came from the living room to see what had been found.

Working for another hour, the man and woman located four more bugs—or so they said. Three on the computers and one more on the telephone, located upstairs. Once they'd finished and left, John asked Sheila why she was holding her breast. After she explained, he made a snide remark to the effect that she might be a masochist. Failing to find the humor in his comment, Sheila told John she was going to stay another night on Fripp.

The young woman, sitting in a van parked a block away, listened in. A smile crept over her face. She too, thought about spending the night on Fripp, her hand dipping down in a familiar repose.

CHAPTER 41

Lying on her chaise lounge as darkness descended across the water, Sheila took a last sip of a frozen Margarita, blended twenty minutes earlier. Her thoughts drifted to the storage chests from 1865 and 1866. Now that the Sentinel building had been swept, they could move the chests to the museum—which for the moment was bug free. And what about that odd couple back at the Sentinel? They never did get their names.

Sheila thought about the thin wiry woman, who seemed to be fixated on her. Probably was. She certainly looked the part. Clutching her still throbbing breast, Sheila thought about the incident earlier in the day. The woman had jumped up and turned so fast that she didn't even have time to react. Maybe the elbow was unintentional, but then again, there was that weird smile the woman had when apologizing. It gave her the heebie-jeebies. Sheila shook her head and banished the woman from her thoughts.

Deciding to give John a ring, she picked up the cell lying on the table next to the chaise and hit the speed dial button for *Sweetheart*. Maybe she should change that to *Asshole*. Fortunately for John, he answered on the first ring and apologized for being a stubborn jerk. Apology accepted. They moved on to talk about what they might find, or find missing, in the storage chests. From there, the conversation went back to how much they missed each other. John offered to drive up, but then remembered that she had his car. Sheila told him not to bother James for his. She could live one more night without him.

"But tomorrow night is another story. I'm wound up pretty tight."

"Well, I better rest up then and get a good night's sleep," John replied.

"That's right buddy, I don't want no slackers."

They said their goodbyes, which lasted another ten minutes as goodbyes often do between new lovers. John said something that made her laugh before hanging up.

Sheila decided to call it a night and do some reading in bed to help her fall asleep. She placed the empty glass on the kitchen counter, eyed the half-full blender. She began to pour it out into the sink, and quickly stopped. *Ah, what the hell,* she thought, and salvaged three-quarters of a glass to take into the bedroom. Entering the bedroom, she fumbled around in the dark, placed her glass on the nightstand and turned on the lamp. She stood up and let her robe drop to the floor.

From the darkness in the other room, a pair of eyes eagerly watched. Sheila took a two-minute shower to wash off the salt water that had accumulated from a quick dip in the ocean before the sun had gone down. Standing in front of the mirror, she spread a little lotion onto her hands and smoothed it on her legs. She did the best she could on her back, wishing John were there to help. Rubbing the lotion onto her arms, she admired her reflection in the mirror as she thought about making love to John. Slowly, sensuously, she rubbed the lotion onto her stomach and ribcage, kneaded it into her breasts—becoming more aroused as she fantasized about tomorrow night. Also fantasizing and becoming more aroused was the woman behind the peering eyes, looking in from the dark.

Sheila pulled the sheet to the side and lay naked on the bed, letting the soft ocean breeze caress her. She tried to focus on a novel—*Dark Passage*—that James had lying around the house. Something about a group of Arab terrorists traveling through a time portal to assassinate Jesus. Sheila had James pegged more for a noir fan than a science fiction aficionado. It was probably his look, that Casper Gutman impersonation. She looked at her three-quarters empty Margarita, amazed at how peaceful she felt. So wound up a few minutes earlier, now so relaxed. Must be the ocean breeze coming through the window and the rhythmic sound of the waves crashing onto the shore. *God, I wish John were here,* she thought. *This is so perfect.* As she drained the last of the Margarita, those thoughts ended—along with Sheila's consciousness.

* * *

The woman stood over Sheila's still body. She set a black handbag down on the bed, removed her clothes, carefully folded them, laid them neatly on a nearby dresser. She walked back to the bed and stared down at her obsession: fingered herself, moved her hands up the sides of her torso, squeezed her small budding breasts. She looked at her watch. Enough time had passed to make it safe to administer the syringe. She turned Sheila over and gave her an intramuscular injection in the folds where the thigh and buttocks intersected. The injection would take about fifteen minutes to take effect. At approximately the same time, the drugs dropped into the margarita blender would be out of Sheila's system.

Enough time to get ready.

She smiled, baring small rodent-like teeth.

Fifteen minutes later the woman returned to the bedroom wearing a strap-on dildo. She went over to Sheila's motionless body and yanked her arm; she spun and raised her to a sitting position. Placing her arms under and around Sheila's chest, the young woman dragged her roughly out of bed and onto the robe lying on the hardwood floor. She grabbed Sheila's left arm and dragged her naked, unconscious body into the living room, like a child would drag a play doll. Surrounded by a dozen glowing candles, she hoisted the body onto the couch and propped it up. Sheila's head lolled on the back of the couch.

The woman picked up a glass of wine from the coffee table and took a sip, drinking in the full scope of Sheila's nakedness. She took the fingers of one hand and dipped it into the wine. With her other hand she grabbed a handful of Sheila's hair and pulled her head forward. She ran her wine-dipped fingers across Sheila's mouth. Kissing her gently, she tasted both her and the wine. The woman ran her mouth and tongue down Sheila's neck, down between her breasts, all the way down to her vagina. She lingered there: licking, nibbling; surprised at how moist she was. No need for any extra lubrication, she thought to herself. Again—that weird smile.

She curled up for awhile with her head on Sheila's lap before getting back up. Grabbing Sheila's hair again, pulling her face towards her, she stared for a long while. Her smile slowly turned from worshipful to rage. She picked up her stiletto from the coffee table with her right hand and flicked the blade open. Roughly, she grabbed a handful of Sheila's left breast and pulled it upwards, fully exposing the underneath portion. She placed the tip of the stiletto at the spot where breast met ribcage.

This is where I'll plunge the knife.

She imagined killing her mother again. She ran the knife up the milky white underside and released her hold on Sheila's breast; the tip of the knife brushed areola and nipple, leaving a faint red scratch.

Starting to become more worked up with rage and arousal, the woman poked the tip of the stiletto into Sheila's areola and nipple. The softness gave way under the prodding of the knife's point. The woman continued to jab, just at the point of drawing blood. She got a little carried away: the knifepoint pierced slightly, just underneath the left nipple. A drop of blood appeared, and slowly grew in size. The blood had a calming effect on the woman. She watched, mesmerized. The drop continued to grow, slowly making its way down to the underside of the breast. The woman bent over and licked the blood off Sheila's breast. She began sucking on the nipple, moaning softly—continuing until the blood no longer flowed.

"Time for bed." The woman gazed longingly into Sheila's closed eyes. This time she grabbed Sheila by the legs and let her head thump on the floor as she dragged the beautiful rag doll back to the bedroom. She hoisted up Sheila's dead weight with surprising ease and placed her on the bed: legs spread wide, a pillow underneath her bottom. Baring those rodent-like teeth, she smiled as she entered.

"Now it's Daddy's turn."

CHAPTER 42

Ted couldn't believe what a tease Adrienne had been. First, she spent over an hour shopping, on the pretext of getting a blanket, then another thirty minutes picking out a bottle of wine and some cheese. The short walk that she promised would lead to a beautiful shade tree on the side of a hill with breathtaking views turned into an hour-long hike.

It's such a beautiful day. Let's walk and enjoy the fresh air . . . the sights, the sounds—it'll be so romantic. You'll just fall in love with the view.

Well she certainly had him going. It turned out that the shade tree was no longer there. And the beautiful view of the village? That turned into a view of the back of a box-like apartment building.

Adrienne apologized profusely to Ted, still steaming mad as they arrived at Jacques' cottage. She promised him that they had all summer to make up for it. Ted felt that Adrienne was just playing him, still not trusting his intentions with Jacques and the story of Henri Richaud. Well, she could just float away for all he cared. But he had a job to do; he would be patient.

They found the old man sitting in his usual spot on the sofa, staring at the fire. Ted immediately greeted Jacques in French and plopped down on the rocking chair. After a few pleasantries about the weather, Ted got right to the point: asking about Henri's meeting with Napoleon. As he did so, he reached into his pocket to turn on the recorder but found it missing.

Damn! It must have fallen out with all that scrambling around on the blanket. And all for nothing. And I thought French women were so sophisticated.

"*So!*" the old man barked, snapping Ted back to attention. "Napoleon had not seen his old friend since 1792 when they witnessed the storming of King Louis XVI's palace. Henri made a remark to Napoleon about his Corsican accent not having improved since their last meeting, to which Napoleon replied, 'Perhaps it was your teaching methods that were lacking.' The two old friends shared a few stories, and then Henri unveiled to Napoleon his magnificent floating machine. Napoleon was initially disappointed in Henri's creation. Looking at it solely for military applications, he thought it too small to have any value."

"Are there any descriptions of Henri's machine?" Ted asked.

"It had a circular base with a long round center pole, like a broomstick, but much thicker around, covered in thin silver plating. A small seat and arm rests containing the controls were attached. Inside the center pole were batteries encased in a fluid that Henri had formulated, based on Berthollet's research. The fluid acted as a superconductor. Foot pedals that turned like a bicycle helped generate some residual energy to the machine's batteries. The base was just over four feet in diameter. Several thin silver discs rotated inside. Ring-like discs moved in a planetary fashion, rotating in the opposite direction around the central discs, offset... like the planets around the sun. Small brushes comprised of thin wires brushed up against protuberances at various spots located on the discs. Electricity flowed from disc to disc at these spots, in a pulsating fashion. The disc assembly was configured to act like a gyroscopic ring. Pierre-Simon Laplace had been in contact with the great German scientist, Johann Bohnenberger, who would go on to develop a much larger and cruder version of a gyroscope. But of course, Henri took the early research of Laplace and Bohnenberger and developed it to a degree not seen for another hundred years."

Jacques paused for a moment before calling out to Adrienne, sitting inside the kitchen. "Aren't you going to take this down for our guest?"

Adrienne replied in a loud voice; "I've been typing it all up in the kitchen so as not to disturb you."

Jacques looked totally perplexed.

Pitching in for Adrienne, Ted said, "I heard her typing away, Jacques."

"My ears must be going," he said, and returned to the story. "*So!*"

That fucking annoying grunt again, Ted thought, as outwardly he maintained a calm demeanor.

"Henri showed off the machine for Napoleon, making several passes over the rooftops of Arcueil. A seat was attached opposite Henri's. Napoleon eagerly jumped onboard. Soaring high over the countryside, Napoleon was enthralled. In his mind, he saw this as a tool to finally rid France of her greatest enemy—the British. Still smarting over the loss of the French and Spanish fleet, he saw Henri's device as the means to finally eliminate Britain's naval superiority."

"How would you know what is in Napoleon's mind?" Ted asked curiously.

"Remember, Ted, this is my father talking to me at night . . . a bedtime story. Like Henri's riddles, I will leave it up to you to ferret out the truth. So! Napoleon, acting like a general, immediately made designs to enlarge the base so Berthollet's bombs could be placed onboard. Over Henri's vigorous objections the base was enlarged, and the floating machine transported two hundred kilometers to Le Havre, which means harbor. Of course, speaking French, you already knew that. Anyway,"—*Ted was pleasantly surprised when the old man didn't shout 'So!'*—"Napoleon had a couple of old Spanish man-of-war ships from the disaster at Trafalgar lying at anchor. He instructed his men to load three bombs aboard the floating machine. Henri flew over the ships with three soldiers onboard. All had lanyards attached to the center pole so they would not fall off. The machine unsteadily rose to a height of one hundred meters over the first ship. The soldiers pushed the first bomb over the side. A miss! The bomb fell harmlessly into the sea. The second bomb hit its target and the ship sank within minutes. The machine began to fly erratically after it dropped the final bomb, sinking a second ship. Henri, unable to recalibrate the machine for this sudden loss of weight—this is what he told Napoleon later—could no longer control the floating machine. It crashed into the sea. Henri nearly lost his life. Fortunately, he was pulled from the sea by French fishermen. The three soldiers, attached to the device in full uniform, were not so fortunate."

Jacques went to the fireplace. In a familiar routine, he placed another log on the pile—poking and prodding with the stoker until the flames were dancing once again. Jacques sat back down, looked at his watch. "Just another minute and that will be all for today."

Ted wondered about the great gift that Adrienne had mentioned, but decided not to press his luck.

"Did they recover the machine?"

"No, it is still down there somewhere," Jacques said.

His mind fixated on the fire for a few moments before returning to conclude that day's tale.

"It was when they returned to Arcueil that Henri noticed the change in Napoleon, and not for the better. I remember my dad saying that both men had been changed by history. Henri, witnessing firsthand the manipulation of the mob that led to the execution of King Louis, became repelled by power. Napoleon became intoxicated by it.

"It became a clash of wills between the two old friends. Napoleon pushed Henri to make a bigger machine, but Henri cleverly resisted, using scientific doublespeak and stalling tactics. Arcueil became an armed camp as Napoleon tried to force the great scientists to recreate Henri's invention. But none of them had the complete symphony; they could only play their parts. Napoleon eventually became fed up; he had Henri imprisoned. The search for Henri's secrets continued throughout the remainder of Napoleon's reign. Secrets that lay coded among his research papers."

"And your father burned them all up," Ted said glumly as he got up to leave.

"There are secrets, and there are secrets. I am sure your American government has more than enough documents to solve the puzzle. It was your Americans that looted Arcueil's archives in 1871, and they were attempting to do the same after the Great War."

"Is that your gift?" Ted said a bit dejectedly.

"Perhaps," Jacques replied with a small smile.

CHAPTER 43

The late morning sun was streaming through the window by the time Sheila awoke. She lay on her back thinking about the weird dreams she had. That strange woman from the sweep team was in one of them: chasing her around the house and on the beach with that scanner device. The scanner device turned into a taser gun. She remembered electricity shooting through her body, paralyzing her. Then the woman turned into John, and he carried her into the bedroom. She remembered John tossing her in the air and doing all sorts of contortions with her—some not humanly possible. She smiled at the thought of trying out a few of the more possible ones before getting up to take a shower.

As she showered, she couldn't help but notice how sore she was between her legs. She had never had a sexual dream do that before. Perhaps it was the separation from John. Then she noticed what looked like red fingernail marks on her breast, and a scratch running across her nipple.

Could I have been that wound up?

She looked at her fingernails and ran them across her stomach. They were certainly sharp enough, she observed.

Maybe I should file them down. Or better yet, wear gloves to bed. Explain to John that it was for both his and my protection.

* * *

It was nearly three in the afternoon by the time Sheila got back to the museum. She arrived just as the last storage chests from the 1800s were being unloaded from Elmer's pickup truck. Earlier, John had called to say that he and James would wait for her before checking out the chests.

"Well, if it isn't little Miss perfect," Elmer said from the back of his pickup, struggling to set a chest down on a dolly, leering as Sheila walked past. "You *could* give me a hand with one of these big chests."

Glaring at him stonily, Sheila walked to the back of the pickup truck, grabbed a storage chest by one of the end handles and pulled it towards her. At the end of the tailgate she picked up the heavy box. Without changing the stone expression on her face, she set it down on the dolly. "Maybe if you didn't drink so much, it wouldn't be so difficult for you."

She gave Elmer a dismissive smile and walked up the stairs, leaving Elmer standing slack-jawed and speechless in her wake.

Making quite a fuss about the exhibit as Sheila walked up, Maggie had John about at the end of his rope: moving chests into different configurations at her direction, stacking and unstacking them. Meanwhile, off to the side, James, nibbling on his cocoa beans looked on in amusement.

"James, how long are you going to let Maggie torture me?" John said as sweat rolled down his face.

"You're right," James replied, handing a kneeling John a piece of cocoa bean. Then, as if talking to a puppy, he said, "You've been a good little boy. Oh *yes* you have. Come on boy, let's check out the chests in the office. That's it."

John got off his knees and stood up, not looking too amused as James continued his puppy talk.

"Attaboy, follow me," James said while walking backwards towards the office, dangling another cocoa bean in front of John. "Attaboy! You're *such* a good little boy. Oh yes you are."

As they entered the office next to Maggie's, James turned to Sheila. "You really have done a marvelous job with him. So well trained."

Sheila replied deadpan, "Now if I can only break him of the habit of humping my leg."

"You know John, if I was a bit younger, I think I could steal this girl from you."

"I don't think there's any doubt about that at all," John replied.

Sheila went over and put her head on James shoulder.

"Well then, shall we open up Pandora's box?" James asked, taking Sheila's hand and leading her and John to the chests that sat atop the desk.

John went through the 1865 storage chest. Sheila went through 1866. James sat in his desk chair observing them, continually nibbling on his cocoa beans—his magic elixir from the Kuna Indians. He occasionally offered a piece to Sheila and John. Both perfunctorily refused as they continued their examination of the chests. James shrugged. It was their loss.

It only took John several minutes to go through the entire 1865 chest. He pronounced that all fifty-two editions were there; and in order.

James wasn't surprised.

Sheila, midway through her chest, looked up with a furrowed brow.

"What is it She? You find something missing?" John sat on the edge of the desk next to her and peered over her shoulder.

"I don't know, but it's not in order. So that means that someone must have been looking for something."

"Let's write down the order of each edition and see if we come up with anything," John offered.

"That's a splendid idea," James said. He opened the center desk drawer and pulled out a pad of paper and pen.

After several minutes they had compiled a list with the order of the newspapers in the chest. All fifty-two editions were accounted for—all in the wrong order. They had come up empty . . . or rather, all full.

"Well maybe it was not such a splendid idea," James said.

"All we can conclude is that someone was looking through these editions for something," John said.

"And maybe something is there, and maybe something isn't there," Sheila replied.

"The only way to find out is to read each edition from cover to cover and hope we find something." James paused for a moment before adding, "Too many somethings and not enough anythings."

"Let's hope whoever else was looking didn't find any of your anythings," John added.

"I'll have Maggie make copies so we can all have a set."

James got up to get Maggie, but was stopped by Sheila before he reached the door. She suggested they divide the task between the four of them. Each had thirteen editions to copy. Maggie would use the office copier, James the copier at home, and Sheila and John would use local copy outlets around town. When finished, they would all meet back at James'.

Eager to get started, the four parted ways and got down to the task at hand. Sheila bet John a bottle of whiskey that she would be the first to finish. James got in on the bet for a bottle of scotch. Maggie, a teetotaler, declined.

Sheila used her feminine charms to enlist a few high school kids who worked at the local copy store.

She won.

"*Not fair,*" John said.

James agreed.

CHAPTER 44

Over the next few days, they spent their time reading the Beaufort Sentinel newspapers from 1866. John's method was to read the front page of each edition. *"Never bury the lead,"* he had told them over dinner at James' the night each had brought over their copies. Sheila preferred to scan each edition, hoping something jumped out at her. James, on the other hand, pored over each line, taking notes. Sheila remarked that at the speed he was reading it would be several weeks before he finished.

In full on Casper Gutman mode, with eyes bulging, James had replied, *"Something hidden for one hundred fifty years my dear, would not so easily be found."*

John discovered what he thought was a significant story on the front page of the August 10, 1866 edition. The entire front page was devoted to the life and death of Chief John Ross. The Chief of the Cherokee nation had passed away a week earlier on August 1. It was unusual to have only one story on the front page; but understandable, since the Chief and the founding editor of the Sentinel, Robert Campbell, had been such close friends.

The story itself was a straight forward recitation of the man's life. Beginning with his birth in 1790 and early childhood on Lookout Mountain, it followed John Ross's exploits as a young Lieutenant, fighting alongside Sam Houston and General Andrew

Jackson during the Creek Indian War. In the decisive battle of Horseshoe Bend, John Ross helped turn the tide by swimming the icy waters of the Tallapoosa River and stealing the Creek's canoes. Stationed for a strategic retreat, the Creek's canoes were used against them by the Cherokee, who attacked from the rear.

The bulk of the story, however, concerned the election of John Ross to Chief, and his futile court efforts to block Andrew Jackson's removal of the Cherokee from their lands. The story concluded with an account of the horrors suffered during the forced march of the Cherokee Nation to Oklahoma: a one thousand mile march that became known as the Trail of Tears.

At the back of the edition, Sheila discovered a small editor's note from Robert Campbell concerning his friendship with Chief John Ross. All agreed it was significant, but John and Sheila laughed when James said there had to be a clue in the note.

James got up and shook his head.

"Kids!" he growled, storming off.

* * *

Late the next evening, James peered over his forebear's note at the back of the August 10, edition of the Sentinel.

Editor's note: I am most humbled to have been a close friend of Guwisguwi, Chief John Ross, for most of my adult life. We shared many adventures together and many sorrows. Our story is a long one. It begins with his battles with the National Government to prevent the removal of his people. The Indian Removal Act may have sealed the fate of his people but did not break his spirit. Our end as a nation of just peoples is yet to be determined. My friend who has gone on to his home among the seven heavens sleeps peacefully. Is written the ultimate fate of the Indian people? Where? Where does our story end? We must look to the past to find our future.

Robert Campbell, Editor Beaufort Sentinel

James knew his forebear's writing style and thought the note oddly worded. He reflected on the long relationship Robert Campbell had with Chief John Ross, and remembered the article concerning shots fired at Henri in Georgetown. Cherokee Indians were seen riding off. He started to play around with the wording of the note. After many trials and errors he came up with the answer—or rather, an answer. On a secure phone he called John and Sheila.

"Meet me at the museum at eight tomorrow morning."

They asked him what was up.

He simply said, "Goodnight."

God this is beginning to become great fun.

James lay in bed thinking of what he hoped to uncover at the museum the next morning.

CHAPTER 45

It was a little past ten in the evening when the man received a phone call. After hanging up, he turned to the woman.

"They want us to snoop around the museum. Whatever they were copying around town may have some significance," he said in a monotone.

"That's it? Just snoop around?" the woman sneered. "This is so much bullshit."

"Well, orders are orders . . . and besides, we get paid well," the man said with a shrug of his shoulders.

"Don't you ever wonder *who* exactly we work for?"

"No, not really," he sighed. "I did a long time ago; not anymore."

"You never wonder what department or agency we work for?"

"I was a kid facing an adult sentence for murder, you were too. The program gave us a second chance. As long as we follow orders and don't fuck up, we're free to live our lives."

"We're not free. We don't have any choice." The woman glared at the man with a fierce look in her eyes. "Well I'm tired of following orders. I'm going to kill that bitch, and take my sweet time doing it."

"Your obsession is going to get us both killed," he said; his eyes matched hers in intensity.

"You don't have to worry. I'll leave you out of it. But I'm going to have my fun . . . and this time she'll be wide awake."

Her mind drifted to a dark reverie.

* * *

The man had no problem with the lock on the back door of the museum. They walked across the exhibition floor to the offices of James and Maggie. Copies of the Sentinel were found in the trash basket next to the copier in Maggie's office. The woman, noting two different dates, both for 1866, showed them to her partner. He made a call. He spoke. He listened. He hung up. The call lasted less than a minute.

"We're to find the chest for 1866 and leave it with the car in the motel parking lot."

"Bullshit."

* * *

Elmer heard a muffled conversation from outside his hiding place in the storage room of the museum. He had no idea what time it was. He remembered sneaking into the room around two in the afternoon to sleep off his drunk. It might be around five in the afternoon, maybe a little later, considering how sober he felt. He listened at the door. The voices didn't sound like Maggie or James, or John and Sheila for that matter.

Some damn kids.

Turning the light on in the storage closet, Elmer noticed the half-finished bottle on the shelf above the light switch, and grabbed it. As soon as he got the kids out, he would go home and finish off the rest of the bottle. He had done pretty good he thought. Gone almost a week without a drink.

Elmer opened the door and found himself face-to-face with a young man carrying one of the storage chests. A young woman stood next to him.

The young man looked more amused than startled. His eyes fixated on the blonde toupee perched lopsidedly on Elmer's head.

"Where did you pick up the rug, from George Burns' estate sale?"

Elmer looked totally confused. "Who are you?"

The woman smiled at Elmer. "We're here to pick up the chest for James."

Suspicious, Elmer said, "I've never seen you two before. And James didn't tell me anything about no chest being moved. They just moved them in here. Why would they move one out?"

As the young man bent over to place the chest on the floor, it dawned on Elmer.

Spies!

Elmer took his bottle and smacked the man on the back of his head just as he was setting the chest down. The young man crumpled over the chest. Elmer ran for the door with the young woman in close pursuit. She caught up and grabbed him by the arm. With surprising strength, she spun him around and put out her leg. At the same time, she grabbed the back of his head to flip him karate style to the ground—remembering Elmer's bad toupee an instant too late. The momentum caused them both to tumble to the floor. Elmer landed on top. The young woman still held onto Elmer's blonde toupee as the back of her head struck the floor hard, stunning her.

Elmer started to choke the still stunned woman as she clawed sluggishly at his face. Despite her woozy state she managed to claw the corner of Elmer's right eye. He relented on the choking for a moment. The young woman took in a lungful of air in one big gasp, just as Elmer's fist came crashing down on her face, breaking her nose. Blood squirted in his face.

The woman lay unconscious.

Elmer paused to catch his breath before standing up and making a beeline to the door.

He reached the door.

A spear sailed towards his back.

During the fight, the young man had come to and grabbed a spear off the Cherokee exhibit on the wall next to the storage closet. He had struggled to catch up as Elmer made his beeline for the exit, but was still about twenty feet away when Elmer reached for the knob.

Elmer's hand turned the door knob just as the spear arrived, striking a glancing blow on the top of his left shoulder before impaling harmlessly in the wall just left of the door. The door flew open. Elmer grabbed his shoulder, spun around, and glared at the man.

"Spies my ass. You're a bunch of amateurs," Elmer said. And

then he gave one last parting shot to the still shaky young man. "No one fucks with Elmer Gaskins, remember that."

As he turned to go through the door, Elmer felt a light thumping sensation.

One, two, three times he counted.

That's odd.

Elmer looked down, noticed the blood on the front of his shirt.

He smiled.

I really gave it to that woman.

And then, realizing it was his own blood pouring from his mouth, Elmer crumpled to the ground.

The young man turned to look at his partner. Blood flowed from her nose. Her elbows were propped on the floor, holding the still smoking Glock 22 with suppressor.

She smiled up at him.

"That certainly went well."

CHAPTER 46

James was the first to arrive at the museum and discover the body. He immediately called 911. Arriving moments before John and Sheila, the police questioned James for about an hour before ushering him out of the museum. By noon, yellow police tape was strung across all the entrances to the museum—now officially a crime scene.

Retreating to James' house, the three huddled together in his screened back sunroom; the humming of a ceiling fan broke the stillness.

"Elmer must have put up one hell of a fight," James said. "I saw two pools of blood. His toupee was on the floor a few feet away from one of the pools of blood. A spear was in the wall to the left of the front door by the other pool of blood. That's where I found Elmer."

"I talked to Max while you were being questioned," John said quietly to James. "He's going to call his FBI friend: the one who set up surveillance for us and is looking into Rachel's death. It'll be interesting to see what the museum surveillance video shows. We should have been monitoring it from day one."

Sheila looked up at James.

"I suppose you told the police about the surveillance cameras?"

James looked a bit taken aback.

"I didn't think of it until halfway through the interview . . . and then I figured it might be best not to mention it."

"We have the instructions to remotely retrieve downloads for the surveillance cameras. Have either of you set it up on your computers?" John asked.

"I haven't, no," Sheila said.

She looked at James; he averted his eyes.

"*James?* Have you?"

Looking a bit sheepish, he replied almost inaudibly; "I set it up on my laptop."

"*And?*" Sheila leaned over and stared at him.

"I looked at the feeds for the museum," he said a bit uncomfortably. "Keeping tabs on Maggie."

James slowly rose from his rattan chair. In a reluctant voice he said, "I'll go get it."

He returned a few minutes later carrying the laptop and a scotch and water.

Sheila remarked that it was a bit early for that: meaning the scotch and water. John responded by getting up to make a drink. Giving in to the prevailing mood, Sheila soon followed suit. In the kitchen, she remarked to John that perhaps he was starting to drink too much again. He replied they both were, and blamed it on stress. When they returned to the sunroom, James was already logged into the surveillance system and had retrieved both audio and video feeds for the previous night.

John and Sheila gave each other a look as they watched James forward through the scene at the museum, effortlessly changing from one camera to another. It was clear he had been doing his own bit of snooping.

"Here we go," James said as the back door to the museum opened.

Two figures appeared.

Sheila gasped as she recognized the man and woman.

"Those are the two that swept the Sentinel."

"Well, now we know that the Sentinel is still bugged," John replied glumly.

They watched the man and woman enter the office area, heard the woman mutter *bullshit* as the two went out onto the exhibition floor and over to the storage chests. They sat mesmerized and horrified, watching Elmer's last moments of life. After the gun shots, James zoomed in on the woman's face. Blood streaming from her nose, the woman appeared to look up and smile right into the camera, *"that certainly went well."*

Sheila shuddered. She put her arms around herself, looked at the woman lying on the floor, smiling, with the smoking gun in her hands.

"That's the same creepy smile she gave me the other day."

"She sure seems to enjoy her work," James said in an aside, instantly drawing daggers from John and Sheila.

"I'm just saying," James continued defensively.

John was the first one to crack a little smile. Sheila shook her head and put a hand to her forehead.

The maudlin spell was broken.

Sheila smiled to herself, thinking of Elmer's last words.

No one fucks with Elmer Gaskins, remember that.

She would remember. They all would.

"James, what was so important that you wanted us to meet you at the museum?" Sheila asked, remembering there was a reason other than murder for their morning museum visit.

James, who was replaying the video feed, finally drew himself away from the screen.

"I think I found out where my double g hid the story of Henri."

"*Really?*" Sheila said astonished.

"You're kidding," John added.

"Well, I think I have. It's just a theory until we can go back to the museum and check it out."

"That could be a few days," John said.

Sheila turned to John.

"Perhaps Max could get his FBI friend to intercede."

Ignoring Sheila's remark, John asked James, "Where is it?"

"Not so fast. Let's see if you can find what I found hidden in my double g's note."

"Fair enough," Sheila said.

"Good. Ted told Max that Henri liked to test the other scientists, so it's only fair that I test you."

James handed each of them a copy of Robert Campbell's note.

John and Sheila pored over the note from James' great-great-grandfather. It helped distract them from that morning's grisly discovery.

Editor's note: I am most humbled to have been a close friend of Guwisguwi, Chief John Ross, for most of my adult life. We shared many adventures together and many sorrows. Our story is a long one. It begins with his battles with the National Government to prevent the removal of his people. The Indian Removal Act may have sealed the fate of his people but did not break his spirit. Our end as a nation of just peoples is yet to be determined. My friend who has gone on to his home among the seven heavens sleeps peacefully. Is written the ultimate fate of the Indian people? Where? Where does our story end? We must look to the past to find our future.
Robert Campbell, Editor Beaufort Sentinel

After a few minutes, John proclaimed that he had solved the riddle.

"It's clear that the note is all about Chief John Ross. His portrait that he presented to Robert Campbell hangs in the museum. So the story must be behind the portrait."

"Very good," James said. "I didn't think of that. There might be part of the story behind the portrait too."

"Too?" Sheila said.

"Both Henri and my forbear loved puzzles, so I decided to fool around with the note: highlighting what I believe is the message within the message. I'll read it to you," James said.

James got up and took the edited note from his pocket. Milking the moment for all it was worth, he slowly unfolded the note and smoothed it out.

"James, *please*, just read the fucking note," John said exasperated.

"Pretty please?" James replied in his Casper Gutman character.

"Pretty please," John echoed back.

"Very well, sir, let's get to it then." James looked over at Sheila; she rolled her eyes at his little charade; he gave her a harrumph and read the note. "I am most humbled to have been a close friend of Guwisguwi, Chief John Ross, for most of my adult life. We shared many adventures together and many sorrows. Our story is a long one. It begins with the Indian Removal Act. Our end, my friend who has gone, is written. Where does our story end? We must look to the past to find our future."

"So the beginning of the story is behind the signed copy of the Indian Removal Act on display at the museum, right?" John asked James.

"Hopefully."

"And for the end to the story, the really good part, we need to look into the past," Sheila sighed.

"Only thirty-six years worth of newspapers," James said cheerfully.

CHAPTER 47

Ted hung up the phone. A look of concern showed on his face. He sat down, got back up and made a cup of instant coffee. After taking a few sips, he made a call to his editor, Max Baker. Max picked up on the third ring.

"Hello."

"Max, it's Ted. I received some bad news today. I'm going to have to rush back to Washington for a few weeks."

"Why? What's up?" Max said evenly.

"It's my sister," Ted said slowly. "She has kidney failure, and I'm a match."

"I'm sorry, Ted. I didn't even know you had a sister. What's her name?"

"Susan. I didn't know I had a sister either, until last year. She lives in Seattle. We were both adopted by different parents shortly after birth. Anyway, she found me last year when her kidney disease began to get worse. She wanted to see me before she died . . . and . . . so, naturally, I took a test to see if I was a good match. Turns out I am."

"What hospital is she in? I'd like to send flowers."

"She just called, she's still at home; she has dialysis equipment there. Listen, I have to pack and tie up a few loose ends here before I catch a flight, so—"

"Sure, no problem. Besides, it sounded earlier like our man Jacques had spun his last tale."

The two talked for a few more minutes. Max ended his half of the conversation with another note of sympathy, and wished Ted a safe trip.

"Thanks Max, gotta run. I want to say goodbye to Adrienne and Jacques before I leave. I'll keep in touch."

* * *

Ted arrived at Jacques' cottage just after nine in the evening. Adrienne was surprised to see him at that late hour. She made him a cup of coffee. The two sat at the kitchen table. Adrienne listened; her eyes searched Ted's with what looked like genuine concern as he told her about his sister's kidney disease.

She put her hand on top of his, gently patted it and got up.

"Let me check on Jacques and see if he's still awake."

A few minutes later she ushered him into Jacques' room. The two talked for a half hour. Ted was grateful that Jacques did not go into one of his long stories.

Just before Ted was about to leave, the old man made a decision.

"Ted, before you go, I want you to take something back with you. In the corner over there." Jacques glanced towards the near corner next to the headboard. "The spy cane: It has your secrets on the film inside. It's not mine anyway. It belonged to one of your American spies. An early forerunner to the James Bond type, only not so good, eh?"

Ted went over and picked up the cane. Examining the long black stock and ornate gold plated handle, he said, "It's beautiful, Jacques. You can trust me to do the right thing with it."

"We'll see," Jacques said with a small smile. "Philippe caught him using that cane to snap some pictures. Your American spy apparently knew what he was looking for. Once my father saw what was on the film, he knew he had to burn down the chateau to keep the secrets safe."

"Your father was a very wise man, Jacques, as are you."

Adrienne, listening just outside, entered the bedroom and escorted Ted to the door.

"I'm sorry about your sister. What you're doing is a wonderful thing."

"I would do it even if she wasn't my sister," Ted replied instinctively, thinking more about what he was carrying in his hands. His attention quickly returned to Adrienne. "I'll miss you, Adrienne, even though you did lead me on the other day."

She gave him a seductive look.

"Perhaps when this game is over, you can come back and visit. Maybe I will treat you a little better next time we meet."

And with that, Adrienne gave Ted a lingering kiss.

I'll definitely be back.

* * *

Adrienne brought Jacques a glass of water and a pill. As he took the pill she stroked his forehead.

"How is the pain today?"

"Every day is a bit worse. It won't be much longer," he said unconcerned.

Her eyes began to tear up.

"What am I going to do without you?"

"Live your life. You're young and beautiful. Youth should not be spent doting on the old."

Through tears she blurted, "Maybe I will give Ted a try."

Jacques looked away with a disgusted look. "You do, and I promise I will never die."

"Are you sure of what you're doing?" Adrienne bent down and checked the drawer of Jacques' nightstand, making sure everything was in order. "Why now?" she asked.

"I don't want you to have the burden of Henri's secrets. And no, I am not sure. But the wheels are in motion. Soon we will know, or you will know."

CHAPTER 48

John and Sheila lay out on the chaise lounge soaking up the morning sun. Sheila had no trouble persuading John to stay at the beach house on Fripp. They both needed to clear their heads. She had insisted that James come up too, but he declined. While they waited for the crime scene at the museum to be lifted, there was nothing to do other than pore over old newspapers; neither of them felt like doing that.

Just before noon, Max called. He had spoken to Mike Kelley. A close friend and FBI agent, Mike was on the list that Henry Smith had given to Sheila. John put Max on speakerphone. They listened intently as he described developments. Keeping tabs on the investigation, Mike had informed Max that the blood pools found at the museum had come from Elmer; something they already knew from the surveillance video. No fingerprints other than theirs were found. Again, something they already knew from watching the man and woman cleaning up on the surveillance video.

"Has anyone monitored the surveillance since the murder?" Max asked.

"No. James just gave us a crash course on how the system works," John said. "We'll check it out on our laptop later."

"Right now we just want to chill out for a little while," Sheila added.

"Understandable," Max said. He paused before continuing. "How much do we tell Mike? At some point we are going to have to let him in on the surveillance. Just a little matter of obstruction of justice involved."

"Let us check out the museum surveillance first, and make sure the police did not discover anything," John said.

Sheila leaned towards the phone and placed her hand on John's knee.

"I'll check the video first thing tomorrow morning. If you don't hear from us by noon, then go ahead and give your FBI friend access, if you feel you can trust him."

Max could tell that neither of them were up for an extended conversation. He quickly ended the call, leaving for another day the news from France.

After an hour with Sheila curled up in his arms, John decided to go for a swim. Sheila begged off, which was unusual for her. As she watched John swim out into the ocean, she pulled her left breast out of her bikini top and examined her inflamed swollen nipple. She couldn't believe how much she had hurt herself while dreaming. Just moving around was painful. It felt better, exposed, not rubbing up against the fabric of the bikini.

John returned twenty minutes later. He smiled at the sight of Sheila lying on the chaise lounge with one breast out.

"Letting one of your babies have some air?" he grinned.

"Look."

Sheila showed John her reddened nipple and scratch marks, then told him about the violent sexual dreams she had had a couple nights previous.

John went inside. He returned with an antibiotic cream, some ice cubes and a small towel. He softly rubbed a little ointment on the inflamed area, wrapped ice cubes in the towel and laid it over her breast.

"Hope that helps." He went back to his chaise lounge, stretched out, and stared at the undulating surf. "Stress can do a lot of strange things. Let's just try to forget about the last few weeks . . . if only for today."

"Maybe you should tie my hands behind my back tonight," Sheila said half jokingly.

Soon they were both sound asleep.

They slept on and off the rest of the morning and part of the afternoon. Stress had definitely wrought havoc on their bodies. Around five, they got up. John boiled lobster tails. Sheila grilled vegetables. After dinner they laid back down on their chaise lounges: she in a light robe, he in a tee and swimsuit. Sharing a half-full bottle of wine that was in the refrigerator, each good-naturedly accused the other of drinking the first half without the other's knowledge. As the last rays of sunlight disappeared over the ocean, Sheila fell fast asleep. John carried her into the bedroom. He gently laid her on the bed and kissed her forehead before turning off the light and returning to the deck.

Poor girl, she's really been through a lot.

His thoughts turned to Rachel and Elmer, not so much Elmer, more Rachel.

We've all been through a lot.

He got up and made a large whiskey on the rocks—more whiskey then rocks.

A few hours and a few whiskeys later he went to bed

* * *

John woke up alone; the first faint rays of sunlight peeked through the window. He went into the living room, still dark except for the glowing screen of Sheila's laptop. He found Sheila naked on the couch. Her arms tightly crossed over her chest. She leaned, hunched forward, rocking back and forth, making mewing sounds. Her robe lay on the floor next to her.

He rushed over. With alarm in his voice he said, "Honey, what's wrong."

In a trance, she could not hear John. She just kept rocking, back and forth, staring at the floor, making those wounded cat-like sounds.

John picked up her robe, placed it over her.

"No!" she said violently, throwing the robe to the other side of the room. Tears streamed down her face. She resumed her rocking, arms tighter around her chest.

John sat down on the couch next to Sheila. He put his hand on her shoulder. She was oblivious. He looked at the screen and saw a frozen shot of the young woman from the museum, naked, dragging Sheila by her legs into the bedroom. His hair stood on end as he saw the same weird smile he had seen earlier on the museum video. John quickly closed the laptop. He got up, went to the linen closet and retrieved a light blanket, placing it over Sheila. He went into the kitchen and made a cup of hot tea with lemon and honey—the way she liked it—and set it on the coffee table in front of her. He sat down on the couch next to Sheila, leaving a little space between the two of them. He didn't know what else to do, so he sat quietly as she rocked and mewed for the next hour.

John was just about to get up and call the hospital when Sheila finally stopped mewing. She reached for the cup of tea. She took a sip. Said one word: "Cold."

John took the cup, got up, left, and returned with a fresh cup of tea.

"Better," she said.

The rocking slowed down, and then, at last, stopped.

John felt it safe to put his hand back on her shoulder. After a short while, Sheila got up and told John she needed to take a shower.

"Pack up our clothes," she said before entering the bathroom.

John made a reservation just down the road at the Golf and Beach resort for a small one bedroom ocean cottage. He packed up. While Sheila showered, he placed a set of clothes on the bathroom vanity for her to wear. When she stepped out, fully dressed, twenty minutes later, John asked, "All set?"

"Wait a second."

Sheila walked over to the robe—the same one from the video—picked it up and took it outside to the fire pit. Grabbing lighter fluid from the charcoal grill, she doused it and set it aflame.

She watched until the robe was reduced to ashes.

She turned to John: a cold, determined look on her face.

"Now we can go."

CHAPTER 49

Ted Dody booked a flight from Charles De Gaulle Airport to Washington, departing at ten-fifty the next morning. He sat down in a faded, upholstery chair in the small sitting room of his tiny apartment and looked out the window.

Paris at night.

He would miss it. And Adrienne.

He picked up the cane: admired its gently tapered ebony shaft with the elaborate gold plated handle. Inside, were the secrets of the Society d' Arcueil. He peered into the small camera lens, surrounded by a raised, gold etched flower.

So this is what men have died for.

He ran his hand down the ebony shaft.

Two hundred years. Now I alone hold the secrets.

Ted stared off into the Paris night, thinking of how the world would change with this discovery.

His phone rang.

Ted answered and listened for a short while. He protested weakly the instructions he received.

"Is this absolutely necessary?" He paused, listened to the response. "Wouldn't it be wise to verify—" Ted was cut off before he could finish. His head slumped to his chest. He listened for another minute, said, "Yes sir, I understand," and with a shaky hand hit the end key.

* * *

Ted made the trip to Lisieux in a little over two hours. He parked the car about a half mile away from the cottage. This was one aspect of the job he was not going to enjoy. Had he known exactly what he was getting into, he would never have agreed to get into the program.

I would have been out of prison by now, he thought wistfully. *They don't lock up juveniles forever. Not even for murder.*

Ted entered the cottage through the back door. It was unlocked.

So trusting, these French.

A deep longing arose in his heart. Thoughts of turning back, disobeying, for the first time in his life, raced through his mind—quickly banished. He realized he would never be free. Ted made his way down the narrow hallway and noticed a small light coming from Jacques' bedroom. He peered through the partially open door; the old man was in bed, reading. What were the odds he'd still be awake at two in the morning? Pretty good, apparently. He stood for a few moments at the door, wondering what the best way to proceed was.

I'm not very good at this.

Ted took a deep breath, pushed the door wide open and walked in, very naturally.

Jacques looked up as his bedroom door opened with a familiar squeak.

"Hello, Ted." Jacques put the book down on his lap, disappointment showed on his face.

"You don't seem surprised to see me," Ted said in a matter-of-fact voice as he sat down on the edge of the bed.

"Disappointed, but not surprised. I took a pill to stay awake."

"*Oh?*" Ted looked around the room suspiciously.

Jacques wheezed a small chuckle. "Not to worry my friend. We are alone. I sent Adrienne to her mother's house."

"Did you know all along that I, that I . . ." Ted started to stammer, Jacques helped him finish the sentence.

"That you were not who you said you were?" Jacques paused. "It took a little while."

"How did you know?" Ted was anxious to hear his response.

"You lack a certain humanity. The eyes are the mirror to the soul. It's not just a cliché. They show fear, longing, nervousness, the whole range of human emotions."

"And what emotions do my eyes show?" Ted said almost pleadingly.

"Up until now, no emotion."

Jacques patted Ted's knee with an almost fatherly touch. "Your eyes are always analyzing, calculating. Even Adrienne noticed it. She told me about your day in the village. Most men would have given in to their heart. I may be an old man, Ted, but I still know beauty. And Adrienne is a beautiful, sensual woman. But you carefully chose every word, even when love presented itself to you. Some snot about truth and the arc of justice . . . really, Ted." Jacques shook his head sadly.

"You said up until now I showed no emotion. What do you see now?"

"I see a mixture of fear and sadness, a kind of desperation. Your life is out of control. Am I right?"

Jacques looked directly into Ted's eyes.

For the first time in his life, Ted looked away from another human being, feeling inadequate. "You're right," he said sadly. "I have no past, no future; and I'm not going to enjoy what I'm about to do."

"Before you kill me, will you honor one last request?"

Ted nodded.

Jacques continued; "I have told you my story, almost succeeded in boring you to death at times, no?"

Ted smiled a genuine smile for the first time in his life.

Jacques took hold of his hand.

"I would like to hear your story."

Ted felt a heavy burden being lifted as he told Jacques his story of childhood abuse. The old man clucked sympathetically at various points of the story, holding Ted's hand and patting it with his free hand.

"I was only fourteen when I finally snapped. Got my Dad's revolver out of his nightstand and shot him while he was sleeping. The prosecutor moved to try me as an adult. That would have meant a life sentence. I was so grateful when a man from the Justice

Department said I could plea bargain and enroll in a special government program for public service. It soon became clear to me that this was no Department of Justice program—and no public service. But by then it was too late.

"I was housed dormitory style with other young boys and girls who had committed similar crimes. Along with a first rate education, sprinkled with a heavy dose of patriotism, we were given a grueling physical exercise regimen and weapons training. Weekly sessions with a so-called psychiatrist ensured that we remained screwed up and obedient to our new parents."

Ted paused.

"And who were your new parents?" Jacques asked quietly.

"Basically, anyone wearing a uniform, or suit and tie. We were taught to respect authority."

"So one form of abuse was supplanted by another form of abuse . . . *incredible*." Jacques pulled the blanket up to his chin—suddenly very cold. "Who are your parents now?"

"You mean who gives me my orders? I don't even know. We were sent out into the world with certain skill sets. I had an aptitude for writing and investigation, so I was set up with a phony resume and given a job with the Washington Post. I have a bank account that receives regular monthly deposits. From time to time I get a call from someone who identifies himself by a sequential code known only to me and my parents. When the code is given, I follow orders. Simple as that. After an assignment, my bank account increases substantially. I was told that I could eventually retire, but that's never going to happen. Who would I even call to notify?"

Ted slumped, his head fell on his chest as cathartic tears streamed down his face.

Jacques gently said, "How many people have you killed?"

"Just my father. Two, if we're counting you." Ted smiled sadly.

"Yes, I see. Well let's get on with it then, shall we? How are you going to do it?"

"I planned to put a pillow over your face and smother you while you slept."

"That would have been considerate."

"I thought so." Ted grinned. "But I've changed my mind."

"And now?" Jacques looked at Ted warily.

Ted laughed out loud.

"Don't worry, Jacques, I've changed my mind. How can I kill you now? For the first time in my life I feel like a member of the human family. I have you to thank for that."

"But Ted, you *have* to kill me." Jacques sat up straighter in bed, grabbed Ted's arm. He stared resolutely for a moment before weakly barking out, "You have your orders."

Ted got up and pulled away from Jacques' grip. Without warning he leaned over and kissed Jacques on the forehead before turning to walk out the door.

"Tell Adrienne I'll miss her."

In a surprisingly strong voice, Jacques shouted, "Ted, stop! They will kill you! I know these people!"

"I know them too, Jacques." Ted paused at the door and turned to face Jacques. "You don't understand. I don't care anymore. I'm finally free."

"But they will kill you, I'm sure of it. I'm dying anyway, so what does it matter?"

"It matters to me, old man. My conscience is clear. Just honor this walking dead man one final request . . . if you would be so kind."

"What is it, Ted?" Jacques craned his head towards his delinquent assassin.

Smiling slyly, Ted said, "Next time you tell someone your stories, stop with the . . . *So!* And the . . . *Question!* All the time, Jesus Christ, it drove me nuts."

The old man smiled.

"Adrienne says the same thing."

Ted was already out the door.

Jacques took a notepad from his nightstand and wrote out a long note.

* * *

In the morning, Adrienne found Jacques in bed with a smile on his face. She read the note and saw the empty pill bottle on the nightstand. She kissed her grandfather on the forehead for the last time. A smile broke through her tears.

CHAPTER 50

In the wake of what Sheila was going through, both she and John had forgotten all about reviewing the surveillance video for Max. After checking in and unpacking, they did a quick survey of their one bedroom cottage at the Golf and Beach resort. While a step down from James' beach house, it was still very cozy, and offered Sheila the added comfort of not having been defiled by a crazed young woman.

John made sure the doors and windows were kept locked, whether they were inside or out. He missed the ocean breeze coming through the windows, but that was a small sacrifice to secure Sheila's well-being. Sheila was slowly coming around. She didn't talk for most of the afternoon. Sitting out on the small deck staring at the ocean, she would wave John off when he occasionally asked if she needed anything.

Around five in the afternoon, she turned to John—patiently sitting and reading in a deck chair a few feet away—and asked about dinner. She didn't want to leave the cottage. They decided to order out for pizza. An hour later, a horrible, cheesy pizza, along with a free liter of soda arrived—just what the doctor ordered. The cheese was like a spider web. Whenever Sheila took a bite, it would stretch endlessly, tangling up even worse when she grabbed the strands with her fingers. She began to get frustrated. John saved the day by going to the kitchen drawer and pulling out a scissors. Sheila gave him a wary look as he sat next to her, scissors in hand. He just smiled. She took another bite of pizza. As the cheese began to stretch from her mouth back to the slice, John very adeptly took the scissors and snipped the cheese.

The pall that had settled over Sheila finally broke. She cracked up and spit out her food to keep from choking. She took a drink of soda. John smiled mischievously, clicking the scissors open and shut, cracking her up further and causing soda to spurt from her nose. After she recovered, he handed her the scissors. Soon she was snipping away, bite after bite.

After dinner, she opened up to John about her feelings. They morphed from humiliation, to lack of control, to fear, and finally, anger. Anger was good. It reached a crescendo when she described what she was going to do to that crazy psycho bitch—one of her many affectionate terms for the woman.

She was just finishing her rant when she suddenly remembered her promise to Max to review the museum surveillance. She asked John to get the laptop. He wanted to spare her the trauma of revisiting the site of Elmer's murder at the hand of the psycho bitch—he liked that phrase, it seemed to empower Sheila more—but she insisted on reviewing the video with him.

They skipped over the murder of Elmer and went to the part where James entered the museum and found his body lying in a pool of blood. They watched as the police took measurements, blood samples, photos, and fingerprints. John was fascinated by the interview conducted with James, who remained remarkably composed throughout the ordeal. Nothing else out of the ordinary occurred. Omitting, of course, the last few weeks in its entirety.

After finishing a review of the video, John gave Max a call. Max said he'd already given his FBI friend, Mike Kelley, the access code to the surveillance cameras. Mike had called back to say that a colleague at the FBI's Operational Technology Division was going to run the pair through a facial recognition program. He said the police were cooperating, and an FBI team was on its way to follow up.

From a review of the surveillance, Mike had identified a few places the police missed in their fingerprint search. Hopefully something would pop—his words—when they ran prints through the IAFIS: the FBI's Integrated Automated Fingerprint Identification System.

John was taken aback when Sheila told Max to have Mike review the surveillance from the beach house. She gave him the date and time—her face a look of fierce determination. She didn't tell Max what Mike would find.

After they hung up, Sheila turned to John and sighed, "He's certainly in for an eyeful."

Max called Sheila back less than an hour later. She listened as he said, "I don't know what was on that video, but Mike wanted me to assure you that he would personally see to it that this gets the highest priority. He also wanted me to give you his direct line and cell number. Whatever resources you feel you need, give him a call. He'll see that you get it."

"And you *trust* him, Max?" Sheila said quietly.

"He's one of the good guys, Sheila. Yes, I trust him," Max said in a reassuring tone.

"Alright . . . I guess."

Sheila took down the number that Max's FBI friend had given him.

After hanging up, she hugged herself. A cold rain coursed through her body.

Why is it that I feel less and less reassured when someone tries to reassure me?

CHAPTER 51

Just before noon the next day, James called. The police had released the museum. John and Sheila hopped into the Grand Marquis and made the short drive from the island to the museum. They hurried up the steps. Once inside, they took a quick glance around before entering the office. James sat behind the desk, his hands clasped over his rotund belly. The Indian Removal Act signed by President Andrew Jackson lay in front of him, still inside its large wooden frame.

"I thought I'd wait for you before trying to find out what's inside," James said. "I feel like a kid at Christmas waiting to open his present."

Noticing the set of tools next to the framed copy, John remarked, "I see you came prepared."

James smiled. "Shall we get on with it then?"

"The sooner we get to the bottom of this, the better," Sheila replied. "Maybe then we can get our lives back."

James looked up, a bit embarrassed. "Yes . . . well . . ." His voice trailed off as he picked up the frame with its several layers of ornate wood trim.

"It's certainly thick enough to hold a lot of papers, even a book," John said.

James examined the frame. "I suppose the bottom trim piece

would be the logical place to start."

Very delicately, he began to pry the wood.

Not wanting to damage the frame, James only managed to raise the bottom trim piece an eighth of an inch after twenty minutes of careful prying. Sheila remarked that James was trying to kill them with suspense.

Fifteen minutes later the trim was raised a quarter inch. James took a small penlight and peered inside.

"Nothing but another wooden bottom."

He slowly continued to pry the trim. Five minutes later, James, exasperated, said, "The hell with it," and started to pry with a lot more authority. The edges of the trim started popping from the frame. Finally, the bottom layer of trim started to give way from the rest of the frame. John and Sheila held down the ends of the bottom layer as James lifted the frame from both sides. After a little wiggling and tugging, they noticed a distinct pungent smell.

James stopped and looked at John, then Sheila.

"Do you smell that? Camphorwood."

He continued to tug at the top of the frame. It pulled free. The force of the last pull caused a box enclosed inside the frame to pop out onto the desk, along with the bottom layer.

The three of them stared down at a miniature version of the camphorwood storage chests that held the Sentinel newspapers. Identical, right down to the lock.

James opened his desk drawer and reached in. With key in hand, he turned to John.

"Would you like to have the honor?"

Sheila, remembering the episode at the beach house when John pretended the key didn't fit, intercepted.

"I'll take that," she said, snatching the key from James' hand.

Smiling triumphantly at John, she turned the key. A look of concern spread across her face as she jiggled the key in the lock.

"It doesn't fit!"

"Sorry." James fumbled in his drawer until he found what he was looking for. "I gave you the key for the storage chests at the house. Here, try this one."

She took the key and inserted it into the lock. The key turned. *Finally!*

She lifted the lid of the small chest. There, sitting on top, was the special edition of the Beaufort Sentinel from Friday, June 18, 1830.

Sheila read the headline. James and John leaned over to read along.

Floating Man Flies Over Beaufort.

She laid the newspaper down on the desk.

Looking back into the chest, Sheila paused, and said, *"Wow"* in a low gasp.

She slowly lifted a leather-bound book out of the box and placed it on the desk. The title, embossed in gold, stared up at them from centuries past: *My Adventures with Henri Richaud, the Amazing Floating Man, by Robert Campbell.*

They stood over the desk, stunned. John gave James a nod.

"I think you should be the first to handle the book. After all, it's your great-great-grandfather's memoirs."

James ran his hands across the cover of the pristine book, bound in rich brown leather with raised gold lettering.

"Almost two hundred years old. Unbelievable."

He slowly paged through the book.

"I'm tempted to just go to the last page."

He started to flip back and forth through the pages and give a short running commentary, pausing here and there.

"Chief John Ross is in it . . ." A little further on, James said, "Andrew Jackson."

Flipping past another twenty pages, James paused, muttered in a low voice, "Bastard."

"Andrew Jackson?" Sheila asked.

James nodded, flipped ahead further.

"Harriott Horry." He paused to look up at John: "Your Horrible Hairy woman," and paused another moment before continuing.

"Coachman Isaac . . . wonder who he was and what role he played?"

James flipped toward the end of the book and chuckled.

"Sorry, couldn't help myself . . . I peeked."

* * *

Sitting around the desk, each took turns examining the book, flipping through the pages.

Sheila, the last to examine the book, asked, "Well, shall we start reading cover to cover?"

"No, we need to put the book back into the frame," John said.

"What?" James asked, taken aback.

"John's right," Sheila said. "Nobody is aware of the existence of the book except for us. It needs to go back into the frame, along with the newspaper, as soon as we get done making copies."

"We better get started," John said. "That's a lot of pages,"

With that settled, they got up and went to the copier.

Two hours and three sets later, James returned the book and June 18 edition of the Sentinel to the chest, placed it snugly back into the frame and refastened the trim. The framed copy of the Indian Removal Act was returned to its former perch alongside the portrait of Chief John Ross. James took down the portrait of the Chief, examined it, and pronounced it too light and thin to be holding any secret compartment.

Before leaving the museum, they agreed that James would stick to his normal routine and go straight home, with the copies safely locked inside his briefcase. Knowing that their place was bugged, John and Sheila would go back to the Sentinel and act as if nothing out of the ordinary had occurred. They would then go out to dinner. Afterwards, they would drive to James', taking a circuitous route to insure that they were not being followed.

CHAPTER 52

It was after midnight by the time they finished reviewing the surveillance tapes, satisfying themselves that they were indeed alone, free from any prying eyes—human or otherwise. James offered to make drinks. John readily accepted. This drew a quick stare and comment from Sheila about it being a little late in the day. John's reply was to look up at the clock and say it was early. James returned with a scotch and water for himself, a whiskey on the rocks for John.

Sheila got up.

"What the hell," she said, and went into the kitchen to make herself a drink. She returned, plopping back down on the sofa next to John. All settled in, they listened to James read the article from the long missing edition of the Sentinel.

"Floating Man Flies Over Beaufort. This past Saturday, the residents of the small town of Beaufort were treated to what will possibly be the most wondrous sight ever to be witnessed in their lifetimes. The great Floating Man from France, Henri Richaud, astride his antigravity device, performed maneuvers in the skies that seemingly defy the laws of nature and God.

"As throngs assembled in Union Square with great anticipation, a low buzzing sound, like that of a hummingbird, seemed to come at us from beyond the houses. The sound grew in crescendo until it was painful to the senses. Many in the crowd covered their ears and began to run away. All at once, seemingly out of nowhere, Henri appeared overhead on what looked like a large, flying, butter churn. The circular base of the device had an approximate width of four feet, with its height appearing to be just over two. A long center pole adorned with sections of gleaming silver bands protruded some twelve feet from the center of the base. On the pole was attached a seat. Near the base were footrests that Henri continually turned. A small cross handle, attached midway up, provided a rest for his hands, and I was later to learn, allowed Henri to steer the device.

"As Henri first appeared above the crowd, at a height this observer would approximate at thirty feet, the device hovered in place, neither rising nor falling. Henri then guided the device to the perimeter of the crowd and slowly circled, before moving back to the center and descending. The crowd made way as Henri settled the device mere inches above the ground. He hovered there for several moments, the more curious in the crowd slowly approaching. And then, without warning, he shot up into the sky, almost to the point of disappearing. A great murmur went up among the crowd. Then, just as rapidly as he had ascended, he descended. Hurtling towards the earth, the crowd began to scatter in fear. It appeared to all, that this Frenchman, Henri Richaud, was falling to his death, only to be saved at the last moment when the device abruptly stopped ten feet above the crowd. Henri then further mesmerized the crowd: flying very much like a hummingbird, darting here and there, stopping and hovering in place before darting to another part of the square. After several more minutes, Henri disappeared over the houses and the performance was over.

"It was only by chance that I was later able to meet this most illustrious fellow. During the performance, I happened to spy an old friend of mine, Chief John Ross of the Cherokee nation. As a young man, working for the Washington Gazette, it had been my esteemed privilege to interview him. At the time, Chief John Ross had been visiting the capitol for the purpose of defending the Cherokee's right to their lands. Lands that the government was most eager to possess. I greatly admired his passion and intellect in resisting the government's insistence that he relinquish title to

Cherokee lands and move westward. So persuaded was I by this great man's oratory, that I began to write passionately in his defense. So much so, that I soon found myself removed from my position at the Gazette: having ruffled the feathers of some very powerful politicians.

"To my great delight, the Chief took this young man under his wing, and allowed me passage on his carriage, back to my home in Beaufort. We have kept up a correspondence ever since. And so it was with exceeding joy that I found myself amongst the crowd last Saturday, next to the Chief and a lady friend from Charleston: one Miss Harriott Pinckney Horry, in whose home Henri was residing. As it turned out, the Chief had been attending the performance of the Floating Man the previous week in Savannah when the crowd became unruly and stormed the carriage of Miss Horry. Chief John Ross, along with several of his Cherokee companions, came riding to the aid of Henri and Miss Horry. The Chief offered to provide security for the remainder of Henri's tour, scheduled to conclude in Washington. An offer readily accepted.

"After the Chief escorted me and my assistant to Miss Horry's carriage, we rode off several miles in a westerly direction, to a rendezvous point where Henri Richaud and his device waited. The Chief introduced me to the great man: small in stature, and looking quite frail. Upon my entreaty, Mr. Richaud graciously allowed me and my assistant to accompany him back to the residence of Miss Harriott Pinckney Horry. Thereupon, I enjoyed a delightful dinner; and with the assistance of Chief John Ross, procured a position as Mr. Richaud's biographer for the remainder of his summer tour.

"So, my dear readers, it is with much regret that I send my assistant, with this dispatch, to inform you that this will be the last edition of the Sentinel until the conclusion of the tour. After which, I hope to regale you all with some most amazing stories of this great man and his invention. Until then, I bid you *au revoir*, as Henri would say.

"As always, your faithful editor, Robert Campbell."

James put the newspaper down and picked up the paper copy memoirs of his forebear's gold embossed book.

"And now, for the pièce de résistance."

CHAPTER 53

Hampton Plantation, June 11, 1830
Memoirs of Robert Campbell

    Guided expertly by Coachman Isaac, a large Negro possessing uncanny abilities to navigate a patchy trail through coastal pine forests and swampy wetlands in waning sunlight, to a degree I thought impossible, our party made its way to Hampton Plantation. I thought it most odd that Henri spent most of the journey on top, next to Coachman Isaac. Miss Horry explained to me that Henri was fascinated with the division of labor employed at the plantation, and wished to learn all he could about the culture of the South and its peoples.
    "He is the most inquisitive man I have ever met, I do believe," Harriott had remarked to me.
    I remember Chief John Ross replying, "He has remarkable empathy for those who find themselves in less fortunate circumstance through no result of their own."
    "He was treated terribly by the French. And his own friend, Napoleon, treated him the worst. We would never treat our slaves that way. You'll see, Mr. Campbell, we are very enlightened at Hampton Plantation. We have never to my recollection whipped any of our slaves, and neither have we separated their families,"

Harriott remarked.

"But they are still enslaved, are they not?" Chief John Ross replied.

"That is an unfortunate circumstance of history," I remember Harriott replying.

Along the journey to Hampton I inquired as to how it was that Henri had made Harriott's acquaintance. She explained that her brother, Charles, living in France and married to a French lady, met a rather eccentric man in a Paris café one afternoon. Henri had recently been released from prison; Charles noticed him writing mathematical formulas on a piece of paper while drinking coffee. Charles introduced himself as an American, and struck up a conversation with Henri, who then proceeded to tell him the most amazing story of his scientific discovery and imprisonment by Napoleon. Charles thought him quite mad, until Henri pointed out a man at another table who appeared to be watching them. Harriott's brother soon satisfied himself that Henri was indeed under close observation. The two developed a friendship. Henri regaled Charles with stories of his youth, and in return, Charles told him of the wonders of America.

Over the next few weeks, Charles watched his newfound friend's condition deteriorate under the pressure of constant surveillance. He offered Henri an escape from his torment. Charles wrote to his mother, the elder Harriott, and a plan was devised whereby Henri would be smuggled aboard a sailing ship bound for America. Harriott would fund a laboratory at Charles' home at Wambaw Plantation. In return, Charles agreed to the lending of his slaves.

Henri, smuggled from France to England, set sail from Liverpool to Boston in the late summer of 1827. He was met by Coachman Isaac and transported to Hampton, arriving in a most weakened condition. According to Harriott, so frail and wracked with cold was Henri, that they did not expect him to survive. He spent months convalescing at Hampton before he was able to visit the room at Wambaw where his laboratory was to be set up, and another two years gathering materials needed to recreate his antigravity device.

The replication of his greatest achievement brought a most delightful change in Henri's spirit. He was like a child with a new plaything: constantly tinkering and refining his antigravity device. For the first few months, he performed only for the residents of the plantation, delighting the field hands with his acrobatic maneuvers. The matriarch of the family, the elder Harriott, was not so amused when Henri would fly low across the rice fields, leaving a five-foot swath flattened in his wake. But all in all, the spirits of everyone were raised, along with Henri's. Soon, Henri was anxious to unveil his discovery to the rest of America.

* * *

It was well after nightfall, on the eleventh, when we arrived at the edge of Hampton Plantation. The sandy path leading to the main house was lined with torches, as our arrival had been expected. We pulled up in front of a magnificent portico with six, gleaming white columns. Standing there to greet us was Little Daphne, one of Harriott's key slaves, who warmly ushered us inside. Awaiting us was a pitcher of sweet camellia tea, followed by a rich chicken jambalaya mixture. Little Daphne, Harriott later explained, was indispensible to the running of the main house. After the death of her mother, Big Daphne, she became Harriott's constant companion. Now an adult, she was in charge of supervising the other house servants.

Little Daphne was especially attentive to Henri. Harriott recounted that when Henri arrived at Hampton almost three years previous, frail and wracked with a fever that doctors could not cure, Little Daphne would secretly bring him herbs and potions from Madame Tallulah: an African healer the slaves relied on. Madame Tallulah's remedies slowly restored Henri to health. From that point on, Little Daphne felt a certain responsibility for Henri. Watching her dote on him, much to the amusement of Harriott, it was evident the two had formed a close bond: much like father and daughter.

Continuing the story of Little Daphne, Harriott remarked in confidence just before we repaired to the front portico for an evening taste of Kentucky Whiskey, the following:

"Little Daphne lost her stepfather, Old Sibb, to fever right before Henri arrived. The poor woman tried everything to save him. She gave him herbal teas and wrapped him in poultices; she even prevailed upon me to send for Doctor Garden of Charleston, who could do little to help. Right before Old Sibb died, Little

Daphne asked Madame Tallulah to work her magic, but it was too late. She said the greater part of his spirit had already left his body and could not be summoned back. Little Daphne was devastated. When Henri, filled with fever, arrived almost at the instant of Old Sibb's passing, she took it as a sign that a small part of her stepfather's spirit had entered Henri's body."

Harriott told me that the guilt Little Daphne felt was relieved when Henri recovered, and for the past three years, she had been his constant companion and assistant. Harriott was a little annoyed at first, as Little Daphne had neglected some of her duties, but for Harriott, seeing the joy return to Little Daphne outweighed the annoyance.

* * *

After dinner we enjoyed a superb Kentucky Whiskey on the front portico. The light from fires, ablaze in the cooking chimneys of slave cabins, darted and flickered through the trees as we looked out upon the night sky. The smell of herbs from hanging pots used to ward off mosquitoes blended with the sounds of African spirituals, drifting by on the evening breeze.

My eyebrows rose a little when Old William the butler, Little Daphne, and a little later, Coachman Isaac, joined us on the porch for some whiskey.

Harriott sensed my discomfort.

"We are all family here, Mr. Campbell, some more, some less, but family nonetheless."

A bit tipsy, she laughed at her unintended rhyme.

Another astonishment, for me, came soon thereafter when Coachman Isaac addressed Harriott.

"Miz Harriott, I rubbed down dem horses, but dat mare be a might old, and she be slowin down dem others. You mights wanna be considerin—"

At this point Henri interrupted.

"Isaac, quit with the pretense. Robert is our guest."

I became slack-jawed when Coachman Isaac responded in perfect gentleman's English.

"As you wish. Like I was saying Miss Harriott, you really should consider buying a new horse on our next visit to Charleston, Betsy is getting too old to pull her fair share of the load."

And then, noticing my astonished countenance, he said directly to me, "Don't be alarmed Mr. Campbell. Most of the house servants speak perfect English. We choose not to, so as not to alarm the white folks."

Henri added, "It makes the masters feel less guilty if their slaves are seen as a bit less civilized."

"I hate when you put it like that, Henri," Harriott replied.

"But it is true, is it not?"

Harriott looked down.

"Still, it is a bit unnerving to think of it that way."

I could not believe the conversation we were having, and then Coachman Isaac explained.

"Shortly after Henri arrived, I drove him down to see Doctor Garden in Charleston, talking along the way in the slave idiom we use. Henri began to question me. Do you remember, Henri? You were still quite delirious."

"Of course. I asked you how it could be that you worked around white folks your whole life, but still spoke broken English."

"And I replied by saying, I don'ts know what you iz talkin bout suh. To which you then chastised me by saying,"—at this point Coachman Isaac mimicked Henri's French accent—"Oh come now, jou cannot fool me-e-e-e. I learned englaze in Frunce and have only spoken zeet for a couple years and can speak better than jou. And I can tell that jou are no one's fool."

Henri continued for Isaac at this point.

"And then in perfect English, you said it makes our masters feel better about themselves."

Old William stood leaning against one of the portico columns, laughing hysterically, trying in vain to do it quietly.

Harriott, a bit put off, said rather testily, "William, if you can pull yourself together, please refill our guest's glass."

William, still chuckling, walked over and poured me another drink, and said, to what I am sure was a still astonished look on my face, "I do pray that you will keep our little secret, sir."

As the songs of slaves drifted from the woods, the night ended with me thinking what a strange world we live in.

Made even stranger with the addition of Henri Richaud.

CHAPTER 54

Waking up a little past eight the next morning with a faint recollection of a buzzing noise in my ears, I proceeded to the kitchen where Old William was making a pot of coffee.

"A little late for breakfast," he said. Which I thought, an unusual thing for a slave to say to a white man. Old William, without prodding, then said in a most casual manner that Harriott was out inspecting floodgates along some of the dikes used to flood the rice fields at high tide. Old Sandy, one of the drivers who supervised the work on the Plantation, had accompanied her, along with one of the trunk minders responsible for the floodgates, which if rotten, could be a disaster for a rice field.

I learned from Old William that I had just missed Little Daphne and Henri. They had taken the antigravity device over to his laboratory on Wambaw Plantation. The humming noise is probably what had awoken me. He also informed me that Chief John Ross had set off earlier with some of his Cherokees to do some scouting for Henri's upcoming trip to Charlestown.

Old William responded to the perplexed look on my face.

"The Chief noticed some suspicious characters in Savannah when Henri performed there. He noticed the same characters talking to a few soldiers in Beaufort, this past Saturday."

"And why would that seem so suspicious to the Chief," I asked

William.

"According to the Chief, one of the men was an aide to John Eaton. Seems he is an important man in Washington. The Chief remembered him as part of the group trying to take his land away," Old William replied.

I informed Old William that John Eaton, Andrew Jackson's secretary of war, was indeed an important man. He just shrugged, brought over a pot of coffee and poured me a cup. My thoughts turned to Henri. I inquired of Old William how long it would take to walk over to the laboratory.

He laughed as if this was the funniest thing he had ever heard.

"You won't be walking to Wambaw Plantation unless you want to trudge through the rice fields. And those mosquitoes just love to get themselves some of that pink flesh, seeing as how their diet is kind of restricted."

Old William said I could normally take a boat up the creek, but all the boats were presently occupied. Noting my crestfallen appearance, he said not to worry; Henri and Little Daphne would be back before dinner at midday.

After pouring my cup of coffee, Old William retreated to the corner of the kitchen, where he remained standing, looking uncomfortable. I inquired as to what was the matter. He replied that on Miss Harriott's orders, he was to remain standing as long as there was a white guest present. I asked if he had to remain standing for Henri, to which he replied, "Oh no, Mr. Henri is family." Then, much to my own amazement, I said that he should consider me family also, and motioned for him to sit down and join me. Old William sat down at the kitchen table, smiled and poured himself a cup of coffee.

I asked him how long he had been at Hampton. He told me the story of how as a young boy living in Senegambia he was taken prisoner by another tribe and sold to slavers. Old William estimated that he arrived in America sometime in the late 1770s or early 1780s, though he could not be sure, as time was not something he often thought about. From his aged appearance, I would venture to guess that perhaps the early 1770s was a more accurate estimation. Old William said he was placed aboard a slave ship with several hundred fellow Africans. With tears rimming his eyes, he recounted the brutal journey of being crammed between decks less than three feet high, shoulder-to-shoulder, sitting amid each other's legs. They slept sitting upright the whole trip, with many men bent over due to the low height of the ceiling. Sitting, crowded together amidst their own waste, stench, and heat, proved too much for many: including William's brother who died sitting next to him. William counted at least thirty-five that died and were thrown overboard during the passage. Offshore, just outside of Charleston, they were deposited on Sullivan Island where they were checked for disease before being allowed into the city. Housed temporarily in an old warehouse, the slaves were fattened up before being auctioned off.

Old William said he considered himself fortunate to end up on Hampton plantation where he was able to raise a family with a reasonable degree of assurance that they would not be split up and sold. His wife Patty was a washerwoman. Their two boys, Caesar and Roger, worked in the rice fields. While telling me stories about his children, I thought I heard a faint humming noise. A few moments later, Old William jumped up, motioning me to follow him out the back door and over to the creek behind the house. The humming grew louder and higher in pitch; a misty spray covered Wambaw Creek. Coming down the center we could make out Henri and Little Daphne aboard his amazing device. Water sprayed in every direction as the device skimmed a few feet above the surface of the creek.

Henri brought the device ashore and hovered near the back door. Coachman Isaac came running up, and to my great surprise, was handed the device from Henri. Coachman Isaac hopped onto the base, hovered magically about a foot above the ground and flew over to the carriage house, maintaining that same foot clearance between the device and the ground. Henri explained that Isaac would be removing the pole which contained batteries in need of charging. The pole would then be connected to the center of an electrical generator wheel turned by horses. As he explained all this, Little Daphne went inside with Old William to prepare dinner. Henri and I repaired to the front porch.

It was my first opportunity to talk to Henri alone, and I did not waste it. After a few pleasantries, followed by harmless comments on the weather, I decided to delve into Henri's past.

"What was Napoleon like, Henri?" I asked.

He stared wistfully into the distance, out past a large oak tree that was saved from being chopped down by no less a personage than the great George Washington. After a few moments in which Henri's memory seemed to transport him deep in time, he came back to the present and simply said, "He was a good friend."

"But Henri," I replied, "did he not imprison you?"

"Well, yes Robert, but you have to understand Napoleon. To him, life was a great game. He loved being at the center of all the action. And most of all he loved a good fight. In the beginning, it did not matter what side he was on or whether he won or lost, as long as it was a good fight. And he viewed every aspect of life as a fight: whether it was winning the love of his life Josephine, or maneuvering through the politics of the Directory, or fielding great armies. It was all the same to him. He had to imprison me. It was his nature. I understood."

Henri became a bit more animated. He broke off his stare of the distant landscape and turned to me. "I think that bothered him a little: the fact that I understood him so well."

"How long were you in prison?" I inquired.

"Eleven years. Napoleon finally gave up trying to persuade me to give up my secrets. He threw me in prison in 1810. I was not released until after his death in 1821."

"And yet you still say Napoleon was a good friend," I said in amazement.

"Yes, he turned into a monster, but he was a good friend," Henri replied.

"How so?"

"I am alive, am I not? He did not kill me. Napoleon had no problem killing anyone who gave him difficulties, and I most certainly gave him that."

"Tell me about the monster in your friend. When did this transformation take place?"

"Like I said: to Napoleon, life was a game. He saw how easily life was destroyed when the revolution turned on itself. All these leaders of the revolution were like so many chess pieces to Napoleon. He decided that in order to win the game of life he would have to control the chess board, not just be a pawn, a bishop, or even a king. By the time I saw my old friend again in the small village of Arcueil, he had already become a monster. He had his opponents rounded up and shot. When he conquered countries, whether it was Spain or Egypt, he rounded up rebels and tortured them before having them executed as a warning to others. I was treated very well by comparison."

"And you were not tortured then?"

"Oh, I was tortured Robert, but if you want to learn about torture, you must talk to Madame Tallulah. She will tell you all about Napoleon's methods of torture. She was one of the few lucky ones to escape Haiti during Napoleon's reign there."

"This Madame Tallulah, she was tortured?"

"Only if you consider watching your family and friends being killed in various ways, torture."

Henri became quite agitated. I was sorry I had brought up the subject.

"Madame Tallulah's family worked in the sugarcane fields. They were forced to wear tin muzzles on their faces to prevent them from eating any of the sugarcane. Napoleon's brother-in-law, General Leclerc, was sent to put down a slave rebellion. At first, rebellious slaves were filled with gunpowder and blown to bits or slowly roasted over fires. Very messy. Later, Napoleon ordered all slaves over the age of twelve to be killed. Various methods were used. Sometimes they would pull the heads off of slaves or chain them with weights and throw them into the sea, but these methods were too slow. One of Napoleon's scientific advisors recommended sealing slaves in cargo ships and using sulfur from the volcanoes to poison them. Ships were crammed with hundreds of slaves. Then sulfur was burned and thrown into the holds of the ship, producing poisonous sulfur dioxide gas. Once the gas cleared, the bodies were thrown overboard into the sea. Thousands and thousands of slaves were killed in this fashion. They were the fortunate ones. Madame Tallulah was forced to watch her husband and children ripped to pieces by dogs. Let her tell you about torture, Robert. I was Napoleon's friend, I survived."

Henri turned his gaze back towards the distance. We both remained silent for a very long time before Henri spoke again.

"That is why I like it here, Robert. They don't torture their slaves. And after all, we are all slaves of one form or another. Are we not?"

Tears began to pool in Henri's eyes. I felt bad for stirring up old memories. Thankfully, Little Daphne came out to announce that dinner was ready. Henri snapped back to the present; his mood brightened considerably.

I made a silent vow to never again bring up the past with Henri.

CHAPTER 55

After dinner, Henri asked if I would like to take a ride on his antigravity machine, as he referred to his amazing device.

"Of course," I replied. And then, much to my disappointment, he told Coachman Isaac to fly me around the plantation after dropping him off at his laboratory.

Henri added more to my discomfort by telling Isaac, "Make sure to drop in on Madame Tallulah. Robert wants to know about torture."

Coachman Isaac gave me a wide toothy grin as he hopped on Henri's amazing device; the two of them flew over to the laboratory at Wambaw. Isaac returned shortly thereafter.

I felt I had not made a very good impression on Henri and said as much to Coachman Isaac before getting onboard. I fastened my safety strap to a ring on the pole and sat on the small but comfortable seat attached opposite Isaac's. With Coachman Isaac at the controls, the machine slowly rose up into the air, stopping several hundred feet above the ground. I noticed that at this height the machine was much quieter: producing only a low humming sound that seemed to vibrate slightly throughout my body.

Coachman Isaac took his hands off the controls, leaned back and crossed his arms. As I looked down at the vast rice fields, I could make out Wambaw Creek, the lower Santee River, and its tributaries. Crisscrossing the great fields were an intricate network of earthen levees with its system of floodgates, dikes, and ditches. The slaves working the fields looked like a swarm of ants crawling slowly around an ant hill. Coachman Isaac said he liked to sit back at this height and look out over the fields. He pointed out the various fields of green rice, noting how by shade of color he could determine which fields needed more water. From this height he could quickly decide when and which floodgates to open.

Isaac rose higher. The air got colder. He pointed out Harriott and Old Sandy on top of a dike. From this great height they looked alike. Coachman Isaac pointed out the pale yellow of Harriott's bonnet, barely discernible.

How incredibly peaceful and serene the world looked from on high.

And then I was brought back to reality when I again remarked that Henri, I feared, did not think very highly of me.

"You have to understand Henri," Coachman Isaac remarked. "He is a child of the French Revolution. He has told me stories of the early days when everyone was caught up in the fervor of freedom and equality. He just wants everyone to come around to his view of the world. And he is usually quite successful at that. His only failure has been Napoleon."

"I too believe in equality and freedom, Coachman Isaac," I replied earnestly.

"Really? Then why do you call me Coachman Isaac? Do I call you Newspaper Robert?"

"I don't understand," I replied exasperated. "That is your name, isn't it?"

"The name given to me by Miss Harriott to designate that I am a special slave with important duties."

Isaac must have noticed the look of shock on my face.

"Don't get me wrong, Robert. I would much rather be Coachman Isaac than Isaac working in the rice fields, knee deep in mud, fighting off the hot sun, snakes, and insects all day long. And Miss Harriott, from what I have been able to gather, is a most enlightened mistress in comparison to others. But at the end of the day, I am still somebody's slave. Hardly equal in yours or any other white man's eyes."

"What about Henri? Does he treat you equally?"

"He comes close." And then with a big grin he added, "Little Daphne and I think he must have some Negro blood in him somewhere."

"Isaac, this is all very unsettling for me, I apologize if I have aggrieved you in any way. What you told me... the way you speak... and... act, I mean,"—I was stumbling around for words to say—"this is all so new to me."

Then, Isaac—which I was determined to call him from now on—did and said a most comforting thing to put me at ease. Placing his hands on my knees, he gave me the most genuine smile and said sweetly, "Don't worry Robert, there is still hope for you yet."

And then he gave me a wink.

"Isaac, is there any chance that, like Henri, I might have just a little bitty amount of—" Before I could finish, Isaac cut me off.

"Not a chance," Isaac replied. We both broke out laughing. "Come on Robert, let's fly around a spell."

For the next twenty minutes we flew around Harriott's vast holdings. Isaac pointed out the plantations of Harriott's sons, and her brother Charles: Wambaw, Harrietta, and the old Belmont Plantation that had been a favorite of Harriott's mother. A few of the slaves working the fields would stop their work, look up, and wave to us, but for the most part they ignored us. Isaac remarked that they had become used to the machine.

As we reached the edge of Wambaw Plantation, Isaac noticed some water seeping into one of the fields. We set the machine down on top of an earthen levee and inspected a rotted floodgate that appeared to be the culprit. Then we flew over to Harriott and Old Sandy to inform them of the floodgate. Harriott inquired as to my wellbeing and remarked that she herself often flew the machine to inspect her holdings. This would have greatly surprised me only a week previous, but after the past two days I now doubted anything could surprise me.

Isaac resumed hovering, high over the rice fields. Suddenly, and without warning, we veered off sideways across one of the tributaries to the Lower Santee River and flew over one of the many cypress swamps dotting the landscape. I asked Isaac where we were going. He just smiled. Soon we were hovering over a small finger of land, almost completely surrounded by water. I could barely make out a cabin, hidden by plants trailing down the roof, climbing up the sides. An old sturdy Negro woman (who I correctly guessed was Madame Tallulah) presently appeared with her hands on her hips, holding a whisk broom made of slender branches, a serious look upon her face.

"Sit dat ting down befoe you wakes de dead," Madame Tallulah said. "Dis old woman cain't gets no sleep wits you buzzin all around."

Isaac set the machine down. We walked over to Madame Tallulah; she gave me what I can only call, an evil eye.

"You must be Mistah Robert," she declared with a Caribbean accent.

"How did you know my name?" I said. Genuinely surprised at this strange woman who seemed to be able to look deep into my soul.

"I looked into a boiling pot of bones and summoned up de spirits of de dead, dats how I knowsed."

Isaac looked at Madame Tallulah, then at me.

"I flew up here yesterday and told her all about you."

Madame Tallulah rushed at Isaac and swatted him with her whisk broom, saying, "Boy, I beats you foe tellin my secrets." Then smiling, she gave Isaac a hug and said, "Well come on in. Let's git aways from dees skitos."

Inside, we sat around a raised fire pit where a pot of herbs boiled, giving off a sweet smell that kept the insects away. Smoke from the fire streamed up through a center hole in the roof. A slight breeze coming in through slots located around the bottom of the cabin—drawn in by the rising heat—made the inside remarkably comfortable.

Isaac spoke very directly to Madame Tallulah.

"Robert is interested in your story of torture."

"Not really," I protested.

"Henri, dat po tomented soul cain't git nuff," Madame Tallulah said, shaking her head sadly.

"What do you mean, Madame Tallulah?" I had no clue as to where this conversation was leading.

"He is a po beautiful fool Mistah Robert. Tinks he sponsible foe de sins of de whole world. He come ta me foe tonement of his sins."

Tallulah got up and took a long tapered switch off the wall.

"I beats him wit dis once a week."

"Why?" is all I could manage to stutter, not understanding.

"I tole him my stury and shows him my back."

Tallulah turned around and pulled up her blouse, revealing horrible raised scars that crisscrossed every inch of her back. She lowered her blouse and turned to face us.

"I tells him dat dis is what his French friends did. I'm jes glad I didn't show him my front side or Ize afraid he woulda made me beat him teh death. Anyway, dats all in de pass. I tells Henri teh gets over it, but he says it makes him feel better teh be beat."

After quite an uncomfortable spell of silence, I spoke, very stupidly: "Other than that, how is life treating you, Madame Tallulah?"

Madame Tallulah stared at me stonily for a few seconds and then busted out laughing; Isaac and I joined in.

"Isaac, where dits yoose gits dis fellow?"

"He is Henri's biographer," Isaac replied.

"Oh lawd, he a mess."

Madame Tallulah continued laughing.

"Who? Me?" I asked smiling.

"Henri . . . And yoose too."

* * *

We flew back to Hampton with Madame Tallulah's cackling laughter drifting through the swamp. I was beginning to feel less and less like an outsider. The more I learned of Henri and the slaves of Hampton, the more amazed I was at the resilient nature of the human spirit . . . and of course, its cruelty.

CHAPTER 56

The remainder of the week was spent avoiding any talk of Henri's past. Instead, I focused on his future plans, which he was most eager to share.

The day that Chief John Ross returned from his scouting of Charleston—which I still did not quite understand the necessity thereof—Henri showed me his laboratory. I was quite surprised to see several Negroes working there. Henri introduced me to Stephen the Blacksmith: working on something Stephen called a magnetic flux rotator. Henri explained that it was an essential part of the planetary electromagnetic discs that comprised the base of his machine. Stephen showed me a series of gears that comprised the rotator, allowing the discs to tilt while moving up and down.

At another station, a slave named Paul—an exceptionally bright fellow that Henri discovered working in the rice fields—was winding very thin, flat copper filaments through various slots in the electromagnetic discs. Henri said these copper filaments, embedded with a silver alloy, conducted electricity far more efficiently than had been previously achieved to date. He was hoping that this advance, along with others, would allow him to build a bigger antigravity machine capable of transporting large groups of people.

At the next station I saw a familiar face: Tailor Will. He had expertly sewn me a pair of trousers the previous evening and was now working on a black disc. Upon closer inspection I noticed that this disc was comprised of what seemed like thousands of tiny holes in which Tailor Will was threading thin iron filaments. I inquired of Tailor Will—as he insisted on being called—the purpose of the black disc, which he referred to as a pulsating magnetic reverberator. Tailor Will replied that as far as he could tell, the only purpose was to make him cross-eyed. Upon hearing this remark, Henri patted Tailor Will on the back and said that perhaps he should take a break.

The remainder of the tour remains a blur in my mind as Henri described various compounds and liquids that comprised his batteries. One piece that stood out however, was a cylindrical sheath called a sliding electrical amplifier that fit over the batteries inside the central pole and slid up and down. At some point, my eyes glazed over; Henri mercifully flew me back to Hampton.

* * *

Shortly after supper, Chief John Ross and several of his Cherokee Indians arrived back from Charleston. After having a bit to eat, he joined Henri, Harriott, and me on the portico. Harriott asked the Chief if he found her residence in Charleston satisfactory. The Chief replied that Harriott's servant, Patty, was a most amenable host and made his stay there most enjoyable. The Chief also thanked Harriott for allowing his fellow Indians to stay there.

Harriott asked the Chief a question that was presently on my mind as well.

"Chief, I still don't understand the necessity of your scouting Charleston. After all, I know it like the back of my hand."

"I am concerned with some of the individuals I observed in Savannah, and then again in Beaufort. In Beaufort, I saw Abel Jenkins, an aide to John Eaton, Andrew Jackson's secretary of war, along with several soldiers."

"But why should that alarm you?" I remember Henri remarking. "After all, I wrote the president of my intention to present him the plans for my antigravity device. I am sure he just wants to guarantee my safety. You know how superstitious some people can be. That crazy preacher in Savannah thought I was the devil and tried to take me into the custody of the Lord, as he put it."

"Henri," the Chief answered. "I would be more assured if the emissary the president sent was anyone but Abel Jenkins. He is a most disagreeable person. If you thought Napoleon was going to use your device to further his own warlike ambitions, what do you think the president will do with it? And why do you think he has sent a representative of his war cabinet here?"

"But my dear Chief, the president does not have anyone to fight," Henri pointed out.

"Excuse me, Henri, but my tribe is in constant peril. The president would dearly love to see us removed from our lands."

"But you are fighting him in the courts. That is what makes this such a great country. Your rule of law is what sets you apart from the rest of the world, Chief."

Henri was most passionate and animated when making this point. He went on for quite awhile until I interrupted, pointing out that the president (although a hero to the young republic) had been brutal in his suppression of Indians during the Creek and Seminole wars. I also reminded Henri, that like Napoleon, Andrew Jackson was not reticent to overstep his authority: taking Florida from Spain when opportunity presented itself.

Henri would not have any of it, declaring, "The president's aide wrote me a letter welcoming me, and he said the president wished me a safe and most satisfactory tour of this republic."

And with that, Henri remarked that he was fatigued and retired for the evening.

Alone with Harriott and the Chief, I remarked that for such an intellectual, Henri could be rather narrow-minded.

The Chief replied, "He does have a remarkable naiveté when it comes to our country. He wants to believe so badly in some idealized democracy. I am afraid it has permanently clouded his judgment."

The Chief confided in Harriott and me that he noticed an alarming increase in the number of soldiers in Charleston, and found out through his sources that Secretary of War, John Eaton planned on attending Henri's exhibition.

"Do you think Henri is in any danger?" I asked.

"I certainly would not discount the possibility. In my scouting, I noticed all the main roads leading into Charleston were manned by soldiers. I did find a few smaller roads that were not manned.

And as of now, we can still safely enter the outskirts of Charleston. I found a secluded spot to park the carriage, from where Henri can fly into the city and return back."

Harriott then remarked, "But Chief, we had a devil of a time getting Henri to agree to a rendezvous spot in Beaufort. I am sure he will want to mingle with the people."

"I have no doubt that if he does that, Eaton's men will take him into custody and seize the machine," the Chief replied.

"But we won't be able to persuade Henri of that, will we?" I said glumly.

"Probably not. But I have devised a plan that will hopefully force him to the rendezvous spot."

The Chief explained his plan to inform Henri of a plot by a religious sect to assassinate him if he were to land amongst the crowd. He would tell Henri to be on the lookout for members of the sect: discernable by their bright red caps.

"I need Tailor Will to make a couple dozen of these right away," he said to Harriott. "I figured a simple cap would be easy for him to make in a hurry."

The Chief went on to say that he would have some of his Cherokees, with mixed blood like himself, dispersed evenly throughout the crowd. He hoped this would induce Henri to fly to the agreed rendezvous point, where we could then safely return to Hampton.

Thinking the plan a bit crazy, I asked the Chief if this was the best he could come up with. Knowing Henri, he replied, the crazier something sounded the more likely he was to believe it. Harriott shook her head, laughed softly and got up, saying she would have Old William instruct Tailor Will to have the red caps ready by midday. Shortly thereafter, the Chief and I retired for the night. Both of us agreed that this tour would end badly if Henri could not be persuaded to curtail it.

CHAPTER 57

The next few days were busily spent in preparation for our trip to Charleston. Henri was putting the finishing touches on an electrical generator that would fit under the horse carriage and allow him to recharge the center pole batteries. Isaac was concerned that the additional drag on the wheels would add an undue burden on the horses. Henri assured him that the drag would be minimal, but Isaac was not convinced: pointing out that Betsy, the old mare, had been laboring on their last trip.

Meanwhile, the Chief and I talked to Harriott's carpenter, Old Moses, about our fears that the carriage might be stopped. If discovered, the antigravity machine along with Henri would most certainly be seized. Old Moses listened intently to our concerns and said he would see what he could do on such short notice.

Two days later Old Moses asked us to inspect the carriage. We looked over the gleaming, freshly painted carriage from stem to stern. After several minutes, the Chief looked quite exasperated. He addressed Old Moses; the irritation dripping from his words was palpable: "Old Moses, I asked you to fashion a secret compartment for the disassembled antigravity machine, not just paint the carriage."

Instead of being chastened by the Chief's remarks, Old Moses seemed unperturbed. "But it sure is a pretty color now, isn't it,

Mistah Chief?" he said with casually crossed arms. As Old Moses admired his work a broad smile crossed his face.

The Chief threw up his hands, smiled back and said, "Alright, where did you put it?"

"Ain't you sposed to be the Indian that can snoops all around and sniff out a trail?" Old Moses said tauntingly, creeping around the carriage low to the ground as if looking for whatever it was he imagined Indians looked for. "Or maybe all that white blood you got, diluted your snooping skills and made you stupid. No offense meant, Mistah Robert."

Old Moses began to laugh. I soon found myself laughing along with him as the Chief now began a more thorough inspection: climbing on top of the carriage, rapping his knuckles against the wooden sides, peering closely at all the joints.

How strange, I thought, as we watched the Chief scramble over the carriage: a month earlier on a different plantation, the insult that Old Moses had made in a lighthearted manner would have resulted in a most severe whipping—which I myself would have seen as perfectly natural. And now? Such a small amount of time and distance effected such a change on my nature. I now found it perfectly natural to be laughing alongside this slave, as we watched the Chief climb into the carriage.

Sitting, looking straight ahead with his black hat and lone Eagle feather sticking up out of the brim, the Chief fumed.

Smiling from ear to ear, Old Moses, with me trailing behind, walked over to the window of the carriage and peered in at the Chief.

"What's a matter Mistah Chief, you stumped?"

The Chief looked around the interior. A few moments later, in resignation, he turned and opened the carriage door. As he got up and began to step out, he said; "I give—" and then the eagle feather of his hat brushed the cloth ceiling of the carriage. The Chief's sullen demeanor changed into a broad smile. He pointed and shouted, "Up!"

The Chief stepped from the carriage onto the ground and began to dance around Old Moses and me.

"Tell me," he said, "do you like my Indian victory dance?"

"I've seen better. If it wasn't for that damn eagle feather, you would have never found it," Moses replied, still smiling. "That's some strong medicine you got there, Chief."

Old Moses climbed onto the carriage and showed us how he had raised the height of the carriage several inches, along with lowering the ceiling inside the passenger compartment. To disguise the raised height, Old Moses had lowered the rails running around the top edge of the carriage that held the luggage. Brightly colored straps for securing the luggage were used to draw attention away from the lowered rails, he explained.

The Chief remarked that he was indeed drawn to the straps when he went on top.

"You know, Old Moses, you would make a pretty good Indian."

To which, in turn, Old Moses replied; "And you would make a pretty good slave. Of course we would need to work on your dancing."

* * *

With more than a touch of trepidation, we set out for our three-day journey to Charleston. I sat inside next to the Chief. Opposite us, sat Little Daphne and Harriott. Henri, as was his usual want, sat on top next to Isaac. The Chief had sent out several scouts a day earlier to warn us of any new military checkpoints that may have recently sprung up along our route. Isaac had been thoroughly briefed on our circuitous travel plans and assured the Chief that he would have no trouble handling Henri's inquiries when we deviated from our normal route.

Around noon we came to a clearing. Waiting to greet us was one of the Chief's advance scouts with a prepared meal of wild turkey, snap beans, and collards. Making the mistake of complimenting the chef for a delicious meal, I was promptly informed by Little Daphne that the turkey was undercooked, and the collards not seasoned properly. She did concede, however, that the snap beans were delicious—not wanting to insult her host, whom the Chief informed us, was his personal chef. After dinner, Henri insisted on taking his machine out for a tour of the countryside. With Isaac aboard, they flew off into the sky above, returning some thirty minutes later. I expressed concern that Henri might be spotted by federal soldiers. The Chief allayed those fears by pointing out that we were too far from Charleston, but did concede that this could be a problem two days hence.

The remainder of the day was spent wending our way through pine forests and skirting around the edges of the great swamps, shaded by towering, bald, cypress trees. Twice we had to disembark and remove luggage to lighten our load as Isaac struggled to get the carriage through paths that had recently flooded. As usual, Isaac was able to navigate in light too low for the rest of us to see; and with darkness reining us in from all sides, he found our first night's encampment among the pine trees. While Isaac tended to the horses, Little Daphne—much to the irritation of the Chief's chef—helped with the cooking. Harriott and I set about making presentable the small cabin: constructed years earlier by Harriott's father, for their frequent trips to Charleston.

Over a light supper, we listened to Henri's plans for the future. He described a world filled with machines that transformed the landscape, preventing the need for slaves to harvest rice. And great machines of the sky that would transport goods over land and sea to faraway places.

As brilliant as Henri was, I began to feel a certain sadness, knowing he was too far ahead of his time. His path to the future would undoubtedly be fraught with danger. I did not know at the time how right I would be as I sat and listened, enthralled by Henri's vision.

That night I dreamt of Henri's great machines: crawling over the landscape, harvesting crops, constructing houses, flying overhead, bringing food and manufactured goods to the far flung reaches of the globe. Then my dream dissolved into a fitful sleep as these machines, made by man, began to turn on man. I saw great cannons in the sky raining down fiery terror: cities and villages on fire, screaming inhabitants running from their homes.

CHAPTER 58

I awoke to the shadow of a man looming over me. The first rays of sunlight were beginning to break through the dawn. The shadow bent over and took form. Chief John Ross quietly asked that I accompany him to the Santee River and perform the Cherokee going to water ritual: a great honor. We stood along the river's edge and cleansed our bodies: reconnecting our spirits to the air, earth, and water. I listened as the Chief sang the sacred morning song, following along as he brought water six times to the crown of his head and a seventh time to his heart. At the conclusion of the ritual we plunged into the depths of the Santee. We broke the surface and swam to a large limb of a tree, hanging low over the water. Wrapping an arm around a branch just beneath the surface, the Chief, still in a spiritual mood, engaged me in conversation.

"Do white men ever stop and think about the world they are creating? All these technological advances and wonderful machines . . . where does it ultimately lead?"

"In the case of Henri's machine," I replied, "it will lead to faster transportation of people and goods. More efficiency. Someday there will be no more need of slaves or slavery."

The Chief shook his head sadly and looked into my eyes.

"And what will become of your slaves when you no longer need them to work in your fields? Will you drive them from their homes and force them like pigs and cattle into smaller and smaller pens? Lock them away from *civilized* whites, like Jackson is attempting to do with my people? Where does this new world you are creating lead to . . . as a people, Robert? Where does it end?"

As he said this, I thought of the dream I had: machines belching fire, raining terror down from the sky. Men, women and children running in panic. I had no answer for my friend.

The Chief paused: his attention momentarily diverted by a Praying Mantis struggling to reach land, caught in the swirling current of the Santee. As it floated by, he scooped the creature up and placed it on a branch, and then turned his attention back to me.

"The Cherokee believe that in the beginning, all things lived in harmony. Plants and animals communicated with each other. Humans came along much later; and we too lived in harmony. Like your Garden of Eden. In those days all things had a common language. We talked to the bear, the birds of the sky, even the rocks of the earth. All things respected and understood each other, taking only what was needed to survive. But for some reason, man began to change."

The fruit of forbidden knowledge, I thought, as I listened to the Chief.

"We forgot that we are part of the Great Life. We placed ourselves above everything. We began to disrespect other living things, taking more than we needed, upsetting the delicate balance . . . losing the ability to communicate with nature.

"In our legends, the animal nations held a council and declared war on humans. One of the warrior bears picked up a bow and arrow, but because of his long claws he could not fire it with any accuracy. He and other bears offered to cut off their claws so they could make better use of the bow, and kill more humans. The warrior chief of the bears stood up and said, *No!* They would not become like humans. The Great Life provided them all they needed to survive. The council was disbanded; the animals agreed to shun man.

"We did not fare as well with the insects: they rebelled and brought disease. They asked the plants of the world to join them, but plants, being more patient, declined, saying that though humans were young and foolish, there was still hope for them. The plants provided us with cures for all the diseases insects brought."

"And now our scientists are experimenting with plants to create better crops," I said. "Where do you think that will lead?"

"We'll screw it up like we do everything else," the Chief sadly replied. "Eventually the plants will stop providing cures for our diseases. Unless there is a foundation of respect, of reverence for the earth and everything that lies above and below, there is ultimately no hope for man."

"So why do you want to help Henri?"

"If I can keep his device out of the president's hands, perhaps I can keep my people alive for another generation or two. That is all I can hope for. Besides, he is my friend. He believes in cultivating the goodness that lies within man as a means to subjugate the hate and fear that also resides there."

The Chief and I looked off into the faint mist that rose off the water's surface, lost in thought: his (I imagined) was of a past where the world of the Cherokee once again was in balance with nature; mine was of an uncertain future surrounding Henri's invention.

Our thirst for knowledge: Where would it lead us? Would we become Gods? Or would we destroy ourselves in the process?

The Chief snapped me back to the present.

"Today we must try to impress upon Henri our story."

"You are referring to your red-capped assassins?" I replied hesitantly, having not been previously convinced of the Chief's plans.

"Yes. I will have thirty braves of mixed blood stationed at various spots in the town center, wearing the red caps and scarves that Tailor Will made. We need to convince Henri of the grave danger posed by these fanatics."

"And why do these fake fanatics want to assassinate Henri? We should at least get that part of our story together," I said.

We paused for a moment to watch a pair of wood ducks flying low overhead before the Chief returned to the matter at hand.

"What if we tell Henri that this religious sect is a radical offshoot of the Puritans that conducted the witchcraft trials in Massachusetts? So radical, that they were forced to leave and settle in South Carolina. They heard of Henri's machine and believe it to be an abomination. The work of the devil. A witch's broomstick."

"Chief, that was all refuted in the 1700s. You don't really expect Henri to buy any of that nonsense," I said dismissively.

We tried for awhile to come up with some other convincing story, but after much fruitless search could only settle on the Chief's original plan. Before returning to the rest of our party, I asked the Chief the name of this phantom religious sect. The Chief replied without hesitation. "The Brothers of the Supreme Righteousness."

I was immediately paralyzed with fits of laughter. When I had sufficiently recovered, I replied that maybe we should just shorten the name and call the group the Supremes. The Chief thought for a moment before replying that either or both names were amenable to him.

* * *

All morning, Henri sat on top next to Isaac. The Chief fumed inside the carriage. At lunch, Henri ate very little. When the Chief and I brought up the subject of the Brothers of the Supreme Righteousness, Henri immediately turned to Isaac and said they needed to do some work on the generator. As Henri and Isaac worked beneath the carriage, the Chief vainly tried to engage Henri.

During the afternoon portion of our journey, Henri again sat on top beside Isaac. The Chief persisted in his disagreeable mood. Harriott and Little Daphne, sitting opposite us, furtively exchanged worried glances with me concerning the Chief, to which I could only shrug.

The second day of our journey came to a close. We set up tents before sitting down to supper. The Chief failed once again to steer the conversation towards the dangers posed in Charleston. Henri, with Little Daphne at his side, complained of an upset stomach and reproached the Chief for his Chef's inability to properly cook a decent stew. Abruptly repairing to his tent, Henri's foul mood infected us all. Following his lead, we soon retired for the evening.

* * *

Judging from the position of the moon, it must have been close to one in the morning when I awoke to a rustling noise. Leaving the comfort of my tent, I found Isaac dragging the antigravity machine through the moonlight. When I approached, he smiled that wide toothy grin of his and asked me to grab an end of the machine.

We walked a few hundred yards along a path next to the Santee River before he stopped and said, "This should be far enough away not to wake them." He stepped onto the base, and with that most engaging smile of his, said, "Well? Are you coming along?"

We rose straight up into the air; the loud humming noise of the machine dissipating the higher we rose. When we were a few hundred feet up, Isaac stopped our ascent and looked down at the winding river. He explained that he needed to find a few landmarks before setting off. Once assured he could find his way back to our starting point, Isaac took off over the landscape. We flew in a zigzag fashion for about twenty minutes before returning to the Santee River, where we slowly rose several thousand feet into the heavens and hovered in place: suspended equally between the earth and the stars. I noticed the temperature had cooled quite a bit and remarked on this to Isaac.

He leaned back, took his hands off the controls and wrapped them around his body in a now familiar pose.

"One time, I rose so high I actually passed out," he said. His eyes fixated on the heavens. "The air gets thinner and thinner the higher up you go. Luckily for me, the machine was just about out of energy and slowly descended to the ground, or else I would have surely died."

I looked out at the panorama of stars spreading in every direction to the horizon as Isaac pointed out various planets and constellations.

"I wanted to see if I could make it to that bright star over there," he said, pointing to a star directly overhead. "Henri told me about Venus and the other planets. He said there might be people out there just like us. I wanted to see if I could make it. I flew up and up until I passed out, from either the cold or lack of air."

In the moonlight, I noticed tears streaming down Isaac's face. His head slumped to his chest.

"I just wanted to feel free for once. But maybe freedom is just as cold down there as it is up here. I don't know . . . guess I never will. Always be someone's property, I suspect. Someone's Negro."

Wiping away tears with his shirtsleeve, Isaac's wide smile returned.

"I am sorry, Mister Campbell."

"No need to apologize," I said. "And Isaac, you can call me Robert. At least up here, you and I are equals . . . and down there, well, there is always hope for freedom . . . some day. I must confess you live on a most unusual plantation, one unlike any I have ever been witness to. That must be a small comfort."

"Ironically, it just seems to make my condition harder to accept."

I didn't know how to respond. We looked out at the majesty that lay spread all around us.

After a minute or two, Isaac spoke softly: "Robert? Do you mind if I ask you a personal question, seeing as how we are all equals up here?"

"No, Isaac, not at all. What is it?" I replied.

"Well, I couldn't help but notice that you and the Chief seem to be conspiring a lot. I know you are worried about Henri's machine being seized, but there is more to it than that. Isn't there?"

"Isaac," I said in a most direct manner, "I am worried for Henri's safety. The Chief noticed some men in Savannah and in Beaufort that he recognized from Washington."

"And these men... you think they mean to cause Henri harm?"

"The Chief believes so. So do I. They are from the war department. And even though we have tried our best to convince Henri that President Jackson is no friend, he seems unwilling or unable to accept that fact."

"So what do you and the Chief plan to do about it? We cannot let Henri be captured by those men. No offense, Robert, but those government men are the worst kind of white men. Look at what they are doing to the Chief's people."

"I know."

And then I told Isaac about our plans.

He laughed when I told him about the red caps and scarves. He had watched Tailor Will make them and asked him what they were for. Will had replied that it was a secret.

"How did you come up with a crazy name like the Brothers of the Supreme Righteousness?" Isaac chuckled.

"That was the Chief's idea," I replied. "Anyway, the Chief has been unable to get Henri alone, or get him to listen to any of this talk about the group's plan to murder him. But I was thinking that since Henri spends all his time sitting on top of the carriage next to you, maybe you could persuade him of the danger this group poses."

"A group that does not exist," Isaac said, shaking his head. "You sure do not make it easy, do you?"

"I know, sounds ridiculous. But that is all we could come up with," I said in agreement. "So what do you think? Can you make it work?"

"I will do my best, Robert. Henri's our friend. But you and the Chief could have come up with something better."

I shrugged.

Isaac pointed out a few more stars before returning us to earth and reality.

CHAPTER 59

The final day of our journey to Charleston found the Chief and me straining to hear every word of conversation between Isaac and Henri, sitting directly above us. Having reversed our seating arrangement of the previous day, I explained to Harriott and Little Daphne that the Chief and I needed to keep a lookout in case the carriage was being followed. Sitting with our heads leaning back as Little Daphne and Harriott prattled on about the running of Harriott's Charleston residence, the Chief and I listened to Isaac and Henri talk of modifications to the antigravity machine.

Henri was especially interested in a modification allowing two antigravity machines to be connected by a long, scythe like object, to reap rice more efficiently than could be done by hand, thus allowing a second crop of rice to be grown and brought to market. This, Henri explained, would also drastically reduce the burden of field slaves. Isaac pointed out that the machine tended to flatten the rice wherever it went, and offered up an alternative idea. He suggested that Henri make a machine capable of a much larger base. Henri remarked excitedly that he had done this very modification for Napoleon. Isaac's most ingenious idea was to suspend slaves from chains or ropes, attached to the underside of the base. The slaves, suspended and sitting comfortably in slings, could reap the rice as usual, by hand, but without the constant bending or standing, knee deep in snake infested muddy water. Baskets suspended from the base could be used to gather the rice as it was cut. Henri thought this interesting, and remarked that the base would provide shade for the slaves as they worked. After much discussion, this idea was discarded, for reasons I now do not remember.

Henri suggested they attach a long wire to the base, and spin the machine in a circular fashion to cut the rice using centrifugal force. Isaac pointed out that this would send rice flying everywhere, but said the idea had merit for clearing fields of weeds.

All morning and into the afternoon their conversation veered from one idea to another, without mention of the potential dangers Henri faced at the band of the fictional Brothers of the Supreme Righteousness. Finally, the subject was broached as we reached the outskirts of Charleston. Turning off the main road onto an overgrown path that could barely be made out, Isaac knew what Henri did not: the road held a checkpoint of soldiers. Alarmed, Henri asked Isaac why he had turned off the main road.

"I want to avoid some people up ahead. Gave me a little trouble last time I came into Charleston," Isaac said softly, as if the matter were inconsequential. "This road will be just fine, Henri." Isaac smiled at Henri. "Yes sir, just fine."

"What people, Isaac?" Henri asked with a degree of worry.

"Just some people that might like to do me harm. It is no concern of yours, Henri."

"Tell me, Isaac. Who are these people? I must know," Henri implored.

"Well, alright, but it is no big deal. Just a small group of religious fanatics that hate us Negroes, along with pretty much everyone and everything else. They call themselves the Righteous Brothers or the Supremes, something like that. You don't need to pay them no heed."

"The Brothers of the Supreme Righteousness. The Chief mentioned them to me."

"That's them," Isaac excitedly remarked. "They wear these red scarves and soft red caps. Like to cut themselves and drink each other's blood. Renewing themselves in the blood of Jesus they call it. One of those red-capped bastards nearly dragged me off the carriage last time I came to Charleston. Said he was going to cut me and drink my blood. Right down the main road, a half mile from where we turned off. Matter of fact, I was able to pull off his cap. Got me it right here under our seat."

Inside, the Chief looked at me. I just shrugged, not knowing how Isaac had obtained a cap.

Isaac handed the cap to Henri. "This is what those bastards wear."

Henri examined the soft red cap and remarked, "This looks very similar to the cap that symbolizes the French revolution. We call it the liberty cap." Henri put the cap on top of his head and turned to Isaac. "How do I look?"

"Take that abomination off, Henri! It makes me dog-mad to see anyone wear that," Isaac said, his voice rising. Later, he told me that he shook violently for added effect.

"I am sorry, Isaac. I did not know the vileness in which this cap is held here. In France its meaning is much different. Did I ever tell you the story of how I saved King Louis XVI of France from one of these red caps?"

"No, Henri, you never have."

"It's true. A group very much like your Brothers of the Supreme Righteousness offered King Louis the XVI a red liberty cap, placed on the end of a sharpened pole. They planned to run the king through with the pole after he reached for the cap. I saved him Isaac . . . it's true!" Henri spoke excitedly, hoping to calm Isaac down.

"Did the king reward you?"

"No. He never even knew. No one did. Only me and Napoleon."

Within the hour we arrived at Harriott's Charleston residence. After settling in, the Chief and I found Isaac out back, rubbing down old Betsy. After complimenting him on a job well done, Isaac again took the occasion to state that this was the craziest plan he had ever heard. The Chief, not taking too kindly to the remark, listened intently nonetheless, as Isaac suggested a plan that could be employed as a last resort—one involving sharpened poles and red caps.

CHAPTER 60

A beautiful sunlit day greeted us on the day of the exhibition. Harriott, along with Little Daphne and her Charleston house slave, Patty, prepared a large breakfast for us all. Most surprising to me, Isaac was allowed to sit at the table while Harriott and her girls served us. I remembered Isaac's remark made the previous night while we were suspended between heaven and earth: how the relatively benign treatment at Hampton Plantation made his condition harder to accept. Now, looking at him talking and joking in the same high spirits as the rest of us, I thought I detected a slight sadness to his countenance. Maybe it was my imagination; but in any event, I felt a bit embarrassed when Isaac noticed me staring at him.

"Is something wrong, Robert?" he asked.

"No, I was just thinking of how beautiful the stars were the other evening."

"Reminds me of how insignificant we all are," Isaac replied.

"Exactly," Henri joined in, looking resplendent in a green morning coat with red velvet trim. "Did you know that bones from great lizards were discovered in England a few years ago? There are bones of all sorts of animals that are now extinct. Some day, people or beings from another planet will come here and find our bones."

"And what they will say about us?" I wondered aloud.

Little Daphne placed some fresh milk on the table and interjected: "Probably say we died from not eating enough, because we were always talking."

She gave Henri a hard stare. Surprisingly, he looked away and began eating. I noticed Little Daphne smiling to herself as she walked back into the kitchen.

After breakfast, we made our way to the carriage that Isaac had brought around to the front of the residence. Henri did not protest, as was his usual want, at proceeding to the Chief's rendezvous point. Before we were able to get under way however, two soldiers on horseback rode over to us. Henri, looking like the gentleman of the carriage in his green morning coat, was about to board when they asked where he resided. Not wishing to speak with his French accent, Henri made a sweeping gesture with his hand at Harriott's large residence, shook his head dismissively, and hopped on board.

Harriott, seated inside next to Little Daphne, leaned her head out the window and asked the soldiers to state their business. They replied that they were providing security for the exhibition of the Floating Man from France.

"Do we look like a bunch of ruffians?" Harriott sneered.

"No Madam," one of the soldiers replied, "we are only following orders."

The other soldier looked over the carriage from front to back as Harriott engaged his partner.

"It's called a carriage," Harriott said, without losing her sneer. "First time you gentlemen ever see one?"

The soldier continued to look, ignoring Harriott's remark, and once satisfied, waved us on our way.

The Chief turned to Henri.

"So Henri, what do you think they were looking for? . . . Your machine, perhaps?"

Henri, his mood deteriorating slightly, replied, "Your point is well taken Chief. Perhaps I have been a bit foolish in regards to my safety. And in that respect, I may have endangered you all."

We proceeded to the rendezvous point; the Chief's braves had several horses waiting for us. The Chief talked inaudibly for a few moments with Isaac and Henri before mounting his horse and riding along with the rest of us towards the town square. Henri stayed behind with Isaac, giving us sufficient time to arrive at the square.

If all went well, we would reunite later.

If, all went well.

Upon our arrival at the square we noticed a large number of people already assembled. Harriott remarked that there must be close to three thousand. I turned to the Chief and relayed my fears that thirty braves in caps and scarves seemed insufficient to arouse Henri's concern. Riding around the perimeter, we were only able to spot two of the Chief's braves in the crowd. More noticeable and more ominous, was the large number of soldiers dispersed throughout the square. A large knot gathered at the east end. We rode over and tied up our horses a considerable distance away, so as not to draw attention. The Chief pointed out Secretary of War, John Eaton's aide, Abel Jenkins, to me and Harriott. At that same instant, the secretary himself appeared at Abel Jenkins' side. Harriott made an attempt to get close to the secretary and eavesdrop, but was prevented from getting nearer than ten feet by the large number of soldiers present.

Soon, a low humming noise drifted over the large crowd. Everyone became instantly silent. Heads craned every which way to try and discern Henri's approach. The humming grew in volume and pitch. Out of the blue, Henri appeared, no more than twenty feet above the center of the crowd, having descended straight down from a great height. The startled crowd gasped in unison. Henri then did something with the machine I had never witnessed before: He tilted the machine on its edge, parallel to the ground, and staring at us from a prone position, turned in ever widening circles; the top of his central pole pointed at the center of the square. Then with a start, he shot off, straight down Market Street.

I looked over at the secretary of war and his aide, Abel Jenkins, directing the soldiers present. They began to quickly make their way to the center of the square. The Chief seemed to recognize immediately what was happening and took off running. I remained bewildered by it all, not comprehending. The Chief literally jumped on his horse and raced around the edge of the square. The government soldiers, with equal speed, raced towards the center.

I now began to realize what was happening. The soldiers cleared a large diameter of space in the center of the square. No sooner had they accomplished this task then Henri reappeared above the square and began to descend; the crowd cheered wildly. Henri basked in their adulation, drawing to within thirty feet of the ground, hovering, not aware of what awaited him. Racing to the center of the square, I knocked several people over in an effort to get there in time to warn Henri. My task was made harder by many in the crowd retreating from the center: frightened by the noise and concussive force produced by Henri's machine. I was within thirty feet, with a clear view of the soldiers ringing the center. Several had ropes with grap'ling irons in their hands. This did not bode well for Henri.

As Henri descended to twenty feet, I looked back and saw the Chief raise a long pole with a red cap on it. At that instant, I turned my attention back to the center and witnessed two braves break the ring of soldiers... just enough, to see... Little Daphne racing through the gap, stopping directly underneath Henri's machine. Henri looked down with a look of surprise. There beneath him stood Little Daphne with one of Tailor Will's red scarves in her outstretched hands, spread like a banner. Henri shot up in the air, disappearing in an instant. The crowd made a mad rush back to the center, dispersing the soldiers and allowing Little Daphne to escape to the perimeter, where Harriott, the Chief, and I awaited.

On the ride back to the rendezvous point, Little Daphne showed me the red scarf. Two words—FLY AWAY—were stitched in white lettering. Later, I congratulated Isaac on his superb improvisation. He looked at me dumbfounded. Little Daphne had planned it all on her own.

After meeting up, our original plan was to return to Harriott's residence in Charleston, but our cover was now blown, thanks to Henri's striking green morning coat with red velvet trim. He would most surely, by now, be identified as the gentleman boarding the carriage in front of Harriott's residence. After much discussion, it was decided that Henri, along with the Chief's braves would disassemble the machine and leave immediately for Hampton. As Henri and the braves loaded up their horses, the rest of us left for Charleston to face what would undoubtedly be an inquisition.

CHAPTER 61

Arriving in front of Harriott's residence, we were greeted by a phalanx of soldiers stretched completely around the edifice. On the front porch, Patty the housekeeper paced back and forth—a worried look on her face.

Isaac, head bent down between his legs, facing backwards, stared into the carriage through the open slot under his seat.

"Should I continue on? Or do you want to face the music now?"

Harriott replied that now was as good a time as later, and added, "We have nothing to hide Isaac. Let us simply act indignant." And with that, Harriott sprung from the carriage with her small parasol and marched to the front entrance. The rest of us struggled to keep up.

The lady put on a most magnificent performance. Marching up to a young officer that stood immediately in her path, and armed only with her parasol, Harriott firmly struck the officer on his forehead. "Out of the way young man, this is my house. How dare you block a lady." By the time the officer recovered from this indignity, Harriott had already elbowed her way past and marched up the front porch steps, leaving the rest of us to face the wrath of the embarrassed young officer, who now refused us admittance.

Harriott turned to Patty. In a loud voice she said, "Patty, get me my gun. If this soldier refuses to let my guests enter *my* house, by God, I don't care if he is not facing me, I will shoot him in the back where he stands."

As we faced the young officer, we could see what Harriott could not. At the instant Harriott had made her threat, the man's eyes grew big, filling with fear.

I said very quietly, "I think you should let us pass son, I am sure your superiors will understand. It will be easier to explain than having to shoot one of the most prominent ladies of Charleston. And you will have to shoot her, unless of course you want to die here on this most beautiful afternoon."

I could see the young officer thinking. As his eyes darted about, the other soldiers looked to him for instructions. Not wishing to embarrass the young man, I continued on in a firm but soft tone that only he could hear: "She has just been handed her gun. Will you let us pass, son? Or should I step aside so I myself am not struck by the ball passing through your body?"

That last line did the trick. He turned aside, letting us pass up the stairs. I could see, but only in my mind, the look on the young officer's face as his eyes followed us up the empty porch: Harriott having gone inside before I had started my little soliloquy.

As we entered the front room, several soldiers were ago'ing about. I found Harriott in the kitchen with John Eaton and his aide, Abel Jenkins. She was being harassed by Mr. Jenkins as Secretary Eaton looked on a bit uncomfortably. She went over to a cupboard and handed Patty some coffee beans for grinding. All the while, Abel Jenkins was at Harriott's side, peppering her with questions about Henri's whereabouts.

"Just *who* are you again?" Harriott said in a most irritated voice, momentarily stopping.

"I am Abel Jenkins, Madam, chief aide to John Eaton, President Jackson's secretary of war. If you don't sit down *immediately* and submit to my questions, I will have one of my soldiers tie you down," he thundered.

Harriott looked at Mr. Jenkins as if he had taken complete leave of his senses.

"Abel, you are an aide," she said disdainfully. "I sat on George Washington's lap as a young girl. If you proceed in this most disagreeable manner I will have my good friend, President James

Madison, intercede on my behalf with your President Jackson. After which, I will have you tied to a post and whip you myself, until I am thoroughly exhausted. In my entire life I have never whipped one of my slaves, but forgive me Lord, I will take such *extreme* delight in whipping you."

Before Abel Jenkins could respond, Harriott continued: "So Mr. Abel Jenkins, I suggest you sit and make yourself comfortable while Patty and I prepare a pot of coffee and a light supper, after which, we can have a most delightful conversation. Or you can persist in your disagreeable manner of constantly getting underfoot and blustering. It's your choice, Abel. Sit down and relax or get whipped by me at a time to be determined later. Either way, you will get the same answers to your questions."

Just as Abel was about to launch himself at Harriott, he looked over at his boss. John Eaton quickly stepped forward, giving Abel a quick shake of the head.

"Madam, you will have to excuse my aide, he gets a little excited at times."

"Tell him to behave himself," Harriott said with a quick hard glance at Abel. "And if he doesn't, I must *insist* on his being removed. I will not tolerate that kind of behavior in my home. Understood?"

"Yes Madam." Turning to his aide, John Eaton lightly dismissed him: "Abel, go join the soldiers in the front room."

With a defeated look on his face, he walked away silently. Pouring further salt into his open wound, Harriott added, "And have those soldiers removed from my home."

Abel dejectedly looked at his boss, who nodded in assent.

Harriott airily took hold of Secretary Eaton's hand, and in a most soothing and charming voice said, "Now let me introduce you to our guests."

* * *

After a supper of oyster stew, we all repaired to the front room and made ourselves comfortable. Little Daphne brought a tray of drinks made from Harriott's own recipe: rum mixed with pickled peach syrup. Each glass contained a slice of peach. Abel Jenkins' glass, however, did not. Harriott apologized most insincerely that she had run out of peaches. Having been comfortably settled,

Secretary John Eaton began the long expected inquisition on a mild note.

"I rather enjoyed Henri's performance today, didn't you, Harriott? Short though it was."

Harriott responded sweetly. "I thought it delightful. Perhaps Mr. Richaud would have entertained us longer if he had not been so rudely interrupted."

"I do not know what you are referring to, Miss Horry," said the secretary evenly. "The soldiers were only there to clear an area for Mr. Richaud to land . . . and prevent the crowd from harming him."

"Please, call me Harriott. And what about the ropes the soldiers carried?"

"Those were to be used to hold the crowd back, to ensure the safety of Mr. Richaud and his device."

"With *grap'ling* irons attached? You must take this Southern lady for a fool, Mr. Secretary."

Harriott took a sip of her rum, peering at the secretary over the rim of her glass.

The secretary let out some air before responding.

"I assure you, Harriott, those grap'ling irons were only there because the soldiers were from the navy shipyard. They use them to grasp and secure ships, and they were *certainly not* under any orders to try and snare the machine."

"And you expect us to believe such nonsense?"

Harriott drained her glass, popped the peach slice into her mouth and abruptly got up and went into the kitchen.

We sat silently. An awkward air filled the room.

Harriott returned moments later with another glass of peach-spiced rum, complete with another slice of peach. This did not go unnoticed by the secretary's aide; he glowered at Harriott. She in return wrinkled her nose and gave him a sneering smile.

As soon as Harriott was seated, the secretary said imploringly, "Harriott, you completely misread our intentions. As God is my witness, I am under direct orders not to bring any harm to Mr. Richaud and his invention. The president ordered me down here personally, to inform Mr. Richaud that he would be attending his performance in Georgetown. He instructed me to hand Mr. Richaud this letter."

The secretary reached into his breast pocket and pulled out a letter with the presidential wax seal of Andrew Jackson.

"By the way, Harriott, is Mr. Richaud here, so I can present him with this letter?"

"He flew back to France," Harriott said quickly.

She took a sip of her peach rum, staring innocently at the secretary.

Abel Jenkins, sitting on the edge of his seat waiting to pounce, could no longer contain himself.

"This is simply preposterous! It would take him a month to cross the Atlantic."

"Not true, Mr. Jenkins. Henri can cross the Atlantic in under seven hours," Harriott lied.

"Please! This is too much. Mr. Secretary, certainly you do not believe this dribble," Abel Jenkins said scornfully.

The secretary turned to his aide, and more for Harriott's benefit than Mr. Jenkins, said, "What I do or do not believe is irrelevant. We are guests in Miss Horry's home. You shall treat her with requisite respect." Turning to Harriott, the secretary added, "Harriott, please accept my most humble apologies for the behavior of my aide. I do not wish to disturb you or your guests any longer. I also apologize for any inconvenience our visit may have caused. Please, if Mr. Richaud happens to return from . . . France, present him this letter."

And that was it: Secretary John Eaton and his aide, Abel Jenkins, withdrew from the house; the soldiers ringing the house also dispersed. All due to Harriott's most magnificent performance. As they left the porch, Harriott stared daggers at the back of the retreating Abel Jenkins.

"I'll be damned if that *bastard* gets any of my peaches."

And then she roughly slammed the door shut behind them.

CHAPTER 62

Beaufort, South Carolina; Present Day

It was just past two in the morning when James closed the memoirs of Robert Campbell.

"I think this is a good spot to break for the night," James said with a yawn. "Why don't you two stay the night? John will attest to the fact that the guest bedroom is quite comfortable."

"James and I have spent many a hangover here together," John said.

"So you two have slept together? I wouldn't want to make James jealous."

"I'll get over it," James replied. "By the way, I cheated and read ahead a bit. I suggest we visit Hampton Plantation tomorrow, before continuing with the memoirs."

"It *still* exists?" Sheila said with a questioning stare.

"Yep. Stayed in the family until the early 1970s when the last of the Horry Rutledge clan turned it over to the state. It's a state park now, complete with tours. A bit off the beaten path though. Not a lot of people visit, and the insects are pretty bad. Can't imagine what it was like back in the days of the rice plantations."

"Why do we need to go there? What's so urgent?" John asked.

In full-on Casper Gutman mode, complete with bulging eyes,

James leaned over and tapped John's knees.

"Buried treasure my boy."

"Are you telling us they buried the floating machine on the Plantation?" Sheila said, looking intently at James.

Still in character, James patted the book of his forebear.

"It's in the book. These are historical facts, not fiction, not some romanticized history one learns in school."

James sat back with a look of utter contentment and crossed his hands over his rotund belly.

Sheila turned to John.

"Help me out here."

"It's from the Maltese Falcon," John replied. "You'll get used to it."

"The *fatman* character. I definitely need to see the movie."

"It's *Gutman*, my dear," James said softly. "Casper Gutman. But let's get back to the task at hand."

James jumped up and began pacing back and forth.

"We will need to talk to the archivist at Hampton and see if there are any old maps of the slave quarters and carriage house. Old Moses' carpenter shop. And you two might want to talk to Max's FBI friend, Mike Kelley." James stopped pacing and stood over Sheila. "Or your friend Henry Smith . . . see if they can hook us up with some state-of-the-art metal detectors."

"My God, I can't believe this is really happening," Sheila said in disbelief.

"The discovery of the ages," John chimed in.

"The *Black Bird*," James said almost inaudibly, sitting down heavily in his chair.

"What?" Sheila said, not hearing James.

"The Maltese Falcon my dear," John replied. "The stuff that dreams are made of."

CHAPTER 63

The next morning after breakfast, with everyone sitting around James' kitchen table, Sheila made a call to Mike Kelley of the FBI. He answered on the third ring.

"Hi Mike, its Sheila... fine, and you?... Mike, I was wondering if you could help us.... Good, well, we need to get some metal detecting equipment, and we don't have a clue... So you don't either?... Well that'd be great. If you could talk with him and get back to us... you don't have to do that... well, okay, fine. Look forward to meeting you.... No, a couple of days are fine. No rush, just a crazy hunch... we'll tell you all about it when we see you.... Thanks again, Mike, bye."

Turning to John and James, Sheila said, "Mike's going to talk to a colleague who's an expert. He'll get back to us."

"Sounded like he is coming down," James said.

Sheila sensed a bit of irritation in his voice.

"Is there a problem, James?"

"I was kind of hoping we could keep it all in the family. We don't really know this guy."

John tried to reassure his old friend.

"Mike's a source that Max uses. He's also on the list of trusted FBI agents that Henry Smith gave to Sheila. And remember, it was your idea in the first place to call him."

"But I didn't say we should invite anyone down," James protested weakly.

"He sort of invited himself down. What was I supposed to do?" Sheila said, trying to soothe James' ruffled feathers.

"We can't be paranoid of everyone," John added.

"And why not? After all we've been through, especially Sheila, I don't think it is paranoid to trust only ourselves. But it's already been decided," James said, throwing his hands up in a gesture of defeat.

"Why don't we change the subject?" John said, trying to lighten the mood. "If we're going to visit Hampton, we should probably get started. I don't have a clue where it is, do you, James?"

"It's been a few years, but I remember. It'll take about three hours down US 17 the way I drive," he said, still with a sour look on his face.

"So it's only two hours away."

James finally cracked a smile.

"Well, shall the three musketeers be off then?" Sheila said brightly.

"The three blind mice would be more apt," John added—not as brightly.

* * *

Two hours and thirty minutes later, John pulled the Marquis up the drive and parked at the visitor's center for Hampton Plantation in McClellanville. John and Sheila were instantly annoyed by the heat and insects buzzing about. Sheila made the comment that living here would be torture, as she vainly swatted the air, trying to fend the flying creatures off. John stood and nodded, wiping perspiration from his face with his tee shirt.

James, on the other hand—returning from the visitor's center with a map—seemed totally oblivious to the heat and insects. Acting like a hyperactive child, he went running up to a large old oak tree.

"Here it is, John. George Washington's oak tree, just like I told you. In 1791 George Washington was asked whether it should be cut down, as it blocked the view from the portico. And he said no, he rather liked it. And here it is, all these years later. Marvelous."

"Yes, *quite*," Sheila said grimly, swiping at a few more bugs as she followed James up the steps of the portico.

Plopping down in a rocker on the porch, James waved Sheila over to an adjacent rocker. "Sit here, Sheila, you can be Harriott. I'll be Robert. John, I'm sorry, but there are no more chairs. You'll have to play the part of Old William and remain standing."

"Yes, perhaps you can get us some peach-sweetened rum, Old William." Sheila smiled. "Or better yet, come over here and keep the bugs away."

John came over, stood behind her and put his hands around her neck in a mock choking fashion.

James looked out on the surrounding landscape.

"Beautiful, simply beautiful." Looking over at Sheila as she played along with John, pretending to be choking, he continued; "You know dear, if you wouldn't have put on perfume, you might have been spared some of the insects."

Sheila, her eyes bugging out as John continued his pretend choking, raised her hand up with middle finger extended and smiled at James.

"Kids these days," James said while shaking his head, "so disrespecting of their elders." He returned to gazing out over the grounds of Hampton, ignoring the childish antics of his young friends. After a few minutes, James took some cocoa beans out of his pocket, popped them into his mouth and got up.

"Your heart okay, James?" John asked solicitously.

"Fine. Let me show you two around."

James got off the porch and walked to the back of Hampton house.

"Here is where Henri pulled off the creek and up to the back door." Walking a little further away from the back door, he stopped at an open area, devoid of vegetation. "Old Moses' carpenter shop stood here." He walked over to a white clapboard structure and pointed to it. "This is the kitchen house where Little Daphne and Old William worked."

Sheila turned to John, whispering, "How does he know all this?"

"I think he's just making it all up," John whispered back, drawing a snicker from Sheila.

James walked on, pointing out several spots where slave houses once stood. He stopped, knelt down and dug a little with his hands, pulling up some blackened soil.

"Centuries of slaves cooking at a hearth caused this charcoaled soil to be built up."

John and Sheila bent over to take a closer look. They followed James as he continued his tour of the grounds.

"The fields over there would be flooded and hoed four or five times a year, depending on the amount of weeds and the condition of the rice. The freshwater creeks and rivers along here rise and fall with the ocean tides. If you look closely over there,"—James pointed to a far off spot —"you can make out the remains of some old earthen dikes. Wooden gates would be interspersed every hundred yards or so. At high tide the gates would be opened, flooding the fields. You think the insects are bad here, Sheila? Imagine standing knee deep in mud out in those fields. It's estimated that forty percent or more of slave children living on rice plantations died before they reached the age of twelve."

Sheila shuddered at the thought of slaves working in the sweltering heat and humidity, knee deep in dirty water, snakes swimming around, mosquitoes buzzing overhead. She slapped at a mosquito that landed on her arm and turned to James.

"How do you know so much about this?"

"I'm a journalist too, don't forget. I didn't write for over forty years without understanding the souls of the South. Just because I'm from a small town doesn't mean I'm a country bumpkin. A Southern gentleman understands his roots, or should anyway. Come on, I think you've seen enough, unless you want to see the swamps where Madame Tallulah lived and get eaten alive by insects the size of birds."

"You're joking," she said.

"I'm joking. Let's go home."

CHAPTER 64

In Washington, a phone rang.

Recognizing the number, Henry Smith, the president's national security advisor answered. "Yes? . . . What's up? . . . And you think they have finally stumbled onto something? . . . I see. Give them any help they need. . . . No, I wouldn't do that. . . . Just give them what they asked for and then back off. . . . I understand the danger. . . . No, I didn't know that. Sheila hasn't called me since she left. . . . In light of what you've just told me, I understand your concerns. . . . I still insist you give them their space. . . . No it's not."

Henry became a bit perturbed.

"I will provide backup. . . . Discreetly. . . . Don't worry; I won't let anything happen to them. . . . I don't need to remind you that this is a national security issue and you don't have clearance. . . . Again, one last time: I'll take care of it. Provide them the equipment and technical guidance and then back off. I'll provide security. If there are too many agencies and men running around, we'll never get to the bottom of this rogue cell and who is controlling it. Understand?"

Henry Smith sat back in his chair, a bit more relaxed. He listened as the caller acquiesced to his demands. When the caller had run out his string, he ended the call.

"Listen, I appreciate your keeping me informed, I know you

didn't have to do that. I guarantee their safety, Mike. You have my word, so don't worry. . . . You too, Mike, bye."

After hanging up, Henry drummed his fingers on the desk for a few moments before picking up the phone and calling Mike's boss at the FBI.

Ten minutes later, Henry made another call and did all the talking.

"Things are about to break. I need you to make sure they are under our watch at all times. I don't want anything happening to them that will screw this operation up; and I don't want any invasive measures while they're searching. I want them free to go about their business."

Henry hung up and swiveled his chair to look out the window of his west wing office. As he gazed out onto the White House grounds, Henry thought that perhaps he should give Sheila a call. See how she was holding up. He turned around and picked up the phone, hesitated a moment, and then put it back down.

Better to let her have her space. She has enough to deal with.

CHAPTER 65

Hampton Plantation, June 26, 1830

On our return from Charleston we found Henri in a most excited state. Having received a long delayed shipment of chemical compounds from a laboratory in New York, he insisted we accompany him to his workshop at Wambaw Plantation. Tired though we were from our four day journey, none of us wanted to disappoint Henri. So, after a brief respite on the front portico, we all piled into a boat and went up Wambaw Creek, guided by Old William, who insisted he be addressed as Boatsman William—as if this were an honorary title much like Captain. After disembarking, we trudged up a winding path to Henri's workshop, minus Old William who insisted on staying behind.

"A Boatsman must remain with his ship," he declared.

A remark that drew a whispered aside from Harriott; "Old William just wants to take a nap. He could care less about Henri's latest invention."

Lagging considerably behind Henri—who despite his advancing years had the energy of a young colt—we found the great man with Stephan the Blacksmith and Paul, huddled over what appeared to be a cluster of miniature energy poles arranged on a circular base, twice as large as Henri's present machine. The arrival of his newly formulated compounds would enable Henri's new machine (once completed) to generate more battery power, allowing him to fly a considerable distance further.

"Along with the energy poles, I am working on a tandem pedal generator so that passengers can help me recharge the batteries in flight," Henri explained.

Isaac, taking a keen interest in the proceedings, asked, "Why don't you make a lower level to the base, Henri, and ring the edges with pedal generators? That way you can place half-a-dozen slaves or more on the base, and they can all pedal, just like the Roman slaves used to row their warships."

Henri, a bit puzzled, looked at Isaac before responding: "I know you're joking Isaac, but that would actually work out rather well. Weight does not seem to affect the machine's ability. In fact, it seems to add to its performance. I have just about figured out the mathematical formula to support this effect. But right now, I have more practical concerns."

The Chief looked over at Harriott and asked, "Will you be able to fly to France with the new batteries?"

"No, certainly not. Not even with Isaac's half-dozen slaves would that be possible," he replied.

Harriott smiled and shrugged at the Chief.

This was all very interesting I said, but I did not think it sufficient to arouse such enthusiasm in him.

Henri looked over at me with twinkling eyes.

"Come over here, Robert."

In a corner of the workshop he led us to a large, shroud-covered object.

"Underneath this cover is a substance which will change the world. Soon, all manner of objects will be created out of this. It is hard, yet flexible, and can be molded by heat into any shape. It can be transparent or colored, or even both as you shall presently see."

"What is it Henri?" Harriott asked impatiently. "And what do you call it?"

"I don't know, Harriott, I just invented it. It gives man the power to give form to matter."

"The plastic hand of the creator," I casually remarked.

"What's that, Robert?" The Chief asked.

"The definition of plastic, in Daniel Webster's dictionary.

Having the power to give form or fashion to a mass of matter; as, the plastic hand of the creator," I replied.

Turning to Henri, I made a sweeping motion with my arm and said, "Well, let's unveil your new discovery."

Henri grabbed the cloth, and with much flourish flung it from the object underneath.

"Ladies and Gentleman, I give you ... *plastic!* A mixture of pyroxylin, alcohol, and camphor!"

We all stared in stunned silence. Henri beamed at his creation.

Harriott was the first to voice our sentiments.

"Henri, it's just a hunk of round glass."

"No, no, Harriott," Henri exclaimed. "It's much more. It's hard, yet flexible, and will fit over the base of my new machine."

"We came all the way here after a long and arduous trip from Charleston to see a hunk of glass," the Chief said in a most disappointed voice, turning to leave. "Let's go back to the boat."

"I am with you on that," Harriott said. "Let's all have a bit of rum. And then I am going to take a long bath."

We started to leave, very much disappointed.

Henri stayed behind, mumbling, "You don't understand. This is lightweight. It can be made in any shape. Some day you will see."

Harriott turned back to Henri.

"Come along, Henri; leave your plastic for another day."

Henri, still protesting as we boarded the boat, woke up Old William.

"You will see, Harriott. Someday everyone will know of plastic. It's the future I tell you. Plastic. Remember that."

As Henri stepped onboard, he tried one last time to impress us.

"Why, this boat! I could make it out of plastic. We could see through it, at the fish underneath!"

Harriott turned to Henri. With a stern look she said, "Henri, *enough*. Button your lips." And then she started laughing.

"All this way for a round hunk of glass. . . . Good lord."

CHAPTER 66

A little after eight in the evening, we had all settled into our usual spots on the front portico. Old William, standing to one side, looked a bit envious at Isaac, sitting in a rocker next to Henri. Little Daphne sat cross-legged at Henri's feet. Harriott was a little late in joining us, owing to the necessity of a bath after a long journey. I was very much relieved when I saw that she carried the letter from President Jackson in her hand, having thought she might withhold it.

Henri started in again on his invention of plastic: a name which he gave me credit for. Praying the subject would soon change, I was instantly rewarded when the Chief interrupted the great man.

"Henri, you know we had a close call the other day. If it were not for Little Daphne, I am afraid you and your machine would no longer be residing here."

"I hope you were not subjected to any unpleasantness on my account," Henri replied, smiling at Little Daphne and patting her shoulder.

She smiled back and gave a quick glance over to Harriott.

"Miss Harriott took care of everything. You should have seen how she handled those men, Henri, with no assistance from the Chief and Mister Robert, sitting in their seats like dumb school children."

"Daphne! That is no way to talk to our guests. Apologize immediately," Harriott said reproachfully.

"No, no," I insisted. "She is right, Harriott. I am afraid we were not much assistance, though I concluded rather early on that none was required."

The Chief enthusiastically joined in: "I especially enjoyed the part when you told Abel Jenkins he was just an aide, and that you would personally whip him."

"No!" Henri said, unbelieving. "You did not say that, did you Harriott?"

"I most certainly did," she said with fire in her eyes, remembering the moment. "What a disgusting man. And to think he works for our own government. I shall have to write a letter to the president about him."

We proceeded to fill in the events of that day for Henri and Isaac: both, hearing them for the first time. Isaac expressed disbelief that the soldiers would leave so precipitously. I explained that once they realized Henri was not there, they had no reason to stay, if they were to hold to the pretense of meaning no harm to him. The Chief thought it rather dull of Secretary Eaton to continue to protest his benign intentions towards Henri.

And then we came to the letter.

"Is that the letter you brought with you out on the portico?" Henri asked Harriott.

"Yes. I should have burned it. I gave it serious thought, but against my better judgment I thought it was not for me to decide."

"May I, Harriott?" Henri reached his hand towards Harriott. Reluctantly, she gave him the letter.

He examined the seal of the envelope and the writing on the outside before opening it. He took out the letter, straightened the folded sheets across his leg, and then addressed us all.

"I would like to read the letter aloud so you can hear it along with me."

"Please, Henri, by all means," Harriott replied.

"I shall proceed then."

In a loud voice, Henri began to read the letter.

"My dearest Mister Richaud, let me take this moment to personally welcome you to this great republic of ours. I apologize at the tardiness of this missive and hope you will accept my most sincere apologies. I trust you are getting a most generous reception from the citizens of this welcoming land of ours. I was most gratified to have received your letter and looked forward, with much anticipation, to your exhibition on the White House lawn at the end of your summer tour.

"But I would be remiss if I were not to inform you of some disturbing developments that have occurred since your arrival to our great land. Developments, I fear, which put both you and your marvelous invention in grave peril. My administration, through our intelligence resources, has uncovered a plot to assassinate you and destroy your invention. I have been tardy in divulging details of this plot, as they seemed too fantastic to believe. But recently uncovered facts have verified, to my satisfaction, the veracity of these reports. With your forgiveness, I will be blunt in the manner by which I lay out the following facts to you. Shortly after your arrival to this country, we learned of a group of religious fanatics that wish to overthrow the government and establish a religious theocracy."

Henri paused for a moment.

The Chief looked at Isaac and said, "So my plan was *crazy*, you said?"

"Apparently, all white men think alike," Isaac responded. "And it still is, *crazy*."

Henri looked puzzled.

"What did you *say*, Chief?"

Harriott said, "Finish the letter Henri, we will explain after you are done."

With a puzzled look remaining on his face, Henri continued.

"A few adherents of this group observed your exhibition in Savannah. At a subsequent meeting of this group, attended by a government informer, we learned of plans to murder you and seize your machine during your performance in Wilmington, North Carolina.

"My Dearest Mister Richaud, I implore you to be vigilant. Be observant for any suspicious or strangely dressed characters. I have also been informed that several Indians from various tribes have joined this group. This is most ominous, as Indians are primitives that cannot be fully domesticated. Their sudden savagery knows no bounds."

I looked over at the Chief; he sat stock-still, quietly seething.

Henri did not pause: oblivious to the emotions aroused in his friend.

"As I feel responsible for the safety of such an esteemed guest in our country, I have ordered my secretary of war to provide security in the least intrusive manner possible. However, it is imperative that I meet with you personally, along with my scientific advisors, at the earliest possible convenience. I will be presently staying at the Georgetown Inn and invite you to be my guest there, at the conclusion of your performance. I look forward to a most enjoyable visit, and again, extend my very best wishes to you. Most sincerely yours, Andrew Jackson, President of the United States."

Henri put the letter down and said wistfully, "He is coming to see me."

"It's a trap, Henri," I said firmly. "Surely, you do not believe him?"

"But he has warned me of the Brothers of the Supreme Righteousness, has he not?"

"Henri," the Chief said sternly, "I made that all up."

"But Isaac was attacked by these people. He told me so. Isaac, get me the cap."

Isaac immediately got up. With his back to Henri, he made a hush motion—index finger over lips—to the rest of us, before going out into the fading rays of sunlight. He returned a few minutes later with Tailor Will. Each dumped a crate of red caps and scarves on the floor at the feet of an astonished Henri.

"But I don't understand. *Why?*" he said sadly.

Little Daphne shocked me by getting to her feet and sitting on Henri's lap. Taking his face firmly in her hands she addressed him: "Because for such a genius, you can be such a fool when it comes to the danger that is staring you right in your face."

I looked over at Harriott; a perverse smile spread across her face as she got up.

"I *knew* it, I *knew* it."

Shaking her head, she stormed off the portico.

Henri sobbed into Little Daphne's bosom.

We left the two of them alone, on the portico, as night once again won its struggle over day.

CHAPTER 67

Arising late Sunday morning as usual, I came down to the kitchen and found Little Daphne cleaning up after breakfast. Giving me a look that indicated she was not to be trifled with, I went to the stove and poured myself some warm coffee. Little Daphne soon relented somewhat in her attitude towards me and placed toast and peach jam on the table. Inquiring as to how Henri was feeling this morning, Little Daphne informed me that he was very well, and presently at church, where she herself would be if some unnamed person had not taken it upon himself to sleep late. I apologized and said she need not have stayed behind on my account; whereupon I was informed that Harriott had given her explicit instructions to provide me with a hearty breakfast. At hearing this comment, I raised up my slice of toast and jam, looked at it, and then at her, with what I hoped was a look of puzzlement.

"I think you will survive," Little Daphne said, taking off her apron and hanging it on a wall hook by the door. "If there is nothing else, Mister Robert, I will be going to church."

I asked her to please wait, but after giving me a very noticeable sigh, I decided it best to put down coffee and toast, and join her immediately.

Little Daphne led me past a small clapboard church built by Hampton slaves back in the late 1770s and over to a clearing alongside Wambaw Creek, where several pews had been set up. She explained to me that when it was hot, and the breeze was coming off the creek, it was more tolerable to be outside. Most of the field slaves sat or stood behind the pews, further back, under some shade trees.

We found Henri sitting in the back pew and sat down next to him. I noticed he immediately took Little Daphne's hand in his. In front of us sat Old William, his wife Patty, and one of their sons, Roger. I inquired as to Caesar, his oldest son. Old William informed me that Caesar was very ill with fever and being attended to by Madame Tallulah. I began to inquire further but was interrupted by a slave parishioner, who turned around and told me to hush. Having been sufficiently admonished, I turned my attention to Preacher George: a slave appointed by Harriott to lead the congregation.

". . . Just as we toil in the vineyard of the Lord, so do we toil on our earthly vineyard. We will reap in heaven that which we have sown here on earth. Just as a good harvest yields its bounty, so a good obedient life in the service of the Lord yields a bountiful life in Heaven."

As I listened to Preacher George, I looked around and tried to find Isaac among those in attendance, but could not locate him.

"When a man walks in righteousness and follows the Lord's path he will be richly rewarded in Heaven. Did not the Lord suffer mightily? Did not the Lord wash his disciples' feet? Did not the Lord bear the pain of the cross? Surely, the suffering we here on earth experience is nothing compared to our Lord's suffering. And he suffered grievously so that we can all have everlasting life and dwell in the vineyard of the Lord where the harvest is always good. The book of Hebrews, chapter two, verse nine says, 'but we do see Him who has been made for a little while lower than the angels, namely Jesus, because of the suffering of death crowned with glory and honor, that by the grace of God He might taste death for everyone.'"

At this point, Preacher George paused and looked around—as if searching for someone. The sudden silence was quite startling. Even the chirping of birds, croaking of frogs and cacophony of insects stopped. After Preacher George had surveyed his flock, he proceeded again with a louder voice.

"Here you have God's only begotten son, made lower than even the angels, toiling on the earth . . . beside man. Think of that for a moment. Think, when you are out toiling in the rice fields in the mud and hot sun, insects buzzing all around, biting you. Think . . . and remember: The Lord is toiling right at your side. And because he suffered for everyone, what did God do? I ask you . . . what did God do? He, who suffered so much. He, who was made lower than the angels. He, who toiled beside man and was tempted by the devil himself! He, who was crowned in thorns! He, who was denied by his own disciple! He, who was rejected by the Jews! He, who was nailed to a cross so he might taste death for everyone! What did God do? What did God do? He placed him at his right side to prepare a kingdom for all of us: White! Negro! Indian! Young! Old! Rich! Poor! Everlasting life for everyone! That is the power of the Lord! That is the power of suffering! That is the power of Jesus Christ our Lord! Our Savior! Our King! World without End! Amen! Brothers and sisters! Amen! Amen!! Amen!!!"

And as Preacher George gave his rousing finish, each sentence louder and accentuated by the slap of drums; everyone got up and praised the Lord: dancing and singing. To my astonishment, Harriott, the Chief, and even Henri joined in. Soon my inhibitions were shed, and although I must confess to not being a regular churchgoer, I did the best I could, and found the experience most enjoyable.

After church, I took a stroll around the plantation with Henri, Little Daphne, and Isaac. The rice was growing nicely. It was strange to look out over the vast fields and not see any slaves working. Isaac, even though it was Sunday, insisted on checking one of the new floodgates that Old Moses had built to hold back the waters of Wambaw Creek at high tide. There was a small trickle of water running underneath the gate and down the irrigation ditch. Isaac studied the situation for awhile, and once satisfied the matter could wait, we continued our walk.

Taking the lead, Isaac led us over to the slave quarters, where I was astonished to find nearly two hundred slaves milling about the small cabins: standing in knots, sharing a drink, sitting on porches, catching up on the latest news of friends and relatives. On Sundays, Little Daphne informed me, the slaves from nearby Wambaw and Harrietta plantations gathered at Hampton to participate in the services and see family and friends. As she was talking, a shot rang out. I flinched—a bit embarrassed when I noticed that no one else in our party did likewise. Seeing my discomfort, Isaac explained that several men were out hunting to provide the Sunday meal that would be shared by all. Earlier, the men had trussed up a large pig to roast. Several of the ladies were busy stacking wood in a stone pit that stood in the center of a clearing, encircled by slave cabins. Around another stone pit, vegetables were piled high, ready to be cooked.

Isaac walked us over to a cabin porch that held several men, amongst whom I recognized Tailor Will. One of the men offered a large mug to Isaac. He poured a little of the liquid on the ground and said softly, "Big Isaac, Big Hannah, and Toney." Isaac took a drink and passed the mug to Henri.

"To Adrienne and Jean, my beloved parents."

Spilling a bit of the liquid on the ground, Henri added, "To Napoleon, a dear friend who went mad. I forgive you," and poured a little more on the ground before taking a sip and handing the mug to Little Daphne.

"To Big Daphne." After spilling some liquid on the ground, taking a sip and handing me the mug, she looked up at me; a tear formed at the edge of her right eye. "I don't know who my real dad was. Big Daphne would never tell me."

Grasping her arm gently with one hand as she handed me the mug, I continued the rite. "To Robert and Lilly." I turned the mug over; only a few drops fell to the ground.

One of the men on the porch laughed: "The spirits of your ancestors are not going to be very happy." He walked over and took the mug from my hands, refilling it from a pail sitting on the porch. "Here, try that again," he said smiling.

So I did. And once my ancestors were hopefully satisfied, I satisfied myself.

"It's not bad. Not Harriott's peach rum, but it will do," I said to Isaac as another shot rang out from the nearby woods.

"It's a Caribbean drink of rum, water, and molasses. Madame Tallulah says it is good for the joints, and keeps your hair from turning gray," Isaac replied, taking the mug along with another swig.

Sitting on the porch with Tailor Will, we shared several mugs of Madame Tallulah's 'hair tonic' as I called it. Each time the mug reached me it was just about empty. I took it upon myself to refill the mug before passing it back, taking an extra swig in the process. Soon, the smell of roasting meat and vegetables wafted over us. Our spirits were greatly lifted: so much so, that except for Tailor Will, who had a propensity for talking, we all just sat mute—enjoying the sun, the smells, and the sounds of nearby Wambaw Creek, babbling with life.

Our meditation was broken by Harriott, Little Daphne, and Old William, bearing baskets of freshly baked bread. This was the signal that our Sunday meal was about to begin. The men slowly got to their feet, while the ladies scampered about, putting food onto long tables set in a clearing, away from the central fire pit.

Everyone gathered quietly together, heads bowed. Preacher George filled a large mug with wine. Harriott stood by his side holding a basket of bread squares in her hand. Preacher George went up singly to everyone, trailed by Harriott and the bread squares, sharing communion. One by one, he intimately intoned; "This is the body of Christ. Take and eat. This is the blood of Christ. Take and drink."

After Preacher George had finished, there was a murmur from behind. We turned around to see an ancient Negro hobbling towards us, helped by Madame Tallulah. I heard someone nearby excitedly whisper that it was Preacher Sogo. Everyone remained silent. The old man, helped by Madame Tallulah, slowly made his way to the front of the gathering.

Harriott smiled and embraced the old preacher. Returning the smile, he said, "I gave communion to your grandmother Eliza and to the great man himself, under the tree named in his honor."

Turning to face the crowd, Preacher Sogo, said in a firm voice, "I do not get around much anymore, but I wanted to give you my blessings and remind you of the old ways. Changes are coming, and I do not know where it will lead us. As in all things, I fear there will be some bad with the good. The devil will always be nipping at the heels of the Lord, and we must always be mindful of that fact. I had a dream and have seen that my end is near. Soon, I will be with our fathers in heaven. As you pass into a new age, I want you to remember the old age and what has kept us together and safe through the generations. Many of you do not know the old catechism... some of you do. The old catechism may be disappearing, but it has kept us safe and together for a long time. Before I pass, I want to say it one last time for all of you."

The old preacher bowed his head with wrinkled forehead, as if trying to remember. He stayed silent for an uncomfortably long time before he spoke.

"Who is duty bound to give servants comfortable clothing, wholesome and abundant food?" the old preacher intoned.

"The master," the older slaves responded.

"And who is duty bound to instruct servants in a knowledge of the Holy Scriptures, and to give them every opportunity and encouragement to seek their soul's salvation?"

"The master," more slaves responded.

The old man looked out at the crowd and lifted his arms to the sky.

"Who is the master of us all in Heaven?"

"God," everyone replied loudly.

With his voice rising, Preacher Sogo continued the call and response.

"Does God show favour to the master more than to the servant, and just because he is a master?"

"No," the crowd responded.

"What are the servants to count their masters worthy of?"

"All honour," the crowd replied.

"How are they to try to please their masters?"

As the old preacher said this, I looked over at Harriott. She appeared a bit uncomfortable, even more so as the crowd responded, with the words of another time and place.

"Please them well in all things, not answering again."

"Is it right for a servant when commanded to do anything to be sullen and slow, and answering his master again?" Preacher Sogo said this line slow and loud. The crowd stirred a bit before responding.

"No," the crowd said with a little less fervor.

"But suppose the master is hard to please, and threatens and punishes more than he ought, what is the servant to do?" the old man said, concluding his call.

The older slaves in the crowd, remembering, replied; "Do his best to please him."

Then the old preacher said to the crowd, "As I go now to my

resting place, I take the old ways with me. Preacher George leads you forward. Remember me as you pour your spirits on the ground. Also, remember the old ways."

I noticed tears forming in Harriott's and Madame Tallulah's eyes as they helped Preacher Sogo to his knees for what would be his final communion. After receiving the holy sacrament, Harriott and Madame Tallulah helped Preacher Sogo back to the cabin he shared with Preacher George and his family. Little Daphne trailed after them with a plate full of food.

After dinner, most of the slaves retreated to hammocks strung between trees for a midday nap. I noticed that Henri and Little Daphne shared a hammock among Isaac's family. Isaac motioned for me to join them. Two of Isaac's children doubled up in a hammock, leaving one free for me. Helped by the swaying motion of the hammock along with a gentle breeze, I was soon fast asleep.

As usual, I slept longer than everyone else, awakened only by a cacophony of noise. Regaining my senses, the sounds soon took on a rhythmic quality. I walked to the center of the main clearing. A large circle of slaves stomped their feet and slapped their arms, legs, chests, and even their faces, in a rhythmic pattern. Moving closer, I could see an inner circle of slaves dancing in a counter-clockwise fashion, lifting their legs in unison.

I found Isaac along the outer ring. He showed me how to clap my hands in rhythm with the others and pointed out Henri and Little Daphne, dancing in the inner circle. Noticing an empty mug next to Isaac's feet, I raised it up with a questioning look. He glanced at a pail, sitting on a nearby stoop. I walked over, nodded to the men sitting on the stoop and poured a mug of the rum mixture. I gave the mug back to Isaac. He took a swallow, set the mug back down, and rejoined me in clapping and slapping our bodies.

I drank most of Isaac's mug. Feeling brave, I decided to try my hand (or rather my feet) at dancing the Juba. Leaving to join the dancers in the inner circle, I heard him snicker that Harriott would put me to work in the fields if I was not careful.

After another hour of drinking, clapping, dancing, and singing, I joined Henri, Little Daphne, and Isaac on his porch. We sat and watched slaves flow back and forth from porches to circles of Juba dancers and rhythm makers. A rum induced, tingling sensation coursed through my body. With my back against the outer wall of a slave cabin, I sat with closed eyes, listening to one of the Juba songs.

Juba dis an' Juba dat,
 Juba skin dat yaller Cat. Juba! Juba!
Juba jump an' Juba sing.
 Juba, cut dat Pigeon's Wing. Juba! Juba!
Juba, kick off Juba's shoe.
 Juba, dance dat Jubal Jew. Juba! Juba!
Juba, whirl dat foot about.
 Juba, blow dat candle out. Juba! Juba!
Juba circle, Raise de Latch.
 Juba do dat Long Dog Scratch.

Suddenly, the dancing and rhythmic clapping stopped. Craning to look, I saw Madame Tallulah carrying a young boy, who I surmised was Old William's son, Caesar. The Madame called out for someone to get Miss Harriott. In no more than an instant, Harriott appeared, having come to investigate why the music had stopped. She came over to Madame Tallulah. Seeing the boy listless, she called out to Isaac to bring Caesar to the house.

Harriott listened intently as Madame Tallulah spoke.

"Miz Harriott, I did all I could but Ize needs a little of Doctor Garden's magic," the Madame said apologetically.

"That's okay," Harriott said, patting her sympathetically on the shoulder. Looking at Caesar and then back at Madame Tallulah, she asked, "Can he survive another week waiting for Doctor Garden? Charleston is a long way."

Madame Tallulah shook her head no. "Ize bin fightin off de fever but Ize beginning to lose. Maybe tree mo days he cans hold, but dats it."

"We will have to use the drums," Harriott said gravely. "I hope we still have slaves on the other plantations who remember."

"Oh dey remembers, Miss Harriott," Madame Tallulah replied with a sad smile.

Soon the sound of drums drifted across the plantation, picked up and passed along by other plantations. All the way to Charleston. Harriott would have to make amends to plantation owners, who would undoubtedly be outraged at this most serious violation. She sent several slaves on horseback with notes to explain her breach of the long ban on drum communication. In the meantime, Harriott hoped that slaves on other plantations would not be too severely beaten. Isaac and Henri took the carriage to the farthest distance the antigravity machine could travel and waited for Doctor Garden's carriage, whereupon the doctor would be flown back to Hampton.

Three hours later, the sound of a distant drum could be heard. Little Daphne informed a worried Harriott that Patty had received the message in Charleston. Doctor Garden was prepared to leave by carriage for Hampton, immediately.

Before retiring for the evening, Harriott looked in on Caesar, struggling to breathe, lying on a small cot in the pantry room. Watching attentively over the boy, worry etched on her face, stood Madame Tallulah.

CHAPTER 68

On the morning of the third day, shortly after sunrise, I was awakened by a familiar buzzing sound. Throwing some clothes on, I ran downstairs just as Henri and Doctor Garden arrived at the back door. Little Daphne ushered the doctor into the pantry, where the little boy Caesar lay.

Madame Tallulah rushed to greet her old friend with a hug.

"Doctor Garden, de fever broke early dis moning jes befoe sunrise. Ize sorry yoose made de trip foe nuhting."

"Well, let us have a look, as long as I am here."

Doctor Garden went over to the little boy and examined him. Pressing a wooden tube to the boy's chest, he pressed the other end to his ear. He listened for a minute and then looked up at Madame Tallulah; "Little Caesar's heart is beating smooth and strong. It is a good thing I arrived when I did. Had I been here sooner, I probably would have killed him trying to help."

Madame Tallulah laughed, relieved. "Aint dat de trut. I thought foe sure I kilt him myself, givin him too much of my beet roots and chamomile tea."

"Sometimes the best medicine is a strong heart and a will to live," Doctor Garden replied. "Look at what our profession did to poor George Washington—bled the poor man to death. Had a common cold. The best doctors of the day decided to take some of his blood. When he started to get better, they took more and more until he had no more to give."

Madame Tallulah and Doctor Garden shared a laugh, interrupted by Preacher George who came running in to announce that Preacher Sogo had died sometime in the early morning hours.

"Maybe de Preacher done took de boy's fever wit him, cuz I thought foe sure de boy wuz on his las bret dis morning, and den suddenly he look up at me and smile. Like someone jes turned on the dawn."

"I have seen a lot of strange things in my life. That is as good an explanation as any, I suspect," Doctor Garden replied.

* * *

Later that morning a funeral service was held. A mixture of joy and sadness permeated the ceremony as news of Preacher Sogo's final miracle spread among the slaves in attendance. After Preacher Sogo was laid to rest in the slave cemetery, the slaves returned to their rice fields filled with the Holy Spirit. Their singing, especially strong, was easily heard from the portico where we all sat, enjoying Harriott's peach rum. All, except for Doctor Garden, who accompanied Madame Tallulah to the cypress swamps to collect herbs for their medicines.

I was especially struck by something Doctor Garden had said, about Madame Tallulah teaching him as much as he taught her. I watched the two walk as colleagues, deep in animated discourse. How different they appeared on the surface, yet how alike they were in substance.

While I thought about how far we had come as a civilized race and how far we still had to travel, Harriott recounted Preacher Sogo's long life. Rumored to be nearly one hundred years old, he had been one of Daniel Horry's first slaves in the 1740s. It was Preacher Sogo who aided Francis Marion, the Swamp Fox, by helping him escape through the back door of Hampton: leading him across Wambaw Creek and the rice fields, while Harriott's mother seduced the British Commander, Colonel Tarleton, at the front door, using her considerable charms. Afterwards, the elder Harriott took a bath for several hours to wipe the British stench off of her body.

I inquired as to how Sogo became a preacher. Harriott obliged me. As a young boy, Sogo had stolen a Bible belonging to Harriott's grandmother, Eliza Horry. One Sunday morning while out fishing, the then master of the Plantation, Daniel Huger Horry, found Sogo down by a shallow bend of the creek, baptizing slaves. He brought Sogo to his mother. Sogo immediately confessed his sin to Eliza and begged that she crucify him. She said that he had to prove that he was worthy of suffering the same fate as the Lord. Asked what he had learned from her Bible, Sogo began to recite the holy book, word for word. Impressed, Eliza let him keep her Bible.

Shortly thereafter, Sogo was preaching alongside his fellow slaves as they worked the rice fields. Alarmed at first, and fearful of a slave rebellion, Eliza's fears turned to surprise and relief as productivity and morale among the slaves began to increase. Once assured he would not foment a rebellion, she asked Sogo to lead the Hampton slave congregation.

Word of his oratory began to spread, and not only amongst the slaves. Soon, members of the white congregation began attending. Eliza eventually combined the white and slave congregations into one service, relieving the white preacher of his pastoral duties.

At this point, Harriott broke down in genuine grief. The rest of us sat in silence for a long time, listening to the songs of slaves working knee deep in the muddy rice fields.

Henri broke the silence with a stunning announcement.

"I am planning to go to Georgetown to meet President Jackson."

We looked at Henri with disbelief.

The Chief, expressing our sentiments, said, "Surely you are joking, Henri?"

"No, my friends," Henri replied. "I am tired of running. At some point, I have to trust that my invention will be used for the good that I intended. And that point has arrived. America, for all its faults, still holds the best promise of peace for mankind."

"But President Jackson is no saint, Henri," I interjected.

Henri turned to me and said, "Robert, President Jackson will not be president forever. Your American system ensures renewal every four years. That is unlike any other system in the world. I will take my chances with your American president."

The Chief tried his best to dissuade our friend.

"Henri, you must understand that you will be taken into

custody along with your machine."

"I am sure you are right, Chief," Henri said. "But I do not care. I am tired of all the intrigue. I just want to lead a normal life from now on. President Jackson can have the damn thing."

He smiled at Little Daphne and took hold of her hand. Turning to look out across the grounds of Hampton, he said, "I just want a normal life, and return to France. I grew up in a vineyard. The other day when Preacher George talked about toiling in the vineyards of the Lord, it brought me back to when I was a little boy, toiling in my father's vineyard. I want that for my son."

"Henri! Stop talking nonsense," Harriott said. "You do not even have a son."

"I will, if you let me buy Little Daphne's freedom."

"Oh my Lord!" Harriott shrieked. She abruptly stood up and stormed inside.

"She will be alright," Little Daphne said to Henri. "She is just in shock at the moment. This is all so new to her."

"I know," Henri replied, gazing at Little Daphne, oblivious to the Chief and I sitting with our mouths agape.

Little Daphne got up and pulled Henri to a standing position.

"Come, Henri, let us tell Big Daphne the news."

The Chief and I watched Henri and Little Daphne walk over to the slave cemetery. The songs of slaves filled the air, the spirit of Preacher Sogo locked in their hearts.

CHAPTER 69

The trip to Georgetown was a complete disaster. Leaving Doctor Garden behind to continue his foraging with Madame Tallulah, the rest of us piled into the carriage for the one-day trip to meet President Jackson. Arriving at the rendezvous site, it was decided that I would stay with the carriage. The first part of our plan was for the Chief to ride ahead with his braves. The Chief (who had fought alongside President Jackson during the Creek Indian wars) would request a presidential audience and try and discern Jackson's true intentions towards Henri. I would later learn that his request had been summarily rebuffed.

The next part of our plan was for Henri and Isaac to fly together to the Georgetown Inn, where Henri would literally be dropped off to meet with the president. While Isaac performed for the crowds assembled nearby, Henri would present documents to the president and his scientific advisors, detailing his invention and its underlying scientific principles. There would, of course, be a few gaps in the papers that could only be filled in by the acquisition of the antigravity machine. Once finished performing for the crowds, Isaac would return to the rendezvous point and await the results of negotiations with the president.

Henri, with the assistance of the Chief, would work out an exchange: Henri for the machine. If all went well, President Jackson would have the most amazing invention of our times and Henri would have the freedom to live a normal life.

All did not go well.

The following narrative of the calamity in Georgetown was provided by Harriott, Little Daphne, Isaac, and the Chief. I have attempted to piece it together, as if I myself were witness to the events that occurred there.

The Chief, being of suspicious nature, kept a safe distance. With five of his braves he rode to within fifty yards of the entrance to the Georgetown Inn. He related to me that the whole town was like an armed camp. Not being one to trust the president, the Chief sent a message with one of his braves to what appeared to be a senior officer, standing with his men in front of the Inn. The officer went inside.

A few minutes later, the president, along with Secretary of War, John Eaton and Abel Jenkins, appeared. Abel began to look out over the surrounding area as if searching for someone. His eyes, like that of an eagle (the Chief's words) fixed on the Chief. Abel remarked something to the president.

Shortly thereafter, several soldiers advanced in the Chief's direction. As the soldiers neared, he smelled a trap and took off with his braves. This was quickly followed by gunshots and lead balls whizzing past their heads. Before splitting off from his braves, the Chief instructed them to follow the alternate plan, devised to ensure Henri and Isaac's safety.

Little did he know at the time, the tragic consequences of that plan.

The Chief drew the soldiers in his direction, enabling his braves to withdraw and set up in predetermined positions. Once he had evaded his pursuers, the Chief headed back towards the rendezvous point.

Meanwhile, Harriott and Little Daphne had tied up their horses at a spot away from the assembled crowd that afforded them a good view of Henri and Isaac's arrival. Moments later, a familiar distant buzzing sound could be heard. Growing in intensity, it seemed to come from every direction, reverberating off the buildings. The crowd began to stir and crane their heads every which way. Henri, with Isaac aboard, appeared about forty feet above the crowd. Slowly traveling over the amassed crowds jamming Main Street, they headed for the Georgetown Inn.

The Floating Man

Henri—ever the showman—stopped for a minute and hovered. Then, with a sudden start, he quickly rose a few hundred feet straight up into the air before descending back down to about fifty. At the intersection of Elm and Main, Henri turned onto Elm and continued towards the Inn where the president awaited them.

It was a beautiful sunny day. Harriott turned to Little Daphne to make the comment that the crowds were certainly in a festive mood, when suddenly, three shots in quick succession rang out. Harriott thought the shots came from a building behind her. Little Daphne was just as insistent that the shots came from the front, near a grassy knoll located behind a fence between two buildings. In any event, they both observed Henri's machine flying erratically after the shots were fired.

Isaac, aboard the antigravity machine with Henri, heard the first shot ring out and whiz overhead. The second shot made a ringing sound as it ricocheted off the machine and appeared to hit Henri; his hands immediately went from the controls to his chest. As the third shot rang out, Isaac took control of the machine and swerved it violently. He observed Henri's head snap back and towards the left. His limp body swung like a rag doll from the attachment point that kept him from falling to the ground. Isaac then flew in a zigzag fashion with a heavily bleeding Henri to the Rendezvous point.

As Isaac descended, I sensed something was terribly wrong and rushed over. I pressed my hand against the gaping wound to Henri's upper left chest to stanch the flow of blood. Isaac worked furiously on disassembling the energy pole and attaching it to the generator located underneath the carriage. While I tried to stop the flow of blood, Isaac drove the carriage in circles, trying to restore energy to the batteries. Henri, lying in the road and bleeding heavily, mumbled something in French, which I could not understand. Shortly thereafter, the Chief arrived, and we got Henri aboard the carriage. He explained that it was too risky to await the arrival of Harriott and Little Daphne. The four of us took off for Hampton with Henri crying out in correspondence to every bump in the road. Isaac apologetically said we needed to generate enough energy to enable the machine to make it to Hampton, where medical attention in the form of Madame Tallulah and Doctor Garden waited. Harriott and Little Daphne would hopefully catch up, but that was not a pressing matter at the moment.

After twenty minutes of Isaac furiously driving the carriage, Henri's eyes began to flutter. A ghostly gray pallor appeared upon his countenance. Isaac pulled the carriage over, jumped down, and immediately unfastened the energy pole from underneath the carriage. He then reattached the pole to the base of the machine and furiously used the less efficient pedal generators to try and pump life back into the batteries. When Isaac's energy flagged, I traded places with him; the Chief, in turn, relieved me when my energy waned.

Another thirty minutes brought the arrival of Harriott and Little Daphne, along with the announcement that Jackson's soldiers were not very far behind. Little Daphne rushed to Henri's aid and bravely attended to Henri's wound, providing him much needed emotional and physical comfort. The Chief ushered everyone back into the carriage. Climbing on top with the antigravity machine, I pedaled as fast as I could from a supine position, trying desperately to restore energy to the batteries.

Isaac again drove the carriage furiously, but after about ten minutes another catastrophe occurred: Old Betsy collapsed and died. It took almost fifteen minutes to unhook the dead mare and pull her away from the carriage. The Chief hopped onto his horse and went riding off to the top of a nearby hill, returning ten minutes later to give us the distressing news that the soldiers were only minutes away. Isaac jumped on the machine but sadly announced that there was still not enough energy. Harriott and the Chief got out their rifles from the carriage, ready to make a final stand as Isaac resumed pedaling. It appeared we would all die on this patchy road leading to Hampton Plantation.

Until—

I remembered something Henri had said to Isaac a week earlier.

I ran over to him and said excitedly, "Isaac! Remember when you had that idea for a lower level with a half-dozen slaves pedaling, like the old Roman slaves rowing a ship?"

He looked at me as if I were mad and continued to pedal.

"Robert, now is not the time for theoretical musings."

"No! Remember what Henri said about added weight making his machine perform better?" I pleaded.

Isaac's eyes lit up.

"Go get everyone. *Hurry!*"

We gathered around the machine. At Isaac's direction we carried it off into the woods near a clearing some forty yards distant.

Resuming his pedaling, Isaac hurriedly addressed the Chief: "I need you to take your rifle and two of your horses, set up at a distance that you feel comfortable with, across the road. When the soldiers come, which will probably be any minute now, start shooting; draw them away from us. After they start chasing you, shake them off your trail and return to Hampton where we hopefully will already be. If we are not there, then hopefully, we will still be here. You can send Doctor Garden and Madame Tallulah to help. Henri will most likely be dead, but that will be the only hope we have left, if this machine of his fails to get off the ground."

The Chief gave a quick nod and raced to his horse; time was not a thing to be spared. A few minutes later we heard the sound of horse hooves galloping up, suddenly stopping at the sight of a carriage with one horse standing, one dead.

Shots rang out.

The soldiers took cover behind the carriage, with us only forty yards away in the woods.

I looked over at Isaac and said, "Let's *go*."

Isaac shook his head no, and kept pedaling. Several soldiers fanned out in the direction of the rifle shots, but just as many stayed near the carriage. After the passage of another few minutes, the shots went from intermittent to zero. Soldiers behind the carriage—at the direction of their commanding officer—began to move out into the woods, in our direction.

It was do or die for us.

Henri and Isaac were attached to the pole; Little Daphne wrapped herself around Henri, her hand pressed firmly against his wound. Harriott clung to Isaac, and I sat on the base with my legs wrapped around Henri's in an attempt to keep his body still.

Isaac started up the antigravity device.

The buzzing noise began.

The soldiers momentarily froze in position, some twenty yards away. Once they had regained their bearings, they headed for the source of the noise. I can only assume that everyone was as frightened as I myself was. The soldiers had drawn to within ten yards, and the machine still had not risen.

Finally!

The machine rose.

I thought for sure the soldiers would fire on us. They clearly had us easily within range, and had demonstrated earlier in Georgetown that they were not afraid to use deadly force. But for some reason, they held their fire. I was to learn later (from the Chief) a possible answer for this. We looked down at the soldiers from about twenty feet; their eyes, filled with wonderment, looked up at us—rifles at their sides.

Our machine fully engaged. We quickly rose to a height of a hundred feet, soaring over the woods, swamps, and rivers that led to Hampton Plantation. Leaving the awe struck soldiers far behind.

CHAPTER 70

We arrived at Hampton after a flight of some twenty minutes—a flight that would have taken half a day by carriage. Hovering near the portico of the mansion, suspended a foot off the ground, Little Daphne and Harriott hopped off the antigravity machine and went racing for Doctor Garden. They ran into Old William; he informed them that the doctor was visiting Madame Tallulah. Grabbing the doctor's bag of surgical tools, Little Daphne ran over to me, holding the hem of her dress with one hand and handing me the bag with the other. She gave Henri a quick kiss on the forehead. And then, much to my surprise and despite a quick protestation on my part, Little Daphne insisted on staying behind with Harriott, claiming she would just be in the way.

We flew on without them to Madame Tallulah's small cabin, deep in the cypress swamp, landing just as Madame Tallulah and Doctor Garden came walking up, each carrying a plant-laden basket. Isaac and I brought Henri into the cabin and laid him gently on a straw mat. Going quickly to work, Madame Tallulah handed Doctor Garden a cloth and a bottle, the contents of which he poured over and into the wound.

Setting a couple pots of water over the perpetually burning fire at the center of her cabin, Madame Tallulah began boiling plants in one pot while Doctor Garden placed his surgical instruments in the other.

"I knowse why Ize boil deeze plants, Doctor Garden, but why on eart iz yoose boilin dem tools? Ain't gonna make no poultice from de metal stew is yoose?" the Madame said, stirring her pot.

"I have a hunch that it is better to boil them before using," Doctor Garden replied. "You can get sick and die from drinking dirty water, but boil that same water for a soup and it does not have the same effect. So I have a theory that boiling burns away any bad things in the water, and maybe it does the same for my tools."

Doctor Garden took out his wooden tube and listened to Henri's heart. He quickly looked up at Madame Tallulah and said with alarm, "His heart is beating too fast. He will bleed to death, and I don't have anything in my bag for that."

Madame Tallulah went to a cupboard in the corner of her room, grabbed a small bottle and sat down next to Henri. Pouring a little of the liquid down his throat, she turned to Doctor Garden: "It's an extract of Lavender, Hawthorne and a few other plants I don't have de names foe. Takes bouts ten minutes teh work."

"I hope we have enough time. I need to tie a few ligatures around these damaged blood vessels and find that lead ball."

Doctor Garden retrieved a tool from the boiling pot and began to probe Henri's wound.

Madame Tallulah set a pot of smoking herbs near Henri's face and told me to fan the aromatic vapors towards his nose. She instructed Isaac to go out back and fetch some eggs from her chicken coop.

Continuing his probe of Henri's wound, the doctor soon found a sharp fragment of the lead ball that must have split when it ricocheted off Henri's machine. After pouring a little more liquid into the wound so he could see what he was doing, Doctor Garden began using a thread to tie off the damaged arteries.

Henri began to moan and mumble in French.

"*Dis à Daphné que je l'aime.*"

Madame Tallulah stroked Henri's head, replying softly, "*Oui, mon amour. Calme-toi, calme-toi.*"

Isaac came back with a half-dozen eggs. Madame Tallulah directed him to crack and pour the yolks into a small bowl. Isaac then took Madame Tallulah's place, stroking Henri's forehead, trying to calm him. I continued to fan the pleasant smelling vapors, while Doctor Garden tied off bleeding blood vessels as best he could. With deliberate speed, Madame Tallulah added what smelled like turpentine and some sweet smelling oil to the egg yolks. She brought the mixture over to Doctor Garden, applying the last of his ligatures to Henri's torn, bleeding arteries.

Madame Tallulah bent down next to Doctor Garden and gave him the mixture. He poured it into the wound in an effort to stop the bleeding. Madame Tallulah ripped a clean piece of cloth and soaked it in the boiling pot of herbs and plants. She covered the wound with the wet cloth and waited awhile before handing Doctor Garden a dry cloth, which he then placed over the other.

Sitting back upright, Doctor Garden nervously rubbed his hands.

"Now we wait . . . and hope."

"Always de hardes part," Madame Tallulah said, and went outside to stretch her legs.

Isaac and I, hovering over Henri, looked up at each other at the sound of a drum.

"That is Little Daphne. She is summoning all the slaves to gather at Wambaw Plantation."

"Why?" I asked Isaac.

"I think I know," Isaac replied. "The soldiers are going to be here in a few hours; she probably doesn't want them to find anything."

"The laboratory. But where will they take everything?"

"Deep into the swamps where it will never be found."

I continued fanning the vapors while Isaac soothed Henri's forehead.

The sound of the drum continued to ring out.

Henri restlessly mumbled in French.

Isaac repeated Madame Tallulah's last words to Henri.

"*Calme-toi, calme-toi.*"

CHAPTER 71

From across the rice fields came the slaves of Hampton, Harrietta, and Belmont. Close to three hundred heeded the sound of Little Daphne's drum, assembling in front of the mansion at Wambaw.

With Old William by her side, Little Daphne addressed friends and relatives, gathered on all sides around her.

"My dear brothers and sisters, listen up! We are all in grave peril. Soon these fields and our homes will be swarming with troops led by President Andrew Jackson. He and his men will not be here on a friendly visit. He is an *evil* man, parading as a just man. Do not fall for any of his lies. Under his orders he has had Henri shot. The father of my soon to be child lies grievously wounded and near death as I speak. If President Jackson, this *evil* man, finds any trace of Henri's inventions, he will burn these plantations to the ground and put us all to death. We must gather up all of Henri's things and leave no trace of him or his work. Go now to his laboratory. Take it apart, piece by piece. Bury everything in the swamps. Hurry my friends. We must be finished before the troops arrive."

Little Daphne later described to me the sight of men, women and children scurrying about, gathering up all of Henri's supplies. Pots and wire bales were piled onto large mats and dragged. Women bundled up various tools and pots in their dresses, while others, in the old African tradition, placed baskets filled with objects on top of their heads—all marching off to the swamps. Most amazing of all was the sight of Harriott, with her contingent of house slaves, marching along with the others: down earthen dikes, crossing canals, and wading into the swamps.

After Little Daphne had finished addressing her fellow slaves, she and Old William went to the laboratory. They unscrewed the energy rod for Henri's new machine and carried it to Madame Tallulah's. She told Isaac and me about the dismantling of Henri's laboratory, and said we needed to use the antigravity machine to dispose of some of the heavier pieces. Once accomplished, we were to destroy the antigravity machine and leave no trace of its existence. Isaac quickly jumped up and told me to stay. He would get Old Moses to help him dispose of Henri's heavy machinery. I immediately suspected Isaac was up to something: that he had his own plans concerning the machine. I believe Little Daphne would have been suspicious also, if not for being preoccupied with the condition of her beloved Henri: lying gravely ill, taking shallow breaths.

After Isaac flew off, I left Little Daphne alone with Henri, and joined Madame Tallulah and Doctor Garden, standing outside by a plot where she grew her herbs. We talked for awhile about Henri's chances, which both the doctor and Madame agreed, were not very good.

Our conversation was interrupted by Little Daphne, running out of the cabin.

"Why aren't you in there helping him? Do something! He is struggling to breathe."

Little Daphne's eyes darted back and forth between Doctor Garden and Madame Tallulah, frantically looking for some sign of hope.

Doctor Garden took Little Daphne's hands in both of his and said very gently, "We have done all we can Little Daphne. Done quite a lot in fact. The rest is between him and God."

Little Daphne, with a look of panic in her eyes, turned to Madame Tallulah. With a sad smile and comforting hand, the Madame said, "De best ting yoose cans do foe Henri is teh let him know yoose by his side. Lay down wit him and let him feel yo bret on his face. Yo hand on his heart."

Little Daphne went back inside. Heeding Madame Tallulah's instructions, she lay down next to Henri, putting her hand on his heart and her face next to his.

He could feel her breath as he lay there, suspended, halfway between life and death.

* * *

Just before nightfall, I returned to Hampton, leaving Madame Tallulah, Doctor Garden, and Little Daphne with Henri. I walked back through the rice fields amongst the slaves returning from the swamps. An eerie quiet covered the fields. Men, women, and children walked silently, heads bowed, as if some impending doom were gathering above them. The contrast with the normal sight of slaves working and doing their call and response songs unnerved me, sending a chill up my spine.

After finding the dirt path that led to the mansion, I spotted Old William's son, Roger. He looked up at me and asked if I knew what would happen once the soldiers came. I told him I did not know. Some of the other slaves heard Roger, and gathered around me, inquiring if I thought the soldiers would arrive before morning. I told them about our close call earlier in the afternoon and said they would most likely make camp and come at sunrise. Everyone listened intently, nodding as if I had some special knowledge, which of course, I did not; but it seemed to give everyone a small measure of comfort. Further down the path, I came across Harriott, walking alone, her dress mud soaked, red insect bites dotting her arms.

"Are you alright?" I said.

"Never mind me, how is Henri?" she asked stoically.

"He lies between life and death. Doctor Garden says it is up to Henri and God now."

"And Little Daphne? Is she there?"

"Yes, Harriott, she is by his side."

"Good," Harriott said brusquely. "She would never forgive herself, or me, if Henri were to die alone."

We walked together in silence. Harriott broke it only once: asking one of the slaves (whom I recognized as one of her overseers) if everything had been disposed of. She received an affirmative answer and continued—grim faced and silent—the long walk back to Hampton.

THE FLOATING MAN

We climbed the steps of the portico; Harriott paused at the sound of a distant drum. She listened, frozen for a minute, and then turned to me.

"The troops have made camp just outside Harrietta Plantation. Better get a good night's sleep, Robert. We are going to need it."

She turned and walked inside.

Despite her mud-soaked clothes, a regal air seemed to surround her.

* * *

Too bound up by worry to sleep, I sat on the portico long after the sun went down. A little after midnight, Isaac walked up. He had changed his clothes. Perspiring profusely, he ran a cloth across his face, patted me on the shoulder and went inside, returning a little while later with two mugs of peach-sweetened rum.

Isaac handed me a mug, took a sip of his, and stretched his back before sitting down next to me.

"Sure beats that damn molasses water and rum all to hell," he said staring out into the dark.

"Looks like you have been working pretty hard. Is Henri's secret, safe?"

Isaac grinned. "Old Moses and I worked all afternoon and evening. We took it apart and boxed it up. Then we buried it here and there. You want to know where?"

"No," I replied, thinking that if the troops tortured me I would not be able to keep a secret.

"Good. I was not going to tell you anyway," Isaac said, still grinning. As he looked into the darkness, his grin got wider.

"What about the troops, if they go digging up the place?"

Isaac turned to me. His eyes gleamed.

"You know how Henri likes his little games . . . his puzzles, Robert?"

"Yes, he told me of the games he played on the scientists in Arcueil."

"Well, I made my own little puzzle. They may dig it all up, Robert, but it is still up in the air whether they can figure it all out," Isaac said with a look that I can only describe as one of supreme satisfaction.

I raised my mug in salute and drained it. Isaac got up, but I motioned him to sit back down, taking his mug and mine inside to replenish.

Handing Isaac his refilled mug, he asked, "So, how does it feel to be a slave?"

"Not bad," I replied, "as long as it is only for a little while."

"Exactly," Isaac beamed. "You would make a good house slave, Robert, but I do not know about being a field slave."

"I do not think that would work out too well. For one, I cannot carry a tune. On top of that, I have a bad back and hate being out in the hot sun all day. And you know what else, Isaac?"

"What?"

"I am kind of lazy."

Isaac and I laughed together.

Turning back to face the darkness, Isaac got up with a start.

"Damn, Chief!" he said as the Chief appeared from the darkness and sat down next to us. "Quit playing like an Indian; give a proper announcement of your arrival. Almost scared the black out of me. And if Robert turned any paler, he would disappear."

"Is Henri dead?" the Chief asked solemnly.

Isaac answered: "No, we would have heard Madame Tallulah or Little Daphne announce his death; but the drum has been silent."

"Doctor Garden does not have a lot of hope," I added.

The Chief buried his head in his hands and sobbed.

"It is all my fault," he said.

"What are you talking about?" Isaac asked. "You could not have known what that crazy Andrew Jackson was up to."

"It is my fault." The Chief stood up and walked over to one of the portico columns, using it as a brace. Staring out into the darkness, he continued; "I told my braves to fire warning shots and make it close, so that Henri would turn back. A little too close, as it turned out."

Both Isaac and I tried to console the Chief. He remained oblivious to our entreaties. We left him there.

Alone.

On the portico.

Sobbing, into the dark.

CHAPTER 72

Beaufort, South Carolina; Present Day

James got up and went into the kitchen to make a pot of coffee, drawing a snide remark from Sheila.

"What's the matter, James? Too early for your scotch and water?"

"It's never too early or too late. It's a frame of mind, dear. And right now, my mind is a little fuzzy. Not enough sleep."

"Did you cheat and read ahead?"

"No, but I should have. My mind kept racing all night. You guys want a cup?"

"Yeah," Sheila said. "We couldn't sleep either."

Sitting around James' kitchen table, the three discussed Robert Campbell's memoirs.

"It's amazing. This one woman ran a large plantation all by herself," Sheila said. "Where were all the men?"

"Harriott's husband, Frederick Rutledge, died in 1824. Her brother, Charles, who befriended Henri in Paris, died in 1828. Our Harriott ran the plantation with her mother, Harriott Pinckney Horry. Both had the same name until the younger Harriott married Frederick."

James stopped to rub his eyes. He poured a little more coffee before continuing.

"From time to time, Harriott's sons would help out, but they were usually away, working on their own careers. For the most part, Hampton plantation has always been run by women. Eliza, our Harriott's grandmother, ran three plantations at the tender age of fifteen, while her father was off running a large holding in Antigua. Soon after Eliza married Charles Pinckney, he left for England to attend to business matters, leaving Eliza once again in charge, along with her daughter. The elder Harriott inherited the plantation upon Eliza's death. And our Harriott took over day-to-day operations from her mother, sometime in the late 1820's."

"Why no mention in the memoirs of the elder Harriott," John said, interrupting James.

"That's a good question. Harriott the elder, lived for sixty years at Hampton. In 1828 she moved to their Charleston residence and left the running of the plantation to our Harriott. Her mother died sometime in 1830, but my research doesn't give a date. I meant to ask the archivist about that when we visited the park . . . totally slipped my mind."

"You know, James, the memoir sounds awfully modern. It doesn't sound like it was written nearly two hundred years ago."

"What are you getting at?" Sheila asked John.

"Some of the wording doesn't sound like nineteenth-century literature. That's all."

"You think it's a forgery?" Sheila, upset, jumped out of her seat. With her hands on the table, she leaned over and glowered at John. "Elmer was murdered for a *forgery*? And I was raped by some psycho bitch for a . . . *forgery*!"

"Timeout!" the normally placid James shouted, bringing John and Sheila to a halt. "John's right."

"What?" Sheila couldn't believe what she was hearing.

In a softer tone, James said, "John's right, it doesn't sound authentic." He reached into his pocket and retrieved a few of his cocoa beans. "Forgive me, but forty years of editing copy dies hard. I thought I would edit as I read." James paused before changing the subject. "On a lighter note, any word from our FBI friend on the psycho bitch and her male companion?"

"No," Sheila said, sitting back down with a worn look on her face.

CHAPTER 73

Defense Intelligence Agency Headquarters: Joint Base Anacostia, Washington, DC

General Eric Stebbins sat at his desk reviewing intelligence reports from AFRICOM (US Africa Command center). Henry Smith, the president's national security advisor was concerned about the activities of Ansar al-Sharia, an Al Qaeda offshoot operating out of the southern Abyan province of Yemen. Rumors were swirling in the port city of Aden of various plots. One involved an assassination attempt on the Queen of England during her Jubilee celebration. Another, an attack on the 2012 London Olympics.

The general's men worked every asset they had. After digging for a week, they could find no evidence of any Ansar al-Sharia operations outside of Abyan province.

They simply do not have the operational capability for such an attack. Still, there's plenty to worry about.

The general buzzed his aide.

"Sir?"

"Stan, see if you can dig a little deeper over at NSA and find out what Henry's boys have on this Ansar al-Sharia business. Other than blowing up local officials in and around Aden . . . we've got nothing."

"Yes sir," Stan replied. And making the same mistake countless aides have made over the millennia, added, "anything else sir?"

"Let's broaden our scope on this thing. Get me all the latest intel on operational capabilities for Al Qaeda affiliates working in the region."

"Do you want raw data or analysis?"

"Both. Analysis and supporting data."

"Yes sir." Again, Stan made the fatal mistake common to aides. "Will that be all then?"

"Yes, Stan, that will be all."

But before the door completely closed, the general said, "Wait a second!"

"Yesss?" Stan slowly opened the door enough to look in.

"That asshole reporter who fucked us in that bid rigging scandal, John . . . what the *fuck's* his—"

"Hill, sir."

"Right. We find anything in the sweep of his office?"

"Nothing, sir. No bugs."

"And now?" the general's eyes bored in.

"Yes sir, top to bottom now."

"Good." The general went back to his reports. In an aside, without looking up, he asked, "What about Henry's eye candy."

"She's sleeping with him."

The general looked up. "*Henry?*"

"No sir, the reporter."

"Keep me up to date on any developments."

"You want camera feeds?"

"Stan, I'm not a peeping tom for Christ's sake. Any information on that Frenchman's antigravity device, I want. Anything, no matter how small. Understood?"

"Yes, sir. If I may, sir, why are we so interested in a piece of technology that is two hundred years old?"

"The machine may be two hundred years old, but the technology is cutting edge. Imagine fighter jets suddenly stopping, then dropping like a rock only to stop again and shoot up in the air, moving multi-directionally at the same time. Picture special ops forces outfitted with these devices, flitting around the battlefield. The possibilities are endless."

"If you say so, sir. Frankly, I think it's a waste of time. Hate to see resources tied up in what will probably turn out be a glorified balloon with a propeller. Meanwhile, we have Al Qaeda planning attacks against the Queen and the upcoming London summer Olympics."

"That's why you're an aide. You worry too much. And since when did you become so concerned about the use of resources? And Stan? That's not a question. You can go now. Remember, anything on this . . . I want to know. Immediately."

Stan nodded and closed the door on the general.

CHAPTER 74

President Jackson Arrives at Hampton Plantation: from the memoirs of Robert Campbell

For a change, I awoke at the first rays of dawn. Looking out my bedroom window I feared the worst, and those fears were realized: Federal troops were camped out on the grounds of Hampton. Coming down to breakfast, I found a nervous looking Harriott fussing with Old William by the stove. Presently, the sound of many men stomping up the steps of the front portico brought us to a halt, quickly followed by a thunderous knocking at the door.

"What the *hell!* Forgive me, Lord." Harriott stormed out of the kitchen followed by Old William and me. She flung the front door open with a furious look on her face. Standing on the porch, surrounded by men with rifles and bayonets was . . . Abel Jenkins!

"You again!" Harriott thundered. "Where is John Eaton, your boss?"

"I am afraid the secretary does not have much stomach for this kind of business," Abel replied. "The president sent him packing, back to Washington. I am not going to play with you Harriott. Hand over Henri or else suffer the consequences."

With her look of fury changing to one of utter contempt, Harriott took a swing at Abel's face. He intercepted the strike with his left hand while simultaneously striking Harriott with his right, flush on the side of her face. I quickly ran to her aid and was roughly shoved by two of the many soldiers gathered on the porch. At that same instant, a distinguished looking older man on horseback rode up to the steps of the portico. Surrounded by officers, he dismounted and climbed the steps. As he got closer, I could see that it was the great man himself, President Andrew Jackson.

Harriott recognized him also, and ran up to him.

"Mr. President, I must *insist* that you remove this vulgar man from my property immediately."

"And why should I do that, Madam?" the president asked.

"He struck me on the side of my face. The man has no civility, and does not know his proper place."

Abel turned to the president.

"Better watch out, Mr. President. Harriott sat on George Washington's lap. She is friends with President James Madison. Did I get that correct, Harriott?"

It looked to me as if Harriott's head—turning a purplish shade of red—would explode and erupt from her body at any moment. She tried to speak but could only gag.

Abel continued with much delight.

"That oak tree over there, Mr. President, was saved by George Washington and is named in his honor."

"Is that *so*?" the president replied. "Well, I do not particularly care for it. It blocks the view. If you like, Harriott, I will have my men chop it down for you."

"Mr. President, *please*." Harriott began to recover a bit of her dignity. She realized the gravity of the situation called for diplomacy. "Can we not discuss this civilly, inside? You are always welcome in my home."

Unfortunately, the president was not in a diplomatic mood this day.

"But my dear Harriott, this is no longer *your* home. Now it is *mine*. I am an old man and have had a long ride. I need my rest. You understand—I am sure."

And then the president turned to go inside, followed by the detestable Abel Jenkins.

"But of course, sir." Harriott turned and began to follow.

The president halted. He turned back around and grabbed Harriott roughly, spinning her around. With her shoulders held firmly by the president, a shocked Harriott looked out at an intermingling of troops and slaves; all gathered to see what the commotion was about. Suddenly, and without warning, she was flung down the steps. Harriott landed on her back, at the foot of the steps, looking up in utter disbelief.

The president pointed to one of the slave cabins and spoke in a booming voice: "*There* is your new home, Harriott. Now leave me in peace. Oh, and by the way, the day is a wasting. I suggest you get out in your rice fields and get to work, or I shall have you whipped." Then, the president gallantly took off his hat and gave her a bow, saying, "I bid you adieu, Madam," before turning on his heel and entering the mansion, followed by a laughing Abel Jenkins.

As Old William and I went past them down the steps to help Harriott, Abel Jenkins grabbed Old William firmly by the wrist. He and the president were now his masters. In a gratuitous insult, he addressed William while smiling at a stricken Harriott. "I hear the former owner of this house has some wonderful peach-sweetened rum. Please be so kind and fetch a mug for the president and me. Oh . . . and make sure you put an *extra* peach slice in mine."

* * *

With Isaac's assistance, I helped Harriott to her feet. We led her to the cabin of Preacher George. He graciously offered her the late Preacher Sogo's straw sleeping mat. Harriott sat very still for a long time on the straw mat. I was worried that she might have suffered from apoplexy; so it gave me much relief when Harriott smilingly accepted a mug of hot tea from Preacher George.

The preacher informed us that there were soldiers at all the Plantations owned by Harriott's family, and estimated their approximate number at five thousand. Shortly after he had finished speaking, a young soldier of no more than nineteen entered the cabin and looked around. Upon seeing Harriott, his face went beet red. I surmised that he must have been witness to President Jackson's most indecent display of manners.

Assuring himself that there was no Henri Richaud in the cabin, the young soldier tipped his head towards Harriott and softly said, "Ma'am, my apologies for the intrusion." He then turned and left the cabin. Not many moments later, other soldiers arrived and ordered everybody out of their cabins and into the rice fields. This was done—we later learned—at Wambaw, Harrietta, and Belmont plantations at approximately the same time. The soldiers wanted us out of our homes so they could make a thorough search of every slave cabin, every room of the mansions, carriage house, boathouse, and kitchen house. In fact, no standing structure was left unsearched. Not even the chicken coops or pig pens were spared.

After a long day in the rice fields I was exhausted, though I didn't even get my feet wet. Accompanying Harriott and Old Sandy, we had walked along the dikes and inspected floodgates. I could only imagine the exhaustion felt by the men, women, and children, working in those hot muddy rice fields surrounding us. All day long, day after day, week after week, year after year, they toiled. Close to a century at Hampton Plantation, longer at others—they toiled. Harriott once explained that a human being gets used to just about anything. What makes it bearable is family, and the camaraderie one feels, working and singing side by side.

We returned to our cabins at sunset. No one felt like singing this night. Instead, everyone watched silently from their porches, staring in disbelief at the troops surrounding the mansion, camped out across the grounds.

Most of the cabins had been left in a state of disarray. Slaves who would normally be cooking and relaxing, now had to work to get their shelters in order. Isaac, Harriott, and I sat on Isaac's porch watching the comings and goings on the front portico. Our usual nighttime spot was now presently occupied by officers of the Federal Government.

Isaac pointed out Abel Jenkins, striding through the front door onto the porch.

"Look at that fat bastard put that peach in his mouth. No offense, Harriott, but I have this picture of him with his pasty white skin glistening in oil, a peach in his mouth, all trussed up and roasting over an open fire."

"You have quite a lovely imagination, Isaac. I can almost smell the garlic, pepper, and salt penetrating his flesh," Harriott responded, getting into Isaac's reverie.

President Andrew Jackson came out onto the porch and sat down.

"Now what could we do with that old dried-up piece of meat, Isaac?" Harriott asked.

"That's a tough one, Harriott. Maybe we could tan strips of his skin and use them for shoe laces. Other than that or a tough beef jerky, our options are rather limited."

I got into the game, adding, "The president would probably be best put to use ground-up and fed as slop to the pigs. Then we could properly feast on him throughout the year."

"Excellent!" Harriott said. "We can have the president for breakfast, dinner and supper. Bacon in the morning, glazed ham for dinner and pickled pig's feet for supper."

Isaac's wife, Eve, quietly listening from inside while she stirred a pot of stew, spoke up: "You know that would make you all cannibals, don't ya?"

We looked over at her.

She raised the pot by the handle and said, "Supper's ready."

For some reason, except for Eve, we all lost our appetite.

* * *

The three of us continued to sit on the porch, drinking rum, water, and molasses. Looking on in envy as President Jackson and Abel Jenkins drank Harriott's peach-sweetened rum, complete with a slice of peach. We sat mesmerized, watching the president talk animatedly with his aides.

Isaac jumped up with a start.

"*Jesus!* Chief. Quit sneaking up like that," Isaac said as the Chief out of nowhere appeared, sitting next to him.

"I just got back from Madame Tallulah's," the Chief said as we turned to him. "Henri has improved slightly. He regained consciousness earlier this evening and smiled at Little Daphne. He asked for some of Harriott's peach rum."

"Well, why don't you just *sneak* on up there and get some?" Isaac said, still smarting from being snuck up on.

Addressing Isaac, the Chief said in a solemn tone, "I will . . . a little later in the evening."

"*That*, I would like to see," I said.

The Chief's mood darkened.

"Tomorrow is not going to be a good day. Not good for any of us. The president plans to start torturing slaves to find the whereabouts of Henri. I recommend that I get you all out of here. Doctor Garden and Madame Tallulah both agree that Henri cannot be moved for at least another day. If I can create some havoc, perhaps we can buy ourselves some time."

"I am not going anywhere, Chief," Harriott said determinedly. "This is *my* home and I am responsible for the people who live here. I will not let those bastards whip anybody. It has never been done at this plantation, and I am not going to let it start now."

"I am sorry to say this, Harriott, but you do not have much say in the matter at this point. The guy up there drinking your rum is the one in charge now," the Chief said apologetically.

"I hope to hell they find that spoiled jar of peaches and poison themselves," Harriott said. Bidding us all a goodnight, she walked over to Preacher George's cabin and her straw-mat bed.

CHAPTER 75

The sun rose on a hot steamy morning. Thick fog spilled over Wambaw Creek, wafting over and through the slave cabins. From the fog emerged swarms of soldiers going from cabin to cabin, grabbing men, women, and children. Sleeping, half dressed, or completely naked, it did not matter. All of us were roughly taken from our quarters, brought to the front grounds of Hampton plantation and lined up in front of the portico. Soldiers with rifles and bayonets lined up behind us in rows.

We stood like statues for over an hour. During that time, Harriott made a few feeble attempts to break free and march up the portico steps, but each time was restrained. A soldier grabbed each of her arms just beneath her shoulders and held her firmly, making further attempts futile. I looked around for Chief John Ross but did not see him among those assembled. I prayed he had eluded Jackson's troops and rejoined Henri.

Suddenly, a most peculiar assemblage occurred on the porch. Several young soldiers with drums appeared, joined shortly thereafter by soldiers with trumpets and other instruments. A drum roll sounded, followed by several trumpet flourishes. And then, "Hail to the Chief," a song from the play *Lady of the Lake* rang out. It was quite impressive. I learned later in life that President Jackson had formally requested this song be played at all his public appearances. Upon conclusion of the song, President Jackson—in full-dress uniform—walked out the front door onto the portico, followed by several aides: including, of course, Abel Jenkins.

Quite a murmur arose from the slaves. The president held up his hands in a quieting gesture. Silence reigned. Even the birds paid homage.

"Ladies and gentleman," the president began, in a clear confident tone. "Let me first take this moment to apologize to all of you for this most inconvenient disruption of your lives. But grave matters of state sometimes require a few inconveniences, do they not? As your president, I am duty bound to defend with my life, if necessary, this great country, from enemies within and without. In the short life of our glorious republic we have been attacked by foreign powers on several occasions. I have no doubt that the European powers still have designs on our great land. As I speak to you today, scientists from these countries are working on advancements in warfare . . . as are we. Any advantage one country gains over another could be determinant in its survival or extinction.

"My friends, we stand at the crossroads of history today. Right here on this little corner of the world resides an invention so technologically advanced, it could insure our survival as a great republic. It could also insure our extinction, if it were to fall into the hands of a foreign power. We must be eternally vigilant in the defense of freedom.

"The inventor of this device is believed to reside here. A great man who may lie gravely wounded. I mean this man no harm. In fact, I have come here along with my personal physician to render this man aid and comfort. My most fervent wish is to restore this good man to health and prosperity. The creator of this most wonderful invention must be honored and revered. I will provide this man with the wealth and high esteem he so richly deserves, if you will but allow it. My friends; I come to you as your president, but also humbly, as a man, to beseech you in all that is right and good for your country. Come forth now, and tell me where this great man and his invention lies."

As the president looked out over the crowd for someone to come forth, I thought about Little Daphne's speech to her fellow slaves and wondered if the stature of the president standing before them would cause their resolve to wither. Several moments passed. It was clear that Little Daphne had made quite an impression on everyone.

The president spoke softly to an aide. The aide saluted and ran inside. Moments later he returned, holding a small chest. The president briefly smiled and spoke again. This time I was certain the slaves would abandon Little Daphne and her man.

"My friends," the president began as his aide opened the chest revealing gold coins. "I am prepared to offer this treasure to anyone who will come forth with information leading to the recovery of Henri Richaud and his invention. Along with this treasure comes freedom. Freedom not just for the person who comes forth, but freedom for all who work on the plantations owned by Harriott Horry Rutledge and her late husband, Frederick."

The president paused. Nobody came forth . . . so he increased his offer.

"Along with your freedom, each of you will be given a thousand dollars in gold coins."

The president paused again and looked out over the crowd.

He began to diminish in my eyes. His true self revealed. A shrunken dried up shell, desperately trying for renewed greatness— reduced to an ordinary huckster. Any hope of his reaching the slaves was destroyed by his obvious pandering.

"Along with your freedom and a thousand dollars, each slave . . . or rather, I should correct myself, each former slave will be offered fifty acres of land carved from Harriott's plantations or in the newly opened western lands."

The president paused once again and looked out at the crowd before continuing his pitch.

"Also, the Federal Government is prepared to give you each a plow mule . . . wagon . . . and seeds for planting."

At this point, one of the slaves laughed; a fury took hold in the president's eyes.

"All right then," he thundered. "It is clear that you have fallen under the subversive sway of this traitor to our country, Harriott Horry Rutledge. So now you shall see what is done to traitors. Bring that young boy over there to me."

The president pointed to Old William's son, Little Caesar. A soldier dragged the struggling boy over to the president. He was handed a whip by one of his aides.

This was just too much for Harriott to bear. Breaking free of her tormentors, she ran up to the president with a fire in her eyes that matched his.

"Don't you *dare* lay a hand on one of my slaves! I cannot believe the country made such a grave mistake in making you president. You *besmirch* the memory of our founders."

The president smiled. "Whether or not I besmirch the founders is for history to decide. But I will honor your request. Let the boy go, he is not my property. But this woman is. Take her over to her beloved George Washington oak."

As Harriott was led to the oak tree the president added a further humiliation. Before the soldiers could tie her arms around the trunk of the tree, he stopped them.

"Strip off her clothes. There is no distinction between her and her slaves any longer."

Harriott turned and faced the president.

"I am fully capable of removing my own clothes."

In full view of everyone, Harriott, with much dignity, disrobed and addressed the president: "I am not afraid to expose myself, unlike you, who resides underneath the trappings of former greatness, with your ribbons and epaulets to puff your shrunken self up."

Turning to face the tree, Harriott was unable to see the president's face turn a dark red as her arms were lashed round the oak.

The president, regaining his composure, began whipping Harriott's naked back. His first blows were vicious: ripping deeply into Harriott's flesh. Blood ran in rivulets down her back. After the first few blows, I was greatly relieved that the president—a frail man in his sixties—soon lost his vigor. Harriott bravely refused to let out a sound. This seemed to enrage the president even more. He bent over to catch his breath, and then continued his now feeble attempts at meting out his perverted form of justice.

When the president, exhausted, handed the whip over to Abel Jenkins, I had witnessed enough. I fervently hoped the Chief had been successful in his plan to move Henri (revealed to me the previous night). Otherwise, Harriott and Little Daphne would never forgive me for what I was about to do.

"Stop!" I yelled, stepping forward. "I will give you Henri."

A furious and wounded Harriott sputtered, "Don't you dare, Robert! Let the bastard kill me."

"I am sorry, Harriott," I said with much sadness in my voice. "I cannot let this madness go on any longer."

I approached the president. My body felt as if it carried the weight of all those brave souls that had resisted the president's entreaties. In a voice heavy with resignation, I said, "Mr. President, I shall lead you to Henri when I have your assurance that no further harm will come to Harriott, her slaves, or this plantation. I give you my word: When the troops are removed from these grounds, I will lead you to where Henri was taken after being grievously wounded."

I was quickly brought inside the mansion where I stalled for as long as I could while mutually acceptable terms were negotiated. A message was sent by drum to the other plantations to signal when the troops began to withdraw. Once withdrawn across the Santee River, another drum message would attest to that fact. I would then lead President Jackson, along with his personal physician and ten soldiers, to Henri.

Another hour passed before the drums sounded, signaling the withdrawal of troops. I led President Jackson and his party onto the dikes that traversed the rice fields, and into the cypress forests to Madame Tallulah's cabin, praying all the way that Chief John Ross had been successful in his mission to save Henri.

We arrived at the cabin a little after midday, greeted by the Madame herself. Filling up the entrance to her small home, I was crestfallen when Madame Tallulah raised a fuss and would not let us enter. I knew this meant that the Chief had not been successful. As the troops tried to barge their way in, Madame Tallulah, with a strength I had never before witnessed in a woman, pushed them away with a broom handle.

"No one gits in here when dere be a sick man," she said in her French Caribbean accent. "Ize will let yoose knowse when Henri is ready foe company."

"Madame," the president spoke. "I am your president and I will gain entry into your cabin immediately."

"De hell yoose—"

And before Madame Tallulah could finish her sentence, the

president nodded to a soldier who quickly ran his bayonet into Madame Tallulah's side. A look of utter shock crossed her face as she crumpled to the ground. I immediately rushed to her aid.

The president crossed into the cabin with his personal physician.

"So *this* is the great man. Is he alive?" I heard him whisper.

There was a long interval before the president's physician spoke.

"He is unconscious, but his heart is strong and his lungs are clear."

"What about his wound?" I heard the president ask, holding my hand to Madame Tallulah's side.

"It does not appear to be seeping too much blood, Mr. President. And the bandage looks fresh. I would say the lady did a pretty good job."

As the doctor said this, I thought I saw a small smile flicker across Madame Tallulah's face, quickly returning to one of pain.

"Is it safe to move him?" the president asked.

"Yes, I think he will be fine," the doctor replied.

The troops carried Henri out on a stretcher. Ashamed, I could not bear to look. After only ten minutes from our arrival, they were gone.

With much difficulty, I half carried and dragged Madame Tallulah into her cabin. We both collapsed to the floor: her from her grievous wounds, and me from shame.

CHAPTER 76

Alone in her cabin, I was distraught. Not only had I betrayed my friends, I was now responsible for Madame Tallulah, dying on the floor of her cabin. In and out of consciousness, she instructed me on preparing the mixture used the previous day to stop Henri's bleeding. Mixing egg yolks with turpentine and rose oil per Madame Tallulah's instructions, I poured the mixture into the wound. I then saturated a cloth with the mixture and pressed it against the wound, wrapping another cloth around it. I started to tear up when I saw how much blood was on the floor of her cabin.

As she lay dying, Madame Tallulah made a last request: "Mistah Robert, will yoose do me a small comfort?"

"Of course," I replied.

"I aint's knowns a man since Napoleon's men done cut me up so I wernt fit foe no man's touch. It's been so long, could yoose hold me like a man holds a woman? I don't wants teh die alone widout a man's touch."

I pressed myself tight up against her back, my arms surrounding her, gently caressing her flesh, kissing her neck. Soon, we fell fast asleep.

* * *

The next morning I was still holding Madame Tallulah's lifeless body. I pulled away, got up . . . startled to hear, "I aints dead yet."

"Sorry," was all I could think to say. I lay back down again, encircling the Madame in my arms, caressing her.

Shortly before noon the Chief entered the cabin. I quickly apologized for turning Henri over to the president.

The Chief grinned.

"You didn't turn Henri over. That was Doctor Garden."

"What?" I exclaimed.

"He agreed to take Henri's place. Even cut and stitched himself up. He and Madame Tallulah mixed some herbs in a pot. He drank it. Said it would knock him out for over a day. Henri is on a boat in the swamp. One of my braves is watching over him. I followed the president and his men until they reached the road to Georgetown."

It was at this point that the Chief noticed Madame Tallulah's blood-soaked side. He began to move about, inside and out of the cabin, mixing plants and herbs together; remarking to me as he worked that he was making a stew of African, Indian, and White man medicine. After working on Madame Tallulah's injury and placing a new bandage on her, I again took my place at her side. The Chief left to aid Henri.

Towards evening I could not feel Madame Tallulah breathing. I got up and went outside to relieve myself. When I returned, I was shocked to see Madame Tallulah sitting up. I boiled her some soup. Afterwards, she replied that she was still going to die and begged me to hold her some more. We resumed our now familiar positions, soon falling fast asleep.

Upon awakening the next morning, Madame Tallulah was gone.

CHAPTER 77

In a panic, I searched around for Madame Tallulah but was unsuccessful in my attempts to locate her. I trudged dejectedly back to Hampton. Nearing the back entrance, I noticed several Indian ponies tied up. Inside, around the kitchen table, a discussion was going on between Harriott, the Chief, and Little Daphne—which I interrupted. As they looked up, I told them how I had lost Madame Tallulah sometime during the night. I was greatly relieved when everyone assured me that Madame Tallulah was fine; the Chief had carried her on his back to Hampton in the early morning hours to help in the treatment of Henri.

Entering Henri's bedroom accompanied by Little Daphne, I found Madame Tallulah changing Henri's dressing.

"I see you have made a miraculous recovery," I said with a stern look that was a bit put on.

"Maybe I wernt hurt as bad as I taut," Madame Tallulah meekly offered. "Den again, maybe it was yoose magic touch. You ever tink of bein a healer, Mistah Robert?"

I shook my head no, and asked the Madame, "You ever think of being an actor? That was quite a performance you gave me."

"Is yoose mad at me?" she said, smiling a bit too sheepishly.

"Nah, I enjoyed it as much as you. Besides, the rest did us both good," I replied.

Madame Tallulah began to open her mouth to reply, but was interrupted by the sounds of a wheezing Henri. I pulled him up to a sitting position, while she yelled for the Chief to bring some aromatic herbs that she had boiling in a pot. He came in and placed the pot where Henri could breathe in the vapors. Madame Tallulah explained that this would help his lungs from becoming too congested. Once Henri was a little more healed, he could cough up the phlegm that was accumulating.

The next few days were tense as we awaited Henri's recovery and word from the Chief's scouts on the whereabouts of President Jackson and his troops. We also were greatly worried about the safety of Doctor Garden. Once President Jackson realized he had been duped, there was no telling what he might do in a fit of rage.

Earlier, before the president's arrival, Isaac had accompanied the Chief to Madame Tallulah's. He gave Doctor Garden an outline of the scientific principles behind the antigravity machine, along with some of the mechanics of the device. Isaac said Doctor Garden listened intently and asked pertinent questions. But of course, Isaac, like the rest of us, did not know how long the doctor could fool the president and his scientific advisors. Harriott prayed that it would be long enough for her to send a missive to her old friend, President James Madison, asking for intercession on her behalf.

The passage of a week's time found Henri coughing up phlegm and keeping down soup. It was decided that now was the time to talk about his travel plans. At first, Henri was more interested in why Little Daphne had destroyed his invention. The two went at each other like an old married couple; we all found it quite amusing. Little Daphne had the last word on the subject as is usually the case in the affairs of men and women.

"You need to grow up, Henri. You are getting too old to be flying around; you have more earthly matters to worry about. Like taking care of your son," Little Daphne said, exasperated.

"A *son*?" Henri said excitedly. "How can you tell?"

"A woman knows these things, Henri," Little Daphne replied, winking at Harriott who stood to the side, smiling at Daphne's ruse.

"A son . . . yes, that does change things quite a bit." Henri thought for a while, and then pointing to his head, said, "Besides, it's all up here. I can teach him the secrets of my machine."

"Not if you hang around here," Isaac joined in.

"No, I suppose you are right, Isaac. The president will be back for me sooner or later. I guess it is time for me to return to my homeland."

"I have my scouts checking on the Ports of Charleston and Savannah. Right now there is no increased federal activity." The Chief paused for a moment. "But you will not be ready to travel for another week. By that time circumstances may change."

"Do you have an alternative plan, Chief?" Henri asked as Little Daphne held his hand.

"The other plan involves a long journey to the western territories, and then later, a ship from a gulf port."

"But that is so far away," I replied.

"I know the route well, Robert. In due course, this is where President Jackson will force all Cherokees to reside. Negotiations I have had with Jackson and his representatives the past few years make his intentions pretty clear. Already, some of my people have voluntarily moved there. The president's ultimate plan is to weaken and divide us into Western and Eastern Cherokee. Once he has accomplished this, he can play one off the other and eventually remove us by force."

"But you have signed treaties," Harriott said, "by George Washington himself."

"Treaties mean nothing to Jackson, Harriott," the Chief said sadly. "You know what his friends and foes alike call him, don't you?" Not waiting for a reply the Chief continued: "King Andrew. He does not care what the congress or the courts decide; he is a law unto himself. Look at what he did in New Orleans, against orders. He virtually exterminated the Seminoles. It was only his harsh treatment of British civilians that earned him a reprimand . . . and he just laughed that off." Then the Chief very tenderly took Harriott's hands in his, and with much conviction said, "I hope by God your letter to President Madison is a good one that bears fruit, because I am telling you Harriott, with that man, *everything* is personal. I saw the way he looked at you when you were strapped to that tree."

Harriott looked down, ashamed at the memory of her humiliation. The Chief kept hold of her hands. His words to Harriott set the mood. That last week, we all waited with dark anticipation for word of any movement of Jackson's troops and signs of improvement in Henri's condition.

CHAPTER 78

The last Friday—Good Friday as I now refer to it—found Henri in much improved condition. He was able to take a few steps without aid, and his color had returned to normal. He even joined us on the portico at noon for some of Harriott's peach rum, with Little Daphne at his side. We reminisced about Henri's tour, which now seemed so long ago. So much adventure packed in such a short period of time. We told stories of our youth and vowed we would be best friends forever. Avoiding any talk of the inevitable... uncertain future.

It was Isaac who brought us back to the present.

"So Henri, what are you going to name the little bastard?"

"*What?*" Henri said, taken aback.

"Well, the little bastard has to have a name, doesn't he?"

"Why do you refer to my future son as a little bastard, why be so insulting?" Henri appeared genuinely wounded by Isaac's flippant manner of speech.

In a more soothing tone, Isaac replied, "You are not married, Henri, and you are preparing for a long journey. Have you given the matter any thought?"

"No, I am afraid I have not," Henri answered. "I have been so consumed with my invention and theories that I have completely neglected more earthly matters. I owe you all an apology. I have been foolish: thinking I could change the world. I realize, now, perhaps too late, what is most important... your friendship. You have all placed yourselves at considerable risk for me and my folly. Watching over me as I naively went along my merry way. And for that, I will always be grateful."

Harriott was not about to let the mood of the day be ruined.

"Henri, we will have no apologies today. It is time to put this episode behind us and get on with the next act of our lives. Little Daphne, I am sorry dear, but you are going to have to do double duty today and help me with the cooking."

"And *what* is the second duty?" Little Daphne said guardedly.

Harriott, in a most natural tone replied, "Why, you silly former slave, you are going to be a bride. And Isaac, please be so kind and fetch Tailor Will and Preacher George."

Little Daphne, overcome with emotion, broke down and ran inside. I must confess, we were all a bit overwhelmed at Harriott's ability to take charge of the affairs of men in such a solicitous manner.

"What about guests, Harriott?" Henri inquired. "We must have guests for such an occasion."

Harriott gave Henri a look; under her breath she said, "Oh what the hell." She stood up and yelled out to Isaac, who was now some thirty yards distant: "Isaac! Bring in everybody from the fields." And then in an aside to Henri, Harriott added, "If we are going to have a party, might as well make it a good one. Seems of late, I cannot get any work done around here anyway."

Harriott's announcement unleashed a flurry of motion. The Chief and two of his braves joined several slaves on a hunting party, soon returning with several game birds and turkeys. Women busily prepared vegetables and got their fires together. Several pigs were pierced with iron spits, secured at each end by prongs and placed on a large roasting rack, where Old William stood at the ready to turn the crank. Little Daphne and Harriott ran around like a pair of chickens with their heads cut off, doing a lot of directing but not accomplishing much. Tailor Will chased after Little Daphne in an attempt to get her measurements but soon gave up his futile pursuit and went inside to work on altering Harriott's old wedding dress. I jumped on a horse and rode off to Harrietta and Wambaw plantations to inform the slaves that their work was done for the week. They all looked at me as if I were mad, until I explained to them that Little Daphne was to be married.

* * *

We all gathered around the front portico. Little Daphne, looking radiant in Harriott's old wedding dress, stood on the porch. Henri, still too weak to stand for any length of time, sat in a chair next to her, wearing his velvet trimmed morning coat. With Preacher George before them, and Harriott standing off to the side of Little Daphne, the ceremony began.

"Today is a celebration of the Lord's good works," Preacher George intoned. "The Lord has taken two of his servants and brought them together on this day: a man from across a great ocean and a slave girl, raised on a plantation. Truly, the Lord is great. His works provide comfort and hope. As we join these two together as man and wife, let us remember what the good book says: Wherefore they are no more twain, but one flesh. What therefore God hath joined together, let not man put asunder."

Preacher George bent down to help Henri to his feet. Looking him sternly in the eye, he said, "Henri, do you want this woman?"

After a pause, Henri realized he was supposed to answer.

"Yes, of course."

Preacher George turned to Little Daphne. "Do you want this man? He seems a little old for you." Preacher George smiled as he said this, and several in attendance laughed.

With tears of happiness in her eyes, Little Daphne answered.

"Yes."

The preacher turned and nodded to Harriott: "Hold the broom please."

Harriott held the broom behind Little Daphne about a foot off the ground; she jumped over it backwards. Then she held the broom for Henri and placed it a little lower for him.

Henri looked panic stricken. "Am I supposed to jump *backwards* over that?"

Harriott looked over at the Chief, then at me. Taking the hint, we ran up the stairs and took hold of Henri's arms, lifting him over the broomstick. Amid much laughter and clapping, Little Daphne put her arms around Henri and gave him a kiss.

"You know what this means, don't you, Henri?" she said,

looking at the broom.

"No, what does it mean?" Henri looked completely baffled.

"Tell him, Preacher George," Harriott said between laughs.

"Well, Henri," Preacher George began, "the jumping of the broom is a solemn occasion. Whoever jumps highest over the broom is the master of the household and the one that makes the final decisions. And Henri, you cheated by being lifted over, so that means Little Daphne is the head of this household."

Henri replied, "Oh hell, George, I already knew that."

After the laughter died down, Henri asked Preacher George if he had any words of wisdom he wished to impart.

Preacher George smiled and said, "Never marry a woman who has bigger feet than you."

Henri quickly looked down at his and Little Daphne's feet and exclaimed, "My feet are bigger!"

"Then you two should have a long happy marriage." Preacher George raised both arms to the heavens and added, "Let's rejoice and give praise to the Lord."

And that was the signal for the party to begin.

* * *

Have you ever seen three hundred slaves party for three days running? Neither had I. All through Friday night we danced and sang, even Harriott joined in. Although confined to a wheelchair, Henri was in great spirits: lifted, in no small measure, by Little Daphne's suggestive dance that began the festivities. With everyone forming a circle around the two, Little Daphne approached Henri's wheelchair from a distance, slowly circling and moving closer, like a cat stalking her prey. As she got nearer, she began to shake and gyrate her body in a most stimulating and licentious fashion to the beat of drums. She dipped and bent over Henri several times, forward and back; ran her hands through his hair and traced lines upon his face with her long slender fingers. Round and round, Little Daphne circled her delighted husband. Her dress and limbs gently brushed up against him. Henri breathed in deeply, her scent, and began to rise out of his wheelchair, only to be gently forced back down by Daphne. The dance climaxed when Little Daphne climbed athwart Henri's lap, and cradling his head in her hands, gently kissed his forehead and drew him close to her bosom.

With Henri and Little Daphne repairing to a nearby porch to watch the festivities, Isaac taught me the finer points of rhythmical clapping. Soon, I was able to vary my pitch considerably, clapping my cheeks and moving my jaw around in harmony with the other musicians. I lost the rhythm when I tried to add foot stomping and thigh slapping to my repertoire; so I stuck with what I knew best.

Several rings of dancers formed around the burning fires. The tempo began slowly, gradually building to a crescendo, that once reached, continued for several hours. Many appeared to be in a state of ecstasy and fell to the ground in pure delight—aided, no doubt, by a degree of rum intoxication. Others quit the ring from exhaustion, quickly replaced by new dancers.

Around midnight, Isaac informed me that my cheeks were becoming bruised and strongly suggested I give the face clapping a break. He asked me to join him in the ring, dancing to the now familiar lyrics.

Juba, whirl dat foot about . . . Juba, blow dat candle out. Juba! Juba!

To my left, the Chief was dancing with some of his braves in a nearby circle. The more I danced and sang, the farther the difficulties of the past few weeks receded from my consciousness.

Juba circle, Raise de Latch, Juba do dat Long Dog Scratch. Juba! Juba!

Watching the pure joy and intensity in those around me, I began to understand that this was not just a celebration, but a spiritual cleanse: to rid one's soul of the indignity of being another person's property. To momentarily forget a lifetime of exhausting sweat and toil, endured on a daily basis for the rest of their lives. For that brief moment I felt connected. I understood the deep pain necessitating this ritual.

Looking at my friend Isaac—destined to a lifetime of servitude—I saw only joy in his eyes. Now was not the time for contemplation but rather for submission to a communal joy and oneness. Turning my gaze from Isaac, I immersed myself in the rhythms and endless lyrics.

Juba dis an' Juba dat, Juba skin dat yaller Cat. Juba! Juba!

The circle moved faster and faster, the rhythmical clapping and drums coursed through our bodies.

Juba jump an' Juba sing. Juba, cut dat Pigeon's Wing. Juba! Juba!

* * *

The Floating Man

I don't remember, but I must have passed out from exhaustion or intoxication. Waking to the sun breaking through the trees, I felt surprisingly refreshed: attributing it to the dancing, which must have burned away the rum.

The Chief, walking with his braves, gathered everyone up and led us to a large shallow inlet off of Wambaw Creek—swollen from a recent high tide. With everyone following along, the Chief and his braves guided us step-by-step through the sacred going to water ritual: dipping our hands in the cool morning water of Wambaw Creek, six times to the crown of our heads and the seventh time to our hearts. We listened silently as the Chief and his braves sang the sacred morning song. At the conclusion, we plunged into the middle of the creek and gave ourselves a good scrubbing. The slaves were very impressed and commented that they would like to make this part of their daily ritual.

Preacher George asked the Chief and his braves if they would consent to being baptized. The Chief eagerly assented. After a laying on of hands followed by another submersion in the waters of the Wambaw we engaged in some horseplay. The Chief started things off by pushing one of his braves under the water, followed by retaliation in the form of splashing. We soon climbed on each other's shoulders and engaged in mock warfare, trying to pull anyone in our vicinity into the water. After a considerable amount of time had passed, several of the women came marching down and ordered us to get dressed for breakfast.

The rest of Saturday followed the same pattern as Friday; if the reader wishes to get a flavor of what occurred, you may indulge yourself by rereading the previous paragraphs.

I would be remiss, however, if I did not make one additional note: Henri, wheeled around by his new bride, stopped at every cabin and thanked the occupants for their friendship and hospitality.

CHAPTER 79

On Sunday morning, after church, the men brought in the hunt and the women prepared the food. No sooner had we all sat down for dinner, spread across the grounds of Hampton, then the sound of distant drums filled the air. Everyone stopped and listened. Soon there was quite a stirring amongst those present. Not being familiar in drum language, I asked Old William, seated next to me, what the drums said. As I watched the Chief get up and walk off at a brisk pace, William informed me that federal troops were at the port of Charleston (some fifty miles away) and more ominously, were also at Georgetown (less than twenty miles away).

Our last dinner together ended before it had started. It was now clear that the Chief's alternate plan of moving Henri to the newly opened western territories would have to be immediately implemented. Federal troops would be expecting Henri to head for one of the ports, most likely Georgetown or Charleston—not further into the wilderness of the country.

While Little Daphne packed up Henri's clothes, the Chief and I wheeled him over to the carpenter's shop where Old Moses was finishing up work on Henri's horse litter. Consisting of a long, narrow wooden box set on two poles harnessed to horses—one in front, one in back—the litter was more than it seemed. Along the sides ran wooden ribs that arched over the box, covered by a sheet.

Old Moses showed a delighted Henri how he could open and close the cover. As he cranked a small handle connected by cords to a pulley, the ribbed canopy moved forward and back.

The journey west of the Mississippi to the new Indian Territories would be arduous, especially for a man in Henri's condition. The Chief was concerned that Henri would be bounced around too much, reopening his wounds. These concerns were assuaged when Old Moses lifted the cotton-stuffed mattress lining. Underneath, an assembly consisting of flexible wooden slats and rollers acted in concert to absorb energy from any sudden shocks. Listening closely, I was totally lost, but the Chief nodded knowingly as the function of each component part was explained. Later, I asked the Chief if he really understood what Henri and Old Moses were talking about. He replied that he did not have a clue.

Everything happened so quickly. The Chief was impatient to take off while there was still plenty of daylight between the night and the troops. Harriott assembled us all on the portico to say our goodbyes. She gave Little Daphne a hug and officially presented freedom papers to her. She then approached Isaac.

"I know how close you and Henri are," Harriott began. "It does not feel right anymore: the power I have over a human being's life. But I am stuck with one foot in the past and one foot in the present. I am just as enslaved by history as are my slaves. But you do not have to be, Isaac." At this point, Harriott brushed back a tear that had begun to streak down her face. "You have shown you have more humanity than me. All the trips you have taken up north, waiting loyally for me to return, when you could have simply walked off to freedom. My conscience cannot bind you here any longer."

Harriott handed papers to an astonished Isaac, granting freedom to him and his family.

Isaac took the papers, looked at them and began to cry as he handed them back to Harriott.

We looked on dumbfounded.

"I cannot leave here, Miss Harriott. My whole life I have dreamed of freedom. I have dreamed of the great things I would accomplish. How I would walk free down the street and someone might say, 'there goes Isaac the owner and driver of that carriage over there; he is a good man.' But it is far easier to dream than to actually do. I am like a bird that lives its whole life in a cage. Once let out, it will always fly back to the only world it has known. A world that feels safe and secure."

"But Isaac," I said to him, "there is so much more to life out there than these few acres. There are so many possibilities. You can go anywhere."

"Robert," Isaac replied to me, "you mean well, but your naiveté betrays you. *You* can go anywhere, but not me. I have a certain condition that I cannot change."

Isaac rubbed his index finger across his forearm and said, "I cannot even go back to the land of my fathers. I have lost my native tongue. I do not know their ways. So it is best I stay here. But now I have lost not only my freedom but my dreams as well. Knowing I could have been free and did not take it."

Harriott took a sobbing Isaac in her arms and patted him on the back. I heard her whisper in his ear: "Yes you can, Isaac. You can still dream. Take these papers and keep them safe. Your dreams can be even bigger now that they are a step closer to reality. Take all the time you need dear, hold on to your dreams. Make them a reality. When you are ready, your dreams will be waiting for you. You'll see."

After some last goodbyes, Henri was loaded into the horse litter. Together with the Chief, Little Daphne, and three braves, they rode off in a cloud of dust, leaving Harriott, Isaac, and me, alone on the portico, wondering aloud if we would ever see our friends again.

CHAPTER 80

We received our answer thirty minutes later.

Our friends returned, quickly dismounting. Bounding up the portico, the Chief informed us that troops were already in place around the plantation. Old Moses came running up to see what was going on as four of the Chief's braves unharnessed the horse litter and placed it on the ground. The Chief was quite distraught and feared that Henri would soon be in the hands of Jackson's men. Discussions began on where to hide Henri; Old Moses kept trying to interrupt. Harriott finally turned to Moses.

"What is it, Old Moses?"

"Miss Harriott, we can sneak Henri across the Wambaw and rice fields, through the canals and into the swamps. Just like Preacher Sogo did for the Swamp Fox when the British surrounded the place."

Harriott quickly dismissed the idea.

"The boat is at Wambaw plantation and we just had a high tide. Henri cannot possibly get across the Wambaw now, Moses. Besides, Preacher Sogo was the only one who knew those swamps, and he is dead."

Old Moses would not be deterred.

"He showed me as a little boy, Miss Harriott. And do not worry about Henri."

Before she could respond, he turned to Isaac.

"Get the carriage ready for a trip to Georgetown. Use the four-horse harness and harness three of the Chief's horses along with Harriott's remaining mare." Old Moses then looked directly at Harriott: "I hope you're the equal of your mother. You are going to have to charm the soldiers enough to let you pass."

Old Moses sent Little Daphne off to round up several slaves. The Chief and I followed him to his shop and returned with several thick ropes to the banks of the Wambaw, at a spot about twenty yards wide. The Chief and I swam across, each with two ropes tied around us. After climbing the bank on the other side, we strung the ropes around two small bald cypress trees that stood three feet apart. Old Moses did the same on the other side of the Wambaw. We then tied two more ropes on each side of the previous ropes. Little Daphne came running back with thirty slaves as we were finishing up. At Little Daphne's direction, the slaves attached themselves to the outer ropes and spaced themselves equally across the Wambaw. Old Moses drew a map on the ground for the Chief's braves as Harriott looked on.

"Once we get to Madame Tallulah's we have the most treacherous part of the journey. We have to go almost a mile through the swamp. We need to get here, at this part of River Road before the sun starts to set, or we will be eaten by alligators. Have three of your braves go with Harriott on horseback. Harriott, if you make it past the troops and they do not provide an escort, unhook two horses. The Chief's braves can take them with their own and meet us here." Old Moses pointed to a spot on the ground that corresponded with a point along River Road. "If you do not make it past the troops, or if they follow you, then the Chief's braves need to split off and shake the troops."

"That sounds like a very risky plan," I replied.

"Under the circumstances, I cannot think of anything else. I am sure if time afforded us, we could come up with a better plan, but we have to leave, and leave now."

And with that settled, the Chief's Braves followed Isaac and Harriott to the carriage.

The Chief, Old Moses, and I passed the horse litter harnesses to the slaves strung across the Wambaw. From one person to another it was passed, along with our supplies, until all was safely across. With Henri tucked inside, we placed the horse litter crosswise onto the ropes as the slaves took hold of the handles and slid it along. When the horse litter reached the deepest part of the Wambaw, the slaves began to have some difficulty. Their feet did not touch bottom.

The horse litter, with Henri tightly holding on, began to pitch from side to side; the ropes were not as taut as they should have been. It appeared the litter would slide off the guide ropes and into the Wambaw. At the exact moment when disaster appeared imminent, I heard a splash and turned to see Little Daphne entering under the waters of the Wambaw between the guide ropes. She emerged just past the litter and grabbed both ropes with her hands. This made the rope tauter, almost touching the surface. Little Daphne took a breath of air and put her head down; kicking her legs backwards, she wrapped them around the ropes just behind the litter. As she lay wrapped around the ropes, face down in the middle of the Wambaw, the litter was passed across her body from slave to slave until it had crossed the deepest part of the Wambaw. It was long after the litter was safely past the difficult section before Little Daphne finally raised her head and exhaustedly gasped for air. She was almost swept down the Wambaw, but one of the slaves grabbed her hand. She wrapped her other arm around him and lay there for a long time trying to catch her breath.

Safely across, we headed out over muddy rice fields to one of the earthen dikes that crisscrossed the irrigation canals. Atop the dike, we began our march to Madame Tallulah's cabin in the great cypress swamp. At the edge of the pine forest bordering the rice field we paused to look back. Slaves were positioned all along the irrigation canals flowing off the Wambaw. One by one they raised the floodgates; water poured into the rice fields. Once flooded, the federal troops would have a hard time following us. But this also meant that we would have a hard time retreating, if we were to unexpectedly encounter them up ahead.

* * *

We arrived at Madame Tallulah's cabin greeted by Little Caesar: there to help the Madame as she mended. Old William, Little Caesar's father, was more than happy—with Harriott's blessing—to let Little Caesar stay with the Madame. Anything to avoid the backbreaking work in the rice fields. Madame Tallulah was also teaching the boy about herbs and plants to one day replace her as a healer.

As we helped her to a bench on the porch of her cabin, Old Moses drew on the ground the route he planned to take through the swamp.

Madame Tallulah shook her head at Old Moses.

"Yoose boys has a det wish. Yoose sure goin teh be gator droppins by moning. Let me get some herbs teh rubs on yoose, soes at least yoose be tasty for de po creatures."

We looked at each other with what can only be described as sheer fear. I think every one of us thought of turning back; but the flooded rice fields and Wambaw had sealed our fate.

Everyone paid close attention as Madame Tallulah described various landmarks to mark her preferred route. Listening to the twists and turns in Madame Tallulah's tortuous route, our mood became more and more depressed.

At our darkest moment, Little Caesar spoke up.

"I know the way. I can show them."

We turned to Madame Tallulah, the only one with the authority to let him be our guide.

She bent down and stared at Little Caesar for a long while, then said, much to our relief, "Better git goin den."

Getting up, she pulled some vines off the posts holding up her porch.

"Here, take deese and put dem round yoose necks," she said. And as she walked inside her cabin, Madame Tallulah added, "Dey will keep de gators away."

We were ready to leave, but I wanted to say a proper goodbye and asked the party to wait a second. I walked inside and up to the Madame, smiling.

"You expect me to believe that those vines are going to keep alligators away?"

"No, yoose too smart foe yoose own good, de others will believe and dere belief will keep dem from bein scairt. Fear is what will kill ya," Madame Tallulah said.

Now I wished I had not asked about the vines. My fear would probably attract the alligators to me. She sensed my uneasiness.

"Don't yoose worry, dem gators will most likely be sleep. Little

Caesar knows to void dem. And deese vines, dey will hep wit de skeeters."

Then Madame Tallulah walked up to me and we took each other in our arms.

"Yoose stay safe and come back in one piece and maybes I lets yoose play doctor wit me again."

I kissed her on the lips.

"You may be in need of a more thorough examination when I return."

"Yoose best be goin, Mistah Robert, just my luck you be eaten by de gators."

We both laughed: she a bit more heartily than me. And then I left to rejoin the others.

* * *

With Little Caesar and Old Moses leading the way, our slog through the cypress swamp commenced. Instead of following Old Moses' more direct route, we followed Little Caesar on the much longer, winding route suggested by Madame Tallulah. Little Caesar explained that had we taken Old Moses' route, we would have been chest deep in water in many places and would have gone through several alligator infested areas. By taking the longer route, we would avoid the deeper areas of the swamp. We still had to be careful where we stepped; one bite of a water moccasin could prove fatal.

With buzzing mosquitoes and wasps directly overhead, and the sounds of red-cockaded woodpeckers pounding in our ears, we followed behind Little Caesar, carrying Henri aloft in his horse litter like some ancient king.

In a few areas we were waist deep in water. Several alligators lay in wait, sunning themselves on raised mounds less than fifteen feet away. Little Daphne looked a bit worried, so I gave her the alligator repellent vine from around my neck and added it to hers. This made her a little more relaxed as we passed by a large alligator that seemed to be staring directly at us. I alone knew that the vines were fake amulets, incapable of providing protection from alligators.

The sun began to dip low in the sky. We became increasingly anxious. It was feeding time for alligators. Little Caesar pointed off to our left; River Road was just through the trees.

Passing by a large group of alligators to our right—soaking up the last rays of the sun—we heard a disturbance behind us.

So did the alligators.

We turned and saw half-a-dozen soldiers forty yards away. They must have seen us from the road and snuck up on us. We moved as fast as we could, but with the handicap of Henri's litter we could not travel as fast as the troops.

As they neared to within thirty yards, Little Caesar abruptly broke away from us, towards them. Closing to within fifteen yards, he stopped and began slapping the water. I noticed the mass of alligators to our right beginning to stir. A few slid into the water. The troops began to run, sloshing in the knee-deep water towards Little Caesar and past the alligators massed on the mound to their right. At this point, Little Caesar dove into the shallow water and began to swim back towards us. Alerted to the noise, more alligators slipped into the water behind the troops.

Little Daphne, terror in her eyes, pointed behind Little Caesar and shouted: "Little Caesar, look out!"

A lone alligator, ten feet long, swam towards him. Morning Star, one of the Chief's braves, had already seen the alligator and made way towards Little Caesar. Placing himself in danger, he picked Little Caesar up and threw him several yards towards us. At that same instant, the alligator attacked. With snapping jaws grabbing him by the waist, Morning Star screamed in agony. He struck valiantly and repeatedly at the alligator with his knife. Oblivious; the alligator thrashed him to and fro. Little Caesar quickly led us to some cypress trees and dry ground on our left, leaving the soldiers frozen in place, looking on in horror as Morning Star's screams filled the air.

Still frozen in fear, the soldiers' fate was sealed. More and more alligators slid into the water. Most unfortunate for them, but fortunately for us, the soldiers began to retreat backwards—unknowingly—into the alligators.

Scrambling onto dry land, the sound of alligators attacking in a feeding frenzy pierced our ears.

We reached the road.

Behind us, the terrible shrieks of men crying out in fear and agony filled the air. Walking silently down the last mile of River Road, we were accompanied by their dying sounds. One by one their voices were extinguished—swallowed up by the swamp and the alligators.

We never looked back.

CHAPTER 81

Before reaching the meet-up spot along River Road, the Chief's braves came galloping up. Night was beginning to fall. No time for long goodbyes. Henri's horse litter was hooked up. We all shook hands. Henri said he would write some day. I gave his Little Daphne a hug. The Chief would be back to fight for the land rights of his people. A fight in which I would assist.

And then it was over. Off into the night they rode. My last image of Henri brought a smile to my face. Disappearing from view, waving the red cap given to him by Isaac on our trip to Charleston, he shouted, *"Liberté! Au revoir!"*

* * *

Old Moses, Little Caesar, and I settled in for the night: our backs against the base of a giant bald cypress, too afraid to sleep. Throughout the long night, sounds of creatures searching for prey seemed to be all around us. Little Caesar huddled close to me, not knowing that I was probably more frightened than he was. Old Moses started to sing a song to keep us awake. I did not know if this would scare off any wild creatures or merely attract them. At the very moment I had these thoughts, a nearby bobcat snarled and growled, sending shivers through my body. I wished Old Moses would have stopped singing but I was not about to say anything as

The Floating Man

Little Caesar and I huddled together in fear, waiting for night to end.

Finally, the dawn came. I got up to relieve a swollen bladder, being too fearful to get up during the night. Apparently, Old Moses and Little Caesar had the same fear. Soon, three streams were shooting out onto the ground. If there was a prize for the largest bladder, I would have won—which was no consolation, as mosquitoes were buzzing all around.

We decided to snoop around and see if any troops were nearby, since we had to wait until the sun was high and the alligators asleep before heading back. We did not have to snoop long. After walking about three-quarters of a mile, Little Caesar spotted a dozen soldiers camped out. Having not eaten for over a day, we thought about casually walking up to their campfire, but since we had no ready explanation for being there, we retreated and waited for the heat of the day.

Once the sun was high overhead, it was back into the swamp. The return trip was a lot quicker. Our journey past the mass of alligators that had so recently torn into the troops and Morning Star, was the only worrisome part.

Were they satiated by the soldiers?

Or were we now considered a delicacy?

We moved as quietly and as slowly as humanly possible. One of the larger creatures raised its head. For a moment we were frozen in terror, like the soldiers of yesterday. The creature turned and moved a few feet towards us. I was about to make a run for it until Little Caesar grabbed my wrist and nodded his head 'no' very slowly. Thankfully, the creature was only changing position in relation to the sun and soon settled back down to continue basking.

The rest of the trip was uneventful. We soon found ourselves back at Madame Tallulah's cabin, eating a stew that tasted like equal portions of food and medicine. The Madame shook her head sadly at the story of Morning Star, but brightened as I recounted how Little Caesar trapped the troops and calmly led us to safety. After the stew, and with the realization that this could become a habit if I were not careful, I gave the Madame a hug and kiss before leaving. Old Moses and I left Little Caesar with Madame Tallulah and walked back to Hampton, arriving there a little after four in the afternoon. Harriott had not yet returned, so Old Moses and I took the time to avail ourselves of a bath. While we scrubbed the swamp off of us, Old William listened proudly as we recounted how his boy had led us through the swamp, safely past the alligators.

Harriott and Isaac arrived back from Georgetown around six. After freshening up, they joined me on the front portico. We recounted our journeys for each other. Harriott and Isaac's were rather ordinary. The troops, it turned out, gave them nothing more than a cursory look. Harriott noted that they were still stationed around the border of the plantation, and she suspected they would remain there for some time.

Apparently, Harriott's letter to President Madison helped ameliorate her situation. For the rest of Jackson's presidency, troops remained just outside, never violating the grounds of Hampton. All on the slim hope that one day, Henri would return.

As the sun went down, the three of us sat drinking Harriott's peach-sweetened rum. Ever present on our minds were the empty chairs sitting next to us on the portico, formerly occupied by the Chief, Henri, and Little Daphne. I remember wondering whether I would ever see all of us together again. The empty void in my heart gave me the answer.

Shortly thereafter, I was back in Beaufort, hard at work at the Sentinel. From time to time I would return to Hampton to pay Harriott and Isaac a visit. Always making sure to drop in on Tallulah to play doctor and patient with her. On Sundays, I would visit with the slaves in their cabins and share a mug of rum, water, and molasses. Listening to their stories, and hopes of a better future for their children. At night, Isaac, Harriott, Old William, and Little Caesar (who had become one of Harriott's key house slaves) would sit out on the portico and reminisce. Invariably, the subject would come back to Henri and his wonderful machine.

On rare occasions, Doctor Garden and the Chief would join us. I remember sitting captivated the first time the doctor described his involuntary journey to Washington. Barely a day after being transported from Madame Tallulah's cabin, he caught an infection from his self-inflicted wound and almost died. Drifting in and out of consciousness, Doctor Garden remembered snippets of a conversation the president had with one of his advisors concerning Henri's machine. While the President's advisor discussed the possibilities of quicker travel and transport of commerce, Jackson was consumed with the military applications of Henri's device. At one point, Doctor Garden remembered the president talking about equipping a thousand soldiers with Henri's device to hover over Indian villages and pick off the helpless inhabitants at their leisure.

I will never forget the horrified expression on the Chief's face when Doctor Garden quoted President Jackson's exact words: "I am tired of negotiating with these savages. The White Man and the Indian can never live in peace. It is only through the eradication of the Indian that peace can be achieved. No more treaties. No more land. This will be the final resolution."

Upon hearing this, the Chief completely broke down. Harriott came over and consoled him as best she could.

I turned and whispered to Isaac; "I pray your hiding place is as secure as you believe it to be."

Isaac gave me a wink and patted my knee. It was all the reassurance I needed.

When the Chief had recovered his composure, Doctor Garden continued his story.

Once recovered from the infection which took almost two weeks to clear, the interrogations began. The doctor could not convince the president and his science advisors that he was not, in fact, Henri. Not helping matters any was the unfortunate fact that Doctor Garden spoke perfect French. For nearly a week he was severely beaten and tortured. It was only through a coincidence of events that he was finally freed. One of his colleagues, a prominent physician in the capital, happened to mention Doctor Garden by name while attending a White House party. An aide to the president overheard the remark and brought him to the basement cell where Doctor Garden was being held. The physician immediately recognized Doctor Garden, who was shortly thereafter released.

After hearing the doctor's travail, the Chief thought it best to keep certain details of Henri's trip secret. A few years later, because of Jackson's inhumane actions, the Chief's people would be brutally driven down the same trail Henri had taken. The Cherokee would be rounded up and penned in like animals, waiting to be shipped to the western Indian territories. Thousands would die along the trail before the Chief was able to persuade authorities to let him lead his people to the promised land.

Another promised land to be taken away, as the Chief bitterly put it to me years later. The infamous trail, known to history as the Trail of Tears, was just one more link in a long unbroken chain of man's inhumanity to man.

* * *

And Henri? I would only hear from him one more time. A few years after that magical and terrible summer, I received a short note from the great man. Like Henri and Isaac, I too like puzzles and will leave it to whoever reads my papers to find the note. I will now depart from you, my dear reader, with words that will always echo in my memory.
Liberté. Au revoir.

CHAPTER 82

Beaufort, South Carolina; Present Day

James put down the story.

"So now we know a little more of the puzzle."

"I hope Isaac didn't break down the machine into a lot of parts and hide them everywhere—like some damn Easter egg hunt," John replied.

"Well, if James' double g wasn't using poetic license," Sheila said, "I am afraid, Isaac, with . . . how did Robert put it? A supreme look of satisfaction on his face, must have done a pretty good job."

"It's a shame he did not just tell your forbear where he hid it," John said.

"I am afraid that if Robert had known, he would have just spilled the beans. Seems to be a family trait." James flipped back through the pages of Robert's memoirs. "Here it is," he said. John and Sheila got on each side of James; the three of them reread the passage.

A little after midnight, Isaac walked up. He had changed his clothes. Perspiring profusely, he ran a cloth across his face, patted me on the shoulder and went inside, returning a little while later with two mugs of peach-sweetened rum.

Isaac handed me a mug, took a sip of his, and stretched his back before sitting down next to me.

"Sure beats that damn molasses water and rum all to hell," he said staring out into the dark.

"Looks like you have been working pretty hard. Is Henri's secret, safe?"

Isaac grinned. "Old Moses and I worked all afternoon and evening. We took it apart and boxed it up. Then we buried it here and there. You want to know where?"

"No," I replied, thinking that if the troops tortured me I would not be able to keep a secret.

"Good. I was not going to tell you anyway," Isaac said, still grinning. As he looked into the darkness, his grin got wider.

"What about the troops, if they go digging up the place?"

Isaac turned to me. His eyes gleamed.

"You know how Henri likes his little games . . . his puzzles, Robert?"

"Yes, he told me of the games he played on the scientists in Arcueil."

"Well, I made my own little puzzle. They may dig it all up, Robert, but it is still up in the air whether they can figure it all out," Isaac said with a look that I can only describe as one of supreme satisfaction.

John got up and went over to the window.

"I think the clues are right in that passage, James. Assuming Robert had good recall."

"Well, we definitely know it's in several pieces," Sheila added.

"No we don't," John replied. "Read the passage again. Isaac said he took the machine apart; boxed it up and hid it *'here'* and *'there'*. That's only two places."

"And he said *'here'* when he was sitting on the portico with Robert," James said, looking over to Sheila for her thoughts on the subject.

Taking the cue, she responded: "And if we read the passage literally, that means Isaac buried one part in the mansion and the other part somewhere on the grounds."

"I think that settles it." John stretched and sat down on the window ledge. "James, you and Sheila can search the basement of the mansion, while I fight off the mosquitoes and search the grounds."

Turning to Sheila, James asked, "When is your Mike Kelley going to bring us that metal detecting equipment he promised? I'm anxious to get started."

"I talked to Mike the other day. He promised that everything would be ready in a couple of days. He's trying to get something state of the art, but simple to use." Sheila paused, and then added, "Oh, by the way, I forgot to mention that Ted Dody called Max. He's back in Washington. I asked them to fly in with Mike and join the hunt. We have a lot of ground to cover."

"He certainly recovered fast. I guess the kidney transplant for his sister went well."

"It didn't. Ted's sister died just as his plane was landing in Seattle."

"How terribly sad," James sighed.

"Yes, and . . . although Ted gives me the creeps, I'm anxious to hear more about Jacques and his granddaughter, Adrienne."

John got up from his perch on the window ledge and walked over to Sheila.

"Well, while we wait for our equipment and the rest of our hunting party, why don't we retire to the front portico, as Robert so nicely put it?" Taking her by the hand, he led her out to the front porch.

"And I'll bring us some drinks," James interjected, sauntering off to the kitchen.

He returned with a tray that held a large pitcher and three glasses, each containing a slice of peach. Pouring the drinks, he commented; "I think you'll like my version. I used some peach syrup from the can, added some sugar and a dash of sour mix, along with a liberal amount of rum."

"*Excellent*," Sheila said, taking a sip. She raised her glass and added, "Here's to Harriott."

"And Isaac." James raised his glass.

"And my favorite, Madame Tallulah." John smiled and quickly drained his glass.

* * *

Watching the three through darkened windows of a van parked a half block away were the well-dressed man and woman.

The man turned to the woman with the cropped blonde hair.

"*Why* are we doing this? Our assignment's over. We've gotten paid."

"Don't you think it's odd that it ended without a conclusion? We just leave with everything up in the air?"

A look of concern showed on the woman's face.

"What do you care?" the man replied. "It's what we do. Follow orders, get paid, and wait for our next assignment."

"Well, I don't like it," she said, picking up a pair of binoculars and focusing the lens on Sheila. "The whole thing is about to come to a head. I can feel it. And we're just supposed to walk away?"

"Maybe they called in the A-Team," he said, smiling.

She didn't notice the smile. Her focus was on Sheila.

"I never heard of an A-Team."

"I am just saying, you know... everyone has their specialty. Maybe the rest of the job requires a different set of skills."

"*Bullshit.*" She put the binoculars down and glared at him. "We may be off the job, but what we do in between assignments is our own business. Are you going to wimp out on me?"

"You're just obsessed with that big-chested bitch. Can't wait to carve her up, can you?" he said with a look of disgust.

"That's my business. Are you in?" She glanced quickly at him before returning to the binoculars.

"I suppose. Someone has to save your ass," he said, adding, "You know, one of these days you are going to get the both of us killed."

"And who saved whose ass back in the museum?" she said in a parting shot.

"Yeah, right. Whatever," he replied with a look of frustration.

His partner continued to ogle 'the big-chested bitch' sitting on the porch.

"Yeah, whatever."

CHAPTER 83

Washington D.C.

Henry Smith, national security advisor to the president and Sheila's boss, picked up his phone and dialed a familiar number. After three rings, a man answered.

"Yes, sir."

"Mike, how are we coming along?"

"Everything's all set," he replied. "I'm going to fly down with Max and Ted Dody in the morning."

"*Max* is coming along? Isn't he a bit old to be running around?" Henry chuckled.

"I guess everyone has a bit of the child in him when it comes to adventure, sir."

"I suppose so." Henry settled back comfortably in his chair and looked out over the White House grounds. "You know you have a point about the child in the man. I think I might just come down and see what this floating machine looks like myself. Maybe I'll bring General Stebbins along. Have everyone in the same place . . . like a big reunion."

"I still think you ought to have Sheila and her friends stand down and let the professionals handle it."

"No. After all the work Sheila and her friends have done, they at least deserve the honor of discovering the thing. I just need you to be as helpful as you can."

"I'm nothing if not helpful. Your government tax dollars at work."

"I hope you didn't pay full price for the metal detecting equipment. We don't need an audit by the GAO." Henry silently chuckled, and hung up the phone.

After a few minutes lost in thought, he picked up the phone again and dialed over to the Defense Intelligence Agency. He reached the director's office. Colonel Stan Weatherly, General Stebbins' aide, picked up and answered.

"Stan, we found out where our damn machine is," Henry began. "I would like to invite General Stebbins down to South Carolina for the unveiling. Think you can arrange that without too much pomp and circumstance?"

"I think I can arrange that, sir," Stan replied. "He'll want his usual entourage. You know the general. He doesn't even trust his own mother."

"Have you seen Eric's mother? I wouldn't trust her either. Anyway," Henry continued, "he trusts you. So I will leave the details up to you. Book some rooms in Georgetown and call my office back with the final arrangements."

The two talked for a few minutes about logistics and decided to have a helicopter on standby to fly the nineteen miles from Georgetown to Hampton. Colonel Weatherly put his boss through to Henry.

"Well, general, I found out where your Frenchman buried his machine," Henry gloated.

It took a moment for General Stebbins to recover his composure. In the intervening silence, Henry told the general the story of John and Sheila. Everything except for the part about Hampton plantation.

"And you're not going to tell me where it is?" the general said, annoyed.

"Come to Georgetown, Eric, we'll go together once it's dug up," Henry replied.

"Henry, you're acting like a prima donna. Quit playing games. Tell me where it is and we'll get a team down there."

"Nope."

"Why not?"

"You don't have clearance, general."

Henry hung up the phone. He had been waiting to say that ever since the general had so smugly used that same line on him a few weeks earlier.

General Stebbins, visibly annoyed, buzzed his aide.

"Yes, sir?"

"Stan, make arrangements for me to stay in Georgetown, and have a helicopter there on standby. Henry thinks he has found our antigravity machine."

The general paused for a beat and added, "Make sure we have a team in place down there. I don't trust that guy."

"Yes, sir." Colonel Weatherly saluted, turned on his heel, and left.

CHAPTER 84

It was a typical low country day in mid-July when John met Max, Ted, and Mike at Charleston airport—hot and humid. When he pulled up in the Marquis they were already waiting by the curb with their bags. Along with small carryon luggage, Mike and Max each had two identical black bags, approximately two feet long.

"Is that our metal detecting equipment?" John asked Mike.

"Yep, this is it. State of the art," Mike replied. And hoisting one of the bags in the air, he added, "Lightweight, too."

"Kind of small, isn't it?"

"Bigger isn't always better."

"If you say so." John opened the cavernous trunk and piled their stuff inside.

On the ride back to Beaufort, Max was in a pensive mood. Looking out the window at the passing countryside, he said more to himself than anyone present, "It's a shame Rachel isn't here to share in all this."

"We wouldn't have been able to get this far without her contacts, that's for sure," John replied in a comforting tone to his friend and former boss.

"You think whoever killed Rachel is still out there? Following us?"

"That's why I'm here." Mike patted Max's knee and pulled a

gun out of his shoulder holster.

"That's a Springfield, isn't it?" Ted said, glancing back over his shoulder at Mike from the front passenger seat, suddenly interested.

"Yes, it is," Mike said with more than a little curiosity in his voice. "How did you know?"

"You're FBI, and that's not a standard issue Glock. Without taking a closer look, I would guess it's a Springfield Model 1911A1 45 ACP Pistol, preferred by members of the HRT."

Mike's jaw dropped. "You're right. But I'm not a member of the Hostage Rescue Team. You really know your guns, Ted."

"I'm a bit of a gun nut."

Quite a bit of a nut, according to Sheila, John thought, keeping his eyes on the road.

CHAPTER 85

After arriving in Beaufort and checking into their rooms at the appropriately named Hampton Inn, John drove the trio to James' house.

Mike Kelley brought along one of the detector bags: unzipped it and pulled out a detector—holding it up for everyone to see.

"Nice, huh?"

"Wow! It's a metal detector," Sheila said scornfully. "We waited a whole week so you could get us a *metal* detector?"

Defensively, Mike said, "It's not an ordinary metal detector. This one transmits twenty-eight multiple frequencies ranging from 1.5 kilohertz to 100 kilohertz."

"Whoop de doo," Sheila replied. "Mr. FBI guy memorized the operator's manual."

"It's more sensitive than other detectors, Sheila. It tells you how deep to dig."

"It looks exactly like what my grandfather uses on the beach to find coins," Sheila said dismissively. "It's a *metal* detector. We waited a whole week for a *metal* detector."

"Well, okay, you're right, it's a metal detector. But it's one of the more expensive ones," Mike responded bravely.

"You mean it's not even the best?" Sheila groaned.

"Let's try it out in the backyard," James said, trying to save the day. "Mike, why don't you show us how to use it?"

"That's a good idea," John piped in before Sheila could get in another dig.

Ted and Max looked on, totally amused.

They went to the backyard. Mike gave them a brief demonstration of the controls. He had already marked where to set the knobs and switches for their search at Hampton plantation. In the meantime, he set the controls to pick up smaller objects. John and Max stood next to James, who held onto a small garden spade. Ted fixated on Sheila, standing near her the whole time. Although uncomfortably close, Sheila seemed not to notice, paying close attention to Mike's instructions.

Once Mike finished going over the basics, he asked, "Who wants to try it out?"

Sheila immediately volunteered. Noticing Ted nipping at her heels, she twirled around and faced him. "Ted, give me a little space. You're creeping me out here."

"Sorry." Ted gave her a nervous smile. *I'm definitely going to have to work on my people skills.*

"It's okay, Ted." Noticing his embarrassment, she added, "The lady just needs a little room to operate."

And with that, Sheila set off with the detector across the backyard. A minute later the detector pinged.

"Bingo!" she shouted triumphantly. Out of the corner of her eye, Sheila noticed Ted's hangdog look and tried to rescue his wounded feelings.

"Ted, grab that spade from James and see what we've found."

He eagerly jumped at the request and was soon at Sheila's feet, digging a small hole. Thirty seconds and six inches later, he held up a rusted lug nut.

"Well I'll be damned," James exclaimed as he bent down to take a closer look. "Lost that twenty years ago. It's from my old Buick. Wonder how in the hell it got way over here."

"Here you go, old man," Ted said, holding the lug nut up.

"The name is James," he said huffily, "and that old Buick is sitting, rusting away in a junkyard somewhere."

"Sorry, James, I didn't mean anything by it."

Ted thought to himself that maybe he would see a therapist and work on his issues. Of which he had plenty. After leaving

Jacques alive, he was amazed that he was not dead yet. Maybe it was the call he received concerning the film in the spy cane that Jacques had given him. Film, that when developed, turned out not to be all it was supposed to be.

I guess my handlers still need me in the game, Ted thought as he watched everyone take turns roaming James' backyard with the metal detector.

CHAPTER 86

The next day they did a dry run to map out some likely spots on the plantation where they might find Henri's machine. Ted decided to tag along, spending an extra day in Beaufort before returning to Washington. And from there, Paris and Adrienne.

John, Max, and Sheila piled into the Marquis. Ted and Mike rode with James in his Buick. Ted quickly endeared himself to both Mike and James by yelling "*Shotgun*!" and jumping into the front passenger seat ahead of Mike, who was already opening the front passenger door. Plopping down, Ted followed up with an aside to James.

"I thought you said your old Buick was rusting away in a junkyard, James?"

"This Buick is only five years old, Ted," James replied stonily. "It only has thirty thousand miles on it. Not a spot of rust. Never had any problems. It's a Regal."

"A *Regal*? Rather ironically named, don't you think?"

Ted continued to endear himself to James and Mike for the rest of their trip to Hampton Plantation.

Between caustic comments, Ted looked out his side-view mirror and noticed a van a considerable distance back. At one point the van pulled up behind them at a long stoplight where traffic was nonexistent. He noticed a couple familiar faces from the program he had attended long ago. A program of which, Ted sadly noted, he was a lifetime member.

John and James pulled into the drive off Rutledge Road that led to the parking lot of Hampton Plantation. The van pulled over onto the shoulder, near the entrance. The man and woman got out and walked a short distance down the drive; the occupants of the two cars they had trailed were just getting out. The woman focused the binoculars on John's Grand Marquis, zeroing in on Sheila. A man from the other car came over and blocked the woman's view. Frustrated, she was about to put the binoculars down when she noticed something vaguely familiar about the man standing next to Sheila.

"Hey," she said to her partner. "Take a look at the guy next to my girl."

The man picked up the binoculars and focused them on Ted.

"Well, I'll be damned. I remember him from the program. Maybe he's the one relieving us."

"No way!" She snatched the binoculars back and looked at Ted again. "I remember him now. He was the nerd who couldn't shoot straight. I can't believe they need him for this assignment."

"Maybe it calls for brains, not brawn."

"He wasn't *that* smart," she replied.

"Things are coming to a head. Yesterday they were walking all around the yard practicing with a metal detector. And today they are visiting a state park that used to be a plantation." The man continued to watch as John and his friends walked over to the ranger's station. "My guess is that they're doing a bit of scouting and will be back later to try and find their buried treasure."

"Their magic flying carpet," she said. "Betcha it was somewhere in those old newspapers all along."

"You know what you said yesterday about staying on the case? I think you're right. I have a hunch the people who pull our strings will be showing up—sooner or later. And my bet is sooner, *much* sooner."

The woman put the binoculars down.

"You never cared before."

"I know. The money has always been enough for me. But now, my curiosity has been piqued."

"Your curiosity has been *piqued*," she said with a crooked smile.

"Look at you with the big words. Getting all sophisticated on me."

"Fuck you," he replied.

"That's much better," she said and kissed him on the cheek. "Let's get outta here. The show ain't gonna happen today."

* * *

After finishing a tour of the mansion, James asked how he and Sheila would get down into the basement to search.

"We can't just march in with our metal detectors and say hello," James said to Mike.

"Don't worry, James, it's all arranged. I cleared it through the state law enforcement division. We have unrestricted access after the park closes at six. I even have LED headlamps if we need to work in the dark. Supposedly, they don't attract mosquitoes."

"Thank God," Sheila replied.

Walking out onto the grounds of Hampton, John turned to James. "How about a tour for Mike and Max's benefit? Point out some promising places we can search with our metal detectors."

"Absolutely. This way gentlemen."

James proudly proceeded to take them on a tour of the grounds, pointing out where the slave cabins, blacksmith shop, carriage house, and carpenter shop once stood.

John still believed he was making some of the stuff up, but James was in his glory. And John was not about to rain on his parade.

After the tour, they piled back into the cars for the drive back to Beaufort. Ted saw no sign of the van with the two familiar faces on the trip back.

Much to the relief of James and Mike, Ted stared out the window, lost in thought.

Tomorrow should be an interesting day.

CHAPTER 87

Ted left around noon for the trip back to Charleston and his ultimate destination, Paris. The night before, he told them about his talks with Jacques and his pretty granddaughter, Adrienne—leaving out the part about the spy cane and his assignment to kill Jacques. After he left, Sheila commented that Ted had shown signs of improvement in the personal skills department. She noted that he wasn't as creepy as he used to be when they were all working together at the *Post*.

John, Sheila, and James picked up Mike and Max around three-thirty that afternoon for the two-hour drive to Hampton Plantation. Stuffed into the trunk were metal detectors and shovels.

Sheila bent forward from the back seat towards Mike, riding up front with John. Tapping him on the shoulder, she said, "Hey Mike, I thought you had our visit cleared with the authorities."

"I do." Mike turned around to face Sheila. "We have complete, unfettered access."

"Then why do we have shovels? Why not a small caterpillar to dig for us?"

"They don't want a lot of big holes everywhere, Sheila. It's a state historic site and a national landmark. If our metal detectors hit something and we aren't able to dig it up tonight, we can come back tomorrow."

"Still seems like a half-assed way to approach this," she said, slumping back down.

At a quarter to six they pulled into the parking lot and waited for the park to empty out. A grand procession of seven people and three cars slowly exited—a busy day for Hampton Plantation State Historic Site.

Grabbing their metal detectors and shovels, the group headed for the mansion. Sitting down on the front portico they went over their last minute plans. It was evident that John and James had given this considerable thought.

"Sheila," John began, "why don't you and James spend an hour—give or take—north behind the mansion, cross the abandoned rice field over to Wambaw Creek. From there, take the walking trail west along the creek and edge of the rice field before returning to the mansion where you can continue your search inside."

"What if Henri's machine is on the other side of the creek?" Max asked.

Sheila responded: "There was a high tide when they buried the machine. They had a hard enough time getting Henri across."

"Anyway," James interrupted, "let's get back to business. John is going to search west of the mansion and follow the edge of the rice field south, towards Rutledge Road. Max, you'll search east of the mansion to the boundary, then work your way south towards Rutledge Road. When you get there, you and John can work your way to each other and search on each side of the drive leading back to the mansion."

"And what will Mike do?" Sheila asked.

"I'm the roamer." Mike reached into a zippered bag and passed out LED headlamps to each of them. "I search here and there, and check and make sure nobody disturbs us."

"Like those spies at the museum who killed Elmer?" James asked.

"And Rachel," Max added.

As if on cue, a van pulled over to the side of Rutledge road. A man and woman got out. They sprayed each other with mosquito repellant and went off down opposite sides of the drive towards the mansion. The woman wore a small backpack.

While John, Max, and Mike trundled off in search of Henri's

long lost machine, a young park employee named Elizabeth led Sheila and James through the mansion, turning all the lights on as she went, including those in the raised basement. After escorting Elizabeth out, James and Sheila went around to the back of the mansion and headed towards Wambaw Creek.

"Quite a seat of the pants operation, eh?" James remarked to Sheila as they walked along the creek.

"I know. Wouldn't you think that Mike would have at least brought some walkie-talkies for us to communicate?" Sheila shook her head and added, "For an FBI guy, he doesn't seem that prepared."

"Does have a big gun though," James said reassuringly.

"Probably trying to overcompensate, if you know what I mean."

"No, I don't know," James said with a look of bewilderment.

"You know, James, he . . . ah, forget it. Let's just concentrate on finding this thing and try to avoid the mosquitoes."

James tugged at his long sleeved green cotton pullover.

"This is my mosquito repellant right here. Tightly woven so that mosquitoes can't penetrate."

"Looks hot as hell, James," Sheila said, shaking her billowing white blouse. "Now this is the way to avoid mosquitoes. Wear something loose fitting and shake the little suckers off."

"What if they get underneath?"

"*Shit!* I didn't think of that."

"Don't worry; we have enough bug spray on us to kill an elephant."

Just then James metal detector pinged.

"I've got something!"

Sheila bent down with her spade and started digging. After a minute, she pulled up a coin.

"Here you go, don't spend it all in one place."

"This is fun," James said jovially as he examined the coin—a quarter from 1987.

"Looks like you found a new vocation. You can join my grandfather on his beach expeditions."

* * *

As James and Sheila continued along Wambaw Creek, the

young woman snuck inside the mansion and went down into the basement where she set up shop. She found two closely spaced eyehooks in one of the ceiling timbers near the west end of the basement, looped a small chain through them, attaching wrist cuffs to each end. She placed an unlit candle nearby on the floor and stood back up. She looked around a bit before reaching up and pulling the cord, turning off the light bulb.

She took off her clothes and stood still.

Naked.

Waiting.

A gun in one gloved hand, a knife in the other.

In the darkened west end of the basement.

* * *

Mike Kelley made his way back to the parking lot. He stood outside John's car, dialing his boss. Henry Smith answered on the second ring.

"Yes, Mike."

"Henry, I think this is a wild goose chase. Why don't we call this off and get a team to do a geophysical survey of the area?"

"Mike, you give up too easily. Have a little more faith in Sheila and her band of merry men. If I may, I would suggest you search where the slave cabins once stood. Andrew Jackson, with the natural prejudice prevalent at that time, wouldn't have expected the machine to be buried under slave quarters."

Henry turned to General Stebbins aide, Colonel Stan Weatherly, and covered the phone with his hand. "The impatience of youth," he whispered.

"Okay," Mike said, "That's not a bad idea."

He hung up. Laid down on the hood of John's car and took a nap.

Meanwhile, Max was zigzagging down the eastern border of the park—sweating and swatting away mosquitoes. He stopped and sat down on a tree stump.

This is the stupidest thing I have ever done. When I get back to Washington, it's only nightclubs and dinner parties from now on.

After a short while, Max got back up and resumed his search, waving the metal detector back and forth across the ground. A half-hour later he was within sight of Rutledge Road.

Max looked down at the meter of his metal detector and noticed a pair of feet.

He looked up to see a man smiling at him.

"I'm sorry," Max said. "We're doing a geological survey. The park is closed."

"Permanently," the man replied, still smiling.

"*Permanently?*" A bit confused, Max added, "No, just for the night."

"No, permanently," the man insisted.

"Permanently? I don't follow you." Max was totally confused—until he noticed the gun.

"Permanently for you," the man said.

His gun, with silencer attached, made two short muffled sounds. Two spots of blood appeared close together on Max's shirt.

As Max fell, his last thoughts were of Rachel. He crumpled to his knees.

"Are you the one who murdered my Rachel?"

Still smiling, the man said, "No, that was my partner."

And added a final shot to Max's forehead.

* * *

John had the most ground to cover. He slowly made his way west to the edge of the rice field before turning south towards Rutledge Road and the southern boundary of what were now the last remnants of Hampton Plantation. He had a few pings on his metal detector. It indicated small objects. He ignored them. The sun was just beginning to set when he reached Rutledge Road and began walking east, looking for Max. After a little while he grew impatient. He started calling for Max.

Mike, still napping on John's car, heard his shouts. Slowly rousing himself, he headed towards the shouting. He found John near the entrance to the park.

"Have you seen Max?" John asked as Mike came walking up.

"I haven't seen him since we split up."

"Where have you been?" John said curiously.

"I walked along Germantown Road on the western border of the park," Mike lied.

"Well, I'm sure Max will find us eventually. Let's cover some more ground on the way back towards the mansion."

"Sounds good to me. Why don't we do a thorough check of the area where the slave cabins stood? Just a suggestion." Mike paused for a moment before adding, "You know, in Jackson's time they had a natural prejudice and would never think the machine would be buried under a slave's cabin."

"That's not a bad idea. Why didn't I think of that?"

"You're not an FBI agent. We're trained to think in a very analytical way."

The two of them walked along the dirt drive, towards the mansion and the area where the slave cabins once stood.

* * *

Two hours and two coins later, Sheila and James made it back to the mansion. They went down into the basement and started with their metal detectors at the east end. As they neared the west end, James noticed a light bulb had apparently burned out.

Entering the edge of darkness, the light suddenly snapped on.

A young woman stood naked underneath.

"Surprise! Remember me?"

Sheila and James stopped in their tracks, frozen in fear. The young woman who had murdered Elmer and violated Sheila, stood before them: holding a gun in one hand, a stiletto in the other.

"James, dear, be a sweetheart and take Sheila's hand. Cuff her wrist, right there."

She pointed her gun at the cuffs hanging from the eyehooks.

James broke out in a nervous sweat, and began to mumble incomprehensibly.

"I said *now!* You fat fuck!" the woman snarled.

James finally comprehended. With trembling hands he attached Sheila's right wrist to one of the cuffs.

"And now, the other . . . *please*," the young woman impatiently directed.

James, with even more of a tremble, took hold of Sheila's left wrist. Sheila stood on her tiptoes as he attached the cuff to the other eyehook, spaced about three feet away.

As James stood next to Sheila, the young woman handed him her knife while pointing the gun at Sheila.

"James, darling, if you'd please, cut away that lovely blouse for me."

James turned and faced Sheila. A strange expression accompanied the fear stamped on his face, but Sheila could not discern what it was. Blinking uncontrollably, he took the knife to the top button of her blouse and cut it away. He began to tremble more violently. He turned around and faced the young woman. Clutching his chest, eyes bulging out of his reddened face, James staggered towards the young woman. White foamy spittle formed around the edge of his mouth and seeped onto his chin. As James drew nearer, the woman grabbed him by the shoulders and spun him around behind her. He fell roughly onto a workbench that stood along the wall. With his back slumped against the wall, James began to convulse.

"Help, him!" Sheila cried. "He's having a heart attack."

"Well, *good*," the young woman chortled.

The woman watched James body spasm and then relax. His eyes bulged out in a death stare. She walked over to James and pried the knife from his hand. Turning back to Sheila, she smiled.

"Now I won't have to go to all the trouble of shooting him. Though I did want him to truss up your legs behind you before I killed him. Guess if you want things done right, you have to do it yourself."

The young woman went behind Sheila. After removing her pants and panties she put a plastic tie around her ankles. Sheila struggled initially, but after receiving a poke in the buttocks with the stiletto, she relented. The young woman knotted a rope through the plastic tie and made a noose around Sheila's neck. She pulled the noose tight, bringing Sheila's legs up behind her, forcing her head backwards.

Then she walked around to the front and admired her handiwork. Sheila hung limply from her wrists; her head pulled back, her upper torso thrust outward. The young woman went over and lit the scented candle, placing her gun on the window ledge. A pleasant floral scent broke through the musty air. Still holding her stiletto, she lifted her right foot and placed it high on Sheila's stomach, just below her sternum, and gave her a shove, swinging her back and forth. Each time Sheila swung forward, the young woman flicked her stiletto underneath a button, cutting it away.

After the last button fell to the dirt floor of the basement, Sheila continued to swing.

Backwards.
Forward.
Backwards.

As her torso swung forward, the young woman flicked her stiletto between Sheila's breasts, cutting her bra away, nicking her sternum.

A trickle of blood flowed down between her breasts to her navel.

The young woman's eyes lit up, drinking in all of Sheila's exposed flesh.

With her chest arched forward and head pulled back, Sheila could not see any of this as she hung suspended. Only her imagination knew what horrors were in store for her now.

She thought of James, her good friend, lying dead against the wall; and then she thought of the child with John she would never have.

She forgot about her own fear, worried about John.

The young woman's partner was out there.

Lurking, in the now dark night.

Hanging from the ceiling, swinging back and forth, Sheila was somehow able to project her mind outside her body in search of her lover.

She was brought back to reality when the young woman said something about a nipple erection. She felt the blade of the stiletto pierce her areola, once ... twice. Surprised that the pain was not intolerable, Sheila managed to say, "You know, you are one crazy bitch, don't you?"

This brought the young woman to a momentary halt in her activities.

As blood flowed from Sheila's wounds, the young woman spit out a torrent of expletives. Something to the effect that Sheila reminded her of her mother. And all women reminded her of her mother. And her mother watched her being abused. And nobody helped, and this and that, until Sheila finally had had enough, and just wanted to get the whole thing over with.

"*Shut* the *fuck* up! God, there is nothing worse than a whiny little bitch," Sheila screamed at the ceiling timbers. "Just have your fun and get it over with. But don't torture me with any more of your psycho babble bullshit!"

Not expecting this kind of response from someone she was about to kill, the young woman was momentarily taken aback. It had quite a calming effect on her.

"You're right," she said apologetically. "I shouldn't be bothering you with my baggage. You kind of took the fun out of my plans though. I was looking forward to stabbing you repeatedly and licking the blood off your body. But now, I guess the humane thing to do is just stab you in the heart, under your left breast—just like I did my mother. You won't suffer too much."

"Thank you," Sheila said. "Now please, just get it over with."

Sheila could not see the young woman getting ready to thrust the stiletto into her heart. She could only imagine that in the next few seconds she would feel a sharp pain . . . and then it would be all over—her heart would stop.

Instead, Sheila felt a heavy thud against her chest, not the sharp pain she had imagined.

The heavy thing slid down her torso.

And hit the floor—Hard.

Someone was behind her, cutting the ropes, freeing her legs and neck.

She turned her head.

"James!" Sheila said, wide-eyed.

Fear mixed with relief.

"I thought you were dead."

"Part of my Casper Gutman act. I thought I gave you a wink when I cut your blouse button off."

"No, you just had a weird frightened out of your mind look. By the way, what took you so long?"

"Sorry. I had to find something to hit her over the head with and also move about fifteen feet without making a sound. Once she started swearing and getting all worked up I made my move. You almost blew it by calming her down."

"James, I couldn't see a thing. There's nothing more terrifying then not knowing what's about to happen."

"I can't begin to imagine."

He removed her wrists from the cuffs; noticed her blood-streaked body.

"You're a bloody mess."

James took what was left of Sheila's blouse and wiped away the blood. Examining her wounds, he pronounced, "You're not in bad shape. The cuts aren't very deep." And then he took off his green pullover and handed it to Sheila. "*Here*, put this on."

Sheila took the green pullover, slipped into her pants, and went to the window ledge where the woman had laid her pistol. She picked it up and slipped it into the back of her waistband, covering it with the green pullover.

"Come on, let's find John," she said determinedly.

They climbed the stairs and went out into the night.

CHAPTER 88

"I found something!"

John took off his headphones and turned to Mike.

Running his detector over the same spot, Mike heard the familiar ping sound. They'd been looking where the slave cabins once stood, and found nothing. Now, an hour later, they were at the spot that James said had been the site of the carpenter shop.

"It's a large object," Mike said. "Less than three feet down."

They put down their detectors, switched their LED headlamps on, and began to dig. After about five minutes John hit something solid. Bending down to look, he could see metal. Another twenty minutes of furious digging revealed a twelve-foot long, rectangular metal box. John and Mike dug around the sides until they could get their shovels wedged under the edges of the metal lid. Using the elevated soil as a fulcrum point for their shovels, they slowly pried the lid as darkness enveloped them. Once it was loosened all the way around, each took an end; after a little wiggling the snug lid came off.

And there it was!

After almost two hundred years, Henri Richaud's antigravity machine lay before them.

"It's in amazing condition," Mike said, opening his cell phone.

"Who are you calling?"

"Sheila's boss. Henry wanted me to watch out for you guys," Mike said, glancing over at John as Henry Smith picked up the other end of the phone.

"We've got it, sir."

Mike listened while looking at John. " . . . Perfect condition . . . I know, amazing . . . Everything went smooth . . . It's clear to copter in. There is a clearing where we are at, so just hone in on my GPS . . . Right sir, I will. Over."

Mike began to take a step towards John.

"Henry wanted me to congrat—"

Before he could get the word out, Mike fell face down next to the excavated pit just as Sheila and James came walking up from out of the darkness.

Rushing to Mike's side, at the end of the pit, opposite John, Sheila shrieked, "What's wrong with Mike?"

Before John could answer, a well-dressed man walked up behind him, put a gun in his back and whispered in his ear.

"Boo!"

John jumped.

The man grabbed him by the collar and pulled him back. "Don't worry; we're just going to wait until Mike's friends show up. So for now, let's just remain calm and act like old friends."

The man kicked Mike's gun into the pit and directed James and Sheila to drag his body off behind a tree, thirty yards away, with an admonition not to run off or else Sheila's boyfriend would get a bullet in the back.

When Sheila and James returned, the man made some snide remark about James' bare-chested look and his need of some support. He turned to Sheila and surveyed the ill-fitting, blood-streaked green pullover she was wearing.

"I see you ran into my friend. Where is she?"

"We left her in the basement," Sheila replied.

"Dead?" he asked casually.

"No, I'm not dead yet."

The naked young woman came stumbling in out of the dark, holding her stiletto.

"This *fat* fuck over here, hit me in the back of the head with a two-by-four just as I was warming up with my girlfriend."

"Nice of you to dress up for the occasion," the man said. "By the way, where's your gun?"

She scratched her head with the stiletto and thought for a moment.

"I placed it on the window ledge. I wasn't thinking too clearly until I hit the fresh air and started walking."

The woman noticed Henri's machine.

"So *this* is what all the fuss is about. Looks like something out of a Jules Verne novel."

The man turned to the young woman with a look of annoyance on his face.

"Honey, you think you can put some clothes on? In a little while some very important people are going to show up. I haven't quite made up my mind whether to kill them or ask them for a raise. Having you running around naked might scare them off. No offense."

"Just let me kill the bitch first. It'll only take a second."

She smiled sweetly at the man.

Sheila looked on, horrified.

The man held the gun tight against the back of John's head. Sheila needed to distract him so John could get the gun free or else they both would be dead.

Thinking fast, she turned to the naked young woman.

"Let me get out of this green thing and give you something to aim at."

The gleam in the young woman's eyes told Sheila she had just enough time. She bent slightly forward, reached behind and got the gun out of her waistband, concealing it in the folds of the green pullover. She bent further, pulling the green material up and over her head, wrapping it around her hands along with the gun.

Lifting herself upright, she stretched her arms high overhead.

Tits don't fail me now.

And gave them an extra jiggle.

The woman rushed at Sheila with the stiletto held low, letting out a scream of delight.

Unfortunately, Sheila's little show did not distract the man with the gun. Lowering her arms at the onrushing woman, she took aim at her chest. Before she could pull the trigger however, the man noticed her gun. Swinging his around, he took aim at Sheila. John immediately grabbed the gun.

It fired.

The bullet whizzed harmlessly into the night as the two wrestled for control.

Sheila's gun didn't go off.

She squeezed the trigger again and again. Still, nothing.

The woman froze momentarily.

"The safety!"

She struck Sheila in the face before she could recover from the shock of the gun failing to fire. Sheila fell to the ground, stunned. In an instant the woman was on top of her. She slammed the stiletto down next to Sheila's head and grabbed the gun. Clicking the safety off, the woman buried the muzzle of the gun deep into the soft flesh of Sheila's breast.

"Say goodbye, bitch." The woman smiled.

Sheila waited with eyes closed for a gunshot to go off and end her life.

A gunshot went off. She felt a spray of blood, then a thud, as the woman fell on her. Sheila opened her eyes, amazed to be alive.

The woman got back up to a kneeling position, still straddling Sheila, and pointed her gun into the darkness. Blood flowed from her shoulder.

More shots rang out. One struck the ground near Sheila, another whizzed close by.

And then another.

And another.

Until . . . a clicking sound was heard.

The woman, blood streaming down her arm, laughed.

She shouted out into the darkness.

"You always were a lousy shot, Ted—if that's your real name."

Shaking her head and laughing, she stuck the gun back into Sheila's breast.

"I'm sorry for the delay, dear."

Sheila looked up one last time into the young woman's laughing face and closed her eyes.

The gun went off.

The young woman's head exploded.

The next thing Sheila knew, James was lifting the body off of her and helping her to her feet. John stood nearby, holding the gun at the man's back.

"What happened?" Sheila said in a daze.

She noticed Ted picking up the woman's gun.

"Ted, what are you doing here?"

"I figured you might need some help." Ted had a sheepish smile as he walked over to John's captive and fastened a plastic tie around his hands.

"That woman knew you," Sheila said, startled. "How?"

"It's a long story. One for another place and time."

"You saved my life."

"I'm afraid I missed. Your boyfriend here is the one that can shoot straight."

"Well, you both saved my life," Sheila said as the whir of a copter's blades came into range.

John rushed over to comfort her.

"You okay?" he said, placing a hand on her bare shoulder.

"I'm fine," Sheila assured him. Crossing her arms, she nodded towards the young woman lying at their feet. "You sure that crazy bitch is dead?"

Looking down at the woman—half her head missing—John said, "If she's human, she's dead."

"I'm not so sure about the human part," Sheila shuddered as they watched the copter land some thirty yards away.

* * *

Henry Smith, General Eric Stebbins, and his aide, Colonel Stan Weatherly came walking up.

Surveying the mess, Sheila's boss turned to her with a straight face.

"Aren't we taking casual Fridays a little too far, Sheila?"

"Henry," General Stebbins interrupted, "these people need medical attention."

Ignoring the general, Henry asked, "Where's Mike Kelley?"

"Dead, sir," Sheila answered.

"Well, that's unfortunate." Pointing to Ted, Henry continued; "And you must be—"

"Ted Dody, sir."

"And this fellow?" Henry pointed to the man that John held.

The man replied, "I don't know *who* I am. I only know that I work for the same government you do, sir."

"Hardly," Henry Smith scoffed.

The general turned to his aide. "Stan, call for paramedics."

"I'm with Henry, sir," his aide replied.

"What?" General Stebbins bellowed.

"The gig is up, general," Henry said with scorn.

"What the hell are you talking about?" General Stebbins said in exasperation. "For God's sake, don't be a fool. My team's got you surrounded."

Henry Smith just grinned.

You there." The general nodded to Ted, pointed at Henry and said, "Arrest this man."

Ted walked up to General Stebbins.

"I need the code, sir."

"I don't know what the devil you're talking about," General Stebbins sputtered.

"I do." Henry Smith pulled a card from his pocket and began to read off a series of numbers and letters: "YT765GU90." After he finished, he looked up expectantly at Ted.

"That's correct, sir. What do you want me to do?"

"Shoot the traitor," Henry ordered, pointing at the general.

"Yes, sir." Ted saluted the national security advisor. Turning back towards the general he said apologetically, "I'm sorry, sir."

And quickly, from a distance of two feet, Ted Dody pivoted, pointed his pistol directly at Henry Smith's chest and pulled the trigger.

"I may be a bad shot, but it's hard to miss at this distance," Ted said as Henry Smith crumpled to the ground—a smile permanently etched on his lifeless face.

Ted lowered his gun.

He failed to notice Stan pulling his out.

But John didn't.

He had his gun out quicker, killing Stan before he could pull the trigger.

The general, surveying the carnage around him, seemed to be in a state of shock. A few moments later he had recovered enough to say, "Somebody get me a phone . . . please."

John handed him Mike Kelley's cell phone. The same one used thirty minutes earlier to call Henry Smith.

After calling for paramedics and talking to Washington, the

general addressed the group: "After we get you some medical attention you'll be put in protective custody until we can get this thing all sorted out." He paused, then quickly added, "I'm sorry for the inconvenience."

John stepped forward and asked what was probably on everyone's mind.

"Sir, how do we know that you are one of the good guys?"

"You don't. But you damn well know *he* wasn't one." General Stebbins pointed to Henry Smith and let out a heavy sigh. "In my line of work it's a good rule of thumb not to trust anybody." And then turning to look at his deceased aide, he added, "Not even my own aide, apparently."

CHAPTER 89

A team of specialists swarmed over Hampton State Park, performing a geophysical survey of the grounds and surrounding areas that made up Harriott's former holdings. A defense intelligence team was sent to retrieve copies of Robert Campbell's memoirs from James' home and the Beaufort Sentinel.

John, Sheila, James, Ted, and the man (who they learned was named Bob) waited in separate holding cells. Over a period of three days several different interrogators questioned each of them separately. On the fourth day—with the exception of Ted and Bob—they were flown to Washington. Ushered into General Stebbins' office at the Pentagon, the three of them sat around a conference table, stone-faced and silent. The general entered through an interoffice door, plopped a copy of Robert Campbell's memoirs down on the table, and sat down.

"That's quite a story," General Stebbins began. "I reviewed the results of the interviews that were conducted with each of you. You were all very forthcoming. Frankly speaking, you wouldn't make very good spies. I suggest you contact me if you uncover any other secrets and let us handle it. You could have saved quite a few lives if you would have done that from the beginning."

"Actually, we did," Sheila said. "We let the president's national security advisor know."

The general winced.

"Yes . . . well, unfortunately, he was the one behind this whole mess."

General Stebbins paused. He nervously drummed the table with his fingers for a few moments before clasping his hands together and coming to a decision. After taking a deep breath and exhaling, the general plunged on.

"What I'm about to tell you is classified, so I'm not telling you this. And if you ever repeat any of this, I'll have you flown to a foreign country and thrown into a cell where you'll rot the rest of your lives away."

The general sat back and stared at each of them.

"Is that clear?"

"So, what aren't you going to tell us," John asked.

"I'm not going to tell you that Henry Smith had a long and storied career. Army intelligence in Vietnam. The CIA, where he worked his way up from station chief to become the head of counterintelligence. The NSA, NSC, et cetera, et cetera. You already know all that. And I certainly will not tell you that he had an off-the-books budget for special operations. One of which, was to establish a program that involved training young children with special skills. Juveniles caught up in the judicial system for serious crimes, having no living relations.

"A secluded school tucked away in the mountains of Virginia was set up. The administrators didn't know the real identities of these children, nor did they know the ultimate purpose. Every facet of their training was compartmentalized from the other. Once fully trained, they were given new identities different from the ones given them when they entered the school. A card with a control number and bank account was given to them to memorize and then destroy.

"Some were placed in industry. Some, like Ted, with journalistic skills, were placed in various media outlets. Those having more brawn than brains were used as Henry's personal hit squad. Monthly allotments were automatically deposited into their accounts. From time to time they would be called upon to use their skills or focus their rage into projects deemed useful by Henry and his inner circle. It was their own little espionage ring. These kids were groomed to follow orders explicitly. And the beauty of it all? Henry had complete deniability. None of them ever knew the identities of their handlers until the other night."

General Stebbins paused for a moment.

Sheila took the chance to ask a question.

"Why would Henry Smith, one of the most respected men in Washington, get involved in something like that?"

"Good question. The simplest explanation is that knowledge equals power in this town. Secrets . . . even more so. I think from Henry's decades of being involved in the intelligence business, much of it on the covert side, he realized the influence he could wield from that knowledge. Remember; Bob Gates served both President Bush and President Obama as secretary of defense. He spent over twenty-five years in the CIA and the NSC. That's no coincidence. That's secrets. J. Edgar Hoover is a better example. Everyone was afraid of what he knew. Secrets kept him as head of the FBI for decades. Like Henry, only death removed him from office. And like Hoover, the secrets Henry obtained enabled him to stay in power throughout both Democratic and Republican administrations."

"So why did Henry get you involved, and let you in on his secret?" John asked.

"Another good question. Henry learned of your search through Sheila's snooping around." The general turned and stared balefully at Sheila. "You know every keystroke you make on an NSC computer is monitored. Henry was undoubtedly intrigued by your search. He immediately put you all under surveillance using his little spy ring."

Sheila was not going to be cowed by the general. Acting as if she were the one in charge, she leaned towards the general and interrupted him.

"You didn't answer the question! Why did Henry involve you?"

The general held up his hands in mock surrender and laughed.

"I feel like I'm in front of those yokels on the Hill. No offense, I'll answer the question." The general matched Sheila's lean and closed the distance between them. "Henry knew what you were looking for in broad outlines. From the censored newspapers dating back to 1830 he also knew that the government was involved. But Henry didn't have the file on Henri Richaud. We did. After Henry's aide asked if we had any information on this Henri Richaud and his floating machine, we did our own search and found the file.

"Henry learned of the magnitude of the discovery from his mole: my aide, Stan Weatherly. He decided to keep me off balance by calling me into his office and reading me the riot act. Pretending to feign outrage that he knew nothing about the search for Henri Richaud's antigravity machine. Meanwhile, all along, my trusted aide was feeding him information the DIA had collected on this Henri Richaud. Henry was always one step ahead of us.

"I learned from Henry that you were being followed and bugged. He actually had the gall to intimate that I was behind it. Naturally, I assumed it was a rogue cell in my own agency and ordered an internal investigation from top to bottom . . . but I was barking up the wrong tree. Then, Henry tried to distract me with some nonsense about Al Qaeda activity in Yemen, and a nonexistent plot to kill the Queen of England.

"He fooled me *almost* to the very end. Actually, make that the very end. I didn't know he had compromised Stan Weatherly. The only reason I'm here today is thanks to all of you. That, and Ted Dody having some kind of epiphany."

James, who had sat quietly listening throughout the meeting, spoke up.

"So it was Henry's plan from the beginning to kill you, and presumably kill us to get Henri's machine. Why? That doesn't make any sense to me."

The general swiveled in his chair towards James. "No, of course not. Henry never had any intention of killing anyone."

"Except for Rachel," Sheila interrupted. "And Elmer."

Shifting uncomfortably in his chair, the general looked away—pained.

"Yes," he replied. "Henry ordered Rachel's death. Elmer, unfortunately, was in the wrong place at the wrong time."

"What did Rachel discover that necessitated her murder?" John asked.

"I have no idea. It's one of the many remaining mysteries still out there, somewhere."

"And you *still* think he didn't want to kill us or yourself?" James said.

"I'm totally convinced of that. Knowing Henry's modus operandi, I believe he would only kill if absolutely necessary. We learned from Bob that he and his late naked partner were given instructions to stand down. Ted confirmed that he too was told to stand down and fly back to Paris. No, if everything had worked the way Henry had planned it, you would have discovered the most amazing invention of our times. Henry and I would have shared in that glory. And those spies that bugged your office and tormented Sheila would have been long gone, vanished forever. Leaving me to chase ghosts in my own agency. If not for Sheila's obsessive little friend and Ted's suddenly discovering a conscience, everything would have worked out just fine for Henry. I would've been grateful to be involved in the most amazing discovery of our time, and he would have gone on with his little spy ring, leaving me none the wiser."

"Did Ted give you any useful information on the extent of Henry's little spy ring?" Sheila asked.

"A little. I've gotten the real names of some of the graduates of the program. Hopefully, Ted and Bob can identify some of the other graduates by going through our picture databases. But unless something turns up in the judicial records or from Henry's computer or phone records, we won't know if the program is headless or if someone else has popped up to take Henry's place."

"And Max Baker?" John asked, assuming the worst.

"Unfortunately, as you probably already suspected, he's dead. Bob confessed to killing him."

"Was Mike a good guy or a bad guy," Sheila asked.

"Good guy. Mike thought he was protecting you by keeping Henry up to date on what was going on. His intentions were honorable." The general's tone grew more somber. "And I regret to say that on Henry's advice, I appointed Stan as my chief aide. It appears that after several decades, Henry has quite a few of these people, and others more sinister than Stan, liberally sprinkled throughout the intelligence community. We're going to have a devil of a time sorting out the good guys from the bad."

"So I didn't kill an innocent man," John sighed, relieved.

"No. And if you hadn't killed Stan, he would have killed Ted and probably me too."

"What is going to happen to Ted?" James asked.

"Well, since he never killed anybody before Henry, not counting his father, I think he can be rehabilitated. The crime he committed as a juvenile and the mitigating circumstances involved would have allowed him to be free long before now. The real villain in all of this is Henry."

"So are we free to go now?" Sheila asked.

"Of course." General Stebbins stood up to usher them all out. "Just don't snoop around anymore and get into any further trouble."

Before they reached the door, John stopped the general.

"What about Henri's machine? What will you do, now that you have the secret to antigravity?"

The general smiled quizzically.

"The machine was all there except for one part. Isaac and Old Moses must have known what they were doing. Either that, or they were just very lucky."

"How so?" John asked.

"Well, the batteries and controls were there, but we have better battery technology today. The generator was nothing special." General Stebbins paused briefly, weighing whether to stop or continue. And then he reluctantly added, "The key was the planetary discs and the mechanism that generated the electromagnetic fields. And that, my friends, is what's missing."

As the door closed, the general's voice followed the trio out into the hallway.

"But you didn't hear that from me . . . and don't go looking for it either."

CHAPTER 90

Epilogue

Back in Beaufort, the Sentinel was put on hold for several weeks. Sheila spent two weeks recuperating on Fripp Island with John faithfully doting on her. She liked this kind of attention, eager to put the past behind her. It was towards the end of their two-week stay on the island that the past came back. James had spent his time at home going over his great-great-grandfather's papers, looking for the last note from Henri.

And he found it.

"I found it! I found the note," James said over the phone to Sheila, lying on a chaise lounge, soaking up the sun.

Sheila put James on speakerphone and called John over.

"James found the note from Henri."

John sat down on the edge of Sheila's chaise lounge.

"Go ahead and read it."

"I found it in the letters to the editor section of January, 1833."

"Great," John replied. "What does it say?"

"At first I looked for a note signed by Henri Richaud and had no luck. Then I skimmed the notes for anyone with first names beginning with an H, and an R for their last."

It was clear that James was going to take his time revealing his secret, so John snuggled up with Sheila on the lounge. They smiled at each other as James continued on.

"Well, I found a few notes. Let me read some that I thought had possibilities."

James read four short notes before getting back to the subject at hand.

"Obviously, in retrospect, they didn't have any connection with our man. So starting when Robert returned from Hampton and resumed publishing the Sentinel on September 24, 1830, I went paper by paper, line by line. And *bingo!* On January 3, 1833 I came across a note in the letters to the editor section."

James paused for a moment to add to the drama.

Sheila looked at John and laughed.

"Annnd? Haven't I been tortured enough already, James."

"I'm sorry. I always have to have my fun. Anyway, I came across a note signed by the Honorable Francis Marion."

"The Swamp Fox," John said. "But he was long dead by then, wasn't he?"

"Yes, of course. He died in the 1790s. Naturally, I was curious, so I read the note."

James paused again.

"Annnd," John said.

Sheila laughed, holding her healing left breast to keep it from hurting.

"Well you won't believe what it said," James continued.

"I suppose not," Sheila said, trying to keep it together through tears of laughter. "Maybe someday you'll let us know."

"Are you alright, Sheila?" James said paternally. "You sound like you're crying."

John had to answer for Sheila, biting down on a towel to keep from laughing out loud, as what sounded like crying whimpers escaped the corners of her mouth.

"She's just a bit overwhelmed by it all, James. This is such a momentous occasion," he said, not helping matters for Sheila. "Why don't you just leave out anymore suspense and read the note."

"Yes, well, perhaps you're right. The note was signed the Honorable Francis Marion, which after reading the note, I deduced was code for the Floating Man. And the h in honorable could stand for Henri, or might just mean honorable. It doesn't really matter, once you figure out that Francis Marion, FM stands for Floating Man. Taking out honorable leaves you with the initials TFM for The Floating Man. Pretty clever, if I do say so myself. But the note clinches it, and has more code. You ready to hear it?"

"No James, we're both kind of tired. We were just about to take a nap when you called. I'll call you later, when we wake up."

John abruptly hung up the phone.

"You didn't!" Sheila said, astounded, laughing even harder.

"Can you imagine the look on James' face right about now?"

"You better call him back right away."

"Nope," John said, wrapping his arms around Sheila in a loving embrace. "This is the first time you've laughed and smiled like this in weeks. Let's just soak it all in, along with the last rays of the sun."

John kissed Sheila tenderly, and very tenderly they shared their love. James intuitively had the good sense not to call back and interrupt the moment. Afterward, they fell asleep in each other's arms.

The sun slowly set over Fripp Island: free from the worries of crazed spies and . . . ringing phone.

"James?" John said groggily into the phone, looking at his watch which read nine thirty.

"I'll be damned! You *did* take a nap!"

"Of course," John said, kissing a still awakening Sheila on her forehead. "So, are you going to read the note to us now?"

"I suppose I better, before you have dinner or take your evening swim, or whatever you two have planned."

"We're all refreshed and ready for your great discovery," Sheila said, rubbing her eyes.

"Did I tell you how I deduced the note was from Henri?"

"*James!*" Sheila shouted, now fully awake.

"Sorry. My little joke. Okay, here goes. The note reads: Dear Editor, have much enjoyed reading your paper. Your layout is very engaging for the reader, all in the place, right on cue. You sir, are a first rate reporter. Hope all is well with you and your family, as is mine. Yours truly, The Honorable Francis Marion. Well? Pretty amazing stuff, isn't it?"

"James, we are still waking up, could you decipher it for us?" John said.

"Certainly. Henri is saying he returned to the village of Arcueil. All is in the place stands for Pierre-Simon Laplace. And his home where the laboratory was located is right on cue, or Arcueil."

"So," Sheila said, "the old man made it back to France after all and had a family. I wonder if Little Daphne had a boy or girl?"

"We'll probably never know," John said.

"I think we should celebrate this news and have a toast to Henri and Little Daphne," Sheila said.

"And family," added James.

"Let's take a trip to Hampton and bring a jug of peach-sweetened rum," John said. "And do our toasting on the front portico."

Sheila finished the sentence for John.

"Just like they did it in the old days."

CHAPTER 91

A few days later they were sitting on the portico of Hampton Plantation, sipping James' version of Harriott's peach-sweetened rum. John had talked at considerable length over the preceding days to state officials, and finally in exasperation, called General Stebbins to intervene so that the three of them could have unrestricted after-hours use of the park. The one stipulation was that Elizabeth, the state employee who had greeted them on the night of their search, stay behind.

The three of them looked out over the grounds. James turned to John and said, "Before we begin, I would like to bring up one other piece of unfinished business."

"Before we begin what?" Sheila said suspiciously.

"Our wedding," John replied, giving Sheila a sly smile. Nonchalantly, he raised his glass and took a sip.

"Isn't the bride supposed to be the first to know?" Sheila asked, a bit chagrined.

"I wanted it to be a surprise. And also, intimate and informal."

"Intimate? With James sitting over there?" Sheila shook her head in disbelief.

James got up. "I'll go inside for a little bit and pester Elizabeth."

Alone on the portico, John got down on his knees and pulled a small box containing a large, center-cut diamond ring from his pocket. James peeked from inside as John offered the ring to Sheila. It had been James' gift to his late wife Thelma on their fortieth wedding anniversary. He had practically insisted that John accept the ring, saying that if he and Sheila were half as in love as he and Thelma had been, it would be more love than the two of them would ever need. He also said he thought of Sheila as the rambunctious child he never had and wanted to see a part of Thelma stay with her. After that, John could hardly refuse. So here they were: John on his knees, and James inside, peeking out.

"Have you set a date for our wedding, Mr. Smooth?" Sheila asked, looking down at John.

"So is that a yes?" John asked tentatively.

"I kind of like you in that position. Groveling. You know, for a guy who took forever to make a move on me, you now are awfully sure of yourself."

Sheila was thoroughly enjoying the moment.

"That's a *bad* thing?" John began to sweat.

"No, that's a *good* thing. Shows there's hope for you yet. I like my men to be decisive."

"Men?"

"Until I'm married, yes. Men."

"Dammit! Sheila, will you marry me?" John said, frustrated. "I'm sweating like hell and my knees are killing me down here."

"You still haven't answered my question."

"What?" John got off his knees and sat Indian style in front of Sheila.

"When is the wedding?"

"I'd have it right now, if you'd say yes and let me get back on my feet."

"Okay, James," Sheila turned and shouted at the front door. "I know you're spying on us anyway. You can come out now. I think we've made him suffer enough."

John got to his feet. James came out carrying a Bible, followed by Elizabeth: a camera hanging from her neck and a broom in her hand.

Sheila, in a long, flowing white summer dress, took John's hand. James stood in front of them, holding a Bible with a piece of paper sticking out.

Sheila's smile turned into a wide grin.

John turned to her and said, "You knew all along, didn't you?"

"Of course. You know James can't keep a secret."

"I wanted to make sure Sheila was comfortable wearing Thelma's ring," James said. "Besides, you should never leave things to chance, if it can be helped. Let's get started, shall we?"

John and Sheila stood side by side, holding hands, listening to James read a familiar, slightly reworked passage.

"Today is a celebration of the Lord's good works," he began. "The Lord has taken two of his servants and brought them together on this day: a man of the South and a woman from Washington. Truly, the Lord is great. His works provide comfort and hope. As we join these two together as man and wife, let us remember what the good book says: Wherefore they are no more twain, but one flesh. What therefore God hath joined together, let not man put asunder."

James looked John sternly in the eye. "John, do you want this woman?"

After pausing a moment to remember Henri's exact words, John said, "Yes, of course."

James turned to Sheila, and with a big smile on his face said, "Do you want this man? He seems a little old for you."

Sheila laughed. "No he isn't. He's only five years older than me."

"Stick with the script dear," James intoned, and then repeated, "Do you want this man?"

Sheila smiled at John. "Yes."

James nodded to Elizabeth, the park employee. "Hold the broom, please."

"Sure, why not. The state is paying me double time for this."

Elizabeth held the broom behind Sheila, about a foot off the ground. She jumped backwards, easily clearing it. Then she held the broom for John a little higher.

John looked back at Elizabeth and said, "That's not fair."

"Sorry," Elizabeth said, "I'm just following orders."

John took a big leap backwards and almost cleared the broom. Almost.

His left leg hit the broom and he lost his balance, falling backwards.

"Perfect! You know what this means, don't you?" Sheila said, looking down at John.

"Yeah, I read the memoirs too, you know."

John rose to his feet.

"Didn't need no broom to let me know who the boss is," he said as he embraced Sheila. The two of them shared a long wedding kiss.

After waiting for what in James' mind was a sufficient amount of time, he interrupted the newlyweds: "Do you want any words of wisdom?"

John and Sheila looked at each other, turned to James, and in unison, said, "No!"

Elizabeth snapped wedding photos of the three of them on the portico and suggested they take a few by the George Washington oak tree. As they walked down the portico steps, across the lawn and over to the oak tree, Sheila turned to James with a question.

"Before the ceremony, you mentioned something about unfinished business."

"We never found the other part of the machine," James responded. "The planetary discs. Isaac said he planted it here and there."

"If you think I am going back into that basement," Sheila said, her voice rising with tension, "you're crazy."

"No, no, of course not," James assured her. "The feds have searched every square inch of the basement with their equipment."

Elizabeth posed them by the tree and started taking pictures from various angles.

Looking back at the house, a big smile crossed John's face.

"Isaac said he made his own little puzzle. He told Robert they may dig it up, but it's still up in the air whether they can figure it all out. And then he had what Robert called, a look of supreme satisfaction." John pointed at the portico. "Isaac said that while sitting right up there."

"So?" Sheila said.

"It's up in the air. Look!" John pointed at the large eaves of the portico roof.

And then they all saw it.

The circular window in the center of the roofline above the portico, so indicative of Georgian-style mansions, trimmed in a large circle of wood. The trim, with its four compass points jutting from the top, bottom, and sides, seemed overly ornate and large.

"Do you really think it's there?" James said.

"I bet if we go behind the window in the attic, we'll see the handiwork of Old Moses the carpenter."

Sheila walked over to Elizabeth; she had been standing out of earshot, previewing the pictures.

"Elizabeth, we need to get into the attic above the portico."

"I'm not allowed to let anyone into the attic areas. It's park policy," Elizabeth said. And then, looking at their crestfallen faces, she relented. "Aw, what the heck. I am getting paid double time after all. Come on."

Elizabeth led them up to the second floor and stopped in front of a small door that led to the attic area above the portico. As Elizabeth waited nervously outside the door, John, Sheila, and James went to the portico window. The first thing they noticed was that the circular wooden frame around the window was as ornate as the outside. The only difference was that it had not been painted. John looked closely at the circular frame.

"Here it is," he whispered reverently. "*Look*."

Sheila and James came close. John pointed out two faint signatures, scratched almost two hundred years earlier: Isaac and Old Moses. John took a few pictures with the camera and then they left. Leaving behind, the final piece of Henri's machine—the planetary discs—safely hidden beneath the wooden frame of the portico window.

All this time it was just as Isaac had said: "Up in the air."

Through the centuries, as generations of the Horry Rutledge family sat on the portico below, Henri's final puzzle piece had silently kept watch from above.

CHAPTER 92

John was the first to suggest their honeymoon spot.
Paris.
An obvious choice.
After listening to Ted Dody's tales, John and Sheila decided to visit Jacques and Adrienne Allegre—the last living connection to Henri's scientific papers.
And Paris was . . . well, Paris.
The perfect place for young newlyweds.
John tracked down Adrienne; he learned that Jacques, suffering from cancer, had died. He told Adrienne about Robert Campbell's memoirs. She was delighted that he was bringing her a copy. She said that her grandfather knew very little about Henri's time in America. This would make his story complete.
After a few days in Paris doing what newlyweds do, they drove a rental to the little town of Lisieux—a two-and-a-half-hour drive from Paris.
Pulling up in front of Jacques' summer cottage, Sheila remarked that she could see herself living in the Paris countryside.
She got out, walked ahead of John, knocked on the front door.
The door swung open.
She jumped back; startled.
There in front of her stood Ted Dody. She was just about to

run when a beautiful young woman with long, jet-black hair pushed Ted aside.

"You must be Sheila," she said, reaching out her hand. "I'm Adrienne. Don't worry about Ted, he's still a work in progress, but he's coming around."

Adrienne introduced herself to John. Meanwhile, Ted was giving Sheila a surprisingly non-sexual hug.

As if in answer to the look on Sheila's face, Ted said, "I'm going to therapy four times a week, paid for by Uncle Sam. After what they did to me, it's the least they could do."

Ted escorted Sheila inside, trailed by John and Adrienne. He motioned them to the sofa in the front room and said, "Please, make yourselves comfortable."

John sat on the sofa next to Sheila, both still in shock at seeing Ted there.

Adrienne volunteered that Ted had come back to apologize for his behavior and learned that Jacques had killed himself to save him.

"He cried like a baby and told me the whole story of how he ended up in some kind of weird government cell. He was ordered to kill my grandfather but couldn't go through with it. Jacques wrote a lovely note before he killed himself. He told me he saw something special in Ted, and if he ever returned, I should give him a second chance."

"I just couldn't go through with it," Ted said in a whisper. "I'm not a killer, despite the fact that I snapped and killed my dad after being abused for years. You saw yourselves that night. I couldn't even shoot straight. Anyway, that's all in the past now. My therapist says I'm making tremendous strides."

"He's still a bit of an ass," Adrienne commented.

"Yeah . . . well, like she said, I'm still a work in progress."

Adrienne said something to Ted in French. Answering back in French, he got up and left. He returned with a half-bottle of wine and some glasses.

"Jacques' last bottle," Ted said. "I think it's appropriate we complete the circle and finish it off."

As Ted poured, Sheila turned to Adrienne. "How did you do it? He's almost human now."

Adrienne smiled. "Love stills the savage beast. That, and *lots* of therapy."

"I wish James were here to witness this," Sheila said.

"I really did get under his skin." Ted finished pouring the wine and added, "Please apologize to him for me. My people skills are much better now. It's a shame the fat man couldn't be here ... that's a joke, by the way. Didn't really mean it."

Adrienne rolled her eyes. "Like I said, he's still a bit of an ass, but he kind of grows on you."

"If you say so," Sheila said.

Ted stuck his tongue out at Sheila; she returned the gesture.

After an hour of conversation, half about Jacques and half about their search for Henri's machine, Adrienne got up and went over to Ted.

"I think we can trust them," she whispered into his ear. He promptly got up and left the room, returning a minute later with a security box.

Adrienne pulled out some old photographs and sat down between John and Sheila.

"Here's my grandfather as a young man, with his dad, Philippe. He was the last caretaker of the Chateau of Saint-Julien de Mailloc where Pierre-Simon Laplace and Henri's papers were stored. And here is Philippe's dad as a young boy."

Sheila looked at the picture and asked, "What was his father's name?"

"Henri," Adrienne smiled. In answer to the look on Sheila's face, she added, "Junior."

"Our Henri's son?" John said incredulously.

"My great-great-great-grandfather. I'm now the last caretaker of Henri's story. Unless I have a child."

With that, Ted perked up and smiled. Adrienne shot him a withering look.

"*What?*" he said with a wounded look.

Adrienne shook her head and turned to John and Sheila.

"After what you two have been through, I think it is only fitting that you join us as members of the Societe d' Arcueil."

"How many members are there?" John asked.

"Right now, just two. Ted and myself. You and Sheila would make four. Are you in?"

Adrienne looked intently at both John and Sheila.

"What would we have to do?" Sheila asked.

"Just keep the secrets safe, and never reveal them unless we all agree."

Sheila looked at John; he nodded and said, "Okay, we're in."

Taking a picture out of her purse and handing it to Adrienne, Sheila said, "Here is where Henri's planetary discs are: underneath the wooden frame of this window. The rest of the machine, as Ted probably told you, is in the government's hands."

"And here is Henri's final piece of the puzzle," Adrienne said. She took out a yellowed piece of paper. Written on it were three scientific formulas and a diagram. "Jacques said that by correctly recombining these formulas, along with the diagram, you would have the secret of antigravity."

Adrienne pulled out another old picture from the box.

"I almost forgot. Here is a picture of Henri. It's a copy that you can keep. Taken shortly before he died in 1857 at the age of eighty-eight. That's his wife, Daphne, by his side. My thrice-removed Grandmother. I don't know who the others are."

John and Sheila looked at the photo of Henri and Little Daphne. They immediately knew who the others were.

"That's Isaac and his family," John replied. "You can tell by his engaging smile."

To Adrienne's puzzled look, Sheila explained: "Isaac was one of Harriott's slaves who finally got to realize his dream of being a free man. A good friend of Henri's."

"A good man," John added and smiled.

* * *

Sheila and John got up to leave. Adrienne and Ted walked them outside to their car. Adrienne remarked that she looked forward to reading Robert's memoirs. They all agreed to keep in touch.

"So what do you plan on doing now?" Adrienne asked.

About to get in the car, John and Sheila looked at each other—puzzled. After everything they had been through, it was not an easy question to answer.

Sheila grabbed the door handle and turned to Adrienne.

"I'm going to get a breast reduction."

"What?" Adrienne said with a look of shock. "Why on *earth*

would you do that? You have a figure a woman would kill for."

"Exactly."

Sheila slid in and closed the door, leaving Adrienne and Ted with their mouths opened wide.

Their car disappeared in a cloud of dust.

CHAPTER 93

Epilogue to the epilogue

Sheila quit her job at the NSA and returned with John to Beaufort, where along with James, they continue to run the Beaufort Sentinel. James now shares the front porch swing with Maggie. They refuse to get married—claiming they're a thoroughly modern couple. Sheila and John are expecting their first child, as are Adrienne and Ted. Sheila and Adrienne update each other by phone on the latest prenatal exercises and Ted's therapy—which is progressing nicely.

And the breast reduction?

That's on hold for now.

John said it didn't matter one way or the other to him.

He just wants Sheila to be happy.

That's his story, and he is sticking to it.

* * *

Oh, you're probably wondering about Henri's last puzzle.

It's printed on the next page.

I know, it's supposed to be a secret.

Well, this is a work of fiction after all . . . or is it?

Henri's Puzzle

$$x_{n+1} = rx_n(1 - x_n)$$

$$i\hbar \frac{\partial}{\partial t} \psi(r,t)$$

$$= \frac{-\hbar^2}{2m} \nabla^2 \psi(r,t) + V(r,t)\psi(r,t)$$

$L\{f(t)\}$

Acknowledgements

First and foremost I would like to thank my lovely wife for putting up with me during the editing process: a process that turned this normally placid and complacent author into a churlish boor. And coincidentally, her name happens to be Sheila. When the novel veered in directions I hadn't previously anticipated I offered to change Sheila's name (the character, not my wife). However, we couldn't agree on an alternative, so Sheila it was and is!

I would also like to thank Jay Crawford Design for the cover. He's a great artist and also a good guy to have as brother and friend. Steve Gibson (another friend and very talented guy) created my webpage. For those in need of web design, visit his page at http://webpagebysteve.com

A big thank you to the many people that took the time to read early drafts of the novel, pointing out mistakes, content errors and offering constructive criticism: Charles Navurskis, John Bongratz, Pat Kelly, Mary Ann Matyasec, Joe Urbanik, and my cousins, Karen Decker and Ed Johnson.

I would be remiss if I did not mention two remarkable authors: Dina Silver and Gregg Cebrzynski. Dina (author of "One Pink Line") gave me great advice on social media, and Gregg (author of "The Champagne Ladies") allowed me to vent; Gregg's very solid advice on the judicious use of alcohol when the brain starts to freeze was invaluable in aiding the writing process.

A special thanks to Sallie Smith for organizing the "Writers Exchange" group in Kenilworth, Illinois: the support and inspiration provided was just what this author needed to get over the final hurdle.

And last but certainly not least; I would like to give thanks to the Peppermill Lake Book Club for their selection of *The Floating Man* as their book of the month.

About the Author

A graduate of Northwestern, William Crawford began telling stories at the age of five to his cousins late at night while on family vacations in the Great North Woods. This quickly progressed—if you can call two decades quickly progressing— to political satire. In 1996 the author created a parody on the OJ Simpson saga. *My Search for the Real Killer, not by OJ Simpson* became a minor cult classic. The author's real ambition was to become a novelist. Over the years he developed several storylines. Once he retired from his safety position in government he turned that ambition into reality. The result is the *Floating Man*: a mystery thriller that takes place in both past and present. Replete with psychosexual overtones, The *Floating Man* weaves historical figures and events into a story of love, discovery, ambition, greed, death, and redemption.

Made in the USA
Monee, IL
02 November 2023

45676142R00219